$\mathcal{P}$raise for $\mathcal{A}$va $\mathcal{M}$iles

NORA ROBERTS LAND
Selected as one of the Best Books of 2013 alongside Nora Roberts' DARK WITCH and Julia Quinn's SUM OF ALL KISSES.
--USA Today Contributor, Becky Lower, Happily Ever After

"It {NORA ROBERTS LAND} captures the best of what I love in a Nora Roberts novel..."
--BlogCritics

"...finding love like in the pages of a Nora Roberts story."
--Publishers Weekly WW Ladies Book Club

FRENCH ROAST
"An entertaining ride...{and) a full-bodied romance."
--Readers' Favorite

"Her engaging story and characters kept me turning the pages."
--Bookfan

THE GRAND OPENING
"Ava Miles is fast becoming one of my favorite light contemporary romance writers."
--Tome Tender

"The latest book in the Dare Valley series is a continuation of love, family, and romance."
--Mary J. Gramlich

THE HOLIDAY SERENADE
"This story is all romance, steam, and humor with a touch of the holiday spirit..."
--The Book Nympho

THE TOWN SQUARE
"Ms. Miles' words melted into each page until the world receded around me..."
--Tome Tender

COUNTRY HEAVEN
"If ever there was a contemporary romance that rated a 10 on a scale of 1 to 5 for me, this one is it!"
--The Romance Reviews

AVA MILES

To my parents, Mike and Julie, for giving me life, always taking me to the library, letting me buy books even when money was tight, teaching me life lessons, and helping me learn ones on my own. I love you both dearly.

And to my divine entourage, who has the best sense of humor and makes me laugh loudly and frequently.

Acknowledgements

For the abundant help that continues to support my writing journey:

The earth angels of Team Ava, including my incredible assistant, Maggie Mae Gallagher; my editor, the amazing and insightful Angela Polidoro; Gregory Stewart for the updated Dare Valley map, the Don't Soy With Me logo for my swag, and his tremendous support in tons of other things; the Killion Group for the cover art; my copy editor, Helen Hester-Ossa; and Bemis Promotions for continuing to add to the brilliance of my website.

My former agent, Jennifer Schober, and her real love for Peggy and Mac's story.

To my sister, Tabitha, and my brother-in-law, Mark, for their incredible help on the poker scenes. Here's to seeing you with the gold bracelet someday, Mark.

To my Aunt Janie and Uncle Alan, for their professional insights on all things law enforcement.

T.F. You know why.

To my readers, whose outpouring of love and support awe and humble me. Thank you for reading!

Lastly, just a note to say I've played with time regarding the hotel being up and running to make this story come together. That's the fun about fiction. So enjoy.

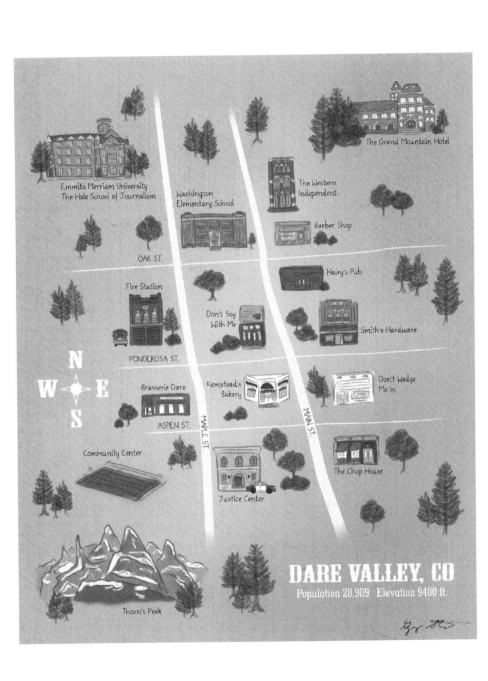

CHAPTER 1

Deputy Sheriff Peggy McBride didn't care what conventional wisdom said about men, meat, and fire. Barbecues had been invented by women.

Some mother had come up with the idea of setting up in the backyard and throwing meat on the grill. Where else could kids run around and howl like banshees with other children while their mothers enjoyed adult beverages, conversation, and chow?

Add in the fact that you didn't have to dress up like you did for a stuffy *inside* party, and BBQs pretty much ruled Peggy's universe. Too bad she lived in the Colorado Rockies now, or she'd do this year round.

"Mom, why didn't you let me bring my new baseball?"

"We don't want anything to happen to another window, do we?"

Her seven-year-old son gave a mulish scowl—so like her own. "Gosh, Mom, it was an accident. Really! Uncle Tanner says things like that happen when you're learning to play ball."

Usually her brother was on her side. She frowned. Maybe his wife, Meredith, would back her up on this one.

"You can play baseball at his house then. Not at Jill's." She hoped he wouldn't ask Jill. Meredith's sister spoiled Keith rotten. Peggy loved that she'd gained an extended family through Tanner, but she hoped Jill would become more of a disciplinarian when she had her twins in a couple of months. Maybe her new husband, Brian, would help with that.

"But Mom..."

She tuned out the whining. If she could tune out a suspect spewing curse words, then she could certainly tune out her own son. And thank God for that. They were less than a month into school vacation, and the whines like *I'm so bored, Mom* were making her crack. She'd mostly gotten over the guilt.

Being a single mother, there wasn't anyone else to share it with.

Keith tugged on her shirt, startling her. She gripped the pie in her hands a little tighter. Walking down Dare Valley's small-town sidewalk carrying a dessert couldn't have embarrassed her more. Did she look like someone from the Colorado Welcome Wagon? Thank God for frozen pie crusts. All she had to do was dump in condensed milk and lime juice, freeze it, and wham, she had a key lime pie. Keith went nuts for it.

His disgruntled symphony finally made her eyelid spasm. "Enough, please. We're going to have a great time today. Jill and Brian know how to throw a party."

"I like her new name. McConnell. Tanner says she's like him now. A 'Mc.'"

Leave it to her brother. McBride and McConnell. Like they were Irish ancestors or something.

"Is Grandpa Hale going to be there too?"

She smiled. Jill and Meredith's grandfather treated Keith like he was his own flesh and blood. They played checkers and went out for ice cream. It warmed her heart.

"Yes, Arthur will be there."

"What about Mr. Maven?"

Her lips twitched into a scowl, and her BBQ giddiness faded. The answer was yes. Jill's boss would probably be there. He was her arch-rival in the community—a poker-playing, hotel-building slickster nicknamed Maverick—but he made her traitorous feminine parts squeal. She'd tried to stop him from building his new boutique poker hotel in town and lost. He'd taken it personally. Who could blame him? They'd basically ignored each other since the city council had approved the plans for the hotel six months ago. Come to think of it, it was pretty impressive that she'd managed to go that long without uttering a word to him, especially since Jill worked for him. He was around all the darn time, making her feel at once guilty and achy.

"Yes, he'll probably be there."

"Okay," Keith muttered, kicking a rock on the street.

Her guilt spiked. Keith loved Maven, so her 'Cold War' with him had her son confused—he was loyal to her, but didn't understand why she had taken such a dislike to his buddy.

How could she explain it to a kid? It was hard enough explaining why she and his dad had broken up and why Frank never seemed to remember Keith's birthday.

"There'll be other kids to play with. You'll like that, right?"

He picked up a stick and heaved it across the street. "Great, 'cause I'm never going to have a baby brother or sister of my own. It stinks. Why can't you just find one when you're working and bring it home?"

Her eye spasm tapped like a telegraph. "Because it's illegal, Keith. We've discussed this before. You're my number one guy."

"I'd help you, Mom. I would, I would."

She wasn't stupid enough to miss the beginnings of a common negotiation. The whole *If I can't have a baby, can I have a puppy?* routine.

The kid was devious. She did the same thing to suspects all the time. The famous McBride genes ran in his veins. It made her proud.

Except when it made her nuts.

"Keith, we'll go home for a time-out if you don't stop this. "

"But the pie will melt." He pointed, his determined chin thrust out. "See, there's already water on the sides. That's consdenforum."

"Condensation," she automatically corrected.

A loud clatter on the sidewalk made her ears cock back. Who was wearing high heels to a BBQ? Someone looking to get laid, but the shoes didn't sound right. More like horse hooves. She looked over her shoulder and froze.

There was a freakin' moose behind them.

She almost dropped the pie. None of her experiences as a cop had prepared her for this *Northern Exposure* moment. God must have had an off-day during Creation Week. It had to be the ugliest, weirdest thing in the animal kingdom. It looked like a tall buffalo with the hump back and sweetheart-shaped face. The ginormous head bounced as it clicked along on legs that looked too spindly to support its massive body. It could have used a serious wax and trim with all that mangy hair sticking out.

Those eerie brown eyes stared at her. Goosebumps skittered across her skin. She'd seen the same look in criminals. This thing wasn't going to leave them alone. He wanted something. Or was it a she? It didn't have any of those horn-thingies. What were they called? Oh, antlers.

Moose didn't eat people, did they?

Why had she moved to the Colorado Rockies again?

She tucked the pie in the crook of her arm and took Keith's hand. "Okay, let's pick up the pace."

She vowed never to walk to Jill's house again. Who cared about gas prices and fluorocarbons when they lived in Wild Kingdom? Heck, she'd heard about bears in people's backyards, but this...

This was nuts. They were on foot with a determined moose in hot pursuit.

Ever attuned to her emotions, Keith tugged on her grip. "What's wrong, Mom?"

"We need to walk faster. There's a moose behind us." She'd always been honest with him. Plus, he was bound to look back and see the freakin' thing. How could you miss a seven-foot ball of hair?

He jerked his head around. "Holy crap!"

She didn't correct his language. Just tugged him along as she snuck glances at the moose over her shoulder.

"What do we do?"

"Umm..." She realized she wasn't sure. She'd heard people talk about deer and bears, but never moose. Or was that mooses? Meese?

Well, except for one thing...*Don't get near one.* Her blood ran cold.

Keith's hand trembled in hers. "It's really big."

Understatement. They turned right. The clip-clop increased. She watched as the moose increased its pace, brown eyes gleaming.

"Mommy, it's walking faster." Keith darted forward, almost jerking her arm out of the socket.

The moose tossed its head. Jeez, that couldn't be good.

Keith was onto something.

"Let's run," she said.

The moose snorted, sending a jolt of pure terror down her spine. Clutching Keith's hand in a vice-like grip, she started sprinting.

The clip-clop shifted to the thundering of hooves. Peggy scanned Juniper Street, looking for options. The tree branches were too tall to climb. The houses in this part of town were tucked back from the street. Plus, what if the owner wasn't home? She and Keith would be cornered.

The moose was gaining on them, even with that weird, lumbering body. The head dipped.

All the saliva drained from her mouth.

If they couldn't make it, she'd have to distract the dumb thing so Keith could get away. Like judo was going to work on this thing. Maybe running in a different direction would keep its attention focused on her? Cold sweat broke out under her clothes.

They were about four blocks from Jill's when the moose halted, stomped its feet like a flamenco dancer, and lowered its head. She could almost hear it yell *Charge!* Its pounding hooves echoed in her ears.

"Run, Keith, run! Don't stop! Get Uncle Tanner." Her brother would know what to do. He always did.

She stopped and turned around, clutching the pie. Maybe she could use it as a shield. Right.

The moose stopped when she did, watching her. Its floppy ears curled back. The grunts issuing from its mouth made her think of the deranged sex offender she'd arrested last year.

She braced her legs, prepared to spring to the side at the last minute if it charged.

A car revved, racing down the street. She was in the middle of the road. God, what a choice—she could be hit by a car or a moose.

A red Ferrari screeched to a halt between them. The beast tossed its head and charged, hitting the car with a resounding thunk. Glass cracked. Metal bent like Superman had put his fists through it.

Shock rolled through her at the sheer destructive power of the thing. The passenger side door swung open as the moose ambled around the side dazedly. "Get in, Peg."

Magically, miraculously, it was Mac Maven, staring at her with his stoplight green eyes, which always made her think of a traffic light telling her, *Yes, go, nothing's stopping you.* She darted for the vehicle as the moose headed her way.

Keith stopped halfway up the block. "Mommy!"

"Run! Get Tanner!"

She jumped into the car and slammed the door, watching Keith run off. Thank God.

The moose circled back and hit Maven's side again, shaking them like clothes in a dryer. Metal whined with the impact. Glass splintered into spider webs.

Her nemesis gripped her shoulders. "Are you all right?"

"There's a moose chasing us!" she sputtered.

He was all but leaning into her lap to evade the shower of glass. "Right. Stupid question."

"Okay, let's get out of here."

The moose stood in their path. Mac revved the engine. "Move, dammit!

"Go!" she yelled. This was not the time to be a granola-loving tree hugger.

His hands tightened on the steering wheel as the animal landed a crushing blow on the hood like a pro-football linebacker. Something popped, and smoke rolled out from the engine, making her nose twitch. The moose stumbled to the side.

The path clear, he hit the gas. The engine sputtered and died, lights flashing on the dashboard.

"You're kidding me," she heaved out.

"Oh, shit! Must have blown something."

"Try again!"

He turned it over. It didn't even fire. "It's like an elephant sat on my car. That thing's gotta weigh close to a thousand pounds."

"How can you joke around at a time like this? Where's your gun?" She dug into his glove compartment.

"I don't have a gun."

The moose circled the car. Tossed its head. Its wild, eerie eyes peered through the shattered windows.

Maven's eyes swept across her, following the moose. "Great, it knows it has us cornered."

She slammed the glove compartment shut. "Why don't you have a gun?"

"I don't like them."

"How unmanly of you." The moose fogged up her window as it peered through the web-like glass. Yuck, moose breath. She hit the window to make it go away, causing more spider cracks.

"I wouldn't do that," Maven cautioned.

It darted back.

"See, it moved! Just needed to show it who's boss."

It lowered its head and charged her side of the car.

Maven tugged her body over the partition between the seats, his strong arms encircling her as he pushed her head against his chest. "Shit. Now you've really pissed it off."

Pie covered her front, its wetness spreading through her shirt. The smell of citrus blended with the smell of burnt car parts hanging thickly in the air.

The moose rammed her side again. The top part of the window blew apart, showering her in glass.

Maven plucked her onto his lap. She flinched at the heat pouring from his body, the sensation of his muscles bunching under her. God, it had been ages since she'd been this close to a man she wasn't handcuffing. Wasn't it her luck they were in mortal danger, and he was her enemy?

"Wait! Give me the pie." He yanked it from her, leaned over, and flung it through the broken part of the window like it was a frisbee.

He gripped her body more tightly against his, a stance so protective she almost fought him. She didn't need anyone protecting her. She was a cop. Then the moose circled the car again. Who was she kidding? Even cops had partners. Damn, she missed her gun.

Suddenly the moose lifted its head as if sniffing the air. It lumbered toward the pie with its clippity-clop gait, bent over, and clamped it between its teeth. After giving them another eerie glance, it ambled down the street.

Maven dropped his face to her shoulder, hugging her. "Jesus, it was hungry. Thank God!"

"Yeah, hungry." What was she saying? Her ears buzzed like they did after a drug raid. She realized they were both breathing hard. His heart was pounding like an anvil in his chest, mirroring hers.

They were both shaking.

He pressed his cheek against hers. "You scared me. I saw you stop and let Keith run ahead." Then he cupped her neck and tunneled his fingers through her short hair.

His concern broke through the power of her hostility toward him. Hell, he'd saved her life. "I had to."

He rubbed their foreheads together, a gesture so tender her heart cracked open.

"I know you did," he murmured. "Mom's instinct. Where's your car?"

His understanding warmed her even more. Maven's breath feathered her lips. She wanted to lean into him, giving herself to the heat, the connection.

"Ah..." What was he saying? Oh. Car. "We walked. It's not far. The weather's nice." Was she babbling? She *never* babbled.

His strong body and spicy scent made her feel safe. God, why did some big scary mountain creature make her feel like such a girl?

He stroked her hair—a gesture she recognized. She did it with Keith when she wanted to soothe him. Well, she didn't want that type of soothing from Maven. His touch burned. Her body switched from fear to heat. Why did he make her feel this way? He was a freakin' poker player.

"Thank God Keith's safe," he uttered in a deep voice.

His words held the power of blazing sunlight on an icicle. She melted a little.

She raised her head and looked down the street. Even from a few blocks away, her eagle eyes made out Tanner and Brian running toward them. Her brother was carrying a shotgun. Sirens whined in the distance.

"Cavalry's coming," Maven murmured, stroking her cheekbone, yanking her awareness back to him.

"It was already here," she responded.

In that instant, all the antagonism between them faded. Those stoplight green eyes peered into her soul, and the long-silent woman inside awoke and whispered, *Yes, him. Let go.*

She swallowed the lump in her throat as he caressed her cheek. A new chill stole over her, and the punch of lust slammed into her belly. Her bottom twitched on his lap. He stilled, his gaze settling on her mouth.

"I'm glad you're safe." His voice was a near whisper, all throaty and soft.

His voice...well, it made things turn liquid that hadn't been liquid for a long, long time. She was no longer an icicle, but a puddle of water.

"Thanks for coming to our rescue."

"Somehow I think you would have managed." His mouth tipped up. "I just couldn't watch from the sidelines this time."

His coal-black hair had fallen onto his forehead, making him look mussed and unkempt, and oh, so totally hot. Her body seemed to flow into him, anchored by their connection.

"I'm glad."

The whole car smelled like citrus. "You ruined my pie," she said to break the tension between them.

His mouth twitched. "Collateral damage. What was it anyway? Wait."

He swept a finger across her diaphragm for a taste, sending a jolt down her thighs. He put it in his mouth, sucking.

"Key lime. Yum. I can see why it satisfied the moose."

The way he said *satisfy* made her insides clench.

Maven's eyes flicked to something over her shoulder. "We should see if we can get out of the car. Tanner and Brian—"

"Right." She turned to angle her body back into the passenger seat.

He gripped her waist and lifted her effortlessly, setting her down gently. She gulped air in a quick inhale.

She settled in as he tried his door. "Jammed shut. Yours?"

"Same," she said after jiggling the handle.

"Okay, lean away from the window." And without further adieu, he stripped off his shirt.

Her mouth gaped. His bronzed chest with all those corded muscles had her heart knocking hard in her chest again. She had the crazy urge to stroke him and never stop.

"What are you doing?" She tried to sound horrified, but was afraid she sounded like a spinster who hadn't seen a naked man in a long while and *really* craved a strip show.

He bit his lip, fighting a smile. "Don't worry, deputy. I'm not planning on having my way with you just now." He wrapped his fist in the shirt. "Come closer. Let's clear the rest of the glass out of the window the moose broke. We'll have to crawl through it."

Tanner finally reached the passenger side of the car, panting from his run. "Jesus, are you guys all right?"

Brian, who was right behind him, repeated the question.

"We're okay. How's Keith?"

"Scared," Tanner said. "He insisted on coming back for you. Threw a fit when I said no, so we compromised. He's in the car with Meredith and Jill." He set the shotgun aside and fished out his phone. "Yeah, it's safe," he said into the speaker. "Bring the little guy over." He shoved the phone back into his pocket.

"Let's get you guys out," Brian said.

Mac pulled Peggy closer with a gentle hand. "I was just about to knock the window out."

It took him and the other men some time to clear the glass away. Peggy went through face first, Brian and Tanner gently pulling her out. She looked back at Maven, and their eyes met. She felt rooted to the spot. Her heart wrenched like someone had stuck one of those long hat pins in it.

"Go to Keith, Peggy. I'll be fine."

She nodded and ran toward Tanner's approaching SUV.

Keith met her by the car door, crying. "Mommy!"

She knelt down beside him, wrapping him up in her arms. "It's okay. You did so great!"

He squeezed her with all his might, and she pulled him onto her lap and stroked his hair. Her sister-in-law and Jill hovered around her, their eyes wide with concern.

"Jeez, Peg, you really know how to get into scrapes," Jill said, holding her round tummy.

"Are you okay?" Meredith asked, patting her shoulder.

She mumbled some response, her attention focused on Maven sliding smoothly from the car, his still-naked chest gleaming in the sunlight.

A few moments later, her fellow officers and the firemen arrived. Maven pointed down the street in the direction of the moose, and the Animal Control SUV took off in hot pursuit. She lifted her hand to her cop buddies. They would want a statement. It would probably be the weirdest one she had ever given.

Maven was gesturing to Officer Barnes with his hands, his gaze swinging back to her every few seconds. Like he wanted to make sure she was all right.

He kept charging into her life at the oddest moments. This wasn't the first time he'd come to their rescue. The first time they'd met was back in February—he had driven up in that same screaming red Ferrari in the nick of time to help Keith with a broken leg.

She knew what would happen if she let him in. The repressed woman inside her would start to dream of him being everything she could want. Protector, companion, partner. Lover. Oh, she couldn't forget lover.

But he was a poker player. She was a cop. Oil and water.

There could never be anything between them.

She was still planning on kicking him out of town. She just didn't know how yet.

He lifted his hand as if asking if Keith were okay and started walking to them. His gaze sought hers, hesitant but hopeful.

The woman inside her rose up in joy, ready to meet him halfway. A smile wanted to spread across her face.

She picked her son up and turned away, shutting them both out.

CHAPTER 2

Mac halted in the middle of the street when Peggy gave him the cut direct. She might as well have driven one of the glass shards littering the ground through his gut. Every time he opened himself up, she rejected him. He stuffed his anger inside.

How could he have let his guard down again? Hadn't he ignored her since she'd tried to damage his character in front of the whole town so they wouldn't approve his plans for the hotel? If she'd gone only after him, he might have forgiven her. Who doesn't respect a good adversary? But she'd picked something personal, exposing his sister and nephew. He couldn't let that go. He'd buried the hurt, pouring his energy into building his hotel. He hoped her panties got in a wad every time she thought about his sparkling poker palace—as he'd been told she called it.

He was going to send her a hand-written invitation to the hotel's grand opening tomorrow to piss her off.

He shook the thoughts off, returning to the present moment as Dare's helpful police force asked him questions about the moose attack. One of the deputies even called a tow truck for him. Tanner—Peggy's brother and his increasingly good friend—hustled back and forth between him and his family.

Peggy stuck close to Tanner's SUV, holding Keith as she delivered her statement to one of her fellow cops.

Wouldn't it have been more efficient for them to give a statement together? Yes, but she couldn't stand to be near him. She'd driven that point home. Her distaste for his profession bordered on unbalanced. Well, he'd worked hard to be treated with respect, and there was nothing wrong with how he made his living or his money.

It baffled him why Peggy, of all women, had dug into him this way. And damn it, he wanted to cut her out. He didn't need another prickly, courageous, confused single mother in his life. He already had one—his sister—who was moving to Dare Valley in a few days to work at the hotel. Isn't that why he understood Peggy?

"You sure you're okay?" Tanner asked.

"Sure. I can add surviving a *moose* to my resume."

"Hell of a thing. We didn't know what to do. Brian had to run to a neighbor's house for a shotgun. Jill hates guns."

Mac surveyed his car. It looked pretty done for. "Peggy took me to task for not having one."

"Yeah, she'd carry one all the time if she could. Summer makes it hard to conceal a clutch piece."

Mac shook his head. "You two speak the same language."

"I might know how to use weapons, but I don't share her fondness for them. Some women like shoes. Peggy likes—"

"Guns. Got it." He circled the car and looked over his shoulder. He let out a long breath. No ugly beastie in sight. "Never knew a moose could do that."

"The cops said it's rare, but happens. It's been dry in the canyon. Not much to eat or drink."

"Well, it liked her pie."

Tanner's laugh snorted out. "That's a miracle. Peg's not the best cook."

There was a crack in the engine. Battery fluid leaked like a tributary onto the concrete. "What a mess. I've never liked Hummers, but I'm seeing them in a new light."

"Or a Range Rover. That's what we always drove on safari."

"I don't consider Dare the Masai Mara."

Tanner's hand gestured to the twisted peaks dotting the valley. "We're living in a mountainous region, and we're crowding the animals out. Hell, if Meredith sees any more deer eating our vegetable garden, I think she might shoot one. And she is *so* not a hunter."

Mac chuckled. "Deer I understand. Now, moose—"

"Fucking ugly." Tanner slapped him on the back as the tow truck pulled up next to the Ferrari. "The cops are done here. Let's head back to Jill and Brian's. Get you a beer."

"I think I could use something a little stronger."

"Whiskey then. We'll toast your Ferrari. She led a good life."

After loading his car—or what remained of it—the tow truck gave them a ride to the party to join the others. Mac fought the sigh. God, he had loved that car...at least he had five others to soften the blow.

When they arrived, Mac followed Tanner into the house.

"Let's get you a shirt. Brian doesn't have your sense of style, though, so you'll have to suck it up."

"No, he sure doesn't." Jill Hale McConnell waddled over to him and pressed herself into his arms. He held her gently, her baby bump pressed firmly against him. She was the main reason his hotel was going through as planned. Besides being his right hand woman, she'd become a dear friend.

When she stepped back, she swept her eyes over him. "Well, now that I think of it, perhaps you should stay shirtless. Add more spice to my BBQ. If I weren't married to Brian..."

He tapped her nose. "Funny. Those twins are short-circuiting your brain."

She held her tummy like the basketball it resembled. "No doubt. You okay?"

"Yeah, but you be careful walking around here, okay? You can't run like you used to if another moose comes through."

Her mouth pinched. "That would seriously suck. Grandpa thinks more animals have been coming into town because of the drought. Still, this moose thing is seriously weird. He says he's going to talk to the Forest Service to see if there's anything Dare citizens need to know. There'll be an article in the paper tomorrow."

"I'm actually doing the article." Tanner poured Mac a whiskey. "We flipped for it. So I'll need a quote. Why do I think Peggy did something to piss the moose off?"

"Well, she did stop to confront it so Keith could run to the house. Maybe it realized she was a worthy opponent." Like he had the moment he met her. He shook his head. "Jill, could you grab me one of Brian's shirts? I'll risk his fashion sense. I'm feeling a little exposed."

"Ah...who knew you were modest?"

"Please."

"Okay, I suppose you deserve a shirt. I'll pick something out."

She waddled off. He drained the whiskey in one shot as people came up and slapped him on the back. He downplayed the whole *hero* talk.

Jill reappeared with a purple shirt with yellow polka-dots. She held it up to his chest. The handful of guests who were mingling in the room laughed. "I realized you could wear one of my maternity shirts instead. Isn't this pretty?"

He pushed the hideous explosion of color away. "Ha-ha. I'm tempted to call your bluff and put this on, but I have too much dignity."

"I think a real hero deserves a *real* shirt," Meredith said, appearing by his side.

Jill stuck out her tongue. "You're so boring, sis."

"Why don't you show me my choices?" Mac said, taking her by the arm.

She led him to Brian's closet, where he selected a simple hunter green T-shirt.

"Mine was better."

He gave her a warm smile. Only Jill would have come up with a stunt like that. "Okay, now it's time for food."

"Follow me. Brian's gone crazy, as usual."

Mac followed her into the backyard. Sure enough, Jill's chef husband had done it up right. Opening the town's hot new restaurant, Brasserie Dare, hadn't lulled him into a cooking comfort zone. A whole pig turned on a spit over a freshly dug fire pit. A BBQ smoker puffed out black clouds, the fragrance of roasted meat, hickory, and spices redolent in the air.

Tanner and Meredith were huddled in a corner with Peggy and Keith. Peggy had also changed her shirt, he noticed. She was wearing a simple navy tee. No polka dots. Her cop sensibilities wouldn't stand for it.

Arthur Hale—Jill and Meredith's curmudgeonly grandpa—let Keith clamber up on his lap and passed the boy a red hot. He waved to Mac, who returned the gesture. The more he knew the journalistic legend from *The*

Western Independent, the more he respected him. He'd walk over to say hello if Peggy weren't emanating her *waves of disgust*, as he'd come to call them.

Jill grabbed his arm. "She'll come around."

Since he knew she meant Peggy, he lifted a shoulder. The gash in his heart still gushed blood. "I don't think so."

"She still calling you by your last name?"

"Let's drop this."

Peggy refused to call him Mac. Jill thought it meant she was fighting her feelings for him; Mac thought it was another sign of her contempt.

She elbowed him. "Is she?"

He picked up a paper plate and scooped up potato salad and a huge helping of pulled pork and dry-rub ribs. "Yes. Now, let's find you somewhere to sit down so you can prop up your feet."

She put her hands on her hips. "I'm fine."

"You're pregnant with twins. Changes everything."

She let him take her hand. "It weirds me out how much you know about pregnant women."

"I went through it with my sister." He shuddered. "You don't forget."

"When are she and your nephew arriving?"

He scanned the eastern part of the mountain where their new house was situated. They'd spend the next couple of years here to launch the hotel. Then, they'd move on to the next spot. He'd used the same model to create boutique poker hotels in six other western locations, to rave reviews.

"Dustin and Abbie will be coming in a couple of days. School finished a few weeks ago. They've been packing up."

"How does Dustin feel about starting out at a new high school?"

He propped her feet up on a cooler and stood over her to block the sun, making her smile. Her red curls bobbed around her face when she sank into the chair.

"He hasn't stopped bitching. I expect we'll hear nothing but complaining for the next few years. We've ruined his life, you see."

"Don't freak out an expectant mom. I'm still trying to wrap my mind around the thought of babies. Teenagers terrify me."

The memory of what it had been like to be a hell-raising teenage boy kept him up at night. The apple didn't fall far from the tree. "Join the club."

"You didn't think about letting them stay in Arizona?"

He took a bite of potato salad. The extra pickle punched it out of the ballpark. "No. We're family. We stick together. Abbie and I made that deal when we built the second hotel. I have to travel between our hotels as part of the business, but we always have a home base together."

She grabbed an olive. "I love that about you. You're like a poker player with a heart of gold—instead of a hooker."

"Leave it to you to twist that phrase into a sick compliment. Have I told you how glad I am you're working with me?"

"Almost every day. It's part of my grand plan to lure you into letting me take over the hotel. You know my aspirations to be a great businesswoman in Dare."

"You already are with the coffee shop. Now, you're just expanding."

He pulled a table with an umbrella closer to Jill. "You need to be in the shade."

"You're right. These munchkins suck all the air conditioning out of me. Not that we have any in the house. We usually don't need it in the mountains, but this is the hottest summer I can remember. I've told Brian he's going to sleep on the couch until he installs a window unit. I can't take it anymore."

Mac's mouth tilted up. "It's the least he could do. You're carrying his kids."

"Exactly!" She grabbed her lemonade.

Mac dragged another chair over to the table. Guests filtered over to discuss the already infamous moose incident and the hotel's grand opening on July 2nd, which was just over a week away. The festivities would include the first big-name poker tournament. Mentioning some of his more famous guests, like the award-winning country singer Rye Crenshaw, had the women swooning. Unfortunately, Mac hadn't been able to convince Rye to sing when the poker tournament ended on July 4th, right before the fireworks show. He was still working on that.

Tanner joined the group with an update on the moose. Officers had followed it back to its one-month-old calf. The poor thing had broken its leg in the stream running adjacent to Brian and Jill's property, probably trying to find water in the drought. The mama had been feeding it Peggy's pie. The cops had used a stun gun on both animals, and a vet was fixing the baby's leg. They'd be released into the wild once the little one recovered. The vet had told the cops that moms always went nuts over their babies. Hadn't Peg?

Mac gave Tanner a few quotes for his article, savored the phenomenal BBQ, and let the chatter and whiskey relax him.

But he couldn't unwind all the way.

Peggy.

Even with his back to her, he could feel her. The watchfulness, the caution, the interest.

God, he had to tune her out again. He'd gotten pretty good at keeping her in the deep freeze. The moose incident had unleashed the primal fire he felt for her.

He switched to beer and let Jill amuse him with her jokes and animated chatter. Her enthusiasm for the hotel matched his own. As they talked about the final training session for the staff, he let himself remember who he was—and how different that was from how Peggy seemed to see him.

A delicate tap on his shoulder made him look back. Keith tucked his hands under his armpits and stared at the ground. Mac fought the instinct to scoop him onto his lap and comfort him. Poor kid had to be terrified. But he'd learned with his nephew that you needed to balance the boy and the growing man, even at this age. Men knew they needed to be brave, scared or not. Especially the sons of single mothers. There was no one to protect their moms, so somehow they felt it was their job. It wasn't, but he'd never crush that spirit.

"Mr. Maven. I wanted to thank you for saving us." His voice could have doubled for a bullfrog's.

"You were doing pretty great before I dropped in. You were brave to run to the house all by yourself."

Keith's head darted up. Those brown eyes—so big and clear like his mom's—widened. "You think so?"

Mac's hand rested on his little shoulder. "I sure do. You know about castles and knights, right?"

Keith nodded emphatically.

"When bad guys surrounded a castle, the knights would always send the bravest person to run for help."

"That's so cool!" His eyes shone as big as dollar coins. "I'm glad you helped my mom. She didn't have her gun."

"She's pretty brave."

"She's the bravest! I can't wait to tell my friends what happened."

His gaze drifted to Peggy. She was watching them. Her facial muscles had softened. He fought off his frustration. He wanted her to soften *with him* regardless of whether he was being kind to her kid.

The mother in her appreciated and trusted him.

The deputy didn't. She'd probably shoot him—not fatally—just to give him a limp. Especially if it delayed the hotel's opening.

"Mom said to tell you thank you."

So, she'd sent a messenger behind enemy lines. He caught Jill looking at him and fought a curse. Peggy could barely say thank you to her brother. Why had he expected her to say it to him?

Because he'd hoped that moment in the car had changed things.

He was a fool.

"You tell your mom I did what anyone would." He ruffled Keith's hair.

The boy took the encouragement and jumped on his lap, chatting like a magpie with Jill, his favorite person in the world. Mac let Keith curl against his body with the total trust of a child.

He remembered how Peggy had curled against him when she was on his lap. Totally different, except for the delicate ribbon of trust that had been created in that moment.

But she'd ripped it in two.

He put an arm around Keith, met her eyes for a full ten seconds, and then looked away.

His heart wasn't staying on his sleeve.

CHAPTER 3

The moose jokes were going to make her crack. Billy Barnes had the audacity to shove a stuffed, furry replica under her desk. It gave a deranged *moo* when she sat down, courtesy of its motion sensor. The guys were yukking it up so hard she hoped they'd choke on their glazed donuts. She'd just hurled the moose at Billy without saying anything.

This was getting ridiculous.

After her lunch break, during which she'd been exposed to a whopping six moose jokes, she stormed back into her office. Usually she could laugh off pranks and jokes, but all the moose talk made her think of Maven. She'd had trouble sleeping two nights in a row courtesy of his stupid, gorgeous face worming its way into her brain. She couldn't stop hearing his dark chocolate voice whisper in her ear.

The pastry box and card on her desk stopped her in her tracks. She eyed it like a bomb tech. The guys wouldn't have gotten her a moose cake, would they? Jeez. See if she'd share it with them. She'd shoot a hole right through its gooey center. That would shut them up.

She lifted the lid one inch at a time. The key lime pie made her snarl. She knew who'd sent it before she tore open the card.

Since you blamed me for ruining your pie, I wanted to replace it.
I hope it matches the care and attention you took with your delicious creation.
I also want to cordially invite you to the hotel's opening on July 4.
The Grand Mountain Hotel looks forward to welcoming you.
Regards,
Mac

She threw the card down. Damn him. Didn't he know this would get her goat? She stopped pacing. Of course he did. Hadn't she seen the hurt in his eyes at the BBQ before he turned into Mr. Cool again?

Her foot kicked her trash can. He was lucky she didn't march over to his hotel and throw the pie in his face. Of all the gall! She rocked on her heels. She simply had to find a way to close him down or make him leave town. Now that she'd found a safe haven at last, she couldn't let gambling ruin it.

She strode out with the pie. "I have a special dessert in my hands. You can have it on one condition. No more moose anything! Understood?"

Fresh-faced Kirby Jenkins stood up. "What kind of pie?"

"What does it matter? It's pie."

"I'm not retiring my moose jokes until I know it's worth it."

"Oh, for crying out loud. It's key lime." Since when did men care what kind of dessert it was?

"Sweet." He grabbed the box. "You're off the hook. I'll see to it." He pointed his finger to the other officers who were lounging with donuts and coffee.

"You'd better. Or I declare war. You know I fight dirty."

Billy Barnes crossed his arms. "You couldn't stop that moose in its tracks."

Her hand waved in the air. "Ha-ha. Don't make me make you eat your words."

She didn't slam her office door, but she wanted to. It was time to get serious. Her key unlocked her storage cabinet. The musty files made her nose twitch. She sneezed and pulled the first faded folder, the dust bunnies shining like starbursts in the sunlight streaming through her office window. The label read *Murder, The Grand Mountain Hotel, 1931*. She'd snuck over to Archives in the early dawn to *borrow* the records.

The murder photos had yellowed with age, but that didn't hide the grisliness. Aaron the Kid, a small-time mobster, had accused the card dealer, Bradford Calvin, of fixing his poker game. Witness statements differed completely. Some said Aaron pulled his weapon first. Others said Bradford had pulled a concealed weapon in self-defense. No one commented on how Lance Kitrick, a local, was involved or why he'd fled the scene.

She'd made her own board about Maven and had been studying this old case for months without any breakthroughs, praying the construction crew would find a skeleton. When they didn't, she locked the cabinet and gave up, but she hadn't been able to put the file back in Archives.

Today, she finally had to admit defeat. Since everyone associated with the crime was dead, she couldn't go back and interview anyone. It was more than a cold case; it was arctic. A murder in 1931 couldn't hurt The Grand Mountain Hotel now.

God, in her desperation to kick Maven out of town, she'd been grasping at straws.

A nasty voice entered her mind. *You're this desperate to make him leave? What does that tell you?* She shut it down and tapped the pencil against her temple. Everybody but her—and the teetotalers and anti-gamblers—wanted this hotel. Her beef with Maven was common knowledge, even though no one understood it.

Her recent "moment" with Maven had reinvigorated her desire to get him out of town. She couldn't ignore him forever. Keith was upset. So was her best friend, Jill. Tanner and Maven had grown close too, dammit, and even Meredith seemed to enjoy laughing with him.

Peggy was odd man out in her family.

Something had to give.

Plus, the ongoing dreams were making her straitjacket crazy.

The sex-crazed ones played out the same fantasy over and over again. She and Maven were tangled up in her bed sheets as he drove into her until she screamed out. Even more mortifying, she came in her sleep every time. She blamed it on the sex drought since her divorce.

The other dreams were about her father. He had been a gambler and a drunk, and the one surety in her young life had been that he would appropriate the money her mom had set aside for her school supplies or prom dress to buy another bottle of Canadian Mist and play some cards. He had never hit her, but he'd always been quick to yell and raise his fists. Tanner had always interceded, diverting his attention.

Peggy blamed her father's behavior on booze and gambling. If he hadn't given into those vices, he'd have been a good father. The cop in her knew it wasn't true, but the young girl she'd been couldn't let go of the belief. She'd channeled her anger into mercilessly upholding the law. No one walked on a drunk driving. Kids drinking underage got arrested.

But she'd never busted anyone for gambling. Hadn't come across it until now.

Maven's legal gambling pissed her off. Why could a hotel offer it, but not a back room? The difference didn't make sense.

What she really needed was to dig up a skeleton in Maven's closet. So far, she hadn't found one. Her first try had ended in total embarrassment, for her.

She shoved the files aside, her nose twitching at the dust. *The Western Independent's* front page drew her gaze. They were running yet another article on the hotel's miraculous transformation, juxtaposing old pictures from its grand opening in 1922 with modern ones. The grainy photos harkened back to a time when men slicked back their hair and wore fedoras and pin-stripe suits.

She tapped a pencil to her lips. These photos were older than the ones in her murder file, but they hadn't yellowed with age. Arthur was beyond resourceful, and he always managed to dig up unusual and obscure scoops. Hell, hadn't he printed the story that Maven was coming to Dare to restore the hotel before it was common knowledge, making Maven accelerate his plans?

Hmm...

Her brain started working. It was time to talk to Arthur. He liked a good story, and maybe together they could find something on Maven.

Cheered, she stood up and decided to visit Tanner. While she was there, she'd pop in to see Arthur. No one would suspect anything.

She locked the files away and strode out. Only a few graham cracker crumbs remained in the bottom of the pastry box. Pigs.

"I'm heading out for a bit," she informed Billy Barnes. His foot tapped like a rabbit on a sugar high.

"See ya, Peg," he called. "Watch out for big, scary—"

"Stop right there!" Kirby warned. "We had pie. We've been paid off."

She gave him a mini-salute for taking charge.

Another slow day in Dare. You had to love it.

She decided to walk. Main Street was decked out in festive red, white, and blue Independence Day banners, and a few shops had planted matching flowers. Who had time for details like that? She was lucky to remember to plant geraniums in a pot on the front steps to cover the crack in the concrete.

The signs *Make Dare Beautiful* baffled her. Who cared? Being clean and safe was enough for her and her kid.

Her eyes zeroed in on a Ferrari the color of a silver bullet. Only one person owned a Ferrari in Dare. Well, he owned two, or he had before the moose had totaled the other one. While his cars had initially branded him as an outsider, they were widely considered cool now, especially since Maven also owned a pick-up truck and an SUV like everyone else. And those weren't his only cars; the guy practically had a fleet. Some people.

She paused, blinded by the car's shine. The metal frame reflected her scowl. Her foot tapped on the sidewalk. The vehicle was over-the-top. The fire hydrant on the corner drew her gaze. His car was parked pretty close to it. Her tape measure was in her office, but she was pretty sure he was breaking the law.

Or so she told herself.

She dug out her notebook and wrote him a ticket. Signing her name gave her a giddy feeling. If only she could see the look on his face when he found it. She hadn't caught him speeding yet, but it was only a matter of time in these babies. When she'd done a background check on him, she'd discovered a pile of speeding tickets. The man liked the fast lane in more things than just poker. Maybe there was more in the fast lane category to uncover about him.

The note fit perfectly under his fancy-schmancy windshield wipers. *Thanks for the pie.* She headed down the street, whistling Dixie.

When she reached the headquarters of *The Independent*, the windows were sparkling in the morning sun. She pushed the door and entered the buzz. Even though it differed from the precinct's energy, she liked the feel. People chasing leads. Talking to sources. Investigating. Stuff she understood.

She waved when a few people lifted their hands. Her shoulder hitched up. She didn't understand this much friendliness. It was like Dare's water supply had candy-striper serum in it. Still, she did her best to respond. Her brother had a corner office with a window—something he appreciated after all of the window-less offices he'd inhabited overseas due to bombs and bullets.

"Hey there," she called out, crossing her arms in his doorway.

He spun around and smiled. "Well, if this isn't a surprise. You wouldn't happen to have the munchkin with you?"

"No. He's probably at the pool with the sitter. Even with all that swimming, he still hates to go to bed. It's a battle every freakin' night."

He rose and gave her a big hug. "I seem to remember you being the same way."

She punched him on the back. "Well, you were the opposite—you always loved going to sleep."

"Still do. You want some coffee?"

"No." She sat in the ancient leather chair across from his desk. It squeaked. She liked that. Gave it character.

He shoved a stack of health care books aside and kicked back. "Any bad dreams?"

Her mouth nearly dropped open. Jeez, his mind-reading thing freaked her out. How did he know she was dreaming about Maven and their dad? "Ah...it's manageable."

His grin confused her. "Do you end up shooting the moose?"

Is that what they were talking about? Whew. "Funny. You should hang out with my crew. They're been cracking moose jokes for days."

"Billy told me he found a stuffed one that mooed at Wal-Mart."

She threw a pencil at him. He ducked.

"You guys need to get a life. Moose don't even moo."

His laughter was as demented as the guys' at the office. "I know. How's Keith? He seemed pretty creeped out."

She scowled. "Well, Maven said something to him about knights and castles—don't ask—and that helped him deal. Still looks over his shoulder, but so do I."

"And that just chaps your hide, right?"

She didn't have to ask which part. "Look, we're not going to agree on this."

Those intense brown eyes—so like hers—studied her face. "I know, which is why I haven't mentioned this before. I understand some of your resistance after Dad, but it's hurting Keith. We saw Mac last night at the ice cream shop. Keith wanted to say hello, but he said he wasn't sure you'd like it. He asked me to call and ask you."

Shame poured over her like hot syrup. "Which you didn't do."

His face softened. "I didn't think there was any need. He's a nice guy, Peg, and Keith likes him. He needs as many men in his life as he can get without his dad around. We both know he's starved for it."

She gripped her knees to keep from lashing out.

Her brother raised a hand. "I'm not saying this to put your back out of line, but it's true. Frank's a dick, and all he'll ever do for Keith is send a few child support payments after you press him. The Hales and Brian love him, but there's no reason to limit the people in his life, is there?"

Her fingernails scraped her tan uniform slacks. "I don't want him confused by all this poker stuff. It's a bad influence."

He didn't say anything for a long while. Just continued studying her in that X-ray-vision way of his. "We both know that's not the issue here. He's nothing like our fuck of a father, Peg."

She stood. "I don't want to talk about this."

His brows only rose.

"Fine," she said. "I'll try to be more reasonable. I don't want Keith to get upset, and I know he has been. But I'm not going to ease up on Maven."

He came over and rubbed her arms, which were locked in place at her side. "Okay, I'll let this go for now, but you know this thing between you and Mac will only get worse, right? The harder you fight it, the bigger it will get."

Her eyes narrowed. Her brother truly *did* have X-ray vision. "Leave it alone."

"I'm not sure either of you has a choice. Okay, changing subjects. David is talking about coming for a visit. What are you going to do then?"

"Take a vacation?" she quipped while the old pain seared through her. Their younger brother had followed in their dad's drinking shoes, covering the family in his shit more than once. Tanner had just finished scraping off a fresh batch involving Meredith, but David was in AA again, so the two of them were talking. Peggy couldn't face him yet. They'd been best friends when they were kids, but then he'd started drinking in high school. Each time he got sober, he'd just fall off the wagon again. It had happened more times than she could count. The hurt and disappointment had unhinged her, so she'd closed it off.

"He still loves you, Peg, and he's not Dad. I know the difference."

Her fingers pinched the bridge of her nose. "It hurts too much." Hard to confess to herself, let alone him.

His sigh gusted out. "Okay, when you want to talk about it, let me know."

Her nod was perfunctory. "I'm going to see Arthur." She turned to leave.

"You mad at me?" Tanner asked.

Her throat cramped like a suspect was strangling her. She coughed. "Yeah." She lifted her tense shoulders. "Sort of."

He sighed and pulled her close. "I'm sorry. I didn't want to make you mad, but seeing tears in Keith's eyes last night upset me. I thought about it and decided I needed to say something."

Her clasp was a stiff as dress blues. "I'll take care of it."

He chucked her under the chin like he used to when she was a kid. "I know you will. You always do the right thing."

She rolled her eyes. "So do you."

"Yeah, it's still part of our rebellion. Dad never did, and we hated it, so we do the opposite."

Her stomach gurgled at the mention of their father. She put a hand to it. "Must be hungry."

"Yeah, must be. I'll see you guys tomorrow night at your house for dinner. Do you want us to bring anything special?"

She liked these monthly family get togethers that everyone took a turn hosting, but it was still weird coordinating a potluck. Did she look like she cared if someone wanted to bring pasta salad or regular salad? Jeez. "I've already talked to Meredith about it."

"Okay. Enjoy your day. Watch out for any wild moose."

Her mouth tipped up, but the smile immediately fell flat when she left the room.

She breathed out a sigh of relief when she walked past Meredith's office. Empty. She really liked her sister-in-law, but she didn't feel like chatting now.

Arthur Hale's office stood in the center of the paper. She liked that he didn't need a window. The clutter of newspapers and chewed-up pencils on his scuffed-up desk made her smile. He had his back to her and was leaning toward the computer screen on the wall-length console.

She walked up behind him. "Hello there," she said awkwardly.

He jumped in his chair and swung those faded blue-jeans eyes at her. "Peggy! What are you doing? Trying to give an old man a heart attack? Didn't you see my AARP sticker on the door?" He huffed and puffed like the wolf in the *Three Little Pigs* story she used to read to Keith.

"Sorry. You were..." She waved at the computer. "Engrossed."

"Yeah, dammit. I can't find my reading glasses. Ticks me off. I think Meredith hid them to get back at me for all the red marks on her Sunday editorial. Man, that girl can hold a grudge. Don't get on her bad side. Ask Tanner. Or Jill." He dug out a red hot. "Want one?"

She grabbed it suspiciously. Wasn't cinnamon supposed to be brown? Still, she popped it in her mouth. The burning flavor had her eyes watering.

"You should see your face." He laughed. "Take a seat. Please. Did you stop by to see Tanner?"

She eyed the door and went ahead and shut it. When she took her seat, he waggled his brow.

"I haven't heard anything of interest on the police scanner this morning. You didn't come across another moose, did you?"

"For crying out loud, are people *ever* going to let that go?"

"Heck no. It's one of the strangest stories in Dare, hands-down. Gossip can't compete. Would you rather hear about who parked in your neighbor's garage last night or a crazed moose?"

She crossed her arms. "People need to get a life."

"I expect so." He leaned toward her over his desk. "So, why did you close the door? My heart pumps harder when people do that."

Her toes scrunched in her shoes. "Well...I wanted to talk about the possibility that we might help each other on something."

The room filled with the crackling of a plastic wrapper as he slowly unwrapped a red hot. "That's pretty vague. Care to be more specific?" His lips twitched, but he leaned back in his chair. A squeak erupted, making her ear drums wince.

She tried to keep a straight face. "It's about Maven."

His mouth moved like he was fighting a smile. "Ah..."

Her toes stopped dancing. "Okay, you don't need to use that tone. This is purely investigative. I was hoping we could make a pact or something... You know, if one of us uncovers something questionable about him or his background, we can share it with each other."

"Struck out with the 1931 murder, did ya?"

Her mouth parted.

"Please, even I knew you were looking into that. Heard you were checking to see if there were any old skeletons on the property."

"Who told you?"

He chewed on the end of a pencil. "Someone I play Bingo with. Okay, let's be honest. You're only doing this because you want to stop Mac Maven."

His bulls-eye made the space between her shoulder blades itch. "His hotel passed the council."

He pointed his pencil in her direction. "And yet, here you are, talking about digging into his background and sharing information with me if I agree to do the same. And in your spare time, I might add. Like a single mom has any."

"Are you saying you won't use something if I find it?"

He threw the pencil down. "No, that's not what I'm saying." He drummed his fingers on the desk. "*If* you find something on Maven or the hotel, I'll print it—*after* it's been confirmed. It's my business. But this topic gives me heartburn. My granddaughter works for the man. The Hale's can usually be neutral, but not Jill—she'll go off like a rocket. I don't like your motives, my dear, but it's not my place as a journalist to judge them."

Jill's reaction *would* be awful. Hadn't she been angry after the city council meeting? Somehow, they'd gotten through it, but she wasn't sure her friend would be as forgiving this time. "I made an investigative board like I would for a case, and I've been looking into him for a while."

"What have you found so far?"

Squat really. She rested her elbows on her knees. "Not much, but I don't give up easily."

"That's one of the things I admire about you, your tenacity." He thumbed through a file drawer and yanked out a green one. "I did my own digging when Maven announced his plan, and Jill told me she was going to work for him. I'll give you what I have on one condition."

Her mouth watered as she stared at that file, wondering if it contained anything she'd missed. "Okay. What is it?"

"If you don't have enough evidence to make a story—any story—this conversation stays between the two of us."

Her brow rose. "That's interesting. Why would you say that?"

"I know you have your reasons for wanting Mac out of business, but I won't be used as a bag man. I'm giving you this information on good faith. I am a journalist, after all. Do we understand one another?"

She nodded.

"I'll make you a copy then."

While she waited, she tapped her feet. God, this just had to work. He could not stay here. She wasn't sure what would happen to her if he did. He was driving her crazy. And none of his gamblers had shown up in town yet. Who knew what would happen to Dare once they did? She just couldn't allow that to happen.

Arthur dropped an envelope in her lap when he returned.

"Thank you. I'll let you know what I discover," she said, "but our agreement goes both ways. I won't mention our pact, and you won't either."

Arthur rubbed his nose. "Tanner doesn't know you're still trying to boot Mac out of town, eh?"

"No."

"Okay. Mum's the word."

"Thanks, Arthur."

His cane clattered to the floor when he stood.

"Don't worry about seeing me out."

He blustered. "Okay. I won't. I'll see you tomorrow night."

"Don't expect the food to be as good as it is at Brasserie Dare. Well, except for whatever Brian brings." She opened the door. "Being his partner, I hear the item you proposed for the restaurant's menu is pretty sweet."

"Well, when I agreed to be Brian's financial backer, he agreed to let me select something. I love a good lamb shank. Had my first one in Rome in 1967. I'll never forget it."

Peggy smiled at the nostalgia on his face. "I'll give it serious consideration next time I eat there."

"You do that." As she left, she knew there was a double meaning there.

Her fingers itched to rip the envelope open and read its contents on the street, but she didn't want to attract attention.

She passed Don't Soy with Me. If she hadn't taken so long at the paper, she'd duck into the coffee shop to see if Jill were in today or at the hotel, her other home. The door jingled behind her. She looked back.

Maven strolled out. His body moved like a burglar she'd once busted, all smooth and quiet as those long, muscular legs ate up the sidewalk. He swung on his reflective sunglasses, covering up his stoplight green eyes. He wore a silky shirt the same gray as his Ferrari, with black slacks that undoubtedly showcased his superior butt.

Her dream exploded in her mind. Of him, naked, breathing hard, pounding into her, her hands on his behind, urging him deeper as she came apart.

A part of her trembled on the sidewalk.

No way was she saying hello. Her power-walk took her well past his car. When she was a safe distance from him, she looked back and watched as he plucked the ticket off the windshield. He tore off his glasses and stared at her, feet planted on the sidewalk. He lifted the ticket and crumpled it into a ball as she watched.

So, it wasn't the smartest thing she'd ever done. Would he contest? It wasn't like he was hurting for cash.

She hustled down the street and ducked into the sheriff's office. Cringed when she heard *Mooooo*.

Her gaze swung to the right. Eerie plastic moose eyes stared back unblinking. Someone had hung the stuffed animal by the door. Repressed laughter reached her ears.

"Okay, that's it!" She sprinted toward the bullpen.
It was time they understood.
She was not a woman to mess with.

CHAPTER 4

"If I hear one more complaint out of your mouth, I swear I'll stop this car right now," Mac gritted out.

His nephew, Dustin, glared at him in the rear-view mirror. A tuft of gelled black hair formed a pyramid on the top of his head in something called a fohawk. Other than hair, looking at Dustin was like looking at a picture of his younger self. They had the same deep-set, dark-lashed green eyes, high cheekbones, and a dimple in their chins.

And wasn't the pissed-off expression familiar? He'd carried a pretty big chip on his shoulder until Abbie had gotten pregnant, requiring him to step up. He'd channeled that 'chip' into poker games and learned to make it work for him, not against him. Dustin didn't have much direction yet, so his shit pretty much splatted on everyone around him.

"Did you hear me?"

"Uh-huh."

When had the kid stopped saying yes? Man, he missed the old days when he was Uncle Mac, a hero in a young boy's life, unable to do any wrong.

His sister's lips twitched. He could all but hear Abbie thinking, *you're losing it*. He'd just picked them up from the airport in Denver a couple of hours ago, and Dustin was already laying on the defiance pretty thick.

"I can't wait to see the hotel, Mac. It was being gutted when we last visited. It might become my favorite."

He slanted his sister a glance. "That's because you're a sucker for old-world elegance."

Didn't even her traveling clothes scream 'lady?' What woman wore a navy linen skirt on a plane unless she was rushing from the airport to the office? Abbie's matching suit jacket fit her petite frame like a glove, but it didn't call attention to her femininity. She always downplayed her prettiness for reasons he'd grown to understand. She was more comfortable that way, and she thought it repelled male attention. Once burned, twice shy. Plus, she had some June Cleaver notion still running in the back of her mind about what a 'good' mother looked like—so totally different from their card-dealing one who'd bleached her hair and favored skin-tight clothes for her job at the casino.

"I am a sucker for the old stuff."

"Too bad the gangsters aren't still around from its heyday. Now that would be cool," his nephew interjected, kicking the back of his seat again.

Mac ground his teeth. "Yes, it'd be nice if some guys would shoot up my hotel."

"Maybe then we'd have to leave."

His hands gripped the wheel. "One can hope."

"It'll be fine, Dustin." Abbie turned in her seat to give him a look.

Mac blew out a breath. The kid had never been so dead set against moving before.

"Oh, look!" Abbie pointed out the window. "There's some deer."

"We've seen those before, Mom."

"Well, I never tire of them. It's a lovely drive, Mac. I know we're going to love Dare. Reminds me of our place in Wyoming. It's nice to see green again after the desert."

"I like the heat."

Mac kept his eyes on the road, even though he wanted to swing his head around and give Dustin a good, old-fashioned stare-down. Funny how these days all Dustin did was stare right back at him. Lately they'd been butting heads like two rams. They were so alike it freaked him out.

Dustin kicked his seat again.

"If you do that one more time, I swear we're going to take your phone away for a day."

"I'm not doing anything!"

"Dustin, why don't you scoot behind me?" Abbie said. "You can see down the canyon better this way. What's it called again?"

"Sardine," Mac growled.

Dustin kicked his seat one last time for good measure. "Oops. Sorry." Mac watched in the rear view mirror as the kid slid to the other side, all slouched body language.

Mac tapped his left foot. Where was his reputable cool? He was a high-stakes poker player, for crying out loud. No one was able to rile him up like Teenage Dustin—sixteen, and newly decked out with a driver's license and a shitty attitude. He took a deep breath, trying to channel calming energy. He spotted a police car up ahead in a speed-trap. He was safe because he didn't speed when he had passengers. He looked for glossy dark hair and high cheekbones, but this cop had a granite jaw and beard stubble.

His mind clicked. Someone else totally broke his cool. Peggy.

She was not a woman to underestimate. He hadn't expected her to nit-pick him from behind her badge. That ticket still pissed him off.

"Here's Dare," he said.

They crested into town, cruising down Main Street.

"Oh, it's exactly how I remember," Abbie said. "So bright and cheerful."

"I think it sucks."

Abbie reached back and patted Dustin's knee. "I know it's hard to move, but you'll like it here. There's so much to do outside."

"There was a lot of stuff to do at home."

"How about we have some lunch at Don't Soy with Me?" Mac interjected. "Jill's there today."

Abbie turned in her seat. "What do you say, Dustin? I'll buy."

"Fine. But I'm getting the tallest coffee they've got."

Mac rolled his eyes. "Okay, then."

He scanned Main Street. Wasn't it his luck that the only open space was the one by the infamous fire hydrant? He wasn't going to risk another ticket. He sped by.

"Hey!" Dustin cried, grabbing his mom's shoulder rest. "What are you doing? Are you going blind? There was a parking space right there."

"That one's defective," he replied. "Trust me."

"No need to cover for your failing vision, Uncle Mac. We know you're getting up there in years."

Even Mac could hear the glee in his voice. Abbie muffled her laughter.

"Keep hoping, kiddo. I can see everything you do just fine. Maybe *you're* the one who's afraid to walk a block."

"In your dreams."

"Yeah."

The banter felt good. He rolled the window down to enjoy the breeze. His family was finally here permanently, and wasn't that a relief. He'd missed them, but he and Abbie had decided it would be best for Dustin to finish out the school year in Arizona. Forming an office in Colorado had involved a lot of travel, but he'd tried to keep it down to only a few nights a week. And when the project had reached its later stages, and the hotel renovations were well underway, he'd moved to Dare full-time, flying down to Arizona every few weeks to see Abbie and Dustin.

He angled into a place down the block, and the three of them headed for Jill's shop. A sheriff's car cruised by. He turned his head slightly to see if it were Peggy. Almost looked back to see if there was anything illegal about his parking job.

"That's the second time you've gotten weird when we've passed a cop. Is something going on?" Abbie peered down her tortoise-shell sunglasses at him. "That female deputy isn't stirring up more trouble, is she?"

Thank God for his poker face. His sister could be pretty intuitive. She didn't need to know he had a thing for the very woman who had revealed their personal business to the whole town.

"Of course not."

His sister raised a brow. "I don't believe you."

"A bicycle co-op," Dustin exclaimed as they walked by. "Sweet. I can't wait to tear up the trails around here. Mom, you remembered to enroll me in the summer soccer league, right?"

Abbie put an arm around him. "I'm sorry. I don't recall my son liking soccer."

He bumped her. "*Hello.* I've played since I was four, Mom. Maybe you're getting old like Uncle Mac." He jogged backwards as Mac made a grab for him.

"No doubt. Yes, you're all signed up. Starts tomorrow."

"Sweet. At least there's a few things to do here. Can I drive the Ferrari?"

"No," they both replied in unison.

He punched the air. "Why not? I have my license. Seriously, it's just another car."

"Then you can drive mine," Abbie said, meeting Mac's gaze.

"Yours so blows, Mom."

"Thank you," she replied primly as Mac opened the door to Don't Soy with Me.

"Why can't I drive the Ferrari?"

"We've covered this, Dustin," Mac replied, waving to people as they walked to the counter.

"Come on. I promise I'll be careful."

"No way."

"But—"

"We're done with this, Dustin," Mac informed him. "You're beating a dead horse."

"It isn't dead yet," he replied mulishly, hunching over.

Mac caught sight of flaming curls behind the counter. "Excuse me, miss, but aren't you supposed to be sitting down?"

Jill looked over her shoulder. "I'm trying to find the almond milk. I'm craving it."

Dustin gagged. "Milk comes from cows, not nuts."

"And hello to you too, Dustin."

"Hey, Jill. Gosh, you've gotten big." His eyes zeroed in on her stomach.

"What can I say?" She gripped the counter to stand up. "Babies grow."

"Where's Margie?" Mac asked, circling the counter to help her.

"I sent her to the post office since we're a little slow right now. I didn't want to walk that far. And Rachel's out sick, so I'm filling in. What would you like? Hey, Abbie."

"Hi, Jill. You're looking radiant."

"Spoken like someone who's cooked a kid. Mothers are usually so much nicer than...pesky teenagers."

"What the heck does 'pesky' mean?"

"Annoying," Mac supplied, bumping Dustin.

He lunged for him, and they wrestled for a moment. Mac couldn't hide his grin. The kid would come around. He always did. Being together is where they belonged.

**

Abbie rested an arm on the counter and watched them grapple as Jill made their drinks. It was good to see them play. When Mac and Dustin fought, her stomach churned up so much she was sure her acid reflux would land her in the hospital. She and Mac hadn't really fought growing up. She hadn't always appreciated his protectiveness, but they'd never gone toe-to-toe over anything.

Now her favorite men were grappling all the time.

She realized her shoulders had hiked up to her ears, so she rolled them down.

"They're a pair, aren't they?" Jill asked, setting down her caramel macchiato.

"Yes. How have you been?"

Her hand patted her expanding tummy. "Well, we're having twin girls. I'll have some shopping buddies besides my sister. I'm psyched."

"Congratulations. I love Dustin, but a shopping companion would be lovely."

She and Jill had spent time together on Abbie's previous visit to Dare, and they'd spoken over the phone frequently about the plans for the hotel. Fortunately, Skype worked like a dream.

"And I love working at the hotel. I can't wait to see what everyone thinks! I know I'm partial, but it's one of the coolest things I've ever been involved in. It's like shining up a penny, but on a bigger scale."

Abbie took a sip and almost sighed. "Well, one thing I don't have to worry about is having bad coffee here. This is so good... I can't wait to see the hotel now that it's finished. I've seen the pictures and the layout, but the real deal is always different. This project holds a pretty special place in Mac's heart, I can tell."

Jill leaned against the counter and brushed back her curls. "Well, he holds one in mine. I'm so glad he came here. He's just the right person to stir things up."

Abbie withdrew a twenty for the drinks. "Once the poker crowd arrives, things will definitely be stirred up around here. Mac told me we have record numbers for the grand opening. Here, why don't you sit down until someone needs a drink?"

She spied an empty circular table and gestured toward it. Mac had told her people packed Jill's place from dawn until midnight, savoring the good food and coffee. The bold red-and-yellow color scheme would certainly keep people awake. That and the funky chartreuse and black brand on the napkins and cups appealed to Abbie. She also liked the local artists' paintings on the walls.

Jill circled the counter and fell into the empty chair. "No, I'll be okay. I might not be able to get up again if I sit. Boys, try not to knock over my new display of local candies and cookies. Your drinks are up, by the way. And please put that money away, Abbie. First round is on the house."

The bill slid back in her wallet. "Thanks. Dustin, your deluxe coffee is ready."

"Sweet!" He lunged for Mac and then picked up the coffee. "Hah! Can't get me now without spilling this all over you."

Mac ruffled his hair. "Well, you'd better watch your back. I'll strike when you least expect it."

Jill clapped her hands. "So, we're having a family dinner at Peggy's tomorrow night. We'd love to welcome you guys."

"Stop meddling," Mac said.

Abbie met her brother's gaze and saw his jaw clench. So, the infamous deputy sheriff was going to be there. She was the last person Abbie wanted to run into. "Jill, really, I'm sorry we can't make it, but Dustin has soccer practice."

Jill put her hands on her hips. "Is this because of Peggy? Mac, I told you she'll come around, but the only way that will happen is if you two interact more."

Her brother went over and gently laid his hands on Jill's shoulders. "We can talk about this later, but I'm not the only one here now."

Her eyes widened. "Oh!"

"Yes," Mac replied.

Acid poured into Abbie's gut. Thanks to Peggy, the whole town knew a man had taken advantage of her so badly that Mac had beaten him up. Thank God, they didn't know the whole story. She glanced at her son. Neither did Dustin. How could she ever tell her son the truth about his father?

"I'm sorry," Jill murmured, grasping her arm. "Peggy wouldn't have said anything if she'd known. Really, she's a great person once you get to know her."

Abbie clutched her purse, unable to reply, remembering that horrible phone call from Mac. She'd been waiting for him to tell her how the city council had voted. Instead, he'd asked her if she was okay with him revealing the reason he'd beaten Richard Wentworth III within an inch of his life. Deputy Sheriff Peggy McBride had called his reputation into question. The future of the hotel was in jeopardy. Abbie hadn't liked the idea of sharing the truth—even without the details—but she'd consented because Mac's business was hers. Still, she wasn't planning on getting chummy with some female deputy who was out to boot her brother from town.

Mac kissed Jill on the cheek. "We need to head up to the house and settle in. I'll see you tomorrow. Stay off your feet."

Jill stood awkwardly and made a move to hug Dustin, but he danced out of reach, blushing like he was eight. "Ah, no offense, but hugging a pregnant chick could ruin my rep."

She wagged a finger at him. "God, don't make me cry. I used to be cute."

Abbie wrapped her arm around her shoulder. "You are! My son has forgotten his manners. We'll see you soon. Maybe we can have lunch at the hotel tomorrow and talk about the opening."

"I'd love that. Dustin, don't think you're off the hook."

He took a step further back, causing everyone to laugh. "Give me a break, Jill," he said.

They left Don't Soy With Me after Mac introduced them to a few more people on the way out. When they returned to the car, Abbie pulled out her notepad and wrote down the names of the people she'd met.

"Okay, tell me more about who I need to remember," she told Mac.

Dustin blew a raspberry. "Man, Mom, do you always have to write everyone up? Wouldn't it be easier to ask the FBI for their backgrounds?"

She turned in her seat. "I know you hate remembering people's names, Dustin, but it's good business for the hotel."

"Well, I don't plan on being part of the business, so I'm not studying any dumb names."

Mac's fingers clenched on the wheel. Before he could respond, she put a hand on his arm. "You're free to be anything you want," she said to her son. "You know that. We only hope you'll be your normal friendly self."

Mac's snort made her look over. "When did you start doing *that*?"

"Jill always snorts when the situation calls for it. I realized it conveys my feelings quite accurately without me needing to say a word."

"Cool! Can I do it too?" Dustin gave a shockingly good imitation of a pig.

"No! It's not polite."

"But Uncle Mac—"

"Is not my son." She narrowed her eyes at Dustin.

He yanked on his seat belt. "I don't get to have any fun."

"No, you have it so bad."

She resumed writing in her makeshift Name Book while Mac peppered her with information about local people and associations. The car climbed, but she didn't look out the window. She made her notations with people's descriptions.

"We're here," Mac announced, parking the car.

Stowing her notepad in her purse, she opened the door. Dustin's foot kicked a rock. She put her arm around him when she noticed he wasn't even looking at the house.

As she'd told Dustin earlier, the weather wasn't the only difference from Arizona. The architecture here had a mountain theme. She'd been to this house before. The rustic log-frame and rock house was two stories, flanked by gray-stone chimneys, with massive bay windows providing a luxurious view of Dare Valley. The front porch already had a table and chairs set up. Mac knew how much she loved to have coffee outside in the morning. He'd also had the flowers she'd selected planted. She looked back and gave him a smile. He winked. He never missed a step.

"It looks different in summertime, doesn't it, Dustin?"

Her son just shrugged. "Whatever."

She let him go when he pulled away. Mac joined her.

"He'll come around," she said, trying to reassure herself as much as her brother.

"Funny, Jill said that about someone else recently. I'm not sure that will come true, either." Mac inserted the key in the lock and swept the door open with an exaggerated bow. "Your new abode, ma'am. Sir."

Abbie laughed. Dustin rolled his eyes.

The open floor plan suited her. The den, dining room, and kitchen were cordoned off with log-frame posts, but each floor had been done in a different hardwood. They flowed into each other like hot caramel into butterscotch. The plush rugs she'd bought in Santa Fe added to the rustic feel.

"You can shift the furniture as much as you want. I did the best I could with the movers."

She hugged him. "You did a great job! I'll barely have to do anything."

Dustin headed up the white birch staircase, turning when he reached the top. She braced herself. His brow was pinched, just like it had when he was a newborn about ready to squall.

"I hate this place! I wanna go home."

His shout closed off her throat.

"You're a pro at this, Dustin," Mac reasoned in a gentle voice, rubbing Abbie's back to calm her. "You know it's hard in the beginning, but you always find your footing."

"I'm tired of starting over! Why can't you get that?" He launched himself down the hall and slammed the door of his third bedroom in six years

"It's going to be a long summer," Mac observed, drawing her close.

Guilt rose over moving Dustin again. Still, they would all find a way to make it work.

They had to if they were to going to stay together as a family—and that was something she'd never let unravel.

CHAPTER 5

Hot-rodding drivers usually pissed Peggy off with their squealing tires and menace to public safety. Yet, the silver Ferrari streaking down Main Street like its tail was on fire made her day. Her mouth stretched from its usual "I'm on duty expression" into a full-out grin.

"You son of a bitch. I *knew* you'd show your true colors!"

Her mind conjured up Maven's ink-black hair and green eyes.

This was what she'd been waiting for.

The thought of pressing that tall, hard frame against his purring, sexy car and cuffing him made an unprofessional ball of lust skyrocket through her. It was embarrassing, yes, but worse, it made her weak. If she could shoot her subconscious, she'd do it—right between the eyes.

She hit her sirens, the sound as delightful as a train whistle to a kid at Christmastime. She longed to see that gorgeous face as he rolled down his window, looking down his nose at her from behind those pricy, reflective sunglasses.

But he didn't reduce his speed. Instead, the car shot several lengths ahead. Surprise tore through her. She gripped the steering wheel.

"So you want to race. Let's see who wins this time, bozo."

She stepped on the gas, mindful of Dare's pedestrian traffic as she cruised down Main Street, which was all decked out in red, white, and blue. Soon the charming shops and restaurants would be hosting hordes of cash-flush, sycophantic poker players. Like pilgrims to that Dali Lama guy, they would come from near and far to play in a tourney against the legend.

"Not if he's in jail," she sang, eyeing the speedometer. She hit fifty when he turned onto the main highway to the canyon. Route 98 had treacherous curves even when snow didn't coat the two-laner. She knew the turns and increased her speed to keep up with the Ferrari. She couldn't catch him head-to-head, but she knew where he was headed. Her car handled, but she might as well be a turtle chasing a jack rabbit.

She called dispatch and gave a terse report of the situation. "Possible suspicious vehicle. Am following. Will advise on cover."

Having four cop cars swarm his hotel with sirens blazing would put his knickers in a wad, but it'd take away from her singular triumph in cuffing his fine ass and hauling him off to jail.

His car continued to zoom down the highway. "You gotta stop

sometime. Then, you and I are going to have it out." She judged his speed to be around one-twenty. Like he was on that freakin' road in Germany everyone always talked about. What was it? Oh, the Autobahn.

She dug into the pedal for more speed and crested to one-hundred. She was glad there weren't any cars on the highway. Weaving through them on a two-laner at this speed would be stupidly dangerous. Keith came to mind. She always tried not to put herself into dicey situations like some rookie. She was all her son had, and she wasn't going anywhere.

Dispatch asked for an update on her radio. "Still following. Will advise."

Her grin faded. That damn jerk was putting her life at risk. When he fishtailed onto the newly paved hotel road, tires squealing, she followed.

"I'm going to kick your ass. I thought you were smarter than this. I've got your plates, make, and model. Plus, you're heading to *your own hotel*. You'd better not be jerking my chain 'cause this cop jerks back. If you want payback for that ticket, this is a stupid way to get it." She crested the hill between the line of trees.

The road flattened out into a lush valley dotted with manicured lawns like a high-priced golf resort, except she could still see the square pattern of newly laid sod. Her foot paused on the pedal when she saw the hotel. Since she knew she had him caged, she eased off the gas as a florist truck approached. The driver pulled over to let her streak by.

The hotel swallowed up her vision as the Ferrari shot into a discrete parking deck in a flash of silver. She followed, taking in the elegant stonework of the three-story building and the shine of glass and brass. It was fancy, with a hint of something out of an old movie—like the Cary Grant dimple in Mac's chin.

It fit him to a T.

She turned off the sirens before entering the parking deck. No sense in making herself deaf from the sound ricocheting off the walls. His car straddled the yellow line, taking up two spaces. Since a nameplate labeled his space, she figured no one would care about his shitty parking job.

She called dispatch. "Have it under control."

Her scan of the deck didn't reveal his whereabouts. She jogged toward a metal door. When she came through the entrance, it took her a minute to gauge her surroundings.

The long corridor had a shiny walnut hardwood floor. She delighted in being the first person to give it scuff marks. The chandeliers in reception shot gas flames into crystal sconces, making her wonder about the utility bill.

"May I help you, Officer?"

She turned to see a stiff-lipped guy in his fifties decked out in a dark burgundy uniform with gold buttons and some fancy epaulettes. The crisp fabric looked like her first police uniform, which had itched like crazy. The guy's shoes even mirrored her reflection when she stepped closer. Cripes, this place simply reeked boutique hotel, right down to the pine scent accenting the cool, circulated air.

"It's Deputy Sheriff. I need to see Maven. Now."

"Mr. Maven is in a meeting. Would you like some coffee while you wait?"

In a meeting. As if. "What part of 'now' don't you understand?"

When he didn't budge, she crowded him. His polite smile thinned, she noted with delight.

"Where's his office?"

"Ah...let me call up for you."

She snagged his arm before he could go behind the cherry wood partition. "No, take me to him. He's done surprising me for the day."

His lips pinched. "Fine, I'd be happy to show you upstairs if you'll kindly remove your hand."

She did, glad to see he had some backbone, and followed him up a sweeping staircase so wide she could have run her car down it with room to spare. The wood's newly polished surface simply screamed custom-built. More gas sconces lined the hallway, interspersed with discreet electric lighting. Workers stopped to watch their progress before continuing on like busy little bees. When they hit the second floor, they wound their way to the main poker room, which was filled with acres of green tables.

An itch developed between her shoulder blades. Her father's face flashed through her mind. She closed it down.

They walked to a closed door at the back, and her helper discreetly knocked. She pushed his hand aside and flung it open.

Like the rest of the hotel, Maven's office was decorated with burnished wood and lush upholstery in burgundy and gold. Bold artwork more suited to the modern school accented the walls in engraved frames. What had she expected, *Dogs Playing Poker*? He might not be from money, but you'd never know it from looking at him in this mega-posh office, wearing a tailored suit that cost as much as her monthly mortgage.

She marched forward. He just steepled his hands and settled back in an embossed leather chair resembling a throne. Fitting for a poker king, she decided as she stopped inches from his desk, ignoring the balding man in the chair next to her, his jaw hanging slack.

"Why, Deputy McBride, what brings you to our humble abode? Did you decide you wanted an advance tour after receiving my invitation? Or didn't you like the pie?"

His smooth-as-cream tone couldn't quite mask the underlying venom.

"Don't pretend you don't know why I'm here. You are *so* under arrest."

Those hot-as-sin lips curved into a smile. "Am I?"

"Mac, what's the meaning of this?" the bald guy blustered. "Lady, you've got the wrong man."

"I don't think so." She smirked at Maven. "Trust you to have an alibi ready, but I got your plates, which register that silver Ferrari to you. You're so busted."

A line appeared between his eyebrows. "This is about my car? Did some parking ticket fly off my windshield?"

The dig made her stomach jump. "Are you saying you didn't park near that fire hydrant the other day?"

His hand reached out and caressed a Waterford paperweight. "I wasn't even close."

"Colorado law states you must not be within fifteen feet of a fire hydrant."

The paperweight dotted the ceiling with prisms when it caught the light streaming in through the windows. There was, she noticed, a killer view of the mountains.

"I was well beyond the limit, and you know it. Just like your harassment today, it was another attempt to show your contempt for my hotel and cause me problems. Right before the grand opening, I might add."

His accusation rocked her back on her heels. "Are you *denying* I just chased your speed-racing ass from downtown up to this...this...Shangri-La?"

He rose from his chair in one sleek line and waved a hand at the huffing bald man. "While I'm impressed with your literary knowledge, yes, I'm denying it. I thought better of you, Peg, but then again, it's not the first time you've made something up about me."

The barb stung like a bee bite. "Did you or did you not beat a man so badly he was hospitalized for days?"

"Dammit, we covered this!" he stormed, surprising her. He usually exhibited an almost eerie control of his emotions. She respected it, since her job required the same. Popping the cork on his volatility had created a few cracks in her own dam. Her heartbeat—already jazzed from the chase—kicked up again.

"I was defending my sister's honor, and the charges were dropped. Not that you care about the details. Only the laws matters." His elegant hands settled on his trim waist. "Well, you've gone too far this time. I don't want any bad blood between us, Deputy, but you're pushing my tolerance. If you leave now, I won't report this to your supervisor."

She sucked in a breath. "How dare you threaten me with a swipe at my professional conduct! I have you cold, mister, for speeding well above the limit and evading law enforcement. You'd better zip it, or I'll throw in harassment for good measure and haul you downtown. Wouldn't that be a nice way to open your hotel?"

"This is outrageous!" the bald guy blasted out, rising to his feet. "Mac, I'm calling security and having Aaron and his guys escort her out."

"No." He lifted his hand like a traffic cop directing cars. "That won't be necessary."

His stoplight green eyes held hers for a long moment. In the silence, she raised her chin, fighting her roiling emotions. Part of her wanted to lash out at him. The other part—quieter, yes, but still there—couldn't believe she'd misjudged him so badly. He was just another truth-allergic jerk who'd say anything to sidestep trouble.

"You seriously believe you chased me up the mountain, don't you?"

"That's what I've been telling you!"

He walked over to a wooden panel and pressed the corner. It slid open, exposing a wall of TV monitors showing the hotel from different vantage points. The white date and timestamp flashed at the top right corner of each screen. He stepped in front of the TVs monitoring three different views of the garage. Each one showed a different parking level.

"My car seems to be badly parked," he said, stroking the dent in his chin. He reached for a remote resembling something NASA might use for the space program and pressed a few buttons. The tape rewound. He paused it when a male form appeared. After slamming the Ferrari's door, the perp—in jeans, tennis shoes, a white T-shirt, and a Yankees ball cap—streaked to the exit door. He had the gangly body of a teenager.

Her head swung to the right. "It wasn't you," she uttered in sheer shock.

Maven looked ready to spit fire. "That little shit," he growled in a voice resplendent with danger.

"Oh, Jesus," the bald man moaned.

"I take it you know who that is. Your new parking attendant?"

It probably wasn't the first time some kid took out one of Mac's cars for the thrill. No wonder he'd run from her like a jackrabbit.

Maven reset the monitor and shut the panels. "I don't suppose you'd let me take care of this."

She could huff as good as the bald man. "Are you kidding? I called it in per procedure. Besides, half of Dare must have seen our car chase."

He stuffed his hands in his pockets, jingling change. "I'll punish him more than you ever could, I promise."

Man, she almost felt sorry for the kid. "Don't ask me to let it slide. He broke the law. I'm sorry if you don't like the bad press it will generate."

"Right. Breaking the law. How could I forget what an unpardonable offense that is?" Maven's sigh was long and gusty. He pinched the bridge of his nose before reaching for the phone. "Dustin? You'd better come to my office. *Now.*"

Peg stood with her legs hip distance apart and stared down at the bald man, who was frowning and tsking under his breath like a mother hen.

"It's not a request. Two minutes." He hung up the phone and exchanged a long look with his colleague. "While we're waiting, Peg, I want you to meet the hotel's manager, Cincinnati Kilkelly. Cince, meet Dare's deputy sheriff, Peggy McBride."

His hand moved hesitantly toward hers like she had the plague or something. The handshake couldn't have been more perfunctory.

Maven undid his jacket and loosened his tie. "Can I offer you a non-alcoholic beverage, Peggy? I realize you're on duty."

She glanced at his crystal clock. "What? Are you planning on drinking? It's not even noon."

"At the moment, it's very tempting."

Before she could ask why, the door burst open. She recognized the perp even without the ball cap.

49

"Deputy, I don't believe you've officially met my nephew, Dustin, newly arrived from Arizona." Maven clamped a hand on the kid's shoulder. The boy looked wild-eyed enough to bolt. "Dustin, please meet Deputy McBride. She wants to haul you off to jail on numerous counts."

The black hair, dimpled chin, and green eyes in the kid's young, thin face dotted with mild acne bore a striking resemblance to Maven. *Do-do-do-do-do-do-do-do* from *The Twilight Zone* streaked through Peggy's head.

"He's your *nephew*? "

"Yes," Maven replied. "Now, let's talk about your wish to arrest him."

The kid pivoted and ran for the door.

CHAPTER 6

$\mathcal{M}$aven sprinted across the room and collared him like an experienced cop. "Not so fast. So you went joy-riding in my car without asking, did you? Dammit, Dustin, we talked about this!"

"Uncle Mac—"

"We have a recording of the whole thing."

The kid's eyes bugged. Then his head lowered, his shoulders hunched. Peg knew the stance. This was no usual trouble maker.

"We've got you—what is the phrase? Dead to rights?"

Peggy nodded and put her hands on her waist for emphasis, fingering her decked-out police belt. "Yes. I have your car clocked, the plates, the whole shebang. Are you even old enough to drive?"

His chin thrust up. "Hell, yes, I just got my license."

"Hey," Mac snapped. "Watch the language."

The kid's jaw clenched. "Yes, ma'am, I do."

She hated being called ma'am, but she wasn't about to give the kid an inch. "So, let's see it."

He fished into his jeans for his wallet and dug out the license. His picture couldn't have been more at odds with his current expression. His dopey grin was the size of Texas, and his eyes sparkled with joy at the new freedom. Man, had she ever looked that excited at the DMV? She considered that place another level of hell. His license was so bright, spanking new it practically shone. The great state of Arizona had issued it just last month.

"Did you flunk the questions on the driving test about speed limits?"

"No, ma'am."

"Fall on your head recently and plumb forgot them?"

His lips twitched, but he kept his head down and muttered, "No, ma'am."

She slapped his license against her fingernail, letting the tapping fill the silence she had intentionally built. He shifted on his feet. Good, no power struggle here. She hated dealing with punk-ass teens who were too stupid or fearless to realize they'd done anything wrong. This kid could learn his lesson, she could tell. So, she'd put the fear of God into him.

"Then you intentionally wish to do harm to yourself, me, and others?"

His eyes flicked up. The first threads of fear shone before he lowered them. "No ma'am."

"So what am I supposed to think about the crap you pulled, racing down Main Street at forty-eight miles per hour and then cresting up to one-twenty on the highway?"

Maven's jaw clenched.

Dustin cleared his throat. "Uh..."

Her radio crackled, so she turned it down. "I'm sorry, I didn't catch that. So you didn't see the mom with the baby carriage coming across the crosswalk when you blew by?"

"Oh my God, no!" he breathed out, turning green.

Maven's eyes shot to hers. Then his brow eased. So, he knew she was lying about the mom and baby. Good for him. Police did it all the time. Plus, it could have happened. He inclined his head as if giving her permission to go hard on his nephew. Like that meant a hill of beans to her.

"Do you know how many families we have strolling down Main Street usually, even more so with the 4th of July coming up next week? What would have happened if someone hadn't been looking? If you'd hit someone?"

The kid grabbed his shirt. "I didn't want to hurt anyone. I just wanted to drive fast. My uncle's car—"

"Isn't a toy. It's a hot car, I'll grant you, but it can kill a pedestrian as easily as any other vehicle."

"I would never—"

"I'm sure you wouldn't mean to. No one *means* to, but people are sent to the hospital or the morgue every day after being hit by crazy-ass speeding drivers like you. Want the statistics?"

His Adams apple moved starkly when he gulped. She rattled them off, still tapping his license against her thumb. "And let's talk about your speed in the canyon and what might have happened there."

As she launched into a litany about the dangers of speeding in a windy canyon on a two-lane highway, Maven crossed his arms, simply watching her. She tried to ignore him, but she couldn't help glancing at him out of the corner of her eye.

"Dustin Michael Maven, age sixteen, this is a serious offense. This isn't just plain ol' speeding. Do you remember the part in the manual where it says you're supposed to pull your car over when an officer hits her sirens?"

He nodded his head slowly. She could tell he was envisioning the worst-case scenarios now. She'd instilled some serious regret in him. *Good*, her job was almost done.

"That's eluding an officer—a class one misdemeanor. You could get fined up to one thousand dollars plus court costs with possible jail time."

"How much are we talking here, Deputy?" that Cincinnati guy finally asked, joining the group.

The kid leaned against him when he put an arm around him like an uncle. Clearly there was affection and history there. The kid was looking at him like a petrified puppy that was about to be sent to the pound.

"A few weeks to one year."

The kid started shaking, but she wouldn't let up. Not yet. "When you display that kind of reckless indifference to the safety of others, it seems like a rather fitting punishment to me."

Cincinnati's face turned ruddy. "Mac, aren't you going to say anything? The kid just got his license. Who doesn't hit the road speeding? I get that he did it in town, where there are tons of people around, but this seems pretty rough. It's the kid's first offense."

She tapped the plastic card and let the silence build again. "Which comes only a few weeks after receiving his license. The court takes this stuff into account."

"Dustin's a good kid, Deputy. I think there's a misunderstanding here."

Maven pursed his lips. "I imagine some sort of community service would work if he receives probation, right?"

Since it was likely, she nodded thoughtfully. "Yes, that's true. Of course, he'd probably have to take the bus. The court might revoke his license. And since he ran from the car, I could add resisting arrest…"

Dustin tried to bolt again, but the older man grabbed him. "It's going to be okay, Dustin. Mac, we need to call the lawyers."

"No, Deputy McBride is right. This is serious. There's also the matter of you stealing my car and trying to get me to take the fall for this. How do you think that would look if it became public knowledge? What the hell were you thinking?"

She didn't know what surprised her more, the lash of his temper or the fact that he was siding with her.

Cincinnati clapped the kid on the back. "Come on, Mac, he wasn't thinking. He's sixteen with a shiny, new license and an uncle who's got a hot car. Tell me you wouldn't have done what he did. Hell, I know I would have."

The kid's eyes widened as he looked at the bald man, clearly pinning all his hopes and dreams on his champion. "I'm sorry I took your car, Uncle Mac. I *never* would have let you get into trouble."

Mac looked down that elegant nose at his nephew.

Dustin hitched his shoulder up. "Really I wouldn't have. I'm sorry."

"Dustin, Deputy McBride is right. You could have killed someone or her."

His eyes locked with Peggy's when he said it. A flame flared between them before he planted his hands on his nephew's shoulders. "She has a boy in second grade she's raising by herself. What would have happened if she'd been killed chasing you down?"

The kid sucked in a breath. "Oh God, I didn't mean it!" He swiveled around and those huge, green eyes fastened on hers. "I'm so sorry. You have to believe me!"

Cincinnati stepped forward. "Mac—"

"What would have happened if you'd gotten yourself killed? Did you ever think how your mother would feel? Or me?" Mac thrust his fist into the air like he was dotting the sentence. The emotion in his voice flashed like lightning and then disappeared just as quickly. He drew in a breath, his composure returning.

Peggy knew love and fear were driving this train. The boy gripped the sides of his shirt like he wanted to run at his uncle full speed for a hug.

"Deputy, this is our new home," Mac said. "We want to set a good example here in Dare. Dustin was in the wrong. Please do what you think is best."

"This is bullshit! You're throwing him to the wolves." Cincinnati planted himself in front of his friend. "Abbie won't like this one bit."

"I didn't want to come here!" Dustin yelled. "I didn't want to leave my friends."

"We discussed this. We're a family. We stick together. Deputy, write up whatever you want. Dustin, I want your cell."

"What for?"

"You're grounded with no phone for a month, maybe more once I talk to your mom."

The boy's eyes turned murderous. "Fine, now that we're stuck in this stupid town, I can't see my friends anyway. Might as well not be able to talk to them either. Why don't you put me in solitary confinement?"

Mac's gaze heated with equal degree. "I'm sure Deputy McBride could arrange it."

Didn't they realize they were cut from the same cloth? Their actions and body language were so eerily alike it made her wonder again about all that DNA stuff.

Dustin slapped the phone in Mac's hand.

"I'm writing you up for the speeding ticket—the full penalty," Peggy said, raising a finger, "and will recommend community service to the city attorney, who will bring it to the judge."

His mouth dropped open. "That's it? You're not taking me to jail?"

The kid's relief turned the burners of her mommy persona on. "Not if you've learned your lesson. Now, if there's a next time—"

"No, ma'am!"

She thought of Keith and wondered if he'd pull something like this someday. Hell, she saw plenty of good parents like herself end up in tight binds with their kids. Joy-riding, shoplifting, even breaking and entering for something as dumb as another kid's mountain bike. All she could ever do was her best. And pray like every other parent in the world that lessons stuck.

She wrote him up. His hands shook so badly when he signed the ticket that she could barely make out his name.

"Don't make me come after you again."

All the life seemed to be sucked out of the kid. No car privileges and no phone. Man, to a sixteen-year-old, it probably felt like prison.

"I'll come up with some chores around here for you to do once I talk with your mother," Mac said.

"Yes. Sir."

The venom couldn't be missed.

Cincinnati shook his head, and patted the teen on the shoulder. "Come on, son."

"Don't you have something to say to Deputy McBride?" Maven asked.

Dustin turned back. "I'm sorry, ma'am. It won't happen again."

She nodded. "See that it doesn't."

With that, Cincinnati led him out of the office. As the door shut behind them, Dustin grabbed the older man in a bear hug.

In the room, Maven asked Peggy, "I think I'm going to have that drink now. Do you want anything?

"I need to get back."

He loosened his collar. "Sit down, Peggy. I'm not done with you yet."

CHAPTER 7

Mac poured two fingers of his new single malt into an Italian crystal glass. He never drank at this time of day, but Dustin had scared a decade off him. Gray hairs were probably popping out of his head like some Chia Pet.

"You ever worry about Keith pulling that crap when he gets older?"

It was the second time today that one of his comments had rocked her back on her heels.

She shrugged. "Sure. All parents do, I think."

"His mother is going to take this hard. She's been trying to stop history from repeating itself—hell, we both have. Maven men. We run wild young." If he included his father in that mix, he'd have to remove the age limit. Maven men ran wild. Period. Until him.

She stayed silent, as if she didn't know what to say or how to handle this side of him. Hell, he wasn't sure how to handle it either. He mentally shook himself.

"Please, sit. That must have been quite an adrenaline rush. I'm sorry he put your life at risk." He gestured to the chair in front of his desk, trying to banish the image of her lying in a tangled, burning metal mass at the bottom of the canyon.

"Do you want a Coke? You wouldn't do the diet stuff, I expect."

She toed her shoe into his carpet like she was deciding whether to stay or go. "Ah, sure."

Mac watched her sit while he poured her drink.

"I'll take the can."

"Indulge me."

She took a healthy sip when he handed it over.

"Dry mouth?"

"A bit. Adrenaline fall-off."

"Yeah, funny how this stuff affects you. I haven't had my palms sweat like this since my first major Vegas tourney."

Her mouth pinched, so he switched the topic. Right, no poker. It put her back up. Stiff as a poker, haha. He wouldn't have much luck quitting his day job for the comedy club.

He spun around a picture of Dustin at age six, riding the Ferris wheel at a state fair.

Peggy took it from him. "The resemblance is unmistakable."

"Yeah. The more he looks like me, the more he reminds me of myself. Scares me shitless, thinking about all the dumbass things he might do. Today, he proved it."

"Let's hope he learned his lesson."

"You did well, going hard on him like that. Thank you for not hauling him off to jail."

She eyed him over the rim of her glass. "You thought I would drag him out in handcuffs?"

With Peggy, he wasn't sure of anything, so he decided to be honest. That, at least, she appreciated. "I wasn't sure."

"Well, if he hadn't been so remorseful, I might have."

He stroked his chin. So she could see more than black and white after all. It was a revelation.

She gulped down the rest of her drink. "Water, please, if you have it."

He handed her a bottle from the small fridge behind his desk. "I should have sold the Ferrari when he got his license, but dammit, I love those cars."

Her mouth twitched. "He probably wouldn't have stolen a mini-van."

"Or Abbie's Subaru."

"Don't blame yourself. I tell parents that all the time. No one forced him to get into that car."

The tough cop was still there, all crisp and polished in her tan slacks and forest-green button-down shirt with the Sheriff patch emblazoned on the shoulder. The police belt holding her radio, gun, mace, and handcuffs seemed too heavy for her frame. Her gold metal badge caught the sun, blinding him with its glory. She'd shoot him if he told her she looked like a stripper in his wildest fantasies.

When the golden halo around her faded, the shared understanding in her eyes made him want to reach for her hand. She had a son. It could have been Keith. She didn't preach to him about his duty as...well, he was the only father Dustin would ever have.

"Do you ever worry about Keith growing up without a father?"

Her eyes veiled immediately.

"I only meant... Well, it struck me that my relationship to Dustin is rather like Tanner's to Keith. I'm the uncle who's always around, trying to fill in."

"When that terrible idea burrows into me on parents' days at school, I think of how much more screwed up Keith would be if his father *were* around."

The chuckle bubbled out before he could stop it. "I'm not laughing at you. I guess I never thought of it that way. I admire your practicality."

She turned her radio down when it sparked to life again. "Let me check in for a minute."

He watched as she turned her back to him and recounted the incident in crisp tones, noting that she'd give more details later. She put her radio away.

"I don't see any reason for beating myself up over what-ifs."

Funny, talking with her was smoothing the knots in his gut better than the single malt. "Yet you sketched out the horrible what-ifs to my nephew and had him about ready to boot his breakfast."

"I'm a trained professional." She capped the water bottle. "I didn't think you'd let me go that far. Your friend sure didn't like it."

"Cince and I play good cop/bad cop with Dustin all the time. His mom usually plays good cop, so we have to pick up the slack when he gets into trouble."

"Does Dustin know that?"

"With two grifters like us, no way."

Her dark eyes fired up again. He hated seeing her turn into a prickly pear cactus when he talked about his card skills.

"If he's not onto you now, he will be soon."

"We'll deal with it."

And they would. He and Abbie and the rest of the family they'd formed together. Dustin would have a better start than they'd had. That promise was forged in steel.

Peggy bit her lip. "So, I guess I owe you an apology."

He cupped his ear. "I'm sorry, what did you say?"

"I said, 'I owe you an apology.' Are you deaf?"

So, her internal compass won out every time. He had to admire it. "Not to my knowledge. I can hear the irritation in your tone just fine." He tugged on his ear to make her squirm. "You said you 'guess.' There's a big difference between guessing and knowing."

She slapped the water bottle down on the desk, showering his papers with condensation from the outside. "You can't make this easy, can you?" She rose and headed to the door. Her masculine tan slacks with the wicked green stripe chasing from hip to ankle only accentuated her small, firm butt.

He followed, the urge to stalk her growing with each step. She challenged him on every single point, and damned if it wasn't refreshing.

"Apologies don't come easy for the two of us, but time doesn't stop when we utter the words. Hell doesn't freeze over either."

"I'm sorry," she ground out like she was sharpening her tongue on a whetstone.

"I'm sorry, *Mac*," he urged, waiting to see how she'd respond.

She crossed her arms, making her uniform stretch tight over her breasts. Her chest could have graced Vegas. He'd bet the size pissed her off. She probably bound them. He couldn't stop himself from imagining how they'd feel in his hands.

"Look, I said I was sorry. What more do you want?"

He pressed his palms against the door, caging her in. Even though her eyes narrowed, he didn't stop, didn't step back. He wanted to touch her, smell the clean scent she wore on her hair and skin. He was taller than she was, something she probably hated. He brushed her shoulder with a finger and made sure it lingered long enough for her to know it wasn't accidental.

"I want you to use my name." She never did, and it bothered him way more than it should.

"Maven works for me."

"I like Mac better." His light tone was a contrast to the war inside him. His heart beat in strong pulses.

She lifted her hand—almost like she was going to flick away a fly—and then let it settle on her waist. "Good for you. Mac's something you'd call a friend. We're not friends."

"Perhaps not, but your resistance makes me think you're not as immune to me as I thought. I wish things were different between us, Peg."

"Don't call me Peg, and don't make this personal."

He dipped his head so he could meet her gaze. She had a caramel-colored ring around those chocolate eyes. The tense line at the corners told him she wouldn't put up with too much more, but in for a penny, in for a pound, as Cince always said.

"I wish I could stop, but it *is* personal, Peg. As personal as it gets. You have no idea how hard it's been to ignore you."

"Ignore me?" she asked as if she hadn't done the same thing.

His mouth curved. He thought about curving it over her unpainted lips. "It was either that or have it out with you in the street. Or show up at your house when I thought Keith was asleep and kiss you senseless. Since I knew you'd likely pull your gun on me in either situation, I chose the path of least resistance." He reached out and traced her chin before she could jerk her head away. "Until the moose madness. You snuck back into my head again. I'm tired of trying to shut you out. Even on my best days, I can't do it."

Something liquid rolled in those dark eyes before a flicker of fear came and went. "This is inappropriate talk. I'm here on official business."

He wanted to slap his hand against the door in pure frustration. "I don't give a shit about inappropriate, and I don't care what kind of business you're here on." He toyed with the ends of her short, page-boy hair. "God, I've missed that wary look. I've wondered how I could ever peel back enough layers to make you open yourself to me. I stopped thinking it was possible when you went after me personally at the city council meeting." Even now, that wound burned, all hot and achy.

She anchored both hands on her police-issue belt. "I was doing my job!"

He shook his head slowly, falling into the rhythm of their energy, the push and pull between them. "No, you were protecting yourself. You didn't want me in town. Face it, you never miss key details in a case, and yet you completely forgot to find out why the charges against me had been dropped."

She didn't flinch from his stare. "I didn't forget."

Understanding dawned, and with it, the wound burned anew. "You *wanted* me to take it personally." He took a jagged breath. "Well, you're goddamn right I did. You maligned my character in front of the whole town. I respected your efforts to stop the project. But you hit below the belt that day. You went after me and my family."

This time she used her palms to nudge him aside. "Step away. I don't like you crowding me."

He pressed closer. Her back hit the door. She shoved at him, but he caught her wrists, careful to contain her without hurting her. Her boot caught him in the instep. He winced.

"You can't trust a man who's interested in you. I realize that now." He leaned his body against hers. That long, tense line shuddered against his raging flesh. Desire thundered through him like a flood, and his blood beat in his ears. "But you can trust me, Peg."

"Step back, or I won't be responsible for what happens," she warned, catching him again with her boot.

He leaned closer. Before there might have been a few inches separating them, but now, there wasn't a hairsbreadth. Their every curve fit together like tongue-and-groove construction. Her breath turned shaky. She shoved, but couldn't dislodge him. Nothing would move him now.

"You opened to me when we were in that car together. Then you stepped back again. Perhaps it's time to try something different."

His mouth descended. He maintained eye contact.

She had to choose him. She had to choose this.

She turned her head, shaking. He forced himself to go completely still, his mouth inches from the delicate line where neck met shoulder. He ran his nose along her starched uniform collar, inhaling the clean scent. She bucked against him. He wasn't sure if she wanted to move him or if she was simply reacting to his touch.

"I want you, Peg," he ground out, his voice vibrating with the desire he couldn't contain. "God, I want you like I've never wanted anyone."

She tipped her face up to him. Those dark eyes were nearly black now. Her right temple beat insistently. Her lips parted, oh so slightly.

Then she rose up on her tiptoes and pressed her mouth to his.

He succumbed. Their first kiss was deep and forceful. After all these long months of longing, denial, and rejection, the shackles he'd forced himself to wear snapped free. When she opened her mouth under his, pressing against his body, her hands clamping his waist, he devoured her. They took from each other, scraping teeth, changing the angle of the kiss, unable to find enough to satiate their furious desire.

When his hands cupped her curves through that coarse fabric, her head twisted against the door, a breathy moan shivering out between them. He pressed his knee between her thighs, wanting to hear another lusty cry from the strong woman he held. She gave it to him, and then another—this one long and tortured—when he rubbed circles around the hard points of her round breasts. His mouth bent to her neck, sucking the delicate skin there. Her hands curved around his butt, grinding her hips against his hardness. When he groaned, he saw a slight smile flash across her lips before he covered them again with his mouth.

He grabbed her hands and pushed them back against the door, dipping his hips into hers, making her moan with the rhythm. God, he hadn't thought about taking her against his office door for the first time, but he wasn't sure he could stop—or wanted to. She was finally letting him see the woman she kept hidden behind her role as a single mom and a cop.

She fought against his hands, so he let them go. She dived to her shirt's buttons and opened them, tugging the material back from her simple white sports bra. He reached for her with trembling hands, eager to touch her soft flesh. He found her mouth. She moaned again as his tongue circled hers in quick passes, his hips following suit.

Someone knocked, but the sound seemed so distant. He couldn't sense anything beyond Peg's heated mouth, the anguished moan from her lips.

The rapid knocking matched his heartbeats.

"Mac! Are you in there? I need to talk to you about Dustin."

Peggy shoved him back and ducked away. He wiped his mouth. Rearranged his clothes. Turned around and saw Peggy doing the same, her face as red as the can of Coke she'd drunk earlier. He motioned her aside and opened the door.

"I'm finishing up with Deputy McBride. I'll find you in a few."

His sister's face was chalk-white and tense, the lines around her mouth visible. "Let me come in, please. I want to apologize. Tell her what a good boy Dustin is."

He had to reach deep for control—and pray his sister didn't notice his loss of composure or his whopping erection. "I already have. Please, Abbie, let me finish this alone. I'll find you."

The movement behind him sent a bolt of frustration through him. Peggy was going to use his sister as her means of escape.

She stepped into view. "I need to go."

If she'd known how fiery her face was, he'd have bet the house she wouldn't have stuck her hand out to his sister. Abbie looked at Peggy and then at him. He veiled his eyes, but who could miss the elephant in the room?

"You're...Deputy McBride." Her hand drew back as she realized who she was. "I'm Abbie Maven," she choked out. "I can't tell you...how sorry I am. I expect Mac has."

Picking up on her tone, he gave her a warning glare.

Peggy went redder. "Yes. I'll see you in court. I need to go and write up my report."

"Peggy," Mac called, but she dashed into the hall. "I'll look forward to picking up that other conversation."

She didn't slow down, not one iota.

Abbie flicked a hand at his still-noticeable erection. "What are you *doing*? That woman tried to destroy our reputations before the city council. You aren't...trying to seduce her so she'll take it easy on Dustin?"

He bristled. "Good God, no! What do you take me for?"

She stared at a place over his shoulder. "Frankly with both you and Dustin, at this moment, I have no idea. Come find me when you *cool* off."

He stepped into his office, resisting the urge to slam the door, and walked over to the ice bucket. Putting some cubes in his silk handkerchief, he pressed it against his neck. It did nothing to cool the furnace inside him. He figured a trip to the Arctic would be the only remedy.

Well, he'd learned one thing today. She wanted him as badly as he wanted her.

But as he watched her car streak down his driveway, he was unsure if things were better or worse between them—and if she'd ever let him touch her again.

"Shit," he uttered to the silent room.

CHAPTER 8

Abbie Maven surveyed the lush mountains through the squeaky clean windows. Her brother had outdone himself again. Only she understood how far he'd come and how much he'd built. As she paced the family quarters Mac always kept at his hotels, she smoothed her hands down her crisp linen dress. Would she be a bad mom if she used ear plugs to buffer the rap music coming from the adjoining room?

She hated rap music. Didn't understand how anyone could like songs with such gutter language and themes. But since Mac liked rap too, she let her son play it. She couldn't keep the world out or make Dustin act like a choir boy.

But listening to questionable music was a big step away from stealing a car for a joy ride and speeding away from a deputy. Since when had her kid become reckless and stupid?

Consequences—teenagers just didn't get them.

Hadn't she been the same way? She poured a Diet Coke into one of Mac's Venetian crystal glasses. Wasn't that why she was the thirty-four-year-old mother of a sixteen-year-old boy? Days like today made her feel older than she was.

The rap music intensified as the door opened. Dustin had on his "defying the world" face. When he was like this, it was hard to reach him.

"Heard you had quite a morning." she casually observed, knowing she needed to walk a fine line. He could spark like a firecracker if she chose the wrong tack.

His chin lifted, the dimple looking like a crater in his still developing face. "Uncle Mac wanted me to go to *jail*, Mom. Can you believe that crap?"

She let the minor language infraction go. "I doubt that very much, Dustin." Since Mac had played the bad guy, and Cince the good guy, she was settling for something in between. God knows it *did* take a village to raise a kid—especially one without a father. "Of course, you could have gone to jail. What you did wasn't simply reckless, it was illegal. You could have gotten hurt or hurt someone else."

"Uncle Mac already hammered that one home. Look, I'm sorry! I just wanted to drive his car. He wouldn't let me." He dived onto the Italian leather sofa. "It's not fair."

She sat across from him. "Seems to me, he was right all along. You didn't drive responsibly."

He lurched up. "I just got my license. Mom, everybody speeds."

Abbie crossed her arms and tried to keep her temper under control. God, she hated when her kid blamed everybody else for his own actions. "Then you should have pulled over when the deputy caught you and accepted your first ticket. Why didn't you?"

He pulled his ball cap lower over his forehead, but his thick black hair still curled around his ears like seaweed. "I didn't want Uncle Mac to find out."

"Do you mean *the* all-knowing Mac Maven? Who's kidding who here, Dustin?"

"I panicked, okay?" He sprung up, his leaf-green eyes fierce, showing the fear of a little boy who was not yet a man. "I didn't want to get into trouble."

"Well, you are in trouble," Mac confirmed as he walked in. "Big time."

Dustin headed for the room he'd claimed. "Fine. Punish me. Send me to jail."

Mac strode across the living area. "Turn the music off and come back here."

"I don't want to talk to you."

Mac angled his bulk in front of the door, and her son stood just inches away from him with clenched fists. Abbie wouldn't be surprised if one of them stomped a foot, lowered a shoulder, and charged like a bull. When they went at it, neither backed down.

"Dustin, close the door and turn the music down. Your uncle and I need to decide on your punishment."

"But he already took my phone."

She shook her head and winced as pain spread up from the base of her neck. Her kid gave her migraines. "That's not enough this time. Let me repeat myself. What you did was serious. This goes beyond anything you've ever pulled."

Mac lowered his arms from the doorframe. "You could have killed someone...or yourself. What kind of stupid, asinine thoughts were going through your head?"

"I don't want to be here! I wanna go home."

Mac ran a hand through his hair. "You know the rules. We're a family, and we always stay together."

"Then stop building these damn hotels! I hate moving every time you need some new Legoland built in your honor."

"Watch it, kid. You're batting zero today with all the crap you've pulled."

Abbie stepped forward and laid a hand on her brother's arm. Since she understood them both, she kept her voice light. "We'll call you when we're done out here, Dustin."

"Don't I even get a say?"

She looked at him and wanted to touch his cheek. No one knew better than a teen mom that growing up could be a bitch. But she was the parent now.

"I'm afraid not. Go in now," she ordered and closed the door.

The music lowered to a faint, persistent beat from the other side. Mac stalked away from her and opened the patio door, stepping onto the skinny balcony. She followed him, shut the door to block out inquiring ears, and put a hand on his back when he lowered his head into his hands.

"God, Abbie. He could have been killed."

She leaned onto his back for a moment, resting there. The moment they put Dustin into her arms at the hospital, the "Imagine Every Horrible Scenario" software had been downloaded into her brain. Mac seemed to have received the same download. They'd shared endless fears over Dustin—record-high fevers, cracking his forehead open—but never anything like this.

"You always tear into him when all you want to do is hug him," she observed.

He sighed and rose to his full height again. "It's not like when he was a kid. He's too big for a hug, and this is serious. Shit. He could have killed Peggy."

Her cheeks flamed, remembering the signs of Mac's lust—not something a sister wanted to see. Ever. She didn't like it—or the deputy—but she wanted to respect Mac's business. "That woman's been eating at you."

"That's not only it. She has a kid, too, Abbie. He's seven."

Since his muscles seemed carved in marble, she rubbed his back. "We can only thank God nothing worse happened."

He grabbed her hand. "Damn Maven genes, right? I'd hoped we'd stamped them out of him. He's giving me gray hair, Abbie, I swear."

"I could find some shoe polish to touch up your roots."

"Funny."

"Might melt if you sweat. Oops, you don't sweat. I forgot."

"Stop trying to make me feel better."

"Is it working?"

"Yes."

She crossed her arms. "Now help me."

He rubbed his chin, considering. "He has more support and resources than we did growing up, and we didn't do so badly."

Her mouth refused to smile. She thought of Dustin's father. Wasn't she really scared of what that gene pool carried? "He's likes the fast lane just like you do, but he's still a good kid. We *have* to keep believing that."

Unlike their own father, she thought, but didn't say. Their old man had called Mac everything from stupid to worthless growing up. Mac had proven him wrong. She hoped Dustin would want to prove them right. God knows he wasn't perfect, but who was?

"Peggy said she'd talk to the city attorney since Dustin's remorseful, and this is his first offense. He'll likely do some community service. But I want to make it up to her."

Abbie pretended to study the scenery. So, he really did have it bad for this deputy who'd tried to stop him from building the hotel. Not his usual no-strings, uncomplicated type. She'd have to check her out more.

"What do you have in mind?"

"What does a single mom need?"

She put her hand under her chin, thinking. "Someone to mow the lawn. It's summertime. Do they have a yard?"

He nodded his head like he was considering it. "Yes, a nice big one for the kid. Good idea. I knew you'd have one."

"I'm a woman. We know what we don't like to do. Of course, we could have Dustin take the garbage out for her." She nudged him gently to diffuse their tenseness.

He pulled her close and tucked her against his side. "Really stinky garbage. Like chicken guts or fish heads—with maggots."

A laugh puffed out, but with it, a bubble of fear so strong, she bit her lip. "Oh, Mac."

His arms pulled her close. They hugged as the mountain sunlight rained over them, the trees whispering secrets as the wind rushed through the valley.

"He's going to be okay, Abbie. I promise."

"I know."

He'd said the same thing to her when the doctors had allowed him to come visit her hospital room more than sixteen years ago. Dustin had been born four months premature. The doctors had scared her to death with talk of brain and lung damage, disabilities. Sick herself from nearly hemorrhaging to death, something inside her had clicked. Given how he'd been conceived, she hadn't completely wanted her baby. That had changed the moment she learned he would need to fight to survive.

Mac had taken her hand that day and made her a promise. Whatever they needed to make Dustin and her better, he'd provide. He'd been as good as his word. Though they hadn't possessed medical insurance at the time, he'd won what they needed playing poker. It had been the start of his grand career. And though their homes might be like musical chairs, they always stayed together.

"Let's go tell him," she said. "And let's chalk this whole thing up to a learning experience."

Mac opened the door for her. "Let's hope he's a fast learner. Otherwise, I'm going to have Peggy throw his ass in jail for a night to scare the shit out of him."

"She looks like she might just do that."

A strange look passed over his face, and then he met her eyes. "She might, indeed." He reached for her arm again. "Wait. I need to tell you something."

His tone caught her off guard as much as his touch. "What is it?"

"Rhett called me. He's coming to the tourney."

She struggled to keep her face from changing into...shock, excitement, fear? It was hard to say how many emotions bubbled through her. "Because Rye's coming..."

"Maybe. You know Rhett. He's spontaneous. He's a late addition, but he's such a crowd pleaser. He knew we'd make room."

Yes, indeed. Rhett Butler Blaylock was anything but methodical—except when it came to poker. His free spirited ways and classic good looks turned heads everywhere he went. For a while, he'd turned hers, starting on a sleepy June morning after an early run when he'd encountered her weeding in her garden. His sweaty, shirtless chest had blown the circuitry in her brain. He must have seen the lust in her eyes because he strode forward, threw the trowel she was holding aside, and kissed her deeply, darkly, until she fell back on the grass, his body covering hers. They'd stumbled to the guest-house and proceeded to have the wildest and most intimate sex imaginable.

Afterward, he'd held her and made her laugh—even as the magnitude of what she'd done hit home. He was Mac's best friend. She'd known him for well over a decade. And he wasn't her type.

But she hadn't been able to stay away from him...or the sex. Their ease with each other inside and outside the bedroom shocked them both. For six months, they met secretly when he came to visit the Mavens in Arizona, or when he and Mac were playing in a poker tournament. She hadn't wanted anyone to know, especially not Mac or Dustin. They'd just be disappointed when it didn't lead anywhere. Plus Rhett's flamboyance and wild lifestyle embarrassed her.

Falling in love hadn't been part of the plan, but it had happened. When she saw him making a beeline for her after a tournament one day, soaked to the bone in champagne after his win, flanked by sequin-clad poker babes and calling out dirty jokes to raucous fans, she'd realized it was time to end things. He had momentarily forgotten their secret arrangement, inebriated on Dom Perignon and the rush of winning another huge pot.

He wasn't husband or father material, and how long could a girl carry on with a man like that without breaking her heart? When she'd told him the next day, his response had been cool, but understanding. It had surprised her when he left the country to play in several international poker tournaments...and it had surprised her more how much she missed him.

"It'll be good to see him," she lied, focusing back on her brother.

"It's been a while." Mac's hand closed over her arm. "You okay?"

His perceptiveness threatened her secret. She needed to walk away. "Why wouldn't I be?" Since he wouldn't release her arm, she halted.

"Did you think I didn't know about you two?"

This conversation could not start. She didn't need him worrying about something that had long since ended.

Discussing her personal business made her cheeks flame, but she tried to downplay her embarrassment. "It wasn't serious. You know Rhett."

He stared at her with that intense gaze she so envied—she couldn't even look at herself in the mirror that way.

"Yes, but I know you. You could never do anything *but* serious."

"I don't want to talk about this, Mac."

He let her go. "Okay, but he's coming. And he means a lot to me."

"I won't mess anything up."

"I wasn't worried you would. I just don't want you two to be at odds."

She smiled to reassure him. "I'm sure he's forgotten all about it. I certainly have."

He dipped his finger into his pocket and took out his lucky piece. He carried one chip for luck—a thousand dollar denomination in canary yellow from his first World Series of Poker win. He tossed it straight up into the air.

"Heads you're lying. Tails, you're telling the truth."

She reached to catch it, but he was too fast for her—like usual. "Heads, Abbie. Better work on that poker face. Rhett will see right through you."

"Oh, shut up," she fumed uncharacteristically. "I have enough to worry about with Dustin turning delinquent and you panting after some female deputy who threw us to the wolves."

He chuckled. "Ah, there's the Maven blood. Always looks good on you when it comes out."

She threw up her hands. They could talk to Dustin after she burned off her anger at the gym. She hoped it would also help her stop thinking about why Rhett Butler Blaylock was coming back now and what he might or might not want from her.

CHAPTER 9

By the time Peggy finished her day job, she could have become NASA's first human test subject to launch into space without a shuttle. God knows she had enough fire in her engines. The dark chocolate bar in her desk had done nothing to curb her appetite. Why did that surprise her? When a woman wanted sex, she wanted sex. Too bad chocolate didn't work as a substitute when a girl was in overdrive.

"Curse Maven's black soul," she muttered, gathering plates to set the dining room table.

"Mom, when are they going to get here?" Keith whined, returning to the kitchen after at least ten sprints to the front door. Did seven-year-olds *ever* get tired?

"When they get here," she replied with little imagination.

Of all the nights, *of course* tonight was the monthly dinner with her new family. It would be a smaller crew than usual because Arthur had called at the last minute, saying he needed to stay at the newspaper and finish a story and couldn't bring the bread, and Meredith and Jill's parents were heading back to town late after a day-long shopping trip to Denver. She'd asked Brian to bring the bread, since nothing was better than his fresh baguettes. She prayed to God he wouldn't wince when he tasted the chicken she'd made. All she'd done was dump Italian dressing on it and pop it in the oven. Cooking for a chef intimidated her, and she didn't intimidate easily. Tanner and Meredith were bringing the green stuff, and Jill and Brian were bringing the dessert, in addition to the bread. God, please let it be chocolate.

A knock on the door made Keith squeal and run for it, reminding her of the Road Runner. She squared her shoulders and tried out a smile. She was so not giving anyone so much as a whiff that something was off with her. What had happened with Maven would stay in that office of his. She refused to indulge in any traitorous mental replays of his mouth and hands on her. Her body was still crying from the interruption to their...what the hell should she call it anyway? Madness? Hormonal attack? No, that sounded too much like PMS.

The logical Peggy had been relieved by his sister's interruption. The sex-starved woman inside her still wanted to howl at the moon or do something crazy—like roll around in Keith's kiddie pool to cool off.

The front foyer sounded like a group booking at the sheriff's office, so she headed over to greet her guests.

"Hey," she cried as she was given as many hugs and kisses as a newborn coming home from the hospital. It still felt weird after growing up in such a non-demonstrative home.

"Brian made double chocolate cake with triple chocolate macadamia nut ice cream just for me," Jill announced.

"It's her theme." Brian rolled his eyes. "Chocolate, chocolate, chocolate. Any form, any time, any way."

"Stop bitc—complaining," Jill said in a good save. They'd agreed on no bad words around Keith.

"You read my mind. And I see you have a shelf for the food," Peggy commented wryly. Jill was balancing the cake and ice cream on her bump, with the baguette at a jaunty angle on top. "I think you're even bigger than you were last weekend."

"Twins," she cried, linking her arm with Meredith's. "It's like having two small trees in here. Seedlings growing into oaks. Just you wait, sis, twins run in the family."

"Trees? Jillie, I thought you were having girls." Keith stared at her stomach as if it might contain aliens.

"She is having girls. She's only using a simile." Tanner gave him a high five. "Your teacher taught you about those in English class, remember?"

Meredith jerked her arm free. "Your scare tactics won't work. I'm *not* having twins when we finally decide to get pregnant. Right, hon?"

Tanner picked Keith up and threw him in the air, making him squeal like a banshee. "Exactly. It's all about the power of the mind."

Jill thrust the food at Peggy, snorting. "Things don't always go the way we plan, but sometimes they turn out perfect all the same." She waddled over to Brian and gave him a smacking kiss on the lips. "Right, babe?"

Brian's grin could have graced a bridal magazine showing a newly married guy doped up on the love drug. Had her ex ever looked at her like that? Peggy didn't think so. Even Tanner had walked around with that look on his face after his wedding to Meredith. Her intense, serious brother couldn't have surprised her more.

"Let's eat," Jill announced.

"Another theme of the past few months," Brian interjected.

"I'm eating for three," she reminded him.

"Dinner's that-a-way," Peggy announced, although everyone knew it.

They chowed down, passing the food back and forth. The guys had a couple of helpings apiece. Peggy's smiles grew easier over the course of the meal. She nearly managed to block out the images of Maven. Then they had dessert, and as soon as the dark chocolate cake hit her mouth, she had a flash of his tongue melting over hers like the frosting. Her face heated. God, she was losing it.

Jill grabbed her napkin and fanned Peggy. "You've got my problem. It's like the babies take all the cold and leave me with the heat. Let me help." She reached into her drink for an ice cube and leaned over to put it down Peggy's collar.

"Don't you dare! I will so take a pregnant woman down," Peggy warned her, laughing in loud gusts as she tried to evade her friend's slippery hands.

Using her new weight, Jill leveraged Peggy against the chair. She got a grip on her collar and popped the ice cube in. The arctic streak actually felt like nirvana against Peggy's heated skin, but she protested to keep up appearances.

Jill's face contorted for a moment, making Peggy think the babies had given her liver a swift kick or something.

"God, Peg, you got bit by some gigantor mosquito." She tugged on Peggy's collar again. Her mouth formed an O. "Is that a hic—" Her face froze. She shot a sheepish grin as Keith zoomed over.

"Let me see!" her son begged. "We've got *huge* bugs in the backyard. Mom says the mountains make them mutant."

"It's a...hiccup," Jill recovered terribly. "I've got hiccups."

Brian nudged her. "Sure you do. Nice one, Red. Hey Keith, let's go throw the ball around in the backyard. Leave the womenfolk alone. Tanner?"

Peggy didn't know what was worse. The shock of actually having a hickey—jeez, was she fifteen?—or having her friends know. Oh, and lying to her son. Maven was dead meat.

Her hand yanked her collar up as Brian led Keith outside, taking his attention away from her, thank God.

Frowning, Tanner rose slowly to his feet. Great, big brother syndrome never seemed to go away.

"Take care of those hic...ups, Jill," he said, following Brian and Keith onto the deck.

Peggy lurched from her seat and bolted to the bathroom. Mirrors never lied. The big, red mark on her neck couldn't have been more obvious.

Mosquito bite, her ass. Maven had bit her? She couldn't recall when. Somewhere between insane and *really* crazy. What in the hell had he been thinking? What in the hell had *she* been thinking? Had she bit him? She hoped he had a "mosquito" bite the size of a big country like...Greenland or something.

Her gaze strayed from the mark to the Hale sisters. They stood in the open doorway with their arms crossed like identical twins.

Meredith's eyebrow rose. "Tell, tell."

"There's only one man in town big and strong enough to bite Peggy and not be dead," Jill mused in a terrible John Wayne voice, "and I didn't hear about her killing anyone today on the news."

"Oh, shut up." Since Jill had zero control over her mouth—and worse, she worked for Maven—Peggy had to make something up, and quickly. She turned from the mirror and leaned back against the vanity. "It's not what you think."

"This girlfriend cries, *bullshit*," Jill sang. "You and Mac finally went at each other. It's about time."

"Seriously, Jill, shut up." Peggy ducked her head, mortified by the heat in her cheeks. She never blushed.

"Look, don't feel bad. It's like you two were in a pressure cooker. Everyone knew the top would finally blow off."

"A pressure cooker? What am I? A pot roast?"

Jill snickered.

"Everyone knew?"

Meredith shrugged. "You two are positively flammable around each other. There should be a warning sticker."

"But we never say anything—"

"Exactly!" Jill rested her hands on her protruding stomach. "You two have ignored each other for months. It had to stop sometime. The whole moose thing changed the status quo. You were fighting for your lives together—"

"It was a moose, Jill. Not a serial killer."

"Whatever. There's way too much attraction between you two for it not to explode. You're like Vesuvius!"

"This is crazy," Peggy muttered, trying to brush past them.

In silent agreement, the sisters blocked her way. "You hurt him, so he got all silent on you," Jill said. "You're scared of how he makes you feel, so you ignored him right back. Don't you think it's time to try something else?"

"I think they just did," Meredith mused. "Seems like it got pretty heated if he marked you. Did you..." She gestured with her hands.

"Give each other the bird?" Peggy asked drolly.

"That was supposed to be that banging-a-chick sign guys always give each other."

Jill's laughter exploded. "Oh, Mere. It's like this." She made a fist and banged it into the air in a pretty lewd way.

"I cannot believe we're standing in my bathroom talking about hickeys and making male banging signs. I feel like I'm at the sheriff's office."

Jill and Meredith started laughing. Peggy couldn't help herself. She finally joined them.

"So how was it really?" Meredith asked when the laughter died.

"Crazy," she replied honestly. "And it's *never* going to happen again."

"A hundred bucks says it will," Jill replied.

Peggy crossed her arms. "See, that's what happens when you start working at a casino. You start betting on every confounded thing... This topic is closed. I'm going to join the guys."

"Tanner's going to be weird about this. I could see it on his face," Jill commented as they all stepped out of the bathroom.

"He's her big brother." Meredith slid the patio door open.

Sure enough, Tanner gave her a look as soon as they emerged from the house. She felt like she was a teenager again, coming in a few minutes past curfew. Dammit, he'd always waited up for her when she was on a date. After their father split, Tanner had been more to her than her big

The Grand Opening

brother. He'd raised her and David. Too bad he'd been little more than a kid himself. Kinda like Mac and his sister, the thought of which only made her want to snarl. *Stop invading my thoughts*, she silently yelled in her head.

"Hey, Jill!" her son called. "Come play with us. Brian taught me how to do a thumb ball."

"It's a knuckle ball, Keith," Tanner corrected.

"Sorry, I can't," Jill announced, dropping into a chair. "Someone knocked me up." She wagged her finger at Brian.

Keith dashed over to join them. "Are you telling a knock-knock joke, Jillie?

"Gosh no, I hate those. Never tell a knock-knock joke, Keith. It's like being in the Humor Torture Squad. Brian and I will have to take you out."

"Not if you can't catch me."

He streaked off.

"Fat chance. Literally. I could out-waddle a duck maybe. I hate this part of pregnancy. It's like aliens have taken over my body. I miss seeing my feet."

"Well, at least you can't complain about how big they are," Meredith mused.

"When did I do that?"

"Like all the time when they hit size eleven in seventh grade. Bri, back me up."

"You did, babe." He darted away when he said it, like he was worried Jill would throw something.

She waved her fist. "*I'll get you my pretty.* Later."

"Can't wait."

"I'll roll over and squash that trim body."

"Good one, Red." He darted up the deck and kissed her smack on the mouth.

"Don't leave a mark." She looked pointedly at Peggy. "Wouldn't that be cute? A preggers chick with a huge hickey."

Peggy expected her cheeks could have been an ad for Red Lobster. "Okay, enough. Seriously. I will kill you."

"Don't hurt my bride. Enough talk, Jill. Come play with us, Peggy."

She jogged into the yard, catching the ball Brian winged her way. She executed the whole pitcher motion and hurled it into his mitt with a smack.

"Got some heat on that one." He rubbed his hand.

No kidding. She had more heat than they had baseballs.

CHAPTER 10

When Peggy heard the knock on the front door, she frowned. Was Tanner picking Keith up early for the baseball game? It wasn't even six o'clock yet. He hadn't eaten.

"Keith," Peggy called as she dredged chicken pieces in flour. "Will you answer that?"

Enraptured by his favorite TV program, it took him a moment to acknowledge her request. Peggy called it the Cartoon Delay—something about imaginary worlds, color, and music altered the synapses in the brain. Her kid usually moved at light speed, his brain processing a heck of a lot faster than hers. But not when he was in what she referred to as Tube Thrall.

He turned to her with glassy, unblinking eyes. "Sure, Mom." His sneakers squeaked when he crossed the linoleum.

"Be right there," Peggy called, speeding up her "dunk and dredge" motion. The pan popped grease as she arranged the chicken strips in the pan. Nothing said summer like fried chicken. The gunk on her hands always required some serious scrubbing. She cocked an ear to hear who it was while she lathered up her hands.

"Hi, Mr. Maven," Keith piped. "Mom! It's Mr. Maven and some other people. Come on in."

Usually his good manners and welcoming spirit would have pleased her. But the name made her frown. She touched a wet hand to her hickey, carefully hidden by a high-neck shirt. Damn if the man's mark hadn't forced her to cover herself up like a nun in this heat. Her own internal fire rose—not from lust this time, but pure, pissed-off rage.

She strode into the hall, ready to send Keith back to his cartoons and then rip Maven a new one for showing up at their home. The sight of his companions stopped her in her tracks. His eyebrow rose like he knew she was raring for battle.

"Peggy, I was just introducing Keith to my sister and nephew. You've already met them—unfortunately under less than desirable circumstances."

They all looked like a bunch of panther people, all of them with the same jet-black hair and stoplight green eyes.

"Hello again," Abbie said like they were meeting after church.

"Dustin, you remember Deputy McBride."

The hunched shoulders conveyed the fact that he'd rather be anywhere but her house, but he met her gaze without flinching. "Deputy McBride, I want to apologize for what happened the other day."

Since no sixteen-year-old talked like that, she suspected he'd had help.

"We came to make amends for putting you in..." Maven smiled at Keith. "A challenging position."

Abbie grabbed her son's hand. "Dustin, please tell Deputy McBride how you'd like to make it up to her."

He toed his red sneaker into her carpet. "I'd like to mow your yard for the summer and do any other yard work you might need."

"Awesome!" Keith all but yelled. "Mom hates mowing the yard. I told her I'd do it, but she says I need to eat more spinach first. I've told her Popeye is so not cool."

Keith's pandering for attention gave her a moment to process the situation. Maven watched her with somber eyes, never looking away. The middle of her back suddenly itched. She ignored it.

"It's really not necessary." She stuffed her hands in the pockets of her shorts, suddenly unsure of what to do with them. "I've already spoken to the...right people." Discussing sheriff matters in front of Keith was something she never did.

"Thank you for that." Abbie strode forward. "But we want to do something for you. I'm a single mom, too, and I know how much it means to have one less chore around the house. Plus, Mac's right. Dustin put you in a difficult situation. He should make amends."

She cast a glance at Keith, whose smile had faded. He was studying all the adults, clearly trying to process the subtext. Little ears had a way of understanding things they didn't need to know about yet.

"Keith, why don't you go back and watch your show?"

"I'm fine here," he replied.

"Keith."

His face fell. "Okay, Mom." His slow gait back to the kitchen magnified the silence in the hallway.

"Dustin, maybe you should wait outside too," Peggy said.

Abbie gave her son a forced smile. He lowered his head and headed out the front door.

Peggy crossed her arms. "I didn't want to say this in front of him, but I'm not sure I want my son spending time around a kid who's stealing cars and taking them out for joy rides."

Abbie's body tensed as if she had used a whip on her. Peggy had a moment of regret—not for speaking the truth, but for hurting another mother.

Maven put a hand on his sister's shoulders and squeezed. With that one touch, Peggy knew how close they were—a team—and that anything affecting Dustin twisted their guts. Her back itched something fierce. Dammit, she didn't want to see this side of him.

"This is the first time he's ever done anything like that. To make sure it never happens again, we want him to understand that there are consequences for his behavior—personal and legal." Mac ran a hand through his hair. "Either Abbie or I will come over with him to mow. If you want to keep Keith out of the way, that's fine."

Abbie wrung her hands. "He's a good kid. I know you don't think much of us, but...please let us do this. This is our home now. We want to be...neighborly."

Peggy caught the edge in her voice. She suspected Abbie knew what she'd done at the city council meeting. Still, she was trying to do the right thing. Peggy admired that.

"Does he know how to mow?"

Mac snorted. "Of course. He doesn't have a PhD in it. Would you like him to go through advanced training?"

His razor-sharp tone made her want to snarl, but his sister didn't need to witness their...banter.

She crossed her arms so she wouldn't fidget with her T-shirt's hem. It felt weird to be around him without her uniform on. "You might think it's funny, but I had a heck of a time starting the mower when I first tried. I wanted to run it over with my car."

That gorgeous mouth that had fit so perfectly to her lips—and bit her—curved. "I blew out our motor when I was a kid running over a whole swarm of toads that invaded our yard." He tapped his sister's nose. "If memory serves, you screamed bloody murder from the window the whole time."

Abbie shivered. "It was disgusting. First I saw the mass of them jumping forward in a unit, and then toad bits were flying everywhere. Yuck."

She was so not getting chummy with Maven. "Not too many toads around here. We should be safe. The mower's in the shed out back. I get to call a halt at any time if he pulls anything."

"Agreed," Maven answered.

"He won't," Abbie declared.

Peggy firmed her shoulders. "Abbie, why don't you tell Dustin? I want to talk to your brother for a moment."

His infernal eyebrow winged up again. She wanted to shave it.

"Thank you, Deputy."

When Abbie extended her hand, Peggy took it, one single mother to another. "Call me Peggy."

The woman's clenched frame eased a bit. "Thank you," she said before easing out the door with barely a sound.

Peggy turned back to Maven. "We need to get something straight."

He crossed his arms way too nonchalantly for her taste. If she had to run him over with a lawn mower for him to understand, she would. They were never ever having a repeat performance of what had happened in his office.

CHAPTER 11

Mac wouldn't have been surprised if Peggy had a weapon nearby, locked and loaded. She'd been hostile toward him from the start, so her attitude wasn't exactly news. The first time they met, she had been under the weather, and while she hadn't looked particularly pretty that day, he'd felt something shift inside him all the same.

That determined chin, those high cheekbones, and that flat out *take no prisoners* attitude had intrigued him. When color had returned to her face, everything had come together—the dark pageboy hair, the brown eyes, the nearly translucent skin—and he'd been rocked back with more than intrigue. Sheer lust had coiled through him until he'd felt strangled. His lack of control and her outright hostility had made her difficult to ignore.

Like a game of cards, life had a way of dealing out surprise hands.

He wasn't ready to fold yet.

He'd tried bluffing—after she went after him publically, he'd ignored her, sending the message that he just didn't give a damn. Then the moose had thrown them together again. And after the insane encounter in his office, a new strategy seemed to be his best bet.

So he'd raise.

"I haven't been able to stop thinking about what happened."

She flinched at his honesty and then firmed her chin like she was preparing for an attack. He wanted to yank her to him and kiss her.

"You bit me."

He blinked for a moment and then scratched his cheek. Of all the things, he thought she'd come back with, that hadn't been one of them. "I did? Let me see."

She tugged her collar up higher when he reached for it. "Not necessary. Look, I have a kid. Hell, I have to walk out of my house every day. My friends saw it. My fellow officers could have. Hell, the whole town." She narrowed her eyes. "Jill thought it was funny."

His lips pursed, trying not to laugh. If Jill knew, he could expect some pithy comment from her about getting a rabies shot.

"Are you sure it was a bite? I might have nipped you a little. Your skin is like silk." He stepped close enough to feel her body heat, smell the flowery aroma of her shampoo. "When you've wanted something for a long time, things can turn a little crazy."

She grabbed her throat like she couldn't swallow all of the sudden. He understood the feeling. His mouth dried up, his body revving, his hands itching to feel those strong curves.

"It can't happen again," she informed him.

He leaned his head closer, so close the golden ring around her iris expanded. "I disagree. It *needs* to happen again. This isn't going away, Peggy. We tried that."

She pushed him back with a palm to his chest. "So we try harder."

His heartbeat seemed to migrate to where she was touching him, pounding in hard, insistent beats. His hand covered hers. "I'm done trying. I want to explore this."

She tried to yank her hand free, but he held it in place.

"Well, I don't. Let go."

He caressed her wrist with delicate strokes. "Not until you admit there's something between us."

She turned into him and, in one quick move, angled her elbow toward his neck. "I'm serious about you letting me go."

She wasn't ready. He wanted to sigh. Hell, his body wanted to weep. When he stepped back, he raised his hands like a white flag of surrender.

"I'll let you go for now, but this is a long way from over." He crossed the hall. "I'll tell Keith goodbye. Then, we'll get out of your way."

"Fine. I'll say goodbye to your sister and nephew." She stormed out.

When he reached the next room, he stopped. Keith stood against the wall, clearly eavesdropping.

"You hear everything?" he asked, not bothering to pretend the situation away. Dustin had been a champ eavesdropper, hiding in cabinets in Mac's office or his mom's room when he wanted to know things they wouldn't tell him, like who his father was. Thank God he still didn't know.

He ducked his head. "Uh-huh. Why'd you bite my mom?"

After talking to Dustin about sex, erections, and other embarrassing things, he didn't squirm. He took a moment to come up with something truthful, but not too explicit.

He hoped to hell, for his own sake, Keith wouldn't ask Peggy the same question. He didn't think she'd shoot him, but he was pretty sure she'd seriously wound him. Funny, hadn't she already?

He crouched down so that he and Keith were eye to eye.

"Keith, I like your mom. You like her too, right?"

The kid's nod couldn't have been more emphatic.

"When you show her how much you like her—like kissing and hugging her—have you ever accidentally squeezed her too hard or anything?"

"Uh-huh."

"So that's what happened with your mom and me. I was too happy to see her."

Keith's eyes narrowed as he tried to work through the puzzle, just like his mom's always did. "You got too excited? Sometimes that happens to me too. Mom tells me to calm down."

Yes, he'd gotten too excited all right. "Yes, that's exactly it."

"She's pretty angry." He glanced around Mac's shoulder like he was looking for Peggy. "You should tell her you're sorry."

"I will. Thanks for reminding me." He wondered if he'd ever been this nice as a kid. "So it's okay if I like your mom?"

"You like her like a girl, don't you?"

His somber expression twisted Mac's stomach. The kid knew how things worked, even if he didn't know all the details.

"Yes, I like her like a girl." And he felt like he was back in junior high, talking about sneaking out of class to practice French kissing with Heather Barlett.

"Mom doesn't really kiss any guys except family—and only on the cheek."

His nerves jumped. The kid had way too much insight for someone his age. Must be a McBride gene. "I'm not family," he said, keeping it simple, but sticking to the truth.

Keith's sneakers squeaked on the linoleum as he shuffled forward. "Be nice to my mom. My dad wasn't. Uncle Tanner said we need to make her happy." His voice was a low whisper, like he was confessing a secret.

Mac's throat squeezed. He'd conspired with Dustin to brighten Abbie's life, trying to fill an impossible void left by the bastard who'd fathered him.

"Your Uncle Tanner's a smart man."

Keith pointed to himself. "I am too. I got all As on my report card."

Mac gave him a high five. "Good for you. Now let's go find your mom."

And he didn't squirm at all when Keith took his hand and walked with him outside to a frowning Peggy.

CHAPTER 12

Usually Wednesday's poker night lifted Mac's mood. Tonight he was having trouble concentrating on his hand—a first—and sliding into the easy male camaraderie he'd come to expect with this group. Brian always joked around. With enough encouragement, Arthur talked about his interviews with influential persons. His son, Alan, bitched about his father smoking bootleg Cuban cigars while he was on his "no more heart attacks" diet. Cince regaled them all with stories about the hands he'd played on gambling steamboats along the Mississippi River, embellishing them like a circus barker. Add in Tanner, and he had a damn good poker group.

The age range covered a wide swath, but Mac liked it that way. Yes, it was lower limit poker, and the people weren't professionals—save Cince—but it was fun. He hadn't gotten into poker originally out of love for the game, so it was nice to be around guys who simply enjoyed it. He could sit back and relax with a cigar between his teeth and a dram of whiskey by his side, savoring the feel of crisp cards in his hands while he talked smack with the other guys as they tried to figure out the one thing that had puzzled men since the beginning of time.

Women.

He figured poker night was like a self-help group for the male species without all the psychological hocus-pocus. They all left feeling a hell of a lot lighter, whether they'd won or lost.

Tonight Tanner was staring him down hard, though, and not over the cards. He must have caught wind of what had happened with Peggy the other day. God, he hoped he hadn't seen the hickey. Mac wasn't one to get uncomfortable when people knew his "female" business, but this situation made his hands itch. Maybe because he was a big brother, too.

"How's the grand opening coming along?" Arthur tapped his cigar on the ashtray and then clamped it between his teeth.

"We're ready. The fun begins on Friday. Just two days away." Cince signaled Mac for another card. "It's a pretty nice location for poker night, though, right? Not that rotating it at everyone's house wasn't nice." They were in one of the six high-roller poker suites Mac had designed for the hotel. Each was fitted with its own sweeping bar named after an indigenous tree growing in the valley. Tonight they were in The Ponderosa

Room.

Brian smoothed his hand over the green felt poker table. "It's like a baby's bottom."

"You'll make a good father, thinking like that, but it's kinda sick, kid," Arthur commented, nudging his new grandson-in-law in the ribs.

Mac reached for a cigar in the embossed wooden case. Smoking one always made him feel like Brett Maverick, minus the western getup. He'd seen every episode of Maverick on reruns growing up. It had helped him pretend his father was like Brett, although Mac had never seen any of the charm or generosity of James Garner's TV character in his dad. Being nicknamed Maverick after his first big tournament couldn't have flattered him more.

"Poker tables are like beds to me," said Mac. "Since I spend so much time at them, I want them to be comfortable. I designed each one myself."

Each table in the hotel focused on a specific type of poker. Some were big, some were small, and groups of all sizes could be accommodated. The stunning ellipse-shaped Hold 'Em table they were using seated nine. The cushioned brown leather armrests supported players' elbows, helping them shield their cards throughout hours of grueling play. Add in the Italian leather throne chairs that curved to the body in ergonomic magic, and Mac could play for days without anything more than a few short breaks.

He couldn't wait to break them in.

"I can see why people pay your prices, Mac. This room is inspired." Alan's head turned away from his cards. "Restoring antiques has always been my favorite hobby, so I've seen some fine wood in my day, but this stuff...it's like you coated the wood in liquid gold."

Mac traced the edges of the table, admiring the room. Yeah, everything looked awesome.

"When the high rollers hit, their mouths are going to drop, I'm telling you. Mac outdid himself with this place. Not that the other hotels aren't freaking ridiculous in their own way," Cincinnati observed.

"Thanks, Cince," Mac replied. "Can't wait to play poker until the sun sets on the 4th of July. Then, we'll top it all off with a big party when the tourney's over. I'm still working on Rye Crenshaw to sing at least one song for us, like 'I'm Proud to be an American' or something."

Cincinnati rattled the ice cubes in his glass. "God, I love that guy, and he's a talented poker player, too. Hope he agrees. Regardless, it's going to be a hell of a show."

Poker night could turn serious, but the easy-going camaraderie was sheer fun. They'd agreed to play low-limit poker—that way no one would lose their shirt. It didn't seem to bother anyone that Mac, Cince, and Tanner took most of the hands, although Arthur tended to surprise them every once in a while. The old guy could bluff like nobody's business. Brian and Alan were improving. He'd whip them all into shape by the end of the summer so they'd be tournament ready.

Mac considered his cards. He had the makings of an ace high straight. He took stock of the cards he suspected everyone else held. The jack he needed would show up.

"The hotel opens to guests on Friday, and the tourney kicks off Saturday morning," Cincinnati informed them. "I'm Mac's biggest opponent."

Mac huffed out a laugh. "In what universe? I beat you with four queens in Vegas at our last tourney. You know I always kick your butt." It wasn't true, but banter was banter.

"Your ass is going to be sore come Monday night. You might be crying after you lose in your new hotel's first tourney."

Arthur harrumphed. "Can't wait to watch. Never did care for all that noise in Vegas. Slot machines erupting and club music blasting. Heard your style is more like a library."

Mac fingered the edge of his king of hearts and stared back at Tanner, who was still stony-silent, his expression cold. "Serious poker players hate all that racket. That's why they always play in the back room."

Arthur put aside his cigar and pulled out one of his signature red hot candies. "Anyone?"

Brian's nose wrinkled. "Doesn't exactly go with beer."

"Shut up and play," Tanner interjected.

Everyone gave him a look, but they did as they'd been commanded. Mac took the hand with the straight. Like always, raking in a pile of colorful casino chips settled him to the core, giving him a feeling of security, success.

Few cared about chips like he did. He'd designed the compression-mold for security, but also to showcase the hotel's brand and logo—The Grand, for The Grand Mountain Hotel. He even dreamed about the sound clay chips made when he ruffled them. *Kalick, kalick, kalick.*

"I'm taking you this time, Mac, my boy." Cince shuffled the cards in the extravagant and gravity-defying Russian style, cards springing from his thumb and pinky and cascading across the table as his hands kept separating them further and further apart.

"Show off," Mac commented, rubbing his lucky piece.

No one could shuffle with more flourish than Cince. He'd been a dealer before becoming a player, and his flourishes had helped him rake in major tips. Now he used all the knowledge he'd picked up from dealing at the tables.

His wide mouth formed an eerie grin. "Let's play."

"You're kicking my ass," Brian commented as Cince raked in the chips on the next hand. "I've got a wife and twins to take care of."

Cince slapped him on the back. "You know the old saying, right? Poker is the hardest way to make an easy living. Besides, Mac won't let Jill go. She's indispensible to the hotel."

"She's got a job for life if she wants it," Mac added. "Jill's a natural."

"Girl's got spunk," her father commented.

"Got all that empire building gumption from her grandfather," Arthur noted, rolling his red hot candy across his front teeth.

"Great, twin girls with spunk. I'm never going to sleep again once they're born. Like Brasserie Dare isn't enough." Brian was half-joking, but Mac caught the shine of new-father fear in his eyes.

"It'll be great. Nothing like kids," Mac murmured, thinking about Dustin and his recent asinine stunt. Kid still wouldn't talk to him. He thought Uncle Mac had sold him out. Well, it wasn't their first boxing match. They'd go a few rounds more.

The group played late. Tanner came on strong, winning two hands in a row—a first. Mac could almost feel the intensity radiating from him like heat off August asphalt. When they called a halt, and everyone headed out of the room, Tanner hung back. Mac started collecting the chips and putting them back in the rack to give them some time.

When the door closed, Tanner put his hands on his hips. "You gave my sister a hickey."

Mac pushed the rack away. A tinge of embarrassment slid up his back. "Since I've got a baby sister myself, I won't tell you to buzz off. But you're not taking a swing at me. I've got a tourney starting. A bruised face would attract the wrong kind of press."

Tanner didn't respond to the joke. His jaw clenched. "I figure since you left a mark—and don't have that black-eye you're so worried about—she wanted it there. At least in the moment. It's the future that worries me."

"Is this the whole 'intentions' talk? We might need another drink."

Tanner waved away the glass he offered. "I'm only warning you to be careful with her. I wasn't home when her ex turned into a fucker, but I'm here now. I won't see her hurt again."

Mac poured himself a single malt and swirled it around, releasing the leather and spice scent. "Hmm...I understand the sentiment. Again, big bro and all. Your sister...well, she's as prickly as a porcupine, so I'm probably the one who's in danger here."

Tanner strode over. "Are you joking about this? 'Cause my funny bone's broke."

Mac held up his hands. "I know she comes with a kid—a great kid." He decided not to tell Tanner about his little talk with Keith. "I watch out for my sister and nephew. I know the drill... Look, if I could stop wanting her, I would."

At Tanner's glare, Mac lifted a shoulder. "It's not just lust." And then he kept his mouth shut. No need to invite a punch.

"Look, Peg had a tough time growing up with our dad, and when she made an effort to be...hell, happy, things turned on her. She went into the police academy all eager-beaver to save the world and then fell in love. Her ex hurt her. Bad. She closed up to everyone except Keith and me. She's just now starting to come out of her shell again with the Hales, and I don't want anything to fuck that up."

Mac's insides slithered, thinking about her being younger and less guarded. Life had a way of kicking people down. No one knew that better than he did. "There's a part of her that wants to open up to me, too. I don't want her hurt either, dammit."

The woman inside wanted to come alive again. He'd seen it from the beginning. In some ways, she was like his hotel—she was on the verge of unveiling herself to new people and experiences. He'd have to nurture her transformation just like he had The Grand Mountain Hotel's, although she'd hate the comparison.

Tanner jabbed his finger in the air. "Fine. You've been warned. Next time I punch you."

His mouth twitched. "Duly noted. We good?"

His friend reached for a glass and poured his own drink. "For the moment."

Mac clinked his glass against Tanner's. "Okay, then let's drink and play some blackjack."

"Are you an ace at this, too?"

"Yeah." Taking a seat, he reached for a new deck of cards. The crisp texture snapped when he shuffled them. "You played well tonight."

Tanner sank into a chair. Put his drink in the embossed drink holder. "International correspondents play a lot of poker. Not much else to do except report the news, play cards, and try not to get killed."

"So cut the damn cards."

As Tanner picked up the stack, Mac realized he and Peggy would deal.

And deal with what was between them very soon.

There was no running from it.

CHAPTER 13

$\mathcal{H}$otel grand openings ran pretty smoothly for Mac after all his test runs. He watched from his office window as guests left their sparkling SUVs at the valet stand, and bellmen carried bags discreetly to an obscure entrance. Gleaming wooden doors swung open for each person, his employees tipping their hats to the ladies—Cince's addition. People signed hotel forms with a flourish, tucking Mac's specially designed room cards away.

Some of the poker players brought their wives or girlfriends, who would hang out at the spa and watch their men in the evenings, resplendent in sequined gowns or cocktail dresses. A few women played, disrupting the whole *boys-only* culture. Mac liked their attendance. It was another challenge.

He left his office periodically to greet an old friend or a high roller. Execs from Fortune 500 companies loved his hotels and frequently rented them out for company retreats. He liked those guests better than the bachelor party crews.

But business was business.

When a gleaming white Bentley pulled up in the far right corner of the security screen, he shook his head and headed out to greet one of his oldest friends, entourage and all. Actually, given the fact that Rye Crenshaw was emerging from the SUV directly behind Rhett's, Mac had to wonder if Rhett wasn't a member of *Rye's* entourage.

Rhett Butler Blaylock—or RBB as he was known on the circuit—had all the flamboyant charm of his namesake. Just like his country singer friend. And given their similar ash blond hair and Southern mannerisms, many people mistakenly assumed they were related.

As usual, Rhett's two poker babes, Raven and Vixen, flanked him, their diamond necklaces sparkling from the gas lighting in the lobby. Their skin-tight dresses in neon orange and electric blue had been designed to draw men's eyes, and they were doing their job well.

Only Mac and a few others knew Rhett planned his entrances and entourages as an off-the-table strategy. People came to see him play, but moreover, they came to watch the spectacle.

"Rhett Butler Blaylock," Mac called out in the lobby as he strode toward him. Everyone was staring anyway, might as well add to the hubbub.

Rhett opened his arms, the turquoise beads on his white leather fringe jacket clicking together. "Mac Maverick Maven. Heck of a place you've got here—like always. Not sure this poor ol' country boy is good enough for this fine establishment. Right, Rye?" he asked of his friend, who was strolling just a few yards behind him with two other men.

Rhett had been poor until he'd developed a knack for poker. Now he was mega-rich, a country boy no more. Mac slapped him on the back, and Rhett pulled him in for a man hug, pounding him heartily in return. Of all the people he called friend, Rhett was the most unusual, but few guys were more loyal.

"And Rye Crenshaw," Mac said, stepping forward as Rhett's poker babes returned to their positions. "Welcome to The Grand Mountain Hotel."

Camera flashes punctuated the lobby like alien fireflies.

Rye shook Mac's hand when he reached him. "And you remember John Parker McGuiness, my lawyer, and Clayton Chandler, my deputy manager."

There were handshakes all around. Mac couldn't help but notice the speculation from all the women in the lobby. This group looked like a crew of actors from one of Rye's country music videos.

"Tell me you've finally decided to sing for us after the tourney ends," Mac threw out there, his voice smooth as silk.

Rhett wrapped an arm around Rye. "I'm working on him, Mac."

"Good. Keep at it," Mac replied easily, imagining the media coverage it would bring. Hell, having Rye here would be great for business regardless of whether he sang. "Just let us know whatever we can do to make your stay more enjoyable."

"Well, I have to tell you, Mac, I am lovin' the name of this town," Rye said. "It's kinda crazy since me and the guys here all live on the Dare River outside of Nashville."

"Oh right. I'd forgotten that," Mac said, remembering that party he'd attended at Rye's house last year, which had been filled with country music's most famous faces. Rye had even talked a few of them into playing a poker game with Mac.

"And tell me about the food," Rye said, adjusting his black cowboy hat.

"Here we go," Clayton muttered at his side.

Rye turned toward his friend. "I don't know why you're bitching about my love of food when you always benefit."

"Because you usually go AWOL after a concert to rustle up something to eat when I have interviews lined up for you."

"Please, that's only happened once."

Clayton stared him down.

"Okay, twice. But who's counting?" He held out his hands like he was some country choir boy. "Maybe I need to hire my own cook."

"I like that idea," Clayton said. "I'll get started on that."

"Aw, you're the best, man," Rye said, slapping his friend on the back.

Mac wondered if Rye and Rhett had trained at the same Aw-Shucks Academy. They had it down to a science.

"There's a fantastic new French restaurant in town called Brasserie Dare," Mac told him. "I'll send up a menu."

"Perfect! Thanks, Mac. Well, if I'm going to eat French food, I need to go work out."

"We'll go with you," Clayton said without pausing.

Rye gave him a warning glare. "These two yahoos are sharing my suite to keep an eye on me."

John Parker laughed. "Maybe we should put Rhett in our suite too. Seems he always manages to raise some Cain, just like you."

Rhett just shook his head. "I don't know what y'all are talking about. Do you, Rye?"

"No, siree. These guys are full of shit. Mac, ladies, I need to take my leave. We'll see y'all later."

"Count on it," Mac replied, blinking as more camera flashes erupted when Rye strode across the lobby.

Cuddling his poker babes close, Rhett kissed each of them on the cheek. "You remember Raven and Vixen."

"Hello, ladies," Mac said with a smile. "Welcome to The Grand."

"It's an incredible hotel, Mac," Raven said, while Vixen nodded her agreement.

"Get us checked in, sweeties," Rhett said. "I'm sure Maverick's got a fine suite all picked out for us."

They simpered and tottered away on the highest "do-me" heels Mac had ever seen.

He almost rolled his eyes. "It's even got windows."

Rhett put his hand on Mac's shoulder. "Seriously, man. I'm so proud of you. Another awesome hotel. We who are about to play poker salute you." And then he executed a perfect one, like he'd been in the military all his life.

"You are so full of it. I had to hire a pooper scooper from the circus when you decided to come at the last minute."

"Aw, shucks, you shouldn't have," he quipped back.

"Been way too long, Rhett."

"Well, this boy needed to see the world. That whole Europe thing, well, it's really old. And out there in Asia, it's like super, duper old."

Knowing Rhett's passion for architecture, Mac could barely contain his laughter. His friend sure liked to keep up his larger-than-life persona. "Slept through world history, huh?"

He waved his hand around. "Never did like all that book learnin' stuff. What I like are practical skills." As another player walked by, Rhett waggled his fingers at his poker babes. "Something I can do with my hands."

Mac played along. Rhett liked to sucker people into thinking he was simple-minded. His success in the tourneys had caused people to dig into his background a little more, though, so the truth was mostly out. After hitting the circuit out of high school, he'd gone back to school, graduating with honors from Vanderbilt University in Nashville right along with Rye Crenshaw and his friends—something neither Rhett nor Rye ever shared in the media. Just didn't fit their images.

When Jill waddled across the lobby, greeting guests, Mac called her by name.

"I heard I missed Rye Crenshaw, darn it." Then her eyes popped open when she saw his companion. "Oh my gosh, you're like Brad Pitt's character in *Fight Club.* "

Rhett took the hand she thrust out and dipped into some weird gallant pose.

"Beats that Liberace jab Mac made a few years back. We had words over that one."

Mac shook his head as Jill's gaze swept over his friend—from the man's gray snakeskin cowboy boots to his silver, gallon-size cowboy hat.

"You're huge!" Jill announced, pointing out the obvious. Rhett topped out at six foot six without the shoes and hat.

"So are you, honey. You look like a tick ready to pop. When are you due?"

Jill caressed her stomach. "A tick, huh? Our twin girls arrive in October. It feels like a long ways away."

"Jeez, Rhett," Mac breathed out. "You *never* tell a woman she's huge."

"It's only nature's way." Rhett looped an arm through Jill's. "This lady shouldn't be on her feet. Aren't there rules against working pregnant women too hard in this state?"

"Gosh, I like you," she said. "I wasn't sure I would after everything I've read about you, but you're fun."

"Been reading up on me, eh?"

"She's married," Mac informed him.

Jill waved her left hand. "Happily and knocked up too. I know a little something about all the high rollers who are coming. Mac believes in personalized service."

"That's the way *I like it,* " Rhett all but purred, white teeth shining from his poster-boy smile.

Mac pointed a finger at Jill. "Don't be taken in by this 'aw shucks' routine. Inside this—"

"Don't say Liberace of Poker," Rhett warned.

"Brad Pitt of Poker?" Jill interjected.

Mac rubbed his lucky poker chip in his pocket. "Inside this *man* beats the heart of a lion who clamps on the jugular every time."

"Why do they call you the 'Rhett Butler' of poker?" Jill asked as Mac led them across the lobby to the bar.

"'Cause that's my legal name. My mama loved *Gone with the Wind* more than any person alive, and she named me after the dashing hero. She works in a profession that keeps her close to the Old South. She designs and sews antebellum ball gowns for Pilgrimage."

"Like Mecca?" Jill asked.

Mac hid his grin behind a cough.

"Good Lord, honey, where are you from? We have a Pilgrimage Festival in Natchez like we used to before the Yanks beat us. Like reenactments," he explained.

"That was a *long* time ago," Jill said, whistling. "So you're basically Rhett incarnate?"

"My mama likes to think so, although I have my own unique style."

This time Mac did roll his eyes. "That's an understatement."

Rhett chuckled, and even to Mac, it had a dirty ring to it. "What Mac is trying to say is that I take things a bit further than a Southern gentleman might, even one on the edges of proper society like the original Rhett Butler."

Mac signaled the bartender. "A bit? That's a whopper. Two bourbons. Buffalo Trace. Rhett, you'll love this brand if you've never had it before. And sparkling water and lime for Jill," he added, knowing it was her pregnancy go-to drink.

"Wish I could join you in the bourbon, fellas, but it's not on the docket. Like coffee." She made a sad face.

"Jill also owns the town's best coffee shop," Mac informed Rhett.

"Ah, a businesswoman," Rhett drawled, tucking the bourbon into the crook of his arm. "If you weren't married and pregnant, we could have something."

Jill huffed out a laugh. "You're what my grandpa would call 'incorrigible.'"

Rhett leaned into her ear. "You bet your lacy under-britches I am."

Jill drained her glass and set it on the bar with a thunk. "I'll leave you men to your poker talk. Good to meet you, Rhett."

He took her hand and bussed it. "You too, honey."

"Mac, we need to put up a sign," she said with a wink. "*Watch out, Dare Valley Females.* Bye, boys."

Mac sipped his bourbon, letting the bold fruit and anise coat his taste buds. "You are way too much sometimes."

Rhett tipped up his cowboy hat with one finger. "All the time. As my mama always says, 'no one remembers you if you don't shake the bushes.'"

"Speaking of bushes," Mac commented as dryly as the bourbon. "Did you have to bring your poker babes? I'm trying to keep a conservative small town happy."

Rhett pulled out a chair. "You know they work for me."

Few knew they both had MBAs from Harvard Business School. They studied and scouted other players for Rhett during tourneys, creating elaborate files on the competitions' tells, betting habits, and strategies.

"Couldn't they wear more...appropriate fashion?" Even as he asked it, he knew better. The way they dressed was all part of the game. He'd missed this ribbing with his friend.

The two women in question had ambled over from the check-in counter and were leaning over the bar, revealing mind-numbing mounds of cleavage. His new bartender fumbled an eighty dollar bottle of tequila before securing it against his chest.

"They're part of the show. You know I haven't paid a hotel bill since I hit the circuit when I was eighteen."

Mac winced. "Yes, I know. Please be nice to me. This isn't Vegas. I can't afford to comp you for the sixty rounds of Jack you bought everyone in the bar at our last tourney."

Rhett grinned. "I'll be good. Scout's honor. Unless there's a hot tub in my room."

"There's not. I made sure."

"You're mean as a snake."

Mac hit his friend on the back. "You're no Boy Scout, and if you think I'd put you in a room with a hot tub after what you pulled last time, you're crazy."

Rhett rubbed his chin. "Now that did get a little crazy." He straightened so suddenly he spilled part of his drink. "Shit, don't say anything. Your sister is coming this way."

Mac fell into poker face mode. "No, she's not. She's only walking to the gym. Hey, Abbie, come say hi."

Abbie halted so quickly it looked like she'd run into a wall. She stopped, face blank, and then forced a lukewarm smile on her face. God love her, he'd tried to teach her a poker face, but she'd never mastered it. Her stride slowed to a shuffle. Her progress over to them couldn't have beaten a snail.

"Why, Rhett. Mac told me you were coming. Welcome to The Grand."

Then she actually extended her hand.

Mac squeezed back against the bar. Sometimes his sister added kerosene to a fire without knowing it. She probably thought she was being nice. After everything the two had shared, he didn't think Rhett would take her gesture well.

Rhett stared at her hand like it held a bag of night crawlers. "You expect me to shake your hand?" he asked in a tone as cold as the mountain stream out back.

Abbie's false smile faltered. "You don't have to. I was only...saying hello."

Rhett had his own poker face. None of the usual good nature or charm shone in his eyes now. They smoldered.

"Hello then, Abigail. I'll pass on the shake. Don't want to hurt my hands. Need to hold my cards, you know."

Mac had to bite his lip to keep from laughing. Then he saw the hurt in Abbie's eyes. So, she really *did* care. Well, shit. Caring about Rhett Butler Blaylock was no easy path.

"Then maybe you should set your bourbon down and use a straw." Her smile had claws now. "Or have your...*girls*...feed it to you."

Rhett stretched out his legs and crossed his ankles. Abbie had to move out of his way as he spread out. "They're my poker babes. I hadn't thought of them feeding me. I'll have to add that to their job description."

Her hands fisted at her sides. "How nice for them. Mac, I'm taking Dustin to soccer practice after I hit the gym. You're staying at the hotel tonight, right?"

Rhett pulled Mac close in a one-arm hug. "Of course, he's staying here. We've got some catching up to do."

Since he loved his sister, Mac decided to give her a boost. "Maybe we can do a family breakfast in the morning before the tourney starts. I'll bring Rhett so he can see the new house. I'm sure Dustin would be delighted. I'll ask Cince too. Be like old times."

Her gaze dipped to the floor and then lifted. Only Mac knew she did that when she was upset and trying to make the best of things.

"Wonderful. I'll get everything ready."

"You still remember I like flapjacks in the morning, right, sweetheart?" Rhett asked in an even more pronounced Southern accent.

Her face blanched. "Funny, it's been so long, I'd forgotten." She all but smirked. "Have fun boys." She turned tail and sped off.

"If I told you not to mess with my sister, would you lay off?" Mac signaled the bartender for another round.

"No." Rhett downed his drink. "I came here to see if I could convince her to marry me."

Mac's glass clattered across the bar before the bartender caught it. "You *what?*"

Rhett crooked his finger to the bartender. When the man came closer, he appropriated the bottle. "We're going to need something to fortify ourselves for this discussion."

"You're pulling my leg, right?" Mac asked. He downed the bourbon Rhett poured for him.

"No, I'm as sober as a Baptist minister in a dry county. I love her, Mac. I tried to forget her when she told me we didn't have a future, but that didn't work."

No, Abbie wouldn't see a future with Rhett. Frankly, until today, Mac had never known Rhett to fall for anyone. How funny the one woman who could break his friend turned out to be his sister.

"You haven't seen each other in a year, have you?"

The slap on his back nearly toppled him over. "Hell, no, we haven't been sneaking around your back this past year."

"Just before," he said. Even though they'd never discussed it, he would've had to be blind to have missed their interactions.

"Do I detect judgment in your tone, *Mr.* Maven? Abbie didn't want anyone to know. Including you." He hunched his shoulders, and for a moment, looked like one of the many guys Mac had seen lose their entire stake playing poker—broke, but even worse, defeated. "She's ashamed of me."

The sigh gusted out before Mac could stop it. "She has a hard time with trust after what happened with Dustin's father." He wished he could tell his friend the whole truth, but that was Abbie's prerogative.

"The fucker ruined it for me," Rhett growled. "But I won't give up on

91

her."

Mac elbowed him in the gut to get his attention. "Good. It's the only way she'll believe you care."

"I know I don't appear to be the stable-raise-kids type," Rhett all but whispered. "But for the right woman, I'll mend my ways. So, I'm stepping back from the circuit and sticking around. I rented a cabin in these fine mountains, and I'm going to try to convince her I can be a good husband to her and stepfather to Dustin." His head turned. "Not that I'd be trying to step into the role you've played with the boy since he was born. I know he's like a son to you."

Mac pushed his glass away when Rhett filled it again, reeling from the news. "But he's not my son. He's my nephew. As he gets older, it's making all the difference in the world." He told him about the incident with the Ferrari.

Rhett continued sipping his bourbon. Man always could drink like a fish.

"Well, some of us run wild when we're young. We find a way to pull it together." He rested his boot on his knee. "Of course, Abbie wouldn't like to wait for it to run its course."

"Honestly, neither do I."

"I hear that."

Mac had run wild, but only in spurts, and always in a controlled way—away from his family. Fucking things up for himself would have meant fucking things up for them. He'd never let them down.

"I want to break the cycle. Have a well adjusted kid who wants to go to college and be a doctor or something."

Rhett whistled. "Who knew Mr. Conventional burned inside The Great Maverick? Of course, building all this...it's your way of being well adjusted. I've got my own plan for that."

Mac narrowed his eyes at his friend. "You?"

His massive shoulder hiked up. "Well...yeah." He downed his bourbon. "I'm asking for your permission to court your sister."

His mouth dropped, his poker face history. "You're asking my permission? Dammit, man, that's the last thing I ever expected you to say to me."

Rhett gave him a flinty look.

He threw up a hand. "Fine. You have it. Just be gentle with her."

"I wish you could tell her to be nice to me, but you best stay out of it. She wouldn't appreciate us having this discussion."

"No, she sure wouldn't."

"So you'll give me your permission to marry her if she agrees."

His head jerked back like he'd been punched in the face. The surprises kept coming. "Two permission requests in one day? On this, Abbie makes up her own mind."

"Yeah, but you're one of my best friends. I don't want to mess things up."

"If she agrees, you're more than welcome to the family" he responded, needing another drink. "Dustin will be over the moon."

Rhett slapped his back. "Good. Damn if I don't love that kid."

Mac had never doubted Rhett's affection for his nephew.

It was going to be an interesting summer.

People continued to buzz across the foyer, but thankfully, the bar stayed quiet. Plus, people were standing on the sidelines, watching Rhett. They didn't usually approach him, never sure what he'd do.

Mac surveyed the floor. He'd molded every inch of every hotel he'd built. He knew how many electric outlets were in the bar. He'd approved liquor lists, added new brands that had pulled in great reviews. Driven himself to prove he was more than a guy who was only good at cards.

Because you could always lose at cards—even though he hadn't. Rhett was right. He had built his empire because he'd wanted to be well established.

And still something was missing.

Peggy's face flashed in his mind. Oh shit. Was she the missing something?

God knows, he'd never chosen the easy road.

"I've got it bad for a woman who doesn't think too much of me, either," he confessed.

"Spill it. Maybe I can tell her what a great guy you are."

"Damn, I missed you, Rhett. Even with all your Liberace ways."

Rhett clapped a meaty hand on his shoulder. "I'll let that one go. Is this woman anything like Abbie?"

"Actually, she's a tougher nut to crack."

"Then you'd best say your prayers, boy," Rhett advised him.

Mac picked up his bourbon and slugged it back. He knew he'd need more than liquid courage to get Peggy to give them a go.

It was time to up the ante.

CHAPTER 14

Peggy knew all about nuts. She'd busted more than her fair share. But the man striding into her office with Maven sported a grin like some Cowboy on Crack. Was he wearing leather chaps? She checked the gun in her holster in case he was having a meltdown.

"I'm not packing, ma'am," the man announced when they reached her desk, the fringe on his leather jacket dancing like Mexican jumping beans. "I'm Rhett Butler Blaylock."

Peggy was sure she blinked twice. "Please tell me that's an alias."

The guy patted her—well slapped her actually—on the back before she could move. "Nah, my mama had a unique obsession with *Gone with the Wind.*"

She crossed her arms, wondering who in the hell this man was and why Maven was with him. Visiting her at the sheriff's office, no less.

"You're kidding me," she responded.

"Nope." Even under his mega-gallon white cowboy hat, his eyes lit up and crinkled at the corners. "I told Mac I wanted to take a tour of the town before the tourney starts tomorrow."

So, he was a high-roller. She suspected he might be some oil executive from Houston—someone with more money than sense.

"So you stopped at the sheriff's office?"

"Well, yes, ma'am, there's no finer way to judge a town than by the officers who serve it."

His smile could have beamed sunshine.

Her eyes narrowed. "Are you punking me?"

He held up his hands, his white leather coat rippling like it had been caught in a strong breeze. "No ma'am. Mac told me how you handled the unfortunate situation with Dustin. He's a good kid. I wanted to thank you in person."

Even to her, this whole song and dance smelled of crap.

"May I speak with you privately, Mr. Maven?"

She hadn't seen him since he'd come to her house the other day. She hadn't needed to appear in court after passing her recommendations along to the city attorney. She knew Dustin had received thirty hours of community service. Frankly, she didn't want Maven around her—ever. Last night, she'd dreamed about him biting her neck again, all vampire-like. She was sick. Truly sick.

She pulled Maven aside, trying not to inhale his spicy forest scent.

"Are you having some private joke at my expense?"

"No. I had a parking ticket to pay." He paused.

She fought a wince.

"My friend wanted to come along and meet the woman who continues to take me down a peg. Ah, bad pun." He leaned closer. "And makes me come back for more."

She shoved him back a step. "That's not funny."

"But true. Even in that masculine uniform. Will you come watch me play poker sometime this weekend?"

Since she didn't want to move closer to his over-the-top friend, she paced in place. "I told you. I don't like gambling."

He tucked his hand in his pocket and nodded. "Okay. How about letting me take you out to dinner after the holiday?"

Her breath hitched. "Are you asking me on a date?"

"Yeah." Those stoplight green eyes burned into her with their intensity.

For a long moment, she couldn't breathe. Her fleeting back itch flared up, and she ached for him to touch her. Then she got herself under control.

"It's not a good idea."

He lifted his hands and walked away. "See, I told you she wouldn't go out with me."

Rhett dug into his coat and pulled out a snakeskin wallet. He withdrew a crisp, one hundred dollar bill. "Damn. She's a tough one."

Peggy clenched her fists. "You *bet* on me?"

"Makes life more interesting," Rhett drawled.

"I could arrest you both right now," she threatened, pulling on her police belt and rocking on her heels.

Maven snorted—actually snorted. "For what?"

She narrowed her eyes. "For gambling. It's only allowed on legitimate premises."

Maven waved the bill in her face. "Better give this to me at the hotel, Rhett."

"The little lady sure means business." Rhett stuffed it into his jacket.

"It's Deputy McBride," she informed him.

Her insufferable nemesis crossed his arms, all nonchalant in khaki dress pants and a white polo shirt with the hotel's logo on it. The Grand. How sporty.

"Yes, we wouldn't want to refer to you as a *woman*. Peg doesn't like to be reminded, Rhett."

"Why the heck not? She's cute as a button." His boots squeaked when he leaned back.

"Cute?" She rose to her full height of five feet five inches, like she did when she tried to intimidate suspects. Since he was tall enough to play in the NBA, it fell flat.

"Sure. You've got a curvy figure, even in that get-up. Nice, thick hair.

Your eyes would be right sparkly if you'd smile more and use some mascara."

"I cannot believe you are talking about my...assets. Get out of my office!" She stalked behind her desk and sat down. "I have work to do."

Rhett strolled over. "Just a minute, now. I only came with Mac here to give you a way out of having Dustin do your yard work, with Mac as his chaperone."

She stopped ruffling through a stack of parking tickets and handed Maven's copy to him.

He scowled.

She smiled her first genuine one of the day. "You did?" It was music to her ears.

The cowboy scratched his stubble. "I heard you weren't happy with the arrangement. I can understand that. Teenage boys are a pain in the...posterior, as my mama always says. I know. I used to be one. And Mac can be...Mac."

Something wasn't right here, but when she studied him, all she saw was eagerness and sympathy. "You're telling me you understand how I feel?"

"Sure do. The kid's having a rough time with the move. And you don't want this guy around."

Mac narrowed his eyes when Rhett jerked his thumb at him.

"That's why I told Mac he should give you a way out. I came along as a neutral party."

He rested a hip on her desk. She decided not to kick him off if he was going to help her.

"Okay, what do you have in mind?"

The cards he pulled out had her sitting up straighter in her chair. "No way!"

"Now, listen here. It's one round of blackjack. I'm the dealer, so even if Mac wanted to cheat, he couldn't—not that he would. The man is honest as the day is long. It's a simple matter. If you win, Mac goes away." He coughed. "And Dustin too, of course." A blur of card suits flashed through his hands as he shuffled.

"And if he wins?"

Rhett looked over his shoulder at Mac, who was watching them quietly from the doorway. Peggy couldn't tell a single thing from his face or posture. The men held eye contact, like two adversaries trying to give the impression of power.

"A meal together," Maven uttered in a velvety voice, finally looking at her.

Her solar plexus tightened. "You won't come by the house?" Of course, she meant Dustin.

Rhett started laughing, so she finally nudged him off her desk. She pushed out of her chair, realizing she was about to break a rule. Was she really willing to gamble for the first time to remove him from her life?

The shuffling stopped. "Blackjack is the easiest game to win."

He was right. It wasn't *real* gambling. It involved two or three cards and lasted a minute. If she lost, it was only a meal, right? Plus, a meal together didn't mean they had to be alone. And if she won, she'd use that leverage to sever any connection between them. Even if he won, she'd outfox him. He didn't realize how devious she could be. She'd pick up three happy meals at McDonald's for them and include Keith. It wasn't like it had to be romantic. She smiled. This was an answer to her prayers.

"Fine. Get it over with and then get out."

Rhett turned around like a semi with a wide load, hands outstretched. "Wonderful. Any woman who can face perps down with a gun can play to win." He shuffled. "So, I'll deal you two cards. You want to come close to the number twenty-one, but not go over. You can have a third card if needed."

"I know how to play it," she steamed. "It's like the most common game out there. An idiot can play."

"Must be why I love it so much," Rhett mused. "Can I clear a spot to deal?"

She moved a stack, certain he'd throw her papers around if he had the chance. The man clearly had no respect for order.

"I'm going to deal your cards facedown. More interesting that way. Mac, are you gonna come over here and play?"

Maven strolled forward with his hands in his pockets. He took out a yellow disc.

"What's that?" she asked.

"My lucky piece. I always rub it before a game."

She rolled her eyes. "Luck is a bunch of hooey."

Rhett chortled. "You don't believe in luck either? Sweetheart, there's a lot I could teach you. How about joining me for dinner tonight?"

"In your dreams," she scoffed.

His laughter erupted again in big barking guffaws. The other officers were probably wondering what in the hell was going on in her office. She had a known gambler and this Cowboy on Crack in her office behind closed doors. They probably thought she'd gotten a concussion without reporting it.

"Well, that rightly puts me in my place. You're smart to refuse me. I wouldn't be able to stop myself from trying to talk you out of your uniform."

"Excuse me?"

"That getup you're wearing is one of my favorite acts in Vegas. Something about the uniform and the handcuffs."

Her eye twitched. "Would you *please* deal the cards?"

"Sure thing, ma'am. I meant no disrespect." He quieted and dealt two cards to each of them.

Maven came around her desk and stood next to her. He was too close, but since she needed to pick up her cards, she couldn't step away. Just inches apart, she could feel his body heat and his pine scent filled her nostrils. Her gaze fell to his hands. The woman inside remembered how they felt rushing over her skin—caressing, squeezing, tantalizing. She tried to take a deep breath without being too obvious about it. He turned his head. The corners of his mouth tipped up like he knew exactly what she was thinking. She frowned. His smile spread wider.

"Okay, now look at your cards. Let me know if you need a hit or want to stay."

Peggy grabbed them and then stepped to the other side of her desk. She wouldn't put it past Maven to cheat. She had a queen of hearts and an eight of spades. Eighteen. She wanted to dance in place.

"I'm good," she replied.

"Sounds like the lady is happy with her hand," Rhett mused, hands resting on his lapels. "Mac?"

He tucked his cards against his chest and smiled at her. Simply smiled. Like the cat who knows he's about to get the cream. "Hit." He took the card Rhett handed him. Looked up and met her gaze. "Ready to lay your cards down?"

"Absolutely." She turned them face up and smiled. Ah, victory.

"The lady's got a nice hand. Mac?"

He laid one card down. A Jack of Diamonds. Then a seven of clubs. Seventeen.

He *had* to have busted with the third card. She put her hands on her hips, feeling the urge to rock back on her heels.

Then he put down a three of spades.

Her lungs stopped functioning. The woman deep inside cried, *Yes, a date!*

"Twenty, Mac. Whew!" Rhett breathed out. "Risky, taking another card."

"I knew Peggy had a good hand, and I always play to win—especially when the pot is something I want so badly."

Her throat stopped working. She couldn't swallow for a minute.

Rhett slapped him on the back. "Damn, this guy likes to take risks. That's why he's building and running hotels, while I'm still a poor gambler trying to cobble together a stake for each tourney."

"You are so full of it. I'll give you a call about dinner, Peggy. And I'll send Dustin over after the tournament. I drove by your house earlier, and I think the lawn can wait a few more days. It looked *incredibly* well attended."

So that hadn't slipped by him, huh? She looked away for a minute. That's because she'd mowed it herself at the crack of dawn. If she took care of it, they wouldn't need to come by. Did he think she didn't have a strategy?

His smile transformed his face into charming again. "When we go out, I'd be happy to find a sitter for Keith, or I'm sure my sister would love to watch him."

Her eyes narrowed to slits. He wasn't boxing her into a corner. "I'll take care of things."

He sauntered around Rhett, who was watching the scene like some demented bulldog. Animal Control needed to be alerted.

Leaning over her desk, Maven tapped her nose before she could react.

"Don't do that," Peg said.

"I couldn't help myself. Rhett's right. You are cute. That green shirt brings out the creaminess of your skin."

"I'm always right about women, Mac. When are you going to realize that?" He threw his arm around Mac's shoulders. "Time for us to head out. Unless you've changed your mind about giving me a tour?" he asked Peggy.

She simply gave him the fish eye.

He lifted his hands. "See, this is why the law and me don't get along. They see this outfit and assume it comes with trouble."

"It does," Maven confirmed, winking at Peggy. "She might be the most mistrustful woman I've ever met, but she's smart."

"Well, I still think Abbie might be more wary, but at least she doesn't pack a gun. If she did, she might have shot me by now. By the way, isn't a 9 mm a more standard weapon for a female officer?"

She caressed her 45 mm Glock and gave him a Cheshire-cat smile. "I'm not that kind of girl."

His hand dropped to his chest, making the heart-beats-for-you motion. "My God, if it weren't for your profession, we'd be soul mates."

Maven snorted, opening the door to her office. "I'll see you soon."

She mimed a fake smile and went back to work, sending a message of her own. He was dismissed.

Rhett didn't take the hint. He walked back to her desk. "I'd kiss your hand, but I expect you'd kick me in the nuts. Since I like my family jewels, I'll simply do like the cowboys of old." He put a finger to his gallon-size hat in a salute. "Good afternoon, ma'am." He followed a grinning Maven out of her office.

Good afternoon, indeed.

She'd just been swindled.

CHAPTER 15

The bark of bawdy laughter made Abbie clench the frying pan. So, he was here in their new home. She checked her watch. For once, Rhett was on time. She whipped off her polka-dot apron and smoothed the lapels of her yellow jacket. Funny, she'd thought wearing something sunny might improve her disposition.

"Mom! Uncle Rhett's here," Dustin called, laughing riotously amidst a scuffle. "Tell me you brought Rye Crenshaw with you."

She froze, praying he hadn't brought any extra guests without asking, especially ones who excelled at getting him into trouble.

"Nope. He had some big Nashville call this morning, but I got him to autograph his newest CD for you."

"Sweet!" her son yelled.

Her summer heels clicked on the tiles as she walked to the doorway. Rhett had Dustin in a barrel hug, lifting him completely off the ground. Her stomach flip-flopped, remembering how he used to do that to her— right before he kissed her senseless. Or threw her on the bed.

Oh heavens.

She firmed a smile on her face instead of fanning herself. "Rhett. Welcome." She couldn't bring herself to say, *It's good to see you.*

His infernal grin made her think he'd read her mind. "Abbie. Don't you look like a drop of sunshine."

She didn't roll her eyes, but she wanted to. Leave it to Rhett to come up with a compliment bordering on poetic. Most men couldn't pull it off, but somehow Rhett got under women's skin with his old-world troubadour act. Well, she wasn't falling for it anymore.

"You exaggerate, as usual. Cince, could you help me in the kitchen?"

"I'll help you," Rhett announced, making her spine straighten.

"No, you catch up with Dustin."

Mac shot her a glance. The more she struggled, the worse it looked.

Rhett squeezed Dustin's shoulders. "I've got something in my car for you, kid. Why don't you run and get it? And maybe after breakfast, you can show me what you can do behind the wheel."

Dustin hugged Rhett one-armed. "Awesome. See! *Someone* trusts me with his car."

"That's because someone's sponsoring his car, so he won't be paying for it if anything happens," Mac replied. "Doesn't change the fact that you're not driving for another month."

Rhett ruffled Dustin's hair and then fished out car keys from his tight jeans. She tried and failed not to look at his inseam. Did he have to flaunt...his family jewels to everybody?

Not her business.

"Cince, let's go check out his Bentley, too," Mac said.

She gave her brother her best glare for leaving her alone with Rhett. Cince tipped his finger to his forehead. So he knew about them too? Gosh, and she thought they had been so discreet. Why couldn't she have gotten the Poker Face gene?

After they filed out, Mac closing the door behind them, Rhett came forward with his arms spread, a lop-sided grin on his face. "Great. Now I can say hello to you proper."

His tone shot sheer lust up her thighs. He was about to kiss her senseless if she didn't stop him. She wanted to turn tail and run, but Rhett would just chase her. She'd fled before. He'd always caught her.

And again, thrown her onto the bed.

Why couldn't she stop thinking about that?

She crossed her arms like she imagined a prim aunt might do—not that she'd had one. "You must have had an accident and become brain damaged on your trip overseas to think I'm ever going to let you greet me 'proper' again."

He didn't stop moving until his snakeskin cowboy boots touched the tips of her jonquil sandals. His white leather jacket had beads on it, which drew her attention to his massive chest. She remembered the rippling muscles, the heat, the sweat. Part of her wanted to lock herself in the bathroom. The other part wanted to step into his arms and never leave.

He tipped up her chin. His golden eyes studied her with an intensity he usually only gave to the table at the end of the tourney when the pressure was bone-crushing.

"I missed you, Abbie."

Her heart tore in two. She fought for air, but wouldn't let herself take a deep breath. She clenched her arms tighter around herself. "Don't say that."

He caressed her cheek with one finger. "I always tell the truth. It's how I was raised."

"Bull," she ground out.

His hand dropped. "You know what happens when someone says I'm bluffing."

Her throat went dry, knowing exactly what he was about to say. He put his hand on her arm as if sensing she might dart off.

"I go all in." He brought her hand to his lips and kissed it.

Her bracelets rattled as she trembled.

"I know it will take some time for you to get used to it, and since I know the kind of woman you are, I'm going to give you the words without the contact—for a while."

Her chest constricted. "I don't understand."

"I told Mac I'm in love with you. I went overseas to be as far away from you as I could, so I wouldn't be tempted to come back on a dime and beg." His tense face formed a rigid smile.

She gasped. "What did you say?"

His face clenched from brow to jaw. "I said, 'I love you,' and I'm not leaving here until you agree to marry me. There's nothing you can do to make me walk away again. I don't figure it can hurt any worse than it already has. After living without you for a year, I'll take anything you dish out. All I care about is being close to you."

She'd hurt him? She knew her mouth had fallen open, but she couldn't help it. She had thought she'd only wounded his pride. Believing he loved her was like dark, treacherous waters, and she was wary of drowning.

"You're insane."

He took a deep breath, expanding his massive chest. "Yes, I am. God knows there are easier women out there, but I don't want them. I want you. I've rented a house here, and I plan to stay until you say yes. Then we'll build one or buy one wherever you want to live. I'll even let you take me shopping for some new clothes, but no polo shirts or Dockers—I couldn't take it."

The change-up was like an earthquake under her feet. "No, I'm—"

"Be quiet and listen for once." He drilled her with a gaze she recognized from when he won the World Series of Poker two years ago after losing half his chips. It was his determined look. "I'm not leaving you, Abbie. *Ever again.* I won't hurt you or abandon you."

Wetness shot into her eyes. She blinked rapidly, praying she wouldn't cry.

His face gentled. "I intend to prove I can be a good husband to you and father to Dustin."

"You're...you're..."

He kissed her hand again, his warm lips lingering, making goosebumps trail up her arms. "Take your time. I know you don't think I can change, but I can. There are no other women, Abbie. There haven't been for nearly ten months—a record. I realized I couldn't get you out of my system and hated myself for even trying."

She reeled in her shoes. He'd been celibate? Rhett Butler Blaylock?

"Until you decide to marry me, I'm not going to touch you. I'm going to court you like a gentleman. If you want me to kiss you or make love to you, you'll have to ask for it."

She finally shoved at his chest. "Stop this! Stop this madness right now."

He was unraveling years of carefully imposed self-control.

"I've asked Mac for his blessing. I won't do anything in secret anymore. What's between us is nothing to be ashamed of."

"This isn't only for you to decide."

"No, but I won't hide what I feel for you. You can tell Dustin or let him find out for himself. You're his mama, so you know best, but that boy loves me, and I love him!"

She stayed quiet, shaking from the emotional overload.

"Dammit, Abbie, you know this whole getup of mine is mostly an act. My poker girls have fancy degrees from Harvard."

She stepped back, sucking in air, needing space. "That's not the point."

He stretched out his arms, reminding her of the bald eagle she'd seen soaring over their house earlier that morning. "Then what is?"

"I don't..." She couldn't lie—not to him. "I *can't* love you!"

Silence poured into the room like sand. He titled his head to the side, watching her. His mouth tipped up. "You already do. I'm gambling my life on it." He walked around her, heading into the kitchen. "Now, what did you need help with?"

She bit her lip, fighting the urge to come undone.

Instead, she drew herself up to her full height. Pulled on her jacket. Smoothed it into place. When she turned and followed him, she pasted a smile on her face. "I need that bread buttered for French toast."

He fiddled with the knife on the counter and then cleanly cut the bread in half, just like he'd done to her sense of peace and security. She didn't bother to tell him he'd cut it the wrong way.

"I'm a pro in the kitchen if you recall."

She did and kicked herself for remembering what else he was good at in the kitchen—laying her on granite countertops and making her scream with pleasure.

No one could ever say butter didn't melt in Rhett's mouth.

CHAPTER 16

Poker tournaments had a way of testing everyone's mettle. Mac savored the *kalick, kalick, kalick* as he raked in another stack of chips. It wasn't simply the winning. There was something primal about pitting yourself against another man—or woman, if the rare occasion surfaced. The constant vigilance of a tournament exhausted most people. The need to continually assess opponents and weigh various betting strategies against each other, the constant draining drive to win.

He wasn't most people.

The physical side of the game could be taxing too, he thought, as he sipped a health drink at the front of the room, watching everyone set up. Grueling days of intense play in eight- to twelve-hour blocks with few breaks in between brought out the body's weaknesses.

Mac liked to think the survivor of the fittest principle was alive and well at the poker table, and he planned to survive like he always did—one hand at a time.

In this world, he'd found his bliss, and all from a quirk of fate. If Abbie and Dustin hadn't had complications at birth, he never would have stepped into the Taj Mahal in Atlantic City with the desperate notion of making the money he needed for their medical bills. He'd done more than provide for their needs. He'd discovered he wasn't like his father, who'd lost money in casinos all his life, sucking their family dry right along with his card-dealing wife.

The boy hadn't understood the draw of the deck. He'd hated it because of his parents.

The man could be grateful for the training he'd received at their knees without condoning their mistakes. Redemption came in surprising places. He wasn't one to spit in fate's face.

"You about ready, boy?" Rhett drawled, putting a huge hand on his shoulder, surveying the room with him.

Mac elbowed him in the chest. "Always."

Rhett stuck out his hand—their ritual. "Good luck. Like I just told Rye, for the next few hours, we're no longer friends."

"Why you always insist..." Mac trailed off when he shrugged. Rhett needed a friends' release clause every time they played. Mac grabbed his hand. "Good luck to you, too, Rhett."

"See you at the final table," Rhett called over his shoulder, Raven and Vixen swirling around him in low-cut gowns.

"You can bet on it," he murmured, rubbing his lucky piece, and went to find his seat number, waving to Rye and his buddies as they headed to their tables.

Mac's first table summed up his afternoon. The eight guys sitting around it all watched him approach. He liked watching their reactions. Half lost their poker faces instantly. One muttered, "Oh, shit." A few grinned, probably imagining the dinner party story they'd be able to tell about losing to Mac Maven. The remaining few eyed him with fiery determination, ready to prove they could beat him. He nodded to them and pulled out his card protector—a nineteenth-century poker chip from a Mississippi Riverboat.

Then he started to build his stack of chips.

His world narrowed to the table. The *wisp* the cards made as they were dealt. His intuitive sense for others' cards. The small prayer he sometimes offered up when the dealer presented the last card of the hand. "The River" could make grown men cry like the timeless song. It changed fates and broke hearts.

He lost a few hands early on, but not many.

Built his stack. Watched his opponents. Upped the pressure by raising the bets. Milked the players of their chips, forcing them to bust or cut out in an hour.

Then he moved on to the next table and did it again, only taking a break for the prescribed thirty minutes for every two hours of play.

He played for ten hours, amassing a solid stack. When he stopped for the day, he went over to join his family, who was watching from the sidelines with the rest of the crowd. He kissed Abbie on the cheek. Grabbed Dustin in a bear hug he resisted. The whole community service thing had jacked up his pissiness. Mac was a convenient target.

"You played fierce," Abbie commented.

"You were awesome!" Jill cried, throwing her arms around him as she scooted over. "I've never watched poker before, so it was all totally new. I mean, you don't move a muscle. It's incredible."

Jill continued to gush as Mac nodded to a passing Rhett, who was sandwiched between his poker babes, talking to a reporter who was filming for some news station. She excused herself and rushed over to congratulate him, her mouth dropping when Rye came up and gave Rhett a bear hug. The camera flashes were blinding.

His sister's frown almost made Mac smile. When Rhett put his arms back around his poker babes, he wasn't looking at them. He was looking directly at Abbie, who stared back without blinking.

"How did Rhett do today?" he asked his sister quietly.

She moistened her lips, breaking eye contact with Rhett. "Okay, but he seemed...distracted."

"He kept looking at Mom when she went by," Dustin added, elbowing Mac.

"I don't know what you're talking about," she replied primly, yanking on her jacket. "Don't be ridiculous."

Dustin snickered. "He's always had a thing for you."

Abbie's back went ram-rod straight. "How did you—"

The kid's eyes rolled. "I'm not blind. And I can top that. You've always had a thing for him, too. When are you going to admit it to the rest of the world?"

Mac shifted his weight, watching Abbie's facial muscles tense in shock and then distress. So the kid knew and was giving his permission. Well, well.

"I have some duties to attend to. Mac, you'll want to check out today's stats." She firmed her shoulders and headed off.

His nephew's dopey grin said it all. "No one gets under her skin like Rhett does."

Mac studied Dustin. To his knowledge, no one had talked to him about Rhett's intentions. Maybe it was time to feel him out.

"Sounds like you'd be okay with them getting together," he said.

His nephew's grin could have powered the hotel, so unlike his usual sulky smirk. "I love Uncle Rhett! Mom needs to have more fun. Rhett's the kind of guy you can't help but have fun with."

So true. They'd had their share of fun together. "Your mom needs more than fun, though."

His nephew shrugged. "She's too serious most of the time. I don't want her to end up alone. I'll be leaving for college in two years. What's she going to do then?"

His diaphragm clenched. Two years? Where had the time gone? "Probably what I'll do. Go crazy without you." What the hell was he going to do? This horrible image of him and Abbie living together and growing old together like in some terrible old Gothic movie surfaced in his mind. That was *so* not happening.

Dustin's sulk returned. "Yeah, right."

Mac pulled him in for a one-arm grab. "You doubting my word?"

Dustin studied the floor.

"So, what did you see today?" he asked to distract him.

The kid's eyes widened for a fraction of a second. Then he started to talk. He had serious observation skills when it came to poker. He might be a natural someday. Mac wasn't sure how he felt about that. Abbie hated the idea, but Mac knew one thing.

Everyone had to follow his or her own path.

He put his arm around Dustin and listened to his analysis as they walked to their family suite, enjoying the momentary closeness.

CHAPTER 17

Peggy eyed the shadows of Jill's house as she headed up the drive for their 4th of July BBQ. After the moose incident, she wasn't going to be caught off guard. Keith squeezed her hand harder than usual after they left the car. The fact that he was holding her hand at all indicated he hadn't forgotten either.

Mac had told Jill to take the afternoon off while they were playing poker, and instead of resting, she'd talked Brian into throwing a last-minute BBQ at their place. Brian had complained about the lack of prep time, but he'd eventually given in. Jill sure knew how to get what she wanted.

Meredith opened the door after Peggy knocked. "Hi!" she cried. And proceeded to pepper Keith's face with kisses. He giggled, but took it like a pro.

When her sister-in-law straightened, Peggy gave her the evil eye. "Don't even think about it."

"How about a simple hug?" Meredith asked, holding up her hands.

An eye-roll seemed to be the only appropriate response.

Meredith gave her a light squeeze. "See, that didn't hurt."

"Hey there!" came a booming voice from behind Peggy, and then Tanner grabbed her up, lifting her off the floor.

Her feet dangled. It was weird to be held like a kid. "Put me down, Tanner."

"Oh, you're such a spoil sport."

"And you have become seriously weird since getting hitched," she replied.

"I know," he said as he set her down, plucking Keith off the ground as a replacement. "Happy Independence Day, kiddo."

He grabbed Tanner's shoulders. "You, too! Can I shoot off firecrackers later?"

Tanner shook his head. "They've been banned this year because of the drought."

Keith's face fell.

"But we'll think of something."

They grabbed each other's hands and headed off.

Jill bounded forward, looking like one of those cute hippos in that

Fantasia movie Keith liked to watch. Peggy realized it probably wasn't something she should tell a pregnant woman.

"Hi!" She grabbed her, pressing her bump into Peggy's belly.

"Don't squash the kids," Peggy warned.

"Can't. My belly is rock hard." And proceeded to grab Peggy's hand and place it on her bump.

She yanked it back. Touching another woman's stomach was...well, weird. "Look, I had one, so I know the drill. Don't need to be feeling yours."

Jill snickered. "Fine. Be that way. Let's eat."

Peggy eyed the time. "Now?"

"Yep. When I found out Mac's playing in the final round, I told everyone we have to go up and watch him. Beats sitting around."

Her stomach burned. She'd been planning on a quiet night of eating in the backyard and watching perps shoot off fireworks in disregard of the burn ban.

"I'll pass."

Jill's red curls swung as she bobbed her head. "You've gotta come, Peg! They're playing for over two million dollars."

"Shut the front door."

"Yeah, and that's just first prize! Can you imagine? Seriously, you've never seen anything like this. Mac's ridiculous. He plays like something out of a movie. You'll see him in a whole new light."

Her knee jerk reaction was to stay firm, but then she thought it through. Maybe seeing him like that—gambling—would put out the flames. She'd be disgusted, right?

"Okay, if everyone else is going," she nodded, secretly hoping she was right. "But I draw the line at Keith."

Jill clapped her hands. "I'm sure we can find someone to watch him."

Peggy followed Jill out to the feast in the backyard. Her mouth watered at the smell of roasted meat. Everyone found a spot at the ginormous red-and-white checkered table showcasing an explosion of sunflowers. Brian had outdone himself again, smoking a whole brisket and baby-back ribs. She wasn't sure what was in the barbeque sauce, but it packed a punch and made her dunk her meat in a second time.

Arthur told Keith stories about past 4th of July holidays when Jill and Meredith were little, and their parents chimed in to add details. Keith sat perched on Tanner's knee, nodding with wide eyes, adoring the attention. She caught Tanner's eyes a few times. His grin said it all. Yes, they had a family. While it still made her feel weird sometimes, she was glad her favorite men were happy.

Jill's mom volunteered to take Keith for ice cream so that everyone else could watch the poker tournament. Peggy wavered, worrying about the imposition.

"How long are we talking here?" she asked Jill.

"No more than a couple of hours. I had Abbie text me. They're down to four players from the final nine—Mac, Rhett, Cince, and this kid named Lance. They're shooting fireworks off after the tourney's over."

She frowned. "How'd Maven manage that?"

"He presented the plans to the city council and received special permission," Arthur responded. "The country club received a pass, too, since they're following procedure."

Well, wasn't that peachy?

"I'll bring Keith up for the fireworks," Linda Hale offered. "It'll be fun."

Just not in the hotel, she almost said. "Are you—?"

"She's sure," Jill finished. "Now, let's get you something else to wear."

Peggy looked down at her shorts and T-shirt. "What's wrong with this?"

"You can't wear cutoffs to the hotel." She grabbed her arm and pulled her toward the bedroom. "I'm sure I have something."

Peggy put her hands on her hips as Jill riffled through a closet resembling a box of Crayola crayons. "Seriously, we don't wear the same size, and we certainly don't have the same style."

It was the kindest thing she could have said. She almost patted herself on the back.

Jill made a raspberry with her mouth. "I know just the thing."

Meredith strolled in and joined them. Peggy realized that both of them were wearing sundresses and sandals. Meredith's was a dark blue. Jill's was a neon green. Peggy eyed the door. God, she didn't want to turn into the third member of the Sundress Sisters Club.

"Grab her, Mere, before she makes a run for it." Jill plucked out something yellow with a red pattern.

Meredith's hand locked around Peggy's arm. "We can do this hard, or we can do this easy."

"That's my line. I could have both of you down on the floor in thirty seconds."

"But you won't. Keith and Tanner love us too much," Jill responded. "Now, if we belt this, it'll be perfect."

Peggy winced. "But it's *yellow*. And what are those—"

"They're embroidered dragons." She pushed the dress into Peggy's face. "Makes you think Bruce Lee, right? Or are you afraid to wear something that says you kick ass?"

The dragons intrigued her. Their mouths gaped open, blowing fire. Whoever had put them on a sundress needed their head examined. "I've never worn yellow. I'll look like Big Bird."

"You barely notice the color with the dragons," Meredith said. "Jill, where's your red belt? It'll be the perfect accessory."

"In Brian's closet. I ran out of room in mine. So, strip, sister. We have to be there in twenty minutes."

Peggy held the dress loosely in her hands. "Umm...let me use the bathroom."

"Oh for cripes sakes! We all have the same girl parts."

Giving a frustrated sigh, Peggy yanked off her clothes.

Jill whistled. "Nice rack, but jeez, did you ever think about wearing a real bra? You look like *Yentl* in that."

Great, now they were talking about Barbra Streisand movies. "I work with guys. I don't show my stuff. I can't have them bouncing around."

"We need to go back to Victoria's Secret in Denver," Jill announced.

She shuddered. "I'd rather take a bullet in the leg." The last time the three of them had gone there together, Peggy had spent the whole time watching a pervert paw at the panties.

Meredith giggled. "I'm sorry. I keep seeing you chasing down a suspect, boobs bobbing up and down."

Jill let out a snarky guffaw.

"Sounds like a bad porn flick," Peggy finished, yanking the dress over her head.

Their hilarity died. Their mouths parted. Their eyes widened.

"What?" she demanded, fidgeting under their scrutiny.

"Yellow is a great color on you," Meredith mused.

"You look beautiful!" Jill gushed, bouncing as much as she could, given her girth. "You should wear dresses more often."

Peggy hitched up a shoulder. "It's a little long."

"Perfect, it'll hide those sandals." Jill thrust out a thick red belt, which she'd retrieved from the other closet. "This will help."

As she strapped the belt on, Peggy eyed the dragons on the sleeves. They fluttered each time she moved her arms.

"Take a look," Jill commanded, pointing to the antique standing mirror against the far wall.

Peggy didn't move an inch, her palms suddenly damp. "Do I look presentable?"

"Absolutely," Meredith assured her.

"Then let's go. I don't need to stare at myself." She headed out of the bedroom, rubbing her burning diaphragm. She was afraid to see how she looked, and dammit, that pissed her off.

When she emerged, the stunned faces around her told her plenty. She looked like an idiot.

Keith ran forward. "Wow, Mom! You look super pretty. Doesn't she, Uncle Tanner?"

Tanner studied her as he walked forward. Bent to kiss her cheek. "Don't think I've seen you in a dress since..."

Her wedding day, she realized. She hadn't been able to get away with wearing pants for that.

"You look beautiful, Peg," he muttered.

"A remarkable transformation, my dear," Arthur added.

She fought against the urge to lift her arms to the sky and scream. "Can we go already?"

Tanner's all-knowing smile pissed her off. "Absolutely."

As they left for the hotel, she realized she was treading on thin ice. She was wearing a dress and attending the final poker tournament.

Had aliens invaded her body?

CHAPTER 18

Mac paused briefly as he raked in the chips. He couldn't explain it, but he knew Peggy was there. Somehow he'd willed it. His rational mind told him he was crazy. She hated his hotel and all it stood for—all *he* stood for. But his gut, which he had long since learned to trust, told him she was on site. He arranged his stack, surreptitiously scanning the crowd.

He thanked God for his poker face because, when he spotted her, he was sure all the blood drained out of his body. The first shock was that she was wearing yellow, something too soft for her. The second was that she was wearing a dress. It cascaded down her slender legs to the most hideous sandals he'd ever seen on a woman—flat, scuffed, and muddy brown. She looked...beautiful. Feminine. What the hell?

He brought his gaze back to the table, keeping abreast of everyone's bets before the dealer turned the next card. His eyes wandered back to her again. A red belt outlined her trim waist and sizeable bustline, her breasts curvy and inviting.

Their eyes met. The noise from the table died away, and a buzzing sounded in his ears. He stopped feeling the cards in his hands. Her dark eyes looked smoky today, perhaps an effect of the yellow she wore. They burned with anger and judgment. He could feel her repulsion from across the room. The slice cut him open.

He cursed under his breath. He had seventy percent of the table's chips and was well on his way to victory. He didn't need this distraction.

"Mac," the dealer said. "Call or raise?"

He wanted to kick the legs of the table. He'd lost track of the betting. "Call."

The dealer turned the final card after Cince bet.

The players put down their hands. Mac swore. The River had blown his hand apart.

Cince raked in the chips, grinning at his right. "Something on your mind, Maverick?"

His knowing glance triggered a spurt of irritation. He shrugged and took his cards, now stationed on the button, every poker player's favorite position. Play continued, but his gaze kept drifting to her.

She watched him like a jackal.

He struggled to shut her out.

When he lost the next hand, Cince elbowed him. Hard. "You and Rhett need to get your heads on straight. Don't let the women get to you."

He glanced across the table. Rhett was distracted too—instead of watching the dealer, his eyes were glued on Abbie, who was talking to Lance Jenkins, a professional who'd busted out before the final table. Jenkins was standing a little too close to his sister. Rhett tugged on his jacket's fringe. Mac could all but see the smoke coming out of his ears. Abbie wasn't encouraging the man, but Jenkins always hit on her whenever he was in town. Mac had decided to let her handle it on her own. He hoped Rhett would too. If he left the table, he'd incur a penalty, which would lead to his chips being posted for the ante even though he wasn't there. No one wanted to lose like that.

The next three hands went to Cince. Mac's concentration was split like two forks in the road—half on the table and the other half on the woman whose presence was like a garrote around his neck.

Lance Jenkins finally busted out when Mac forced him to go all in. He fought the urge to look over at Peggy again. Why was she wearing a dress with dragons on it? And why had she come at all?

Cince was playing it loose, throwing it all out on the table. His strategy was effective. Even Rhett was playing tighter as his stack of chips steadily dwindled. Mac changed tactics a couple of times to keep the others guessing, playing conservative one hand and loose the next. He knew the other men at the table like he knew himself. It was time to shake things up.

He bet heavy on the next hand, willing an inside straight, and when the River card appeared, he smiled at Rhett and raked in the pot. The tourney's MC announced a break.

Mac rose, resisting the urge to smooth down his jacket. The dealer announced the totals. He was in the lead with fifty percent of the chips, having lost ten percent after Peggy's sudden arrival. Cince had picked up a serious stack, but he still hovered at thirty-five percent. Rhett's stack had dwindled to fifteen percent, courtesy of Abbie.

Mac wandered to the bar with Cince beside him. "I need to pay that deputy sheriff to watch you play more often," his friend said.

"You don't need to pay me," Peggy replied from behind them.

Mac turned, his blood heating from her proximity—and her venom.

"I'll leave you two," Cince muttered.

"Why are you here?" he asked boldly.

Her stare was unflinching, a total contrast to the softness of the dress. "My BBQ broke up early to see the finals. I decided to tag along."

He unbuttoned his jacket. Planted his hands on his waist. "To do what? Dissect me like an insect?"

The scooped neckline gave him an ample view of her delicate throat as she swallowed. "Your words. Not mine."

"I want you to leave," he demanded before he could stop himself.

Her mouth turned up. "Am I bothering you?"

"No, but I don't like hostile people attending my tourneys. We have a watch list."

She shifted her weight. It only accentuated the curve of her waist. He had the desperate urge to wrap his arms around her. Whether to throw her out or throw her on the floor and have his way with her, he couldn't decide.

"Am I on it?" she sniped.

He grabbed the Perrier with lime his bartender brought to him—his regular drink during breaks—and downed it. "You don't want to watch this."

She made a merciless humming noise. "*Oh, but I do.* My interest is only increasing."

The snideness of her tone cracked his resolve. "Don't fuck with me, Peg."

Her eyes narrowed. "That's not what you said before. Be careful what you wish for." She turned around so fast her dress twirled like she was Ginger Rogers.

"We're fucked," Rhett commented as he appeared by his side, his brow sweating. "Can't we throw the women out?"

Mac eyed the bourbon in his friend's hand. "Abbie has no interest in Jenkins. She's not trying to get your goat on purpose."

"That's what Rye said." He tapped his snakeskin boot. "Well, I can't say the same for your deputy. She's watching you like a cobra would a mongoose. But you're still in the lead. You've got ice for blood, my friend."

Mac didn't respond. If he had ice for blood, he wouldn't have lost ten percent of his stack or engaged in an idiotic battle of wills with Peggy just now. She was making him loose his cool at the worst possible time.

He set his drink down with a snap. "Let's get back to the table. The break's almost over."

As he followed Rhett, he saw Peggy smirking—actually smirking—at him. What was she, twelve? He took his seat.

Cince bumped him again. "Better stop watching the broad, or I'm going to take you to the cleaners."

Mac didn't respond. Usually their banter was friendly and light. But the truth of Cince's statement burned in his stomach like acid. He hated to lose, but he loathed the idea of losing at his hotel's opening.

They changed their chips out after the break because the blinds were being raised again. He fingered a twenty-five thousand piece and forced himself not to look at Peggy.

The first hand started off well. He was on the button and was dealt pocket kings. He put his chip protector over those two gentlemen facedown while everyone put in their ante. Cince posted the small blind of fifty thousand, and Rhett posted the big blind of one hundred.

Mac knew it was time to force Rhett to act. His friend only had seven hundred and fifty thousand left. He could bust him out if he played his cards right. Mac raised to three hundred thousand. He barely heard the token gasps in the crowd. For a fleeting moment, he wondered if Peggy would be impressed. But hell no, she wouldn't be impressed. She'd be disgusted.

Rhett looked up from his cards, his eyes burning. Yeah, he knew what

Mac was doing.

Mac turned to Cince, who fingered his cards and then called the raise.

Rhett glanced at his cards and went all-in. Mac fought a smile as he heard a few more gasps. Rhett had confirmed his instinct that his friend had an ace with a good kicker. There was no way he was going all in on a bluff. Not at the final table.

He eyed Peggy through his peripheral vision. She stood tall, seemingly impervious to the tension permeating the crowd. Hell, she interrogated suspects for a living. Her blood probably ran colder than his. But even as he contemplated the chill she was giving off in arctic blasts, he couldn't stop his blood from heating at the sight of her in that dress.

He brought his mind back to the table with an internal shake. Decided to trap Cince by letting him think he had a weaker hand than he did. Make him bet a little more. Take most of his chips. He loved luring players in. He called the bet, matching Rhett's all-in. Cince's eyes flickered over to him just as he'd hoped they would. He felt the assessment in them.

The dealer dealt the flop. Mac studied the cards—a ten of clubs, jack of hearts, and queen of spades. He tried to tune out Peggy.

Rhett leaned back in his chair. Mac could feel his excitement building. Yeah, he knew he had a good hand.

When Cince's turn came, he went all in.

Rhett bit his lip, assessing whether Cince had something better.

Mac called, making the pot one million three hundred and fifty. Someone was going to lose their shirt on this hand.

The dealer dealt the turn, and Lady Luck shone on Mac once again. The dealer laid the ace down. Mac had an ace high straight—or "the nuts"— the best hand at the moment. Rhett was going to bust out unless a king fell. His pursed lip signaled he knew he was in trouble.

"Here's the river," the dealer announced.

And please don't let me cry in it, Mac thought, wondering how he'd feel having Peggy watch him lose.

The dealer laid down a jack of clubs.

Cince slammed his cards down. "Check this shit out, boys. I've just rivered a full house."

Mac's stomach burned. Cince had beaten him out with a full house, jacks full of aces.

"Don't that beat all. Well, I'm out," Rhett commented. His poker babes—decked out in red and black sequined gowns—flocked to his sides as he shoved his chair back, soothing his back and his heartbreak. Rye grabbed him in a bear hug. Camera flashes punctuated the scene. But even Rye's antics couldn't make Rhett crack a smile. Mac understood. Losing sucked.

The MC called another break. Mac looked at Cince. It was down to the two of them again, and he was going in short-stacked. He headed to the bar for another Perrier to coat his dry throat, running through his plan. He'd have to go all in on the next hand. Cince was going to force it.

"My, how luck can change on a dime," Peggy commented by his side.

Why wouldn't she leave him the fuck alone? "Enjoying yourself?" Mac hissed, nearly calling for a bourbon.

"Yes. I'm especially starting to look forward to our little talks during the breaks."

He turned to her, waving off Jill, who was barreling toward them with pinched lips. He didn't need a pregnant woman to handle this situation for him. He ignored the Perrier his bartender extended and crossed his arms. "I didn't take you for a cruel woman until this moment."

He had the pleasure of watching her flinch before he walked around to talk to Dustin.

The kid grabbed him in a hug. "You'll get it back, Uncle Mac."

Abbie joined them, and put a comforting hand on his arm. "That woman is deliberately aggravating you! Do you want me to have security escort her out?"

"No, she's only doing it because she knows it's bothering me. I need to focus." He kissed the worry line between her eyebrows. "I'll be fine." And he walked back to the table.

But he couldn't get his mental control back. Cince beat him in a single hand. Mac stood and shook the man's hand. He'd come in second before, but, dammit, he'd wanted to come out ahead at his opening. And he certainly hadn't wanted to lose because of Peggy.

Rhett sauntered over, leaving Rye to sign autographs. "Come on, man. Let's get you a drink."

Mac slapped him on the back. "I almost had one during the game."

"That would break a big rule for you, but who can blame you with Ms. Cobra staring you down like that? Bet she'd eat you after sex."

Like he'd care. "You're mixing your metaphors. That's a black widow spider." He caught sight of his head of security making his way toward him through the crowd. Even though Aaron Higgins had an inscrutable poker face, Mac instantly knew something was wrong.

When Aaron reached him, he leaned in close. "We just had a bomb threat from an untraceable phone."

All the blood rushed to Mac's head, and a pounding started at the base of his skull. "Fuck."

"I'm not convinced it's a serious threat, but there isn't any evidence to prove otherwise. What do you want to do?"

His gaze assessed the room in slow motion. Dustin and Abbie were talking with Jill. Peggy was drinking a soda with Tanner. He didn't hesitate. "We evacuate."

Aaron nodded. "We'll need to call in the authorities, but we can start clearing everyone out now."

Mac's eyes locked on to Peggy. "We already have one officer on the premises. Let me talk to her. Then I'll make an announcement."

He made his way over to her on rubbery legs. She separated from Tanner and Meredith at his signal and followed him over to a corner.

"You lost," she commented without preamble. "Planning on tossing me out now?"

He leaned in. When she reached out a hand to shove him back, he grabbed it. "We just had a bomb threat and need to evacuate. I know you're off duty, but I figured this changes things."

Her head turned sharply. Their eyes locked. "When?"

"Minutes ago. Untraceable. My chief of security doesn't think it's serious, but I'm not taking any chances."

She nodded crisply. "We need to get everyone out. Safely. Without panic."

He took his cell phone as one of his security people handed it to him. They were banned from the table. "Right. Will you call it in?"

She reached into her purse, her mouth a hard line. "Yes."

"I'll have one of my officers show you to security. I need to make an announcement."

"I can find it myself. You need to move."

He nodded and walked away. Grabbed the microphone one of his guys handed him.

And prayed for the right words to come.

CHAPTER 19

Mac ran into the room just moments after making a carefully worded announcement over the loudspeakers. Peggy turned to look at him as he came in.

"What do we know?" he asked, unbuttoning his jacket.

His chief of security answered before Peggy could. "We've run the number. It's from a burner phone. Untraceable. Marion in reception said the caller was male. The only thing he said before hanging up was 'There's a bomb in your hotel.' The lack of specifics makes me think it's not a serious threat."

Mac tapped his chin. "The burner phone suggests some knowledge. I can't risk the guests. We have to check everywhere."

Peggy put her hands on her hips, needing to establish the pissing order. "That's not your decision to make. It's mine. You *will* check every floor. There's not enough information for us to take this lightly."

He cut her a glance as cold as the shaved ice sold on Main Street. "Glad we agree. Do you have a detection dog?"

"Yes, it's on the way with the team," she replied.

He studied the hotel blueprints, which were electronically displayed on the main security screen. "Good. We do too, mostly for drugs, but they're cross-trained. Once your officers arrive, have one of them take your dog through. McHenry will take ours. You search by priority."

She wasn't being cut out of the search. "I'll take the dog. The Emergency Response Team should be here shortly."

He shook his head. "No. I want you here, feeding orders to your team, working with mine. I need your mind. Have someone else be the legs."

She studied him, wondering if this was a ruse to keep her out of danger. Most men didn't like putting women into sticky situations. But he was right. The sheriff was on vacation in Wyoming right now, so she was in charge.

"Fine. I want all the available information."

"You'll have it."

She walked closer and leaned in. "I'm glad you're not questioning my wherewithal to pursue this."

"You might want my hotel shut down, but you wouldn't want anyone to get hurt. I know you'll do everything you can to enforce the law, Peg."

The intensity of that stoplight green gaze took her breath away. She could feel adrenaline and lust coursing through her body.

"Thank you. I will. Now let's move."

"Aaron, you have the floor," Mac said. "I'm going to keep the guests as calm and comfortable as possible in the Evacuation Zone."

"Yes, sir," the square-jawed head of security replied.

Although Aaron wore a tailored suit, she could tell he'd been a cop. He didn't break stride, his eyes didn't miss a beat, and his hands never trembled.

He introduced her to the rest of Maven's security team. They had the kind of top-notch edge she'd admired when she'd done a few runs with SWAT. They were hard-nosed, direct, and they had more resources than her last three police departments combined. She decided not to show them who was boss. They were sharing everything with her, from video feeds to heat signatures in the hotel—all of it in real-time on mind-blowing devices featuring the newest technology. She introduced them to her officers when they rushed in with their detection dog.

A few of her guys gaped at her dress, but they wisely kept their lips zipped. She didn't need anyone to point out how ridiculous she looked.

One of Aaron's men brought in their team's German Shepherd, so they prepared to start the search. Thankfully the hotel wasn't enormous, but still...

She couldn't help but be impressed after her brief scan of the hotel's bomb prevention plan. The team had shown her which areas were the most porous in the hotel. There weren't many. The sheer volume of surveillance cameras boggled the mind.

They split into groups—those searching and those feeding the search. Aaron knew his shit. Without any information about the hypothetical bomb and timer, they needed to move fast. He didn't want to take the dogs from room to room, so he suggested starting with priority areas. After searching the mailroom, they checked the delivery entrance and the parking deck. All luggage went through X-ray machines in the bellboy station room, but they couldn't account for packages guests bought in town. In ten minutes, his team had a list of all guests who'd walked into the hotel after shopping and their corresponding room numbers. They searched the shoppers' hotel rooms.

And found nothing.

So they finished off the last rooms with a more cursory scan. Still nothing.

Her gut told her it was a hoax, but the idea of something detonating made her quiver.

She blocked out Keith and what could happen to her.

She didn't need to think about that now.

Maven periodically radioed in for updates. "Don't be alarmed," he informed them on one such call. "We're starting the fireworks earlier than expected to keep the guests entertained."

At the first boom, her guts gripped, that damn fight-or-flight response causing her system to buck against her mental control. She heard laughter and applause over the hotel's security feed and wondered what kind of magician Maven must be to elicit such reactions from the crowd during a bomb scare.

And then the crowd went wild. When Peggy looked up at the security feed, she watched as Rye Crenshaw took the mike from Mac on a raised platform. And then he started to sing. Even though she was totally focused on the search, his smooth baritone raised gooseflesh on her arms as he poured out a heartfelt version of "Proud to be an American." And then he kept singing some of her favorites; his hit songs that played over and over again on her country music station.

The search took ninety minutes. They didn't find anything.

Part of her wanted to kick something. The other part wanted to put her head between her knees.

She and Aaron agreed to give the all-clear. He handed her a cup of strong coffee. She gulped it down and tried to empty her mind.

Damn bomb threat. And in her small town.

Shit like this wasn't supposed to happen here.

When Maven strolled into the security center, he slapped Aaron on the back and shook hands with his guys and the Emergency Response Team. He even gave the dogs a good rubdown, insisting that the chef would broil them T-bones.

Then he walked over to her, his steps quick, his whole body radiating power and determination. He could bend everything to his will. He could do anything, have anything.

He wanted her.

There was no mistaking the desire and concern in his eyes.

He put his hand on her arm, his thumb swiping the place where forearm met elbow. A punch of lust hit her in the gut. She wanted to throw him against the wall and have him. Now.

"You all right?"

Her voice wouldn't work for a moment, paralyzed by the mere rub of his thumb in the shallow of her arm.

"Of course," she finally replied, clearing her throat.

The right side of his mouth tipped up. He put his mouth close to her ear. His breath tickled her lobe. The woman inside her wanted to thrust her head back, urge his mouth to her neck.

"I'm glad. Thank you for taking care of my hotel."

It was her job. She still hated his poker palace.

When he leaned back, he held her gaze, all smoke and fire and...that damned concern.

A lightheadedness permeated her skull, and she wove in place. His hand gripped her arm, still caressing her skin through the totally inappropriate summer dress she was wearing.

She yanked her arm free, aware of the interest from his security team and her fellow officers. "I'm fine. Glad it worked out. I'm heading out to finish up my report." She stepped away. Dug her feet into her sandals as she headed outside, needing air—big fat doses of it.

He was interfering with her job, which was a first. She'd never had a problem closing out her ex when they'd been on the force together.

This had to stop.

The fresh air was a balm to her head, making everything clear.

There was only one thing to do.

She had to sleep with him. Rip him out of her system.

There was no other way.

CHAPTER 20

Mac broke up his meeting early the next day when he heard the distinct ping from security on his hand-held. Deputy McBride was on the premises.

"Jill, we can go over the apology cards later today. Christ, after yesterday I'm going to be comping people hotel suites until the end of the world." But comping Rye Crenshaw for stepping up and giving a free concert wasn't enough of a payback. He'd have to think of something special to do for him.

"It's so unfair! I still can't believe someone would do that."

Mac refrained from kicking his desk. "We should just be grateful there was no bomb."

She put a hand on her belly. "Right. Shit. Oops. Do you know if I can still swear when they're in there? You always know weird trivia like that."

He snorted. "Yes, they can hear you. It'll be a good long while before they parrot you though."

She stacked the cards. "Whew! Good. I keep telling Brian we've got to clean up our mouths. Restaurant people have horrible potty mouths. I told him he'd have to go to potty training before the girls do."

"Haha. Okay, out you go. I need to hear what Peggy has to say."

The smile left her face. "She's coming?"

"Yeah."

"I'm so pissed at her for picking on you yesterday. Abbie said she made you lose your cool."

"Abbie's wrong. No one makes you lose your cool but you."

"Don't tell Brian that. I accuse him of that all the time." She waddled over and kissed his cheek. "It's going to be okay, Mac."

He squeezed her arm. "Christ, I hope so. I've dealt with stupid security issues before, but this goes way beyond anything I've encountered. It's sabotage."

She patted his cheek. "We'll figure it out."

"No, I'll figure it out with the properly trained professionals. You do your job and take care of yourself."

Her electric blue purse's rhinestones sparkled when she swung it over her arm. "Being pregnant, I appreciate the gallantry."

"You should show your purse to Rhett. It might match his outfit."

"Funny. Tell Peggy to pop by my office before she takes off."

"Will do."

He took a deep breath and fell back in his chair. A bomb threat at his hotel! The mother fuckers. His rage had grown into an open fire by the time Peggy appeared in his doorway. He called security and told them he'd let them know when he was ready for them.

"Come in. What do you have for me?"

"I thought your team would be here."

"They'll be along shortly. I wanted to hear what you had first."

She walked toward his desk. "I'm sorry, but not much. We confirmed that the call came from a burner cell. No idea where."

"I know that. What else?" he demanded, unbuttoning his jacket.

"The timing seems odd to me. It came in right after the tournament wrapped up. I don't have anything concrete, but it could have been someone onsite."

He gestured toward the flimsy file Aaron had handed him this morning. "That's what my team thinks too, but they can't find anything to support it. I want a lead."

"Look, with no package, there's not much of an evidence trail."

"So in other words, we're not going to catch this guy."

She rubbed the heel of her police-issue black boot into his carpet. "We'll keep looking. See what—"

"Pops? You should know I'm offering a hundred grand for credible information leading to the perpetrator's arrest."

Her face pinched. "Rewards don't always—"

"I don't care! If it's an inside job, I need to know. I'll do whatever it takes." He drew in the frustration to clear his desk. He inhaled deeply and reached for every ounce of control. "Sorry. I want to punish whoever did this. They ruined my grand opening."

"Yes."

"And now I have a question for you." He stepped forward until he was in her face. "Why the hell did you show up yesterday, anyway?"

She leaned her chin in. "Jill all but dragged me—"

"Bull. No one drags you anywhere. Hell, if I tried to drag you off to bed right now, you'd knee me in the nuts or pull your gun on me."

She pushed him back with a small shove. "You're just pissed you lost yesterday. Do you think I didn't hear Cincinnati-whatever-his-name-is teasing you and Rhett for being distracted by a couple of women?"

He ground his teeth. "Cince lets his mouth run off. I lost because he beat me."

"But you were ahead when I arrived," she sneered. "Are you saying I didn't make you lose your cool?"

"As I told Jill, who was pretty pissed at you, no one can make you lose your cool but you."

The woman had the audacity to snort like some farm animal. "So, you don't think I can make you lose your cool?"

His instinct was to stalk away. Then he realized that it would prove her right. "I won't let you." A rapping sounded at the door. He wondered who in the hell would interrupt him while he was in a meeting. "Not now, dammit!"

She put a hand on her police belt. "Nice way to talk to your worker bees."

"Well, I'm not feeling particularly *nice* today."

She tilted her head back and stared him in the eyes, her expression all flint and fire. "You didn't answer my question."

He leaned forward until he could feel her breath on his face. "I told you. I won't let *anyone* do that to me." And he told himself yesterday was a momentary blip.

"Now *I* say bull. How about we play Texas Hold 'em?"

His head darted back. "You *hate* poker." He scoffed. "Plus, you couldn't beat me."

"Wanna bet?" Peggy lurched forward and grabbed his dick through his slacks.

"Jesus!" He inhaled sharply and tried to disengage her hands, but she squeezed with enough finesse to pump all his blood to that one area. "Ah, *that* type of Hold 'Em. You should use analogies from your own profession. It's misleading when you use mine."

Her smile held power and determination, and a hint of intrigue. "Hmm... Okay. I received the highest marks in police training for my ability with a night stick."

He wrestled her wandering hands up and pulled them between them. Was she serious about this? "Much more appropriate. I don't doubt you know how to handle a...stick. What are you doing, Peg?"

"Proving I *can* make you lose your cool."

"You've proved that on numerous occasions. Satisfied?"

"No," she replied, sneaking a hand loose and giving him another tantalizing caress. "Not by a long shot."

He cupped her face. "Okay, if it's *Hold 'Em* you're after, let's slow down. Find a nicer room. I have one—"

"I only have thirty minutes."

"Don't put us on the clock."

"I'm a single mom. I don't have tons of time."

"Bullshit. Get a sitter. Or I'll get one for you."

Her hand stroked his shirt, fingering the buttons. "What are you so concerned about? Guys don't last that long anyway. We'll have this out of the way in five minutes flat."

He studied her for a moment. "Was that your experience with your ex? Or all men?"

She looked away. "I don't want to talk about that. I just want to get this behind us. It's starting to affect the way I do my job. I didn't want to come out here to give you my report."

He stepped closer, realizing how hard that admission was for her—and why she was finally yielding to temptation. "And here I was hoping you'd know it was me you were making love with."

"You want this."

He pushed her hands away and walked across the room, fighting the urge to down a shot of whiskey. "True, but I want something more. I always have. If we do this now, your way, you've scratched the itch. That's it." He sighed, suddenly sickened by how vast the gulf still was between them. "I don't want it to stop. And I sure as hell haven't waited this long for a quickie. I won't cheat you or myself." He pulled on the front of his pants. "I can't believe I'm saying this."

She stood there, hands on her hips. "So you're turning me down?"

He dropped some ice into a highball and poured himself a sparkling water. He downed it. "Yep."

"You're a tease." She pointed her finger at him like she'd called him out in a crowd.

"No, I think you have to make someone hot to be a tease. I haven't."

She pointed to herself. "How in the hell would you know whether I'm hot for it?"

He raked his hands through his hair. "I've had some experience with women. You're intrigued. And you're pissed."

She fingered her gun. "You bet I am."

He didn't think she'd shoot him, but he kept his eyes on her hand nonetheless. "No, you're pissed that you're weak enough to want this—me. If I take advantage of that, I'll be confirming everything you believe about me, yourself, and...men."

"You bastard."

"No, not today. Think about what I've said. And, Peg, when you really want to be with me, I'm here. All the way... I lied before. You did make me lose my cool yesterday. I saw you standing under those casino lights in that dress, and I lost it. I couldn't concentrate on my game. I kept wondering what you were thinking while you studied me like I was a leper, fascinating and repelling all at once."

Her hand clenched her night stick.

"Now, go before I change my mind. I'll brief the team myself since there's not much to report."

She rocked on her heels. "I wouldn't screw you if you were the last man on earth now."

He chuckled at her reddening face. "Yes. Got that. Think about what I said. You know where to find me if you change your mind. I can take you places you've never gone. Give you pleasure you've never experienced. All you need to do is open yourself up to what's between us."

"You don't get to decide how it's going to be."

"You're wrong. I do. I'm an active participant. I won't take the crumbs you want to hand out. I want more than that."

Her narrowing eyes confirmed fear was lurking behind their slanted corners. "You're insane."

"You've lost a part of yourself. I can help you reclaim it. I want to treat you like a woman...and for you to see me as something other than a sexual itch you're scratching."

"I hate you."

The energy of that verbal arrow flew across the room and landed in his gut. "Right now you do. I hope that changes. Forgive me for not showing you out." She flew out of his office, slamming the door behind her.

He pressed a panel on the wall, revealing the surveillance TVs behind it. Watching them, he felt new hope.

Her shoulders were slumped, and his eagle eyes picked up the slightest tremble in her fingers when she ran her hands through her hair.

When she walked down the hallway, it took all of his self control not to go after her.

But he knew better. She had to come to him willingly.

Or they'd both be destroyed by what was between them.

CHAPTER 21

When Peggy's alarm went off at 5:30 a.m., the first hints of fire and ocean blue permeated the sky. She tugged on shorts and a T-shirt.

There was one perk to mowing the lawn straight out of bed. The vibration of the engine under her hands allowed her to sleep on her feet. All she had to do was remember to push.

She checked to make sure Keith was still sleeping. Cartoons called to him in the mornings like a siren. Thankfully, he was still out, feet dangling from the bed.

Easing out of the house, she decided she'd have her coffee later. Summer mornings were cooler in the mountains than in their previous home, but she always broke a sweat when she worked outside.

Dew covered her shoes as she headed to the shed, the birds chirping happily all around her. What in the hell were they so happy about? She might have to wake up early because she was a mom, but she still hated mornings with a passion. A fellow cop had told her about these adult afternoon naps called siestas somewhere in Europe. She couldn't remember where. It sounded like heaven.

Why was she up at the butt-crack of dawn if she was already thinking about naps? Oh yeah. Because she was trying to ensure Maven didn't show up with his nephew, especially after what had happened between them. What guy refused sex? He was right. She pretty much wanted to maim him permanently right now. Give him a permanent limp. Or a limp dick. The humor of the thought made her feel more awake. Yeah, she could get on board with that one.

Lost in thought, she reached for the shed door and pulled. Nothing happened. She looked down. And froze.

There was a lock on the door!

She fiddled with it, wondering if Tanner had added it for security, and she'd forgotten. She rubbed her face, trying to get her brain going.

Then it clicked.

There was only one person who would have put a lock on her shed.

Maven.

Dammit!

Fully awake now, anger coursing through her blood, she stalked into the house. She had his phone number because he'd called a few times about the mowing—and dinner. There was no way either of those things was going to happen now.

She eyed the clock. If she was up, he was going to be—and he'd better show up with a key in hand. She couldn't shoot the lock off without drawing attention. Plus, she'd have to explain why she'd discharged her weapon on her own shed like an idiot.

She hit the button and put the phone to her ear.

"Good morning, Peg," he muttered, his tone all gravely with sleep.

She was speechless for a minute. Was she programmed into his phone? The woman in her conjured up an image of him swathed in black satin sheets, his hair mussed, the shadow of a beard on his face. And then her imagination took it too far. She'd bet the farm he slept nude. Oh cripes. And all this from "Good morning"? She needed to get a life.

"There's a lock on my shed."

"Yes. I didn't think you'd appreciate it if I sent someone to stake out your place so I could know exactly when *you* were mowing your lawn. This seemed the best option."

"I don't want you here," she said, not bothering to deny it.

"I know, but you made a deal. Abbie wants Dustin to repay you for what happened, and so do I."

"I don't need repayment. The law is taking care of things."

"So the law's the only thing connecting us? Don't kid yourself, Peg." His voice held a warning.

"You've overstepped."

"And you welshed on a bet. I didn't like dancing around when Keith asked me if Dustin and I were still going to come mow your lawn. He said you were tired from doing it in the morning."

Her kid had ratted her out?

"When did you see Keith?"

"When he was getting ice cream with Tanner and Meredith yesterday. I went to Wal-Mart and bought the lock right after that and installed it, praying you wouldn't see me and shoot. I know you don't want me around, especially after our last 'chat,' but I won't let Keith think we don't keep our promises, Peg."

She stalked around the kitchen. "You've boxed me in nicely."

"No, you boxed yourself in. You agreed to have Dustin mow the lawn and do yard work in front of your son and my family. If you back out now, he'll think Abbie and I don't follow through on our punishments."

She kicked a chair. "Dammit, I don't want you here."

"I know, but you don't have a choice. I'm not walking away. From my commitments or what's between us."

"There's nothing between us."

"Liar."

"Are you calling me a *liar*? "

"Would you prefer Pinocchio? I've always found that story incredibly disturbing. You're only pissed because I told you I want to make love to you instead of having a crappy quickie."

127

Her breath hitched at the images he invoked. "Enough!" She stared at Keith's recent drawings on the fridge. The mom in her surfaced. He was right. They were doing more than fighting each other. They were both raising kids. And kids needed to be taught lessons, see things followed through. "Okay. Dustin can come mow the lawn."

"Thank you," he said, surprising her. "We'll be there after I finish work."

"Can't he just come with Abbie while I'm at work?"

The long pause on the line had her dancing in place.

"No, I'm afraid that's not possible. You're not her favorite person right now after the poker tourney. You'll have to deal with me, Peg. Now, when are we going to have dinner?"

"When pigs fly."

"I'll buy some wings today. Are you trying to welsh again?"

She put her hand to her rapidly beating heart. "How about after Dustin mows? We can order pizza."

"You agreed to have a meal *with me*."

The intimacy in his tone stole her breath. "Not alone."

His slight chuckle made her toes curl. "Ah, so that's the way it's going to be, eh? Well, Deputy, you didn't add anyone to the party before we played our hands, so a meal together with me means you and me. Only."

"In your universe."

"That's the only one I'm interested in." There was another murmur—soft and sexy—from his side. "And yours, of course."

"I'm not interested in discussing planetary alignments."

"Fine, when are we having dinner?"

She stayed stubbornly silent, ripping up a paper napkin to give her hands something to do.

"Okay, here are your choices. We get dressed to the nines and go to Brian's or the Chop House. Everyone will see us and start talking. Or I can take you to Denver. It's a long drive at night, so we might want to stay over. Make love."

Her breathing shattered.

"Option number three is that we can have a private dinner at my house. Abbie and Dustin can go see a movie. We're the only ones who will ever need to know we broke bread together."

She didn't like the idea of spending time alone with him, but the other two choices didn't bear contemplating.

"Did I mention I have a private residence in Denver?"

Lothario couldn't have come up with a more seductive offer. She could imagine it. They wouldn't even eat dinner—they'd feast on each other instead. His body would give her all the sustenance she needed, filling her until she was sure she couldn't take anymore. She stopped the fantasy. Was she getting hot in the kitchen at the crack of dawn? She was losing it.

"Your place in Dare then," she agreed. "And in case you're thinking of making a move, I should tell you I'm bringing my gun."

His chuckle reverberated in her ear. "It just makes me look forward to the moment when I disarm you."

"That's never going to happen."

"We'll see. Friday night?"

Since she was a single mom who didn't have a life, her Friday was free. And her Saturday...

"Fine. What can I bring? Besides my gun, I mean."

"Why, Peg, are you flirting with me?"

She stopped, appalled. Was she? She needed a good smack upside the head. "In your dreams."

"Every night."

Okay, she'd walked into that one. "Time?"

"Is seven-thirty all right?"

"I was thinking five-thirty." Later hours made it more of a date.

His throaty murmur made her want to pop him.

"I work a bit later than that. I hope that's not a problem."

He darn well knew it was. "Fine." Time to get off the phone. This conversation was taking too long.

"I'll see you then. And Peg? Thank you for being the first voice I heard this morning. It's a wonderful way to start the day."

"Don't get used to it."

"Too bad I can't talk you into giving me a wakeup call every morning. That would—"

She hung up before he could finish the sentence. Her back had started itching, and her heart was doing funny things. It was warm, like his statement had meant something to her.

She grabbed the coffee pot to give herself something to do, anything to make her forget how his voice had sounded when he said *good morning*, and how easily she could imagine waking up next to him all warm and mussed, too.

CHAPTER 22

Mac silently swore when he spotted the full gasoline can on the deck with a note secured by duct tape. *For the mower.* That infernal woman! She wouldn't even let him take care of the gas. He glared at the house, but didn't see her in the windows. She was probably hiding somewhere.

"Uncle Mac," Dustin hissed out.

Mac turned sharply. "What's wrong?"

He darted forward, tugging on his T-shirt. "I went to get the mower and saw Keith crying behind the shed. I didn't know what to do."

If Keith was out here, his instinct told him he didn't want his mom to know. Dustin used to hide the same way when he was upset, but they had always been able to tell because his lashes would be salt-tipped when he returned.

"Let's see what's wrong."

Dustin followed him to the shed, but hung a few steps back, fidgeting. Mac heard the boy's quiet sobbing as they came closer. Felt a horrible tugging on his heart. The kid was broken-hearted. He wondered if the woman inside was as well. Peggy would never cause this hurt in her kid.

He crouched down in front of Keith and cupped his head. "What's wrong, son?"

The boy launched himself into Mac's arms with surprising force, upsetting his balance. He put an arm on the ground to steady them and wrapped the other around Keith.

"Don't...tell Mom."

"Shh..." Mac stroked his damp hair. "Tell me what's wrong."

Keith sniffed. "My dad...hates...me." He raised his head. His brown eyes shone with huge fat tears. "Mom won't say it, but I know he does."

Mac felt the tugging of another boy long ago who'd said the same thing to him after another father's show-and-tell day at school. An uncle simply hadn't cut it that day. He looked over at Dustin, who was staring at the ground, kicking a rock. His ears were red.

Mac tucked the kid closer. "Why do you think that?"

Keith inhaled jaggedly. "Every time...Mom calls him after I beg her to...and asks him to visit, she always tells me he's too busy...with police stuff. Today she called him about my birthday next month." He started crying again, wetting Mac's shirt. "I know she's lying for him, and she hates lying! She gets so angry she shreds paper. She doesn't think I know. She broke our shredder, so she's really mad. He...he never wants to see me!"

Mac kept a gentle grip on Keith's tense shoulder where the small bones met. "Isn't he a police officer? Perhaps he's working a really hard case right now." He doubted it, but he didn't want to hurt the kid anymore. Plus, he wasn't going to contradict anyone's parenting.

"He never visited me once while we lived in Kansas! He doesn't ever remember my birthday anymore. It's like...he's forgotten all about me! How could he do that? He's my *dad*! "

Mac fought a dirty curse word.

"He's a fucker," Dustin supplied.

"Dustin!" Mac reproached, but it was exactly what he'd been thinking too.

Keith swung his hopeful gaze toward the older boy.

Dustin shuffled forward. "My dad's a fucker too. You're better off without him."

Mac stayed silent, sensing a shift.

Keith's lip quivered. "That's what my best friend at school says, but he *has* a dad. He doesn't understand. Why doesn't my dad like me? I've tried and tried to think of what I did wrong, but he left when I was a baby."

"You didn't do anything," Dustin said. "He's an asshole. Some men shouldn't have kids."

Mac could hear the hurt growing in his nephew's voice. They'd had these same discussions many times over the years. The pain had coalesced into red-hot teenage rage.

Keith nodded, looking much older than his years.

"If you don't think your dad likes you, why do you keep hoping he'll visit?" Dustin asked.

Wiping his runny nose with his hand, Keith said, "So he can see how good I am now."

Mac put both hands on the boy's small shoulders and stared into his eyes. "Now, wait just a minute. You've *always* been good." He took a deep breath. Sometimes you had to go with the truth. He'd learned that with his nephew. "Dustin's right. Some men shouldn't have kids. I had a terrible dad until he left me and my sister. He didn't like me either."

Keith's eyes turned as huge as chocolate circles. "He didn't?"

"No, and I'm a good person, right?" He tried to smile. He'd used the same line on Dustin. It had worked every time.

Dustin put his hand on Mac's shoulder. "You're the best," he replied like he always had.

It had been a long time since he'd heard that from his nephew. Funny how much he needed it. He cleared his throat. "Takes one to know one."

"Did it ever make you cry?" Keith asked.

"Yeah," Mac whispered, remembering how it had felt to be seven years old. The only difference between them was that his mother hadn't bothered to reassure him. She hadn't liked him either. Dustin was right.

Some people should never have kids.

"What about you?" Keith asked Dustin.

His nephew kicked the ground. "I haven't for a long time." He crouched low to the ground. "So you're part of the pack now—guys whose fathers hate them. Look at Uncle Mac. It didn't mess him up."

So the hero lens wasn't completely gone from Dustin's eyes. His nephew's ears flamed when their gazes met.

Mac swallowed thickly and turned back to Keith. "You're gonna be fine. You've got the best uncle around and the best mom except for my sister. Plus, look at the Hales. You've got a whole family who loves you."

"Mom says we have to stick together."

Mac lifted his head and stared at his nephew. "Yes, that's what families do."

Dustin ducked his head to the right. Mac knew he only did that when he wanted to hide his emotions. So Keith was helping everyone with their hurts today.

As with everything life handed out, there was a silver lining.

"Come here," he told Keith. He picked him up, stood, and pulled Dustin in with the other arm. He hugged those two boys hard until it became awkward. Then he jostled them back and forth. "We okay now?"

When Mac put him down, Keith took Dustin's hand. His nephew's brows shot up, but he didn't shake free. Mac's heart grew so huge he wasn't sure it would fit in his chest.

"Okay," Keith murmured, his *Toy Story* T-shirt dotted with wet spots. "Come on, Dustin. I need a boost to climb the tree."

They walked off together, two hurting boys trying to understand why their fathers had abandoned them, trying to become what they were meant to be in spite of it. Pride couldn't exactly describe what Mac was feeling, but it was damn close.

Dustin helped Keith into the tree and then climbed up himself. Keith's higher-pitched voice blended with Dustin's rapidly changing one.

Mac fished his phone out of his pocket and took a picture. He didn't capture many scenes, but he intended to savor this one. Put it in a frame in his office.

Now, it was time to help the kid's mother heal.

He headed inside to see Peggy.

* * *

Peggy gave the paper shredder another kick. "You stupid piece of crap."

"Thank you," a smooth, velvet voice said from behind her.

She whirled around. "I wasn't talking to you. Yet."

"I know. I thought humor might help. It's not the shredder's fault it's jammed." He walked up until he was standing right in front of her—way too close for comfort, but she wasn't going to back away. She was spoiling for a fight. He'd do.

"What are you doing in here? Why aren't you mowing?"

He crossed his arms and gave her that patient look she was coming to know all too well, like he had all the time in the world. "I needed to talk to you."

"You should have knocked."

"I did. You probably couldn't hear me over the beating you were giving the shredder."

"I don't have time for you. Get mowing and get out!"

She tried to step around him, but he grabbed her arm gently. "Dustin and I found Keith crying by the shed."

"What?" She flung his hand off and stalked toward the door.

"Peg, he didn't want you to know. He might be little, but he's got his pride. Dustin and I talked to him. He's better now. See." He gestured to the window and pointed to where the boys were playing in the tree, shoes dangling from the lowest branch.

Somehow the sight of them choked her up. They looked so sweet together. She threw her arms out, the pressure spreading in her chest. "He shouldn't talk to you about this! He should talk to me. *I'm* his mother."

Mac ran his hand down her arm. "He knows you only use the paper shredder when you're upset."

"Shit. He knows—"

"Yes."

"I wanted to rip something apart, but it wouldn't be a good example if I tore into a chair."

Those stoplight green eyes crinkled at the corners. "I understand. I used to go to the driving range and smack the ball as hard as I could. I don't even like golf. Abbie scrubs the grout in the shower."

Her shoulders drooped. Still she wanted to bellow out, do some damage. *Damn* Frank for making Keith cry. "What did he say?"

Mac put his hand to his heart. "I won't divulge a boy's confidence. Deep down, I think you know."

"His dad is a total deadbeat asshole, and it breaks his heart."

"Like it does yours."

She sailed across the room. "He doesn't break my heart anymore, just his son's. And Keith's never done anything wrong."

"He does break your heart—every time he says no to your boy."

She had to blink back tears, so she turned away. Why did he have to see things so clearly? "So you won't tell me?"

"If he chooses to tell you, he will. Don't rush him. I know you find it hard to believe, but Dustin has a good heart. He understands what Keith is feeling. They...bonded today."

She fisted her hands, not sure how she felt about that.

"Sometimes it helps to know you're not the only one who's going through something."

She touched her aching throat. "You never told me—"

"Because you were too busy accusing me of beating up Dustin's dad in front of the whole town. I don't share the details—ever—but since I want you in my life, you might as well know the full story."

Her legs shook at his words. No, he couldn't tie her to him like this. "I need to do laundry."

"I never billed you for a chicken."

"Fine, but it won't change anything."

"Keep telling yourself that. Now, shut the door," he said, his voice all velvety soft with danger.

The shaking moved up her legs to her belly. She did as he asked.

He leaned against the desk, but even she caught the tense line of his body. "Abbie started going out with a college freshman when she was a high school senior. He took her to a frat party. She did some drinking, and he date raped her. She was a virgin. She didn't say anything, not even to me, but when she found out she was pregnant, she finally told me. I wanted to kill him. I went to his house. He told me that it hadn't been rape, that she was a total slut, and the kid could be anyone's. I went for him. You know the rest."

She'd heard similar stories as a police officer, but this time, it was like someone had burned a hole in her stomach with a cigarette. "Why did his family drop the charges against you?" she asked, her voice cracking.

He uncurled from his casual position like a panther poised to attack. "I threatened to press charges for rape. I knew we had no evidence, but they were a family of some notoriety. They didn't want a slur attached to their name or his. I told them we'd never ask for anything if they left us alone. They did."

"If he did that to her, he's done it to others. You should have pressed charges."

"Well, we didn't have any evidence, Deputy," his voice lashed out. "Besides, Abbie didn't want any reminder of what had happened, and we didn't have the money for a lawyer."

"The court would have provided one."

"Right," he scoffed. "They had a family attorney on retainer. They would have eaten us alive. I wasn't about to put her through that. Sometimes, despite what you believe, the law just isn't the right avenue."

The venom in his voice raised the hairs on her neck. She didn't want to argue with him. She studied the tense line of muscles visible through his simple forest green T-shirt. "I'm sorry."

He released an explosive breath. "Dustin doesn't know any of the details. We'll have to tell him soon, but it's not an easy thing to tell a kid."

She shook her head. "No. I can't imagine."

"He knows something's not right, but I don't think he knows it's this bad. It rips my guts out, thinking how much it will hurt him." He turned around and stared out the window.

She reached a hand out to massage the rigid line of his shoulders before she tucked it behind her back. She couldn't comfort him. That would be too...intimate. It would make them friends or something. She joined him by the window. The boys were sitting on the wide tree branch, talking. Even from this distance, Keith's face looked radiant.

"Dustin's surprisingly good with him."

Maven met her gaze. "Sometimes we connect with someone when we least expect it."

Since she was pretty sure he was talking about them, she looked away. "Are you going to tell me what your ex said?"

She kicked the shredder again. "Pretty much what he always says. That's why I'm so pissed. Why do I keep expecting he'll wake up and realize he has the best son in the world, who's waiting to shower him with everything he has?"

"Because you're smart, and—to quote Dustin—he's a fucker." He raised his hands as if expecting a slap-down for his language.

Her mouth turned up, but she fought the smile. "I can't keep doing this. It breaks Keith's heart every time."

"And yours when you have to lie to him again."

"I *hate* lying."

"I know." He leaned back against the window jam. "Do you remember what you said to me in my office after the stunt Dustin pulled?"

Her mind searched for the memory. The first one it found was when Mac had devoured her in his arms. She rubbed her arms briskly and re-wound her memory further. "I said a lot of things. What specifically?"

"When I asked you if you worried about him growing up without a father, you said you were more worried about how screwed up he'd be if his father *was* around."

She huffed out a laugh. "Funny. I forgot that today. I need to type it out and put it in my purse."

He pointed to her computer. "Have at it."

"I want to kill him."

"I get that."

And he did. Hadn't his story helped her understand him more? Her heart contracted. Uh-oh, she wasn't going to feel this...whatever this was—not with him.

"Abbie has to take Dustin to soccer practice in a little while. Why don't you let Keith come along? Might be good for him."

She could do some chores while he was gone. Kick the shredder some more. "She wouldn't mind?"

He shook his head. "No. Then you can come somewhere with me."

Her thighs clenched at the invitation in his velvety voice. "I don't *want* to go anywhere with you."

His smile grew until it stretched across his face. "I won't call you a liar, not to your face, anyway." He walked over and nudged the paper shredder. "I have a better idea for releasing your anger."

She crossed her arms. "How?"

"Let me show you."

"You're going to have to sell it better than that."

He tapped a finger to his lips. "Okay. That's fair. If I were to describe it, I'd say it safely combines one of your best skill sets with an awesome view. I promise you won't be disappointed. I'll bet you a new paper shredder you'll even have fun."

"Stop betting me!"

He took out his phone. "Can I call Abbie? I think Dustin would like spending some time with Keith too. We all need a little hero worship."

Her gaze darted to the window. "He looks up to Dustin?" She fought with her Protective Mommy Syndrome.

"Only on this dad thing. Don't worry."

"Okay, but this had better be good."

His eyes turned smoky, making her long for a fire extinguisher. "Oh, it will be, Peg. It will be."

"And stop calling me Peg!" she fumed, storming out of the office.

When she reached the hall, she glanced toward her bedroom, thinking about checking her appearance in the bathroom. Then she pulled her hair. It was like Jill had said. He made her feel like a girl.

Abbie's coping mechanism sounded appealing, so she headed into the bathroom to clean the tub, forcing herself not to glance in the mirror. The power of her emotions made her afraid to be alone with him.

She was out of control.

CHAPTER 23

When she told Keith he could go to Dustin's soccer practice, his face glowed like he was headed to Disneyworld. Maven didn't say anything, but she saw the smile on his face before he ducked his head.

After seeing them off, Maven opened the passenger side of his SUV and gestured her inside.

She shook her head. "I want to take my own car."

"There's no need." He patted the supple brown leather seat for emphasis.

"But then you'll have to take me all the way back here."

"It's no trouble," he informed her, leaning against the car now like he could wait her out.

They both knew she was stalling. The yard seemed quieter without Keith around. Goosebumps broke out on her arms. Since she was wearing a short-sleeved T-shirt, he could see them. Darn it. And that damn itch on her back was starting up again. She was allergic to him. That was it.

"Where are we going?"

"To a friend's."

The more she hesitated, the more relaxed he became. She walked forward. "You have friends?"

His mouth curved. "More than you know. This one has some equipment I think you might enjoy."

She stopped in front of him. Those slumberous eyes of his glowed in the summer light. "Why does that sound ominous?"

"I think you'll approve of his equipment."

"Is there a joke there?"

He closed the door when she finally jumped inside. "My friend would make one. Buckle up."

"I'm a cop. I always buckle up. And if you speed, I'll give you a ticket."

He turned up the music—rap, of course.

"I never speed with people in the car. Now, stop poking at me."

From what she could tell, he never did anything to put his family or anyone else in jeopardy. He was responsible...to a point.

She settled back and let the primal beat of the bass pulse and throb around her, trying not to notice how smooth the leather felt against the exposed skin where she'd cut her jeans above the knee. It made her think of how his hands felt on her, so she looked out the window to distract herself. The trees flashed bright green as he sped up the mountain road. She wondered where they were going. She'd seen him talking on his cell before they had taken off, laughing like he was demented. She wished she had her gun.

They turned onto a private drive. He gunned the engine to climb the rough road. Whoever lived here would have a bitch of a time getting out once the sky dropped a load of snow. The simple rustic log cabin appealed to her, but when he shut the car off, she gave him her best smirk.

"Why am I not surprised you have a *pied-à-terre?*"

He chuckled. "*Pied-à-terres* are usually in big cities, but I understand your meaning. You think I bring women here?"

The jolt of jealousy surprised her. Why hadn't she kept her mouth shut? "It's your business."

He came around to help her with the door—not that she needed it. He kept his hand on the side of the car, caging her in. "Since you brought it up, I'll *share* my business. Sharing is caring, after all." He studied her for a long moment, as if weighing what he wanted to say.

She squirmed. Oh, this wasn't going to be what she wanted to hear.

"There hasn't been anyone since I met you. I wasn't happy about that, but I've made my peace with it."

His meaning hit her like a slug in her police vest. "You've got to be kidding?" He was, right?

"You believe me deep down or your voice wouldn't squeak that way. You can analyze it later. Come on."

Without waiting for her, he walked up the porch steps. Opened the door. Who doesn't lock their doors? She followed, reeling from his confession. How did a guy like him go all those months...

She wouldn't think about it. Her hands and other parts were growing sweaty. She rubbed her palms against her jean shorts and jogged after him.

The house's interior was filled with the rich textures of leather and suede and burnished wood. The fireplace's stones looked like they'd been underwater a hundred years, as smooth as a baby's bottom. No photos or knickknacks were displayed.

"Who lives here?"

"Rhett's renting it, but don't worry, he's not around right now." Maven walked over to the bar and pulled out a bottle of sparkling water. "What would you like?"

"A Coke would be fine."

He handed it over. "Let's find your surprise."

She hung back, finding it eerie to be alone with him this way. She usually had a buffer. Her gaze fell to his rock-hard butt. God, she was losing it. Her muscles were locking up, thinking about all that hard sinew in his body. He wouldn't be a pushover in bed.

She shook her head to clear it. They passed through a mudroom where dirty hiking boots sat by the back door.

The view took her breath away. Perhaps it was the two bald eagles circling overhead. There was one lone tree in a small flat valley before the next mountain peak rose up in bold, thrusting points dotted with sage and evergreens and craggy, moss-covered rocks.

Maven walked over to a table and pointed. "Your surprise, my lady."

Her eyes took in three guns that had been laid out at precise angles—a Marakov PM Pistol 4.5 mm, a Beretta Elite II 9 mm, and a stunning Winchester 12 gauge shotgun inlaid with cherry wood and a silver insignia pattern.

"Rhett wasn't sure which one you'd like. He always carries a few."

She closed her mouth, certain she must look like some wacko fish in *Finding Nemo*.

"He said to tell you his permits are on his desk if you want to check."

"Huh?" Where was her sense? Her ability to think on her feet?

"He only has left-over beer bottles, but he said they're fun to shoot. He even said you could shoot the full bottles in the fridge if you're still pissed after you make it through the empties. But he draws the line at the pickle jar. That man loves dill pickles. He can eat a whole jar on a card break."

Her mouth opened again. If she didn't cut this out, she was going to inhale one of the bugs zipping along. It would be embarrassing to start gagging. Maybe he'd give her the Heimlich. She quaked at the thought of him pressed against her backside. Get a grip, Peg.

Maven gestured to the table set up a number of yards in the distance, which she somehow hadn't noticed. Sure enough, it held a combination of brown, green, and clear bottles. "He said he'll have someone clean it up, so you're not to worry about that. Just shoot them. He wants your stats. He said he'll join you sometime if you're any good."

She tried to say something, but only managed to sputter like a car backfiring.

His smile never left his face. "Why don't you set up? He only has enough ear protection for one, but he kept the ear plugs he didn't use in business class from Hong Kong, so I'll use those. I'll rustle up some snacks."

He headed into the house before she could find her voice. She shuffled forward, trying to take it all in. He'd set up a mini firing range just for her? Dear God, it might be the nicest thing anyone had ever done.

She picked up each gun, judging the weight. All were freshly cleaned.

Maven came back with a plate of apples, cheese, and grapes. "Rhett's not the healthiest eater, but whoever's been doing his shopping is hoping that will change."

He held out the tray like some waiter at a fancy party. She took a stem of grapes to be polite. Crunched on a few while he bit into an apple. She noticed he didn't throw the core out like she'd warned Keith not to do. He put it in a napkin like Mr. Responsible Nature himself.

Why did he keep surprising her?

"So, will his collection do? I had no idea what you'd like."

She felt him come up beside her, and they studied the view together. "Right. You hate guns." That made this whole surprise even more...

"Well, I knew you couldn't use your service weapon to vent, so this seemed like a good idea. Plus, you can't jam these as easily as your paper shredder."

She'd melt in a puddle at his feet if he didn't stop talking, so she secured her eye and ear protection. She picked up a gun because she didn't know what to say. Swiveled to see him stuffing in yellow ear plugs. He gave her the thumbs up.

She turned before she let loose some giddy grin. Brought the 9 mm up and fired six rounds straight, taking out six bottles from left to right in an explosion of glass.

Maven whistled. "Somehow I knew you'd hit everything," he yelled because of the earplugs.

"Did you make a bet with Rhett?" she yelled back.

He waggled those dark browns. "Sure did. It's what we do."

She picked up the shotgun. Each round took a few seconds longer to unload than it would from her service gun, but she liked the recoil. It made her plant her feet to prepare for the impact. The bottles blew to bits. Part of her enjoyed the destruction. The mommy inside *loved* not having to clean it up.

The pistol fit into her palm like it belonged there. She checked the chamber and sighted her remaining beer bottles. She decided to mix it up. Found her stance. Then she fired from right to left, blowing the bottles from the inside out like a metronome clicking back and forth.

She tore off the goggles and ear protection, wanting to dance in place. Her blood sang as it coursed through her body. Her skin soaked up the wind rushing down the canyon. The sunlight gave everything crystal clarity.

Maven walked to the target area. "You seem to be out of bottles. How about I hold this apple up by its stem? See if you can shoot it?"

Her head lurched back when he did exactly that. His body looked about as relaxed as she'd ever seen it.

"You're crazy! You really must trust me not to shoot you."

"You're a good shot. Plus, doesn't my willingness to do something like this prove how much I care about you?"

His words burned her throat like the gunpowder swirling in the air. Is that what he was doing? Proving himself?

She picked up the weapon and reloaded, watching him from heavy-lidded eyes. Surely, he would back down. Even her fellow officers wouldn't do something this nuts.

He didn't move a muscle. Simply kept smiling, saying nothing.

Well, hadn't he said enough already?

It hit her then. Smack between the eyes. He was waiting for her to make her move. Hadn't he showed her his hand?

Yearning rose within her, a long tortured cry starting at her toes and cruising up her body, gaining speed. She put the safety on and set the gun down. Her feet took a few steps toward him. His smile made her increase her pace until she was running. He threw the apple aside and opened his arms as she hurled herself against him.

"I should have called your bluff."

His hand caressed her cheek. "I still wouldn't have folded. This hand's too important." Then he lowered his head slowly, never taking his eyes off hers, and kissed her.

His gentleness had to stop, so she dug her hands into his hair. Devoured him with teeth and tongue.

She pulled her mouth away and grabbed his face. Looked into those liquid, green eyes. "I want you."

He anchored his hands on her face, fingers stroking her skin. "You remember what I said? It hasn't changed."

Her skin felt sunburned. Inside, her muscles coiled. Shifted. Waited.

She couldn't hold back anymore. She *had* to be with him. She didn't know where it would go, but she knew one thing.

She didn't want only one time with him either. He was right. It wouldn't be enough.

Her fingers caressed his lips. His jaw clenched. The insistent evidence of his desire pressed against her hips, and she angled her pelvis closer. His breath hissed out.

"Fine. We do it your way."

"Thank God." He picked her up like she weighed nothing and carried her into the house.

"You don't have to carry me."

"Don't protest about something silly. Save your energy."

The doorknob turned easily. He made a beeline for a long hallway. "We're not going to use Rhett's bedroom, but I think this one will do."

When he walked inside, she was aware of a tall slanted ceiling and Mission-style beams. Indian weavings hung on the wall in bold oranges and reds. He deposited her on the side of the bed and sat in front of her. Took her hand.

"I don't know how slow I can make this for the first time, but I promise I'll take care of you."

"Slow? Good God, no."

He grinned and cupped her neck, pulling her head closer. "You say that in horror. We'll deal with that later. Let me make love to you, Peg."

The intimacy of his voice made the first ripple of unease spread across her belly, but the jagged edge of desire overrode all thought. She fitted her mouth to his and dug her hands under his T-shirt, caressing his thickly corded chest until he pulled back and yanked the shirt off. She did the same, wanting contact, flesh against flesh, heat. He grabbed her hands when she went for her sports bra.

"Give me a minute to enjoy this."

She pushed him onto the bed and climbed on top. "No."

He grabbed her hips as she ground into him. "So that's how it's going to be."

Her head fell back. She grabbed his hands and put them to her breasts. "If you had any idea how long it's been..."

He flipped her, cutting her off. Tugged on the zipper to her shorts and swept them and her panties away. He lifted her and tugged off her sports bra. Threw it across the room.

When he leaned up, his eyes were all smoke and fire.

"I won't make you wait."

"*Thank you*," she breathed out.

His head lowered. He took her nipple in the sweetest, wettest suction of her life. A tortured moan tumbled out as pleasure surged through her body. His hand swept down her belly, lighting a trail of heat to her core. He parted her with his fingers and began to play. She bucked against him as he switched to her other breast, never breaking his rhythm. The tug, the pull, the flick of his thumb made her convulse, crying out in one long, agonizing refrain.

She panted, her hand over her forehead. He brushed it aside and kissed the side of her mouth. Forcing her eyes open, she almost did a double-take at the tenderness in his face.

"Better?"

A laugh huffed out. "Not really." It hadn't made much of a dent in the raging river inside her.

He pressed his fingers higher inside her, causing her to twist and moan. "I understand the feeling."

"Kiss me," she whispered and wove her hand through his hair when he settled that sweet mouth on hers.

His tongue thrust in time with his fingers. He gently bit on the corner of her mouth and tugged on another sensitive area. Feeling the build, she wanted to scream for the release she knew was right around the corner. He slid his other hand across her breast. Caressed the nipple. Then he pulled. She came again, moaning nonsense words, flushed with sweat, wanting.

"I can't take anymore," he ground out.

His hands left her. She felt him shift away. Her eyes popped open, fearing he was leaving. Instead, she got the best view of her life. Maven naked had to be the hottest sight she'd ever seen, and she'd busted plenty of naked people. He slid back over her body. Held up a packet.

"Do you want to put this on or should I?"

She grabbed it and tore it open. "This single mom thanks you for not making me wait."

He groaned as she rolled it over him. "Well...I didn't think I could stop you. Christ, Peg. Touch me."

His head fell forward until it rested against hers. His breath warmed her face. She gave him a few long, hard strokes before he grabbed her hands. "Enough." He caressed her cheek. "I need you."

He positioned himself over her, fingers caressing her collarbones. She wrapped her legs around him in a bow as he pressed forward, penetrating her slowly, watching her, always watching her. His gaze seemed to look inside her, so she closed her eyes. Focused on him entering her body. She bowed her head on the pillow at the sensation.

"Deeper."

He pulled her hips forward, impaling her to the quick. Her cry sounded tortured. When he propped himself his elbows, she waited for him to move. He didn't, so she opened her eyes. He was gazing at her with heated control and expectation.

"What?" she whispered.

"Say my name."

Her heart's rhythm stopped for a moment, out of sync with the pounding pulse in her body. "Don't stop." She realized it was a plea.

"Say my name," he insisted, his voice as deep and dark as the mountains at night.

The woman inside tore through the barriers she'd erected. She took his face in her hands. "Mac. Mac. Mac."

He pulled out and thrust into her in one hard lunge. Her head dug into the pillow as he fell into a take-no-prisoners rhythm. She gave him back everything she could, wanting to make it good for him. She caressed his back. Dug her fingers into his waist. Called out his name again. He pounded into her, breathing hard. The need for release built in them both. Her legs tightened when he thrust deep. She flew like a dancer across the stage, poised brilliantly in the air, defying gravity. When she landed, her body felt like a feather.

She was conscious of him thrusting in bursts and then freezing above her, calling out her name. Then he folded over her, wheezing in her ear. His hot sweaty skin burned her, but instead of pushing him away, she drew closer, wanting the heat.

Wanting him.

His hand ended up in her hair somehow, caressing her scalp. His chest heaved in time with hers.

Sweet mother of God.

He turned on his side, taking her with him. "Holy freaking Christ."

"My...thoughts...exactly." She tried to inhale deeply, but her lungs wouldn't cooperate.

With their faces inches apart, she saw his eyes crinkle. "Aren't you...glad we waited? I believe it...helped." His breath rushed in and out like a steam engine.

"What?" Were her ears buzzing?

His laugh sputtered out. "I'm usually...pretty quick to turnaround, but...you might have to give me a little time. God, Peg."

Yes, God, she thought to herself, trying to catch her breath. *This* was sex? What the hell had she been having all her life? It was like moving from the romper-room to a graduate program.

He took some deep breaths. Caressed her arm. Brought her hand to his lips. "I've got a pretty good imagination. This was better."

"This was..." What could she say? The best she'd ever had?

He nibbled on her fingers, which seemed ridiculous. "You were saying?"

The truth hit. She'd done it. She'd finally gone to bed with him. Why was it her infernal luck that it was this hot between them? "It was good."

His mouth tipped up. "I know you're not prone to over-dramatizations, so I'll let that piddly word go."

She tried to draw her hand away. "Shouldn't you..." She gestured to the bathroom across the room.

He kissed her full on the lips and then pulled away. "As you wish."

She spun into action when he cleared the door. Why didn't he close it? Somehow that action seemed more intimate than what they'd done. She dove for her shirt and had one arm through it when she heard a clucking sound. She looked over.

He stood in the door, all naked and relaxed. Her mouth went dry.

"I didn't take you for the do-and-dart type."

She usually wasn't. No one had ever made her want to run but him. "Ah...I have to fix Keith dinner."

"Abbie and Dustin are taking him out for pizza if that's all right."

He didn't move from his place. Home Depot would sell more doors if they had him model like that in an ad. She'd buy twenty if they came with a signed photo.

"I..."

"Rhett says there are steaks in the fridge. Why don't we cook some dinner? Then if you want, we can make love again."

Her voice wouldn't work. She pressed a hand to it and swallowed the thick lump in her throat. "You don't need to make me dinner. I can make something when I get home."

He finally uncurled and strode across the room. She'd admired his gracefulness before and wondered if it was his fancy clothes.

It wasn't.

He sat on the bed. "But then you would deprive me of your company, which is what I want."

She blinked. "You want my company?" No one had ever told her that before.

"Yes, I like talking to you. Being with you." He kissed her nose, which made her feel weird. "I can hear the wheels turning already. You did say you understood my position before we started this."

Her gaze dropped to her hands. She had. She simply hadn't realized how it would feel to be with him. Like she was out of control.

Worse, like she needed him.

Want was one thing. Need was another.

He tipped her chin up. "Don't hurt me by saying you've changed your mind."

She flung out her arms. "Why do you keep saying things like that to me? It's making it hard."

His face softened. "I realized that one of us would need to be vulnerable if we were going to have anything. I knew you weren't ready, so I volunteered."

She pulled the sheet over her breasts. "I don't like you saying those things to me."

"Why?"

That damn, patient gaze again. "I don't know. I just don't."

He rose and went to a closet. Shrugged into a robe. Pulled out a man's white, button-up shirt and extended it. "Well, perhaps that's something you should think about then. I'd like to hear something nice from you every now and again, but I don't require it. I know who I am."

She yanked on the shirt. "I'm not the gushing type."

"Bull," he uttered in the quietest voice she'd ever heard him use.

She shot off the bed. "Don't tell me you think you know me."

He belted his robe. "I know some, and I'd like to know more. I've seen how you are with Keith. I know how it feels to have tenderness for a child. That feeling starts to grow inside you, and then it can come out for anyone. *Who* is our choice. Mine seems to come out with you."

When he walked toward the door, she fisted her hands by her side. "I don't want yours to come out with me."

"Too bad. It already has."

The shakes started.

"Stay. It's only dinner, Peg. If you don't want to make love again tonight, we can wait until you do."

Her stomach clenched. She didn't want *that* to stop. Sex was all she thought she could manage, and even that...

"This is new territory for me." It was as honest as she could be.

He reached for her hand. Kissed her gently on the lips, like a boy giving his girl a first kiss in school. Her eyes grew wet, shaming her. When they were face to face, he caressed her cheek.

"It is for both of us. Come on."

He stroked her palm and led her out of the room. She looked back at the bed. The pillows were on the floor. Their clothes were scattered everywhere. It looked like they'd had an orgy.

Yet, the crushing pressure in her chest warring with the warmth in her heart made her know better.

They really had made love.

It might have been a first.

CHAPTER 24

Abbie was an unabashed soccer mom. Some people let loose on the dance floor. She let loose next to yards of white-lined grass and gaudy orange goals. She could yell and express herself here—it was all about supporting her son, right? The initial shocked looks from new parents always amused her. They must glance over, see the conservative Ann Taylor suit, and think, *Holy moly, someone's sure hiding something under her bushel basket.*

Mac teased her about it. Dustin's ears turned red a few times at the level of her enthusiasm, particularly as he grew older, but he'd never told her to quit.

"Come on, Dustin. Cut him off." She didn't yell, but since it was practice, her voice carried across the plush field.

"Wow. He's really good. Isn't he, Ms. Maven?"

Her little companion crunched on the granola bar she'd handed him from her well-stocked mini-cooler. Keith had the sweetness she'd always cherished in second graders when she used to volunteer at Dustin's school. He was starting to know his own mind, but he still liked to cuddle.

She put her arm around the boy. Mac had told her the story about how he and Dustin had found Keith crying behind the shed. It had broken her heart, and she'd teared up when Mac texted her a picture of the two boys sitting in a large oak tree hand in hand. Mac was right. They adored each other. It gave her a warm glow to see her son treat a younger boy so well.

She still didn't like Mac spending time alone with Peggy, but she wouldn't hold that against Keith. He was a sweetheart, and his warm little body curled into her like he'd known her forever. She loved the smell of a little boy who'd played outside. Their sweat seemed purer somehow, just like their motives.

Abbie understood kids. It was adults who sometimes baffled her.

Her gaze lifted to the scenic view above them. The mountains promised a gritty survival she appreciated. The wind could blow. The snow could dump. But they didn't bow or break. They stood tall. She wouldn't mind being a mountain.

Keith's feet bounced in time to music only he could hear. She crossed her legs and wiggled, hoping to get more comfortable. There was no doubt in her mind that metal bleachers had been invented by a man.

Dustin streaked ahead of the pack with the ball, dribbling with a precision honed from year-round Select Soccer Leagues and week-long camps.

"Go Dustin. Go!" she yelled as he cut off another player.

"Yeah! Make a goal, Dustin," Keith added, wiping melted chocolate on his T-shirt from the granola's chocolate chips.

She grabbed a wet wipe.

"Take your shot," a rough-and-tumble Southern voice boomed from the bottom of the bleachers.

Her fingers dropped the wipe in surprise. It fell through the metal slats to the ground.

Dustin shot forward, and kicked the ball. It sailed into the corner of the goal, so powerful the net popped back like a parachute before falling into place.

"Yes!" her son cried out and pumped his fist to the sky—his signature after-goal gesture.

She and Keith clapped together. "Good job, Dustin," she managed, but her attention had shifted to the man who was strolling up the bleachers toward them.

Rhett wore a simple white T-shirt accentuating his long, hard torso— oh heavens—and tight-fitted jeans with the tamest brown leather boots she'd ever seen on him. His cowboy hat was nowhere in sight.

"Awesome, Dustin!" he called over his shoulder.

Her son gave an enthusiastic wave. Rhett returned it.

Abbie grabbed her purse from the bench in front and put it by her side, trying to block him. Rhett grinned, shuffled down the narrow riser, picked up her handbag and returned it to its spot. He sat down, nudging her with his thigh.

Her gaze remained on the field. Where was her self-control?

From her peripheral vision, she saw his gaze crest over her face like he was admiring a painting's many angles.

"Hey, Abigail."

His intimate tone made her bite the side of her cheek. "Rhett." Her voice was as stiff as her back. "I thought you'd be hanging out with Rye and Co."

"They took off last night. I'm sure I'll see them again soon now that I'm back stateside." He bumped her as he reached across her. "Now, who's this little fella?"

Keith responded to Rhett like he did everyone. He grinned.

"I'm Keith. My mom's Deputy Peggy McBride. Who are you?"

Rhett shook his hand, still leaning close enough to brush his arm over the rise of her breasts. Her insides curled up like paper in a fire. She elbowed him. Hard. He grunted and then did it again.

"I'm Rhett Butler Blaylock, a family friend. I play poker like Mac."

She inhaled his infernal cologne—something she used to smell when she missed him, even when he was halfway around the world. The woodsy musk hinted at sex and fun and a little rebellion too. Hadn't she picked this one out for him? She'd thought the name, Narciso Rodriguez Limited Edition, both funny and ironic. Who was more narcissistic than Rhett? He'd laughed, but his mouth had tightened a millimeter. Still, she hadn't stopped him from buying it. When had she become so cruel?

Keith bopped up and down in his seat. "Do you win a lot? My Uncle Tanner says you need nerves of steel to play like it's a real job. Steel's really hard, you know. My mom's got nerves of steel."

"I've met her. She's a lovely woman. You're lucky to have her as your mama."

"Uh-huh," her little companion agreed.

"So how did you come to join our little outing today?"

"My mom got upset. Mr. Maven said he was going to cheer her up. She broke our paper shredder today."

"So I heard. He took her over to my house. We set up something fun for her."

Abbie waited for him to fill her in. So, he was in on this thing with Mac? Why wasn't she surprised? She frowned. She might not like the idea of him getting involved with that woman, but it was his business. If it hurt her and Dustin again, she would interfere, but only then.

"What did you set up?" Keith asked.

"Well, you can ask your mom when she gets home. It's a secret. Do you like secrets?"

He shook his head. "We don't like secrets in my house. Mom says."

Rhett dramatically clapped his hand to his heart. "Crushed to the quick."

"It's *cut* to the quick," she corrected.

He winked.

Keith giggled. "We like surprises though."

"A much better word. Give me a high five."

Their palms met in front of her, so different in size she was amazed they connected.

"I'm not so fond of secrets myself," Rhett bandied back to the boy. "Your mama's a wise woman."

Score a dig for Rhett. She stared at the field, wishing the boys would finish sucking their oranges and start playing again. A distraction would make it easier to ignore him. And, God she needed to ignore him.

"Aren't you going to ask what I'm doing here?" Rhett inquired.

She narrowed her eyes, wishing for sunny skies. Her sunglasses would be on, making it harder for him to study her. "I figure Dustin must have told you about practice."

"You figured right." He pulled a bag of sunflower seeds from his pocket—a Rhett staple—and offered her some.

"No thanks."

"Keith?"

"Sure, but I like the other ones better. You can spit the hard parts on the grass, and no one gets mad. It was kinda hard at first, but I figured it out."

Rhett chuckled in that dirty way of his, sending shivers down her spine.

"I like those too, but Abbie here isn't too fond of men spitting, so I brought the clean kind." Then he had the audacity to wink again.

He darn well knew she didn't like it since she sucked at spitting. He'd tried to teach her how to eat the shelled seeds one time, but she hadn't taken to it. He'd laughed like a loon when she got an icky glob on one of her white sandals. After wiping it off, she'd joined him. Then he'd kissed her senseless and thrown her over his shoulder. She stopped the memory in its tracks.

Keith eyed her with a new regard—like she was some clean-freak mommy type—which she was. She gave Rhett another elbow in the ribs since he continued to lean across her, knotting her stomach.

He grabbed her elbow with his hand and tickled her. She emitted a high-pitched giggle, rising a foot off her seat.

His snicker carried across the field.

She yanked her arm away.

Keith's eyes widened. "Are you okay, Ms. Maven?"

The other parents who'd stayed for practice looked over.

"I'm fine," she replied primly, crossing her arms.

Rhett poked her under her ribs. She giggled again and dug her feet into the metal slab beneath her so she wouldn't jump.

"Stop it," she hissed under her breath.

His infernal grin made her heart pound in her ears. "I can't help it. I love to hear you laugh. Missed it. Doesn't she have a great laugh, Keith?"

The poor kid simply nodded, probably wondering what the heck was going on. "Are you ticklish, Ms. Maven?"

"As the day is long, son," Rhett replied.

His deep voice held a touch of longing, igniting a memory of how much he'd loved tickling her when they were in bed together, making her scream with laughter. Later, she would scream for another reason—usually his hot, pumping body taking her places she'd never imagined could exist for someone like her. She'd thought she was frigid...until Rhett. Part of her missed her ignorance. The other part craved to be let out of her cage.

"My mom likes to tickle me. I have to be careful 'cause sometimes my legs kick. I don't want to hurt her."

Abbie ruffled his hair. "You're a sweet boy. *Some* people could learn from you." She glared over at Rhett, whose shoulders lifted with his hushed chuckle.

Keith swung his feet back and forth. "Are they going to start up again soon?"

"Pretty soon," she replied.

They came back onto the field all juiced up. Dustin took his position as a forward. His teammate kicked off mid-field, and everyone started the dance. The ball bounded down the sidelines. Someone stopped it with their foot. Then it flew across the field again. She considered soccer a kind of poetry. There was a beat and cadence to it, a majesty beyond each individual's actions.

Rhett didn't talk to her. He simply handed over the bag of sunflower seeds periodically so Keith could grab more.

"Come on, Dustin," she cried out when someone kicked him in the shins, digging for the ball.

"Yeah, come on, Dustin," Keith mimed.

God, she missed this age. She remembered how Dustin used to parrot her like that. Follow her around. Ask her opinion. He needed to be his own man, but she was still afraid he wouldn't turn out okay without her help.

"He's a good boy, Abbie," Rhett murmured. "There's so much to be proud of. You've done a great job."

She gripped her knees. He'd always had the ability to read her thoughts, anticipate her needs. For someone who wasn't used to sharing her feelings, he'd short-circuited a major stumbling block between them. He simply knew. Damn his poker player's instincts.

Hadn't that scared her to death?

Worse, he'd wanted to give to her, whatever she'd ever wanted or needed.

She hadn't known what to do about it then. She still didn't.

"Kick it, Dustin!" Rhett yelled.

She watched his hands under her lashes. He'd told her he wouldn't touch her until she asked. God, how much more could she take?

"You have any water?" Rhett asked. "These seeds are pretty salty."

She gestured to the small cooler. He pulled out a bottle, and she watched him from the corner of her eye as he threw back his head and guzzled the whole thing down. His throat moved, all corded and strong.

"So," Rhett said when he was finished. "Are you eating anywhere special tonight?"

"We're going out for pizza," Keith supplied, bouncing in his seat. "It's so cool."

"Mind if I come along?"

Keith looked at her. "You need to ask Ms. Maven, but I'd like it if you came."

He'd boxed her in nicely. She gave him the fakest smile she could muster. "Sure."

He settled back on the bleachers, crossing his ankles on top of the bench in front of them and putting his arms behind his head. The full-on stretch made her body sizzle. She picked up the cooler and dropped it in his crotch before he could move.

"Whoa!" he cried out, grabbing it and setting it down on the bottom slat. "Careful there, Abs. That's special merchandise."

She narrowed her eyes at his use of his intimate nickname for her. "It can be replaced."

His face clenched for a second. She felt bad for hurting him, but she looked away quickly so she wouldn't apologize.

She couldn't give ground. If she started, she'd never stop.

He leaned forward. "Keith? How do you feel about replacing things? I have this old shirt from when I first visited Ole Miss University. It's down south in my home state of Mississippi."

"I can spell Mississippi."

"Show me."

He recited the letters like a spelling bee champion. Rhett gave him a high-five.

"That's pretty good. So, back to my story. I was about Dustin's age when my mama bought me a Rebel T-shirt. That's their mascot," he told an eagerly-listening Keith. "I wore it everywhere. Even until I popped a seam in the shoulder playing softball. But I kept it. It's a bit tight now, but I still wear it sometimes."

Her throat grew hot and dry, so she reached for a water bottle.

He beat her to it. "Let me."

He uncapped it. Cleaned off the condensation by rubbing it against his T-shirt. She stared at the wet spots. Couldn't miss the six-pack under the thin cotton. He reached for her hand and fit it into her palm with slow deliberation. His touch burned—everywhere.

Her throat squeezed, and the urge to cry swept through her. She wanted to reach for him so badly, she locked her hands under her ribs.

"Come on, Keith. Let's get closer to the field." Rhett scooped him up and then transferred him to a piggy-back hold. Keith's smile could have powered a generator.

"Are you coming, Ms. Maven?"

Rhett wiggled like a worm, making Keith giggle and grab his shoulders. "Nah. We'll give her a minute. She knows we'll be back."

His face was expressionless.

She couldn't swallow the water she'd just sipped.

He jogged down the stairs, making Keith squeal, and then bucked like a horse—something he'd done when Dustin was little.

She caressed her throat and somehow managed not to choke.

Dustin dashed to the sidelines for a moment to greet the newcomer, his face beaming as they one-arm hugged.

There was just something about Rhett.

There always had been. She was desperately afraid there always would be.

He gave her space, pushed her to the limit, and then backed off again. The pattern denoted his strategic genius. Keith cheered from his back, making her wonder if Rhett's ears were ringing. He didn't seem to mind. The two talked like old friends.

To an observer, they could be father and son, rooting for an older brother. Without his usual get-up, Rhett looked like a dad. A really hot dad—someone the other girls would swoon over. A few people might mistake them for a family.

Her breath hitched. She reached for her inhaler. Her asthma didn't bother her often, but Rhett seemed to aggravate it by his sheer presence.

She tucked it away and looked back at the field. He was looking at her from over his shoulder, his mouth grim.

When practice ended, Dustin's teammates patted him on the back. Others hung back and talked to him. Good, he was making friends. With school a couple of months away, this was the best place to start. She prayed they would be good friends. God knows he needed them.

When the last boy took off, Dustin jogged back over to Rhett and gave him a bear hug, making Keith laugh. Rhett set the younger boy down and turned his back to Dustin like he was offering to give him a piggyback. Dustin slapped him away, laughing, but Rhett craned his head and gestured to his back again. Her son finally leapt on.

Rhett always had a physical way of showing his affection. Her palms itched, wanting to be the recipient of all that intensity and care. As he raced around with Dustin on his back, Keith ran alongside them. They were cheering something. She cocked her ear.

She knew the cadence before she picked up the words of the Ole Miss cheer, *Hotty Toddy*. She frowned. It wasn't appropriate for Keith, but that hadn't stopped Rhett from teaching it to Dustin years ago on a cool fall Saturday during a football game. Since he sang it frequently, she knew it by heart too—especially since he'd made her sing it to him in bed wearing his old Eli Manning jersey with Number 10 in bold white. Her face flamed. He'd called her Hotty Toddy as he'd licked his way up her belly.

Are you ready?
Hell yes! Damn Right!
Hotty Toddy, Gosh almighty
Who the hell are we, Hey!
Flim Flam, Bim Bam
Ole Miss By Damn!

Rhett pretended to be a fly-by-the-seat-of-his-pants kind of guy, but she knew he was methodical. Diabolical.

He was sending her a message.

Was she ready?

Hell no!

CHAPTER 25

Mac busied himself preparing the steaks while Peggy settled herself on a bar stool at the kitchen counter. She fussed with the shirt's hem. It cruised just below her knees, highlighting her strong, supple calves. He'd have to explore those legs later.

There was a lot to explore.

And she was already putting up walls.

His hand clenched around the package as he tore off the cling-wrap. Why did he feel this resentment over her resistance? Had he thought she'd simply fall at his feet once they made love? Who was he kidding? He knew she'd be as prickly as ever. Patience was a must.

He'd told her the truth. If he hadn't put himself out there, nothing would have happened. He could carry the water for a while. Someday she'd want to help. He was counting on her loving nature. She had it—all you had to do was see her with Keith to know that. She simply wasn't used to sharing it with others. Hadn't he seen her reluctance with Tanner and the Hales? How long was he going to have to wait until she called him Mac again? Her hushed cry had been the sweetest music to his ears.

"So, do you have any more information about the bomb threat now that you've offered the reward?" she asked, fingers pulling down the shirt modestly.

He gave the steaks a good whack with a wooden spoon, more out of frustration than a need to tenderize them. "Peg, we are not going to have any shop talk when we're together."

"But—"

"You've made it clear that you don't want to be seen in public with me. Yet. This is my rule. I want to keep our professional and personal interactions separate. I'll treat you like the deputy sheriff when you're on duty, but when you're with me, I only want to be with *you.*"

She hiked up her shoulder. "That's weird."

"Whatever." He rubbed the steaks with some olive oil and salt and pepper. "So, now that I've seen what a regular Annie Oakley you are, I'm curious. How old were you when you first fired a gun?"

Her hands smoothed her shirt down again. She gave him another pained look, a please-don't-expect-me-to-talk look.

He pointed to the salad mixings in front of her. "Can you slice the vegetables?"

That wary expression again. "Ah...sure."

He used a serrated knife to slice the bread for bruschetta. "You were saying?"

She cut a tomato in half. "Umm... I was seventeen."

He ground his teeth. Never let anyone say Peggy's mouth got away with her. "That's pretty young. Did Tanner show you?"

She shook her head, cutting the cucumber into precise circles. "No. I was dating a boy who really liked the outdoors. He took me hunting. I didn't like killing animals, but he let me shoot his gun. I didn't kill anything—which I was grateful for—but I liked how it felt."

"It made you feel powerful."

"Yes, how did you know?"

He brought a bowl over by her and sat down. "It's a common lure. So did you decide to become a cop that day?"

Her carrot cutting displayed the precision of a julienne. "I don't know when it came to me."

He didn't believe her for a minute, but he didn't call her out on it.

"So, were you one of the best shots in the academy?"

Her mouth curved as she threw the carrots in the bowl he'd provided. "You're not the first to call me Annie Oakley."

"Ever think about going blond?"

Her fingers tentatively brushed her short hair. "No."

"Good. I like brunettes." He kissed her square on the mouth. Her frame tensed up like she wasn't used to being touched. Well, that could be changed.

"So why do you hate guns so much?" Her voice held an edge.

"I'll bet you think some guy I was playing cards with pulled one on me, right?"

She lifted a shoulder, making the shirt peek open. The view distracted him from dicing the green olives Rhett always kept for dirty martinis.

"Well, you're close. I was coming out of a two-day poker game at a casino when I heard some shots near the blackjack tables. The shooter was ten yards away. I'd never seen anyone that crazed before, not even my old man after he'd lost a stack and spent the night drinking. There was a pregnant woman nearby. I remember looking at her. She'd put her hands around her belly. I wondered if she realized what she was doing. Not every parent's first instinct is to protect their child. My parents never had it."

A cucumber rolled when she stopped cutting it.

"I'd talked my old man down a few times when he was in a state. So I held out my hands to this guy and walked toward him. Asked what his name was. Got him talking. It all worked out."

Peggy laid her knife aside. "When was this?"

"About ten years ago."

She snapped her fingers. "In Vegas, right?"

His neck prickled. Damn, he hadn't thought she'd make the connection. "Yes."

"I remember that. Now, who's holding back? *It all worked out.* Right. I seem to remember some famous poker player offering himself up as a hostage. They had pictures in the paper of the perp walking out with a gun to your head. You put him in your car and let him go."

Yes, and he'd thrown up in the bathroom after the police finished questioning him. "And you probably think I was in the wrong for offering up my car. Well, he didn't clear the drive before the cops surrounded him."

"No, it was brilliant." She wagged a celery stalk at him. "After he drove off, you got everyone inside. Saved countless lives."

"He only had four more bullets in the chamber." Not that he'd known that at the time.

"Which he could have emptied into you! I can't believe that didn't come up..."

A smile tugged at his lips. "When you ran me?"

She narrowed those delicious brown eyes. "Of course I ran you. Duh!"

He puffed out his chest playfully. "It probably moved down the search engine after all my championship wins."

She chewed on her lip, making him want to kiss her.

"You didn't mention this during the town meeting when you were trying to obtain the city council's permission for your hotel. You would have been a shoe-in with that story."

"I like to let my work speak for itself."

"Most people would use a heroic gesture like that to pave their way."

"I'm not 'most.'" He bumped her playfully. "So, did you find anything else interesting?"

Her fist punched him in the shoulder, delighting him. "I know you sometimes have a penchant to be Speedy Gonzales with your cars."

Ah, his favorite. *"Hello, pussy cats! You looking for a nice fat mouse for deenner?"* he said in his best imitation.

Her laughter swept through the kitchen like the sound of wind chimes. "Hey, that's pretty good."

"I watched Looney Tunes with Dustin when he was growing up. I can do all the voices. He used to beg me."

He watched in sheer fascination as her luscious mouth curved into a genuine smile. "Who else can you do?"

"Who's your favorite character?"

Her thumb stroked her chin. "Foghorn Leghorn."

Foghorn seemed too silly for her. "You like the chicken? Why does that surprise me? Well, Rhett does a Southern accent better than I can, but let's see what you think of my rendition. *Well, now, ah, well, now that woman's about as cold as a nudist on an iceberg.*"

Her laughter blew out again. "He did *not* say that."

His own laughter surfaced. "He did so. I remember because I had to explain what a nudist was to Dustin. He was six."

"Did you tell him the truth?"

Did she know her eyes sparkled when she laughed? Now that he did, he planned on seeing it again and again. "I always tell him the truth, or as close as I can get. I hate lying."

Her lids fluttered down.

"Something we have in common," he supplied since he knew she was thinking it. "Dustin's response was priceless. He simply *couldn't* understand why anyone would want to run around outside naked for fear of ticks, bug bites, bee stings, and sunburn. And detention would be the worst part about it, he said. Apparently another boy was given detention when he streaked down the hall after gym class, making the girls scream bloody murder. He was so serious I had to bite my lip to keep from losing it."

Her shoulders shook. "Keith does the same thing. He came home after learning about Native Americans and said he'd rather be shot by an arrow than a bullet. When I asked why, he put his hands on his hip like I was the dumbest person alive and informed me in his haughtiest tone possible that you could pull an arrow out with your *hand*. You didn't have to have surgery. I nodded, went into the laundry room, and pressed my face into the ironing board so he wouldn't hear me laughing."

"Dustin would die if he knew I was telling you this."

"Keith's not usually embarrassed, but he has his moments."

They talked about the boys, sharing stories, making each other laugh. Her guard lowered, giving him a glimpse of what he'd always guessed was inside—a fun, warm, loving woman. His heart sputtered as he put the steaks on the grill. She was working beside him, tossing the salad and topping the bruschetta.

Mac talked her into opening a bottle of red wine and tucked her close when she brought it to him. He felt her tense and then relax into his embrace.

She held the plates while he dished out the food. And then he sat back and savored the sheer pleasure of eating a meal with her while she was in a man's shirt.

When they loaded the last dish into the dishwasher, he came up behind her. Took the wine glass from her hand and tugged her into his arms. Took her mouth in a slow, sweet kiss. Let her tell him if she wanted to take it any further.

Her body curled around him, and she opened her mouth to him.

In that instant, his heart lay on the floor.

He picked her up again. Muffled her protests.

When he laid her on the bed, he slowly undid the buttons. Smoothed the shirt open.

"I forgot to say it before." His fingers caressed her breast. "You're beautiful."

Her eyes widened. "You don't have to say that."

He shrugged off his robe and slid over her, letting their skin start a fire. "Don't tell me not to tell the truth."

Her mouth pinched, but she didn't argue, so he put his mouth to hers and kissed her self-doubt away. Touched her until she threw her head back. Let his hands find all the secret places he hadn't discovered the first time.

When she called out his first name, he lost the battle for control. God, it felt incredible not to have to beg her to say it. He slid into her. Pressed his brow to hers when her hips lifted to meet his first thrust. Her breath panted against his mouth as he took them higher, went even deeper. When she convulsed again in his arms, he linked their hands and let go, filled with a new peace, knowing they'd traveled somewhere uncharted tonight.

Her muscles tensed again when he tugged her onto his chest to hold her, but only for a millisecond. Her fingers traced his skin softly. He brought her hand to his lips and kissed it. She buried her face against his shoulder. When she rose to dress, he let her go.

"When are we going to see each other again?" he asked, pulling on his T-shirt.

She smoothed her mussed hair down. "Ah...we'll have to see."

Oh, the walls were going up again. "How about we go to Brasserie Dare Friday night instead of what we'd planned? I like supporting Brian, and there's no better place in town."

Her spine went curtain-rod straight. His guts spilled out.

"I'm still not...ready to make this public."

"Are you ashamed of me?" he made himself ask.

Her throat moved when she swallowed. "No...I...you have to understand. I went against you about the hotel. Being seen together undermines what I did."

He could feel himself shutting down. "And you're not finished trying, is that right?"

Her hands dug into her pockets. "Stop. It's just that we don't know how long this is going to last. I have a son to consider. I'm willing to see you, but let's be discreet. I'm surprised you're not more concerned about your reputation."

Not when it came to his love life. "I don't give a damn what other people think."

"Well, good for you, but I'm an officer of the law in this community—and a woman—which isn't the easiest combination. Plus, I don't want to raise Keith's hopes. He really likes you."

He turned away, fighting with himself. He understood how she felt, even if he didn't agree.

"How long?"

Her shoulder lifted. "Ah...six months—if we make it that long."

"No way I'm waiting until Christmas. I'll do three, but no more." Dammit, they were going to make it that long and more.

"But you—"

"We need to compromise here, Peg. I can't hide what's between us that long. I won't have any shame here. That's final."

She leaned down and tied her shoelaces. "Fine. I don't have men spend the night at my house."

Even though he wanted to strangle her, his mouth tipped up. "Me neither."

Her brow rose.

"Women, I mean. I use the hotel."

"I can't go there."

"I know. I'll talk to Rhett. See if we can come here. Is this secluded enough for you?"

The mockery in his voice made her frown. "So, we're to have a *pied-à-terre* after all?"

"Don't say it like that. You want things this way. I don't."

He turned away, sick at heart, wondering if that's how Rhett had felt when Abbie had chosen to keep their relationship hidden. Funny how he'd gotten boxed into the same corner as his friend—in his house too. "Come on. I'll take you home."

He jolted when she pressed her face into his back. When her hands slid around his chest, his heart flipped over like a pancake. He covered them with his own.

"I'm doing the best I can," she whispered.

The plea couldn't be missed. "I know you are, but there's more inside you."

When she stepped away, he reached for the car keys. She walked forward until they were face to face. "Kiss me before we go."

"Ah, Christ, how am I supposed to fight against that?"

No response came. He hadn't expected one.

He kissed her until they were both senseless and then took her hand. Led her to the car. When he buckled her into her seatbelt, another hard kiss communicated his intent.

"Friday night. Just you and me. Find a sitter. Or I will."

Then he walked around the hood and took her home, the growing silence making the afternoon feel like a dream.

CHAPTER 26

The next morning he called her, which was baffling. When she told him she didn't need the reassurance, he laughed and told her perhaps he did.

In a pig's eye, she said and hung up.

Still, he called or texted her every day until Friday.

She didn't understand it.

Deep down, the emerging woman thought it was sweet and counted down the days until she would see him again.

The day finally dawned. As she swung the car up Tanner's driveway, Keith kept his hand poised on the door handle, practically vibrating with excitement. Nothing beat free babysitting—especially when the babysitter was your responsible older brother. The minute she stopped the car, Keith made a break for it. He whooped and hollered all the way up the stairs. She left the car more slowly, smiling as she watched him greet Meredith and Tanner with hugs.

"How about some ice cream?" Meredith asked.

"Awesome. You still have chocolate brownie crunch?"

"Yep."

"I'll see you in a minute, man," Tanner called as the two of them went inside.

When her brother came down the porch and crossed his arms, she scowled. She hadn't told him where she was going, but he knew. Her back started to itch again. "Thanks for doing this."

"Do you know what you're doing?"

His directness shot her in the gut. "I don't know what you mean."

"You don't go out ever, and even I can see the spring in your step, which Jill calls the Sex Spring—dear God—so I have to ask. I know it's Mac. Again, do you—"

"Stop." She snarled. Great. Jill knew. That meant everyone probably did. She'd lay down the law later. "Yes. No. Not really."

Now his mouth formed a scowl. "Good, I'm glad you're sure."

Her hand was on his arm before she realized it. "I don't want things to be weird, between us or between you and Maven. I know he's a friend."

When she snatched her hand back, he took her shoulder in a gentle grip. "You're my sister. Besides, I've already told him what will happen if he hurts you."

She gaped at him. "You did?"

"You may be a better shot than I am, but I know more devious ways of making a man suffer."

"I'll let you know if I need to call in the special forces, but so far it's been...civil."

She almost had to laugh at her own choice of words. Try hot, steaming...

His foot kicked the gravel. "Civil? Okay, I won't ask for a definition there. Are you sure you don't want Keith to spend the night?"

It seemed wise to suppress a squirm. Maven hadn't asked, but it was only a matter of time before he did. Staying over would be...strange. She didn't want to think about trying to fall asleep with him, listening to his breathing, feeling his arms around her. Relaxation would be impossible. Falling asleep next to a cop on stakeout was easier. Plus, she wasn't ready to make this into something more—even if it was.

"I can tell by your body language that that would be a no. Be back by eleven, or I'll have to ground you."

Walking away, memories of being a teenager surfaced. "Okay. Don't wait up."

She knew he would...he always had.

"Wait a minute. I need to tell you something."

She turned around slowly. "From the look on your face, I can tell I'm not going to like it."

His fingers dug into his temple. "Hell, I'm not sure I like it."

Uh-oh. "Give."

"David's making firmer plans about his visit, but he's not bringing his family. He wants to come up for Labor Day weekend."

"Does he really think he can just show up and say he's sorry for everything? Our brother needs to find a clue."

His face softened. "I said I'd check if you were open to seeing him. He understands if you're not ready."

She didn't think she'd ever be ready to see him again, not when he seemed intent on ruining his life over and over again. Just like their father. "I can't believe Mom hasn't called me yet."

"David told her not to. He's standing on his own, working on being a good husband, father, and city councilman."

"He's done this whole song and dance before."

Tanner's sigh carried across the yard. "I don't want to debate David's choices with you. Just think about it, okay? He's family."

She fidgeted and confessed her deepest fear. "I don't know if I want him around Keith, okay?"

"I know, Peg, but it's not like he's going to offer your son a drink."

"Jeez, that's—"

"The truth. Deal with it. Now I need to go inside and play with my nephew. Have fun with Mac."

"Right." Fun. That wasn't what she'd call it.

She yanked open the car door hard, pissed that David's plans had stirred her up this way. She knew it was part of the AA program, but why did he have to make amends in person? Why couldn't he send a greeting card inscribed *Regrets on Being an Asshole with a Capital A, Thinking of You.*

She flicked the windshield wipers on by accident when she tried to turn on the lights. Great, now she couldn't operate a vehicle properly. She yanked her mind back to what awaited her at Rhett's cabin. Her body turned all hot and tense as she imagined Maven's hands on her. She eyed the speedometer. Thought about speeding. Ratcheted it down. He was *not* going to make her break her rules.

He was waiting for her on the porch. Not doing anything. Just waiting. The sight of him there wrenched her heart, but some weird peace descended as she walked toward him.

His navy T-shirt and khaki cargo shorts gave him a relaxed look. He cupped her face and kissed her on the mouth before she could blink.

"Hi," he said, easing back slowly. "I've been looking forward to this moment all day."

She glanced at her watch to break his intense eye contact. "I'm not late, am I?"

His hand covered hers, shooting fireworks up her arm.

"No, I just missed you."

What could she say? He'd glued her mouth shut with that comment. They went inside and headed into the kitchen.

Her fingers drummed on the kitchen island as he opened the refrigerator. There was pasta bubbling in a pot on the stove, a blood-red tomato sauce with sausage on the front burner. Funny, she'd expected take-out, not a home-cooked meal.

"Ah, where did you learn to cook? And where the heck is Rhett?"

He smiled and brought out a bottle of wine. "Abbie's been a good teacher. And as for Rhett, he's hanging out at the hotel, playing poker likely. I gave him use of the family suite since he's been so generous with this place. Tell me about your day."

Tell him about her day? He might as well be speaking a foreign language. "There wasn't much to it. Any news about the bomb threat?" His head of security, Aaron, had been keeping her well informed, so she didn't really need to ask, but it was something to talk about.

He shook his finger at her. "You know the rule. No work talk."

"But you asked me about my day. That's work stuff."

His level stare made her squirm. "You know what I mean. Let me show you how it's done." He told her about his day as he brought the meal together. The spicy scent of garlic made her mouth water. Poker didn't come up once, she noted, and neither did the whole bomb threat thing.

He fed her a few bites of his meal from his fork. She tried to smile even though it felt weird. When they were through, he insisted on cleaning up while she waited, so she sat there fiddling with her wine stem. A healthy stream of lust shot through her as she watched him do the dishes. Funny how she'd had the same reaction when he'd helped around her yard with Dustin. Clearly, she liked a man who could do chores. She could see the calendar now. Hot hunks vacuuming in their underwear or doing the dishes in leather thongs.

She shook her head and fanned herself.

"Come on," he finally called after drying the last pan.

He led her into the living room where there was a mammoth flat-screen TV as large as a VW bug. Following, she pulled on her T-shirt's hem. When were they going to *get to it* already? She was so hot she might detonate like some bomb.

"What kind of movies do you like?" An on-demand site popped onto the screen when he hit one of the remote's many buttons. "With a sister and a teenager in the house, I'm used to sitting through pretty much anything. I've watched *Beaches* three times. I never cried, even though Abbie swears she saw a tear once. And I've seen *Puss in Boots* seven times—not the whole way through, thank God. I thought about shooting myself every time, but family's family."

Her mouth might as well have dropped to the floor. "We're watching *a movie?*"

He set aside the remote. "Yeah. I thought it would be a nice way to spend the evening."

"Are you serious?"

"Yes. I thought we could do something normal."

Her hand gestured to their fancy surroundings. "This isn't normal."

"Bull. You just don't think you can do 'normal' with me. I told you this wouldn't just be about sex."

She was sure a steady glare would drive her point home. "I thought it would at least be on the menu."

He slid off his shoes and stretched out on the couch. "Did you think I planned to watch the whole movie? I was hoping to eat way too much popcorn and then put my hands on you."

"Oh." Give her the idiot prize.

"Is that all right with you?"

"Why don't we skip the movie then?" Her hip bumped the couch, an invitation.

"Because I want popcorn. Have you ever wondered what it is about the stuff? Even the smell makes me crave it."

Were they really discussing popcorn?

"I hope you like it with butter. I can't make love to you unless you like butter on your popcorn."

She glared at him like he was a suspect she couldn't get a read on—or one who was high on something. "What is wrong with you?"

His arms stretched out. "I'm letting you see how I really am. Did you think I was a serious businessman and poker player all the time? This is pretty much me—making dinner, hanging out, watching a movie. It's how I like to enjoy myself."

Telling him he was weird wouldn't be nice. "You're nothing like I thought."

Those stoplight green eyes never left her face. "Is that a good thing or a bad thing?"

"I don't know." And that was the God's honest truth.

"At least you're honest," he said with a small smile. "Now, my turn. You don't seem to trust me any more now than you ever have. You're as passionate in bed as I expected, but intimacy bothers you. We'll work on it. You're not comfortable with casual conversation because you feel like someone's going to use it against you. I'm not a suspect who's trying to pull one over on you, Peg. I'm looking for the woman who makes goofy faces with her son, like in those photos on your refrigerator."

Her face heated. "That was...an off day."

His hand patted the seat beside him. "I don't think so. You need to let your hair down a little. Relax. It's something else we can work on."

Beaning him with the paperback on Rhett's table sounded like a better idea. "I don't want to work on anything with you."

"Relaxation is a key component of good sex."

An eye-roll seemed appropriate. "Thank you, Dr. Ruth."

"So is tension. Which you have in spades. We'll strike a balance."

"I haven't heard you complain yet." The emerging woman cringed.

"We don't have enough evidence yet. Besides, men are pretty easy to please. It's an aspect of our sex that most women resent."

"It makes you less complicated. At least we know where your brains are." She gazed meaningfully at his crotch.

He laughed. "See, that's the kind of thing we need to do. Joke around more. You're pretty hilarious when you let loose."

"This is...weird."

His fingers chucked her under the chin. "I know, but it won't be weird forever. When's the last time you spent an evening with someone other than family?"

Her mind conducted an audit. "It's been years."

"So, if you don't want to watch a movie right now, how about we go for a walk?"

Her heartbeat was already racing from their conversation. Maybe she could work off some lust in the woods. "Okay."

When they reached the front porch, he took her hand like they were high school sweethearts. She squirmed and almost yanked it away, but he pulled her along.

"Rhett says there's a nice vista on the east side. Come on."

His pace grated on her—it was a slow stroll, the opposite of her preferred power walk. But after a few paces, she grew used to the feel of his fingers curled around hers, the warmth of his palm. When his hand squeezed hers, she didn't return the gesture, but the urge to yank it away lessened.

Dark clouds were rolling in, but she doubted it would rain. After all, clouds like this had shown themselves several times in recent weeks, and the drought was still in full force. They'd be fine.

"My favorite movie is *Aliens*, " she volunteered as they rounded the trail's curve.

"Ah...Sigourney Weaver kicking alien ass. Saving a child and the world at the same time. It sounds like you."

"Thanks," she sputtered.

His feet ate up the path as she tagged along. "We can watch it when we get back. I haven't seen it in a while. Then maybe you can save me."

"From what?" she said, her voice a whisper.

He pushed her against a nearby tree and kissed her deeply, his tongue twisting with hers. When he edged back, his breathing was labored.

"All this wanting I have for you." His mouth found hers again. "I can't stop thinking about you. I'm not sure I'll ever get enough."

She gripped his waist, needing an anchor after his confession. "Fine. Let's get to it then."

His hand cupped her cheek. "I told you we were going to watch a movie and have popcorn. I never go back on my word."

The bark cut into her shirt, adding to her excitement. "I won't tell."

His lips nipped her ear. "But I'll know. I want normal with you, Peg. We won't have anything more than sex if we don't *do* anything but sex."

Her hips jutted forward, lust pooling like water in a hurricane. "I don't care right now."

He jogged backwards, leaving her bereft. "It'll only make it better later. Catch me if you can."

She chased him, her lungs burning from the effort. He zigzagged through the trees like a pro. She finally launched herself at him like he was a suspect. They bounced against each other before hitting the ground. She had his hands wrapped up behind his back before he could resist.

"Don't make me cuff you."

His snort held a tinge of laughter. "Peg, if you wanted me that bad, all you had to do was say so."

She released his hands and nudged him onto his back. "So."

Dirt streaked his shirt. His eyes blazed like the leaves in a final patch of sunlight. "Okay, then. How do you feel about the great outdoors?"

"Shut up," she murmured, yanking her top off and climbing on top of him.

The distant rumble of thunder sounded, echoing the sensation inside her.

"Aren't you afraid a moose might—"

Her mouth slammed against his, her teeth biting as his tongue thrust out. His strong arms flipped her over, and he tugged off his shirt.

Her body went from tingle to full-on power surge at the sight of all those rippling muscles. He undid her shorts and slid them down her legs in a whisper. Then he took off his own. Naked, he cradled her head in his warm hands. The gesture moved her, sending an unusual pang reverberating through her heart. She didn't like it.

She pushed him onto his back again and slid onto his thighs. Reached out and grabbed his erection.

"Be gentle with me," he joked, then groaned when she squeezed.

"Not in this lifetime."

He filled his hands with her breasts, keeping the pressure light until she wanted to beg. When his fingers caressed the triangle between her legs, her head dropped back.

"Mac, please," she finally called, knowing he wanted to hear her say his first name.

His fingers slid inside and started a rhythm as primal as nature's drumbeat. She finally shoved his hand aside.

"Please tell me you have a condom."

He felt along the ground for his pants. Yanked out his wallet and pulled out a packet. She grabbed it, tore it open, and unrolled it over his length. When she slid onto him, she cried out at the fullness. His hands locked around her hips, deepening their connection. When she'd taken all of him, her moan fluttered out into the grove.

"Look at me, Peg," he ordered, his voice husky and tender.

Her eyes opened. The dark ground framed him. She noticed a few rocks by his head and wondered for a split second if he were uncomfortable. Then he touched where they joined, and all thought evaporated. Her lids fluttered shut.

The first drops of rain touched her shoulders. She opened her eyes to see steam rising from the ground as the gentle rain fell. The water felt cleansing, and it cooled her heated flesh.

"The drought's over," Mac murmured, raindrops plopping on his chest.

Yes, she thought, it was. She fit their fingers together, telling herself she needed leverage. But as she slid up and down on him, she knew better.

She took him home—and found a place there for herself.

Huffing and puffing from exertion, she curled onto his slick chest as the warm rain continued to fall. His arms twined around her, as gentle as the rain falling on her back.

The earth's musky fragrance—and their own—tickled her nose. She allowed herself to be held as she came back from the distant place he'd helped her find.

"I'm going to need a real shower when we get back inside," he murmured, nuzzling her neck. "You'll have to wash my back. I've felt at least three bugs crawl under me."

She levered herself up reluctantly and pushed back her wet bangs from her forehead. "You afraid of some little bugs?"

He sat up too, wrapping his hands around her hips, almost hugging her. "Nah, I just want you to wash my back."

She tried to untangle herself from him, but his arms tightened around her.

"Give it a sec. Listen."

She cocked her ear, on alert. "Someone coming?"

His laughter reverberated against her body. "No. The rain."

The crackle of rain against the leaves and trees sounded like its own percussion when she finally tuned in. And after its long absence, Peggy welcomed the summer shower.

"After being in the desert, it's nice to be back in the mountains."

She wiped away the droplets off his chest. "After this, I refuse to watch some boring nature show when we get back inside."

His fingers tucked her hair behind her ear. "I've already had my nature show. And it wasn't in the least bit boring."

She stood, feeling a blush darken her cheeks as the realization dawned on her. She was standing naked outside in the rain. The squirrels even stopped their rain dance to check her out. Her foot kicked in their direction. "You. Move. There's nothing to see here."

"They're simply admiring you."

Her face flamed. "Hah! Why don't you..." She gestured to his clothes.

He tucked his hands behind his head. "In a sec. I like watching the rain kiss your flesh. You really are beautiful, you know. Soft, white skin. Curves in all the right places. And your breasts—"

She made a raspberry sound. "Feel free to sleep out here and grow mold. Personally, I'm heading back."

He pushed off the ground, his naked body streaked with water and dirt. She lost her balance while putting her damp shorts back on, hopping a few extra steps before she firmed her feet on the ground. God, she liked men with a little grime. Isn't that why Aragorn from *Lord of the Rings* was one of her favorite heroes? The dirtier he got, the hotter he looked. She needed help.

Walking over, Mac kissed her lightly on the lips. "Maybe someday you'll believe me when I tell you you're beautiful."

Peg couldn't repress a Gallic shrug. "And maybe someone should get his pants on before those squirrels over there decide to run up his little tree trunk and hide from the rain." She gestured to his penis.

"Little? Now, Peg, there's no need to be mean."

"Well, compared to the tree where they're hiding, it *is* little."

His hands tugged on his clothes. The corner of his mouth winged up. "Be glad I'm not insecure, or I'd have to give you a lesson on how mighty my oak can be."

Her insides quickened again. Jeez, how long could a girl stay horny? "Maybe after

you shower. You look pretty wet and dirty to me." At this rate, she'd be lucky to have a drop of moisture left in her mouth.

His finger stroked the pounding pulse in her neck. "We aren't going to make it to the shower, are we?"

Her heart rate doubled. "We're sick. Truly sick."

His eyes crinkled. "I wouldn't want it to be any other way."

"Let's head inside."

He took her hand again as they walked back through the rain. "I'm glad you came over tonight. Next time, you'll have to stay over. I want to wake up with you."

Her mouth went even drier, but not in a lust way. Rather like a someone-pulled-a-gun-on-her way. "We'll see."

He stopped in his tracks, making her stop, too. "I'm not your son, Peg. You can't satisfy me with empty promises."

She stared at the mountain's tree line on the adjoining ridge dotted with rain clouds, not wanting to make eye contact. "I'm not ready for that yet."

"Then all you need to do is say so."

A nod was all she could manage.

They walked back to the cabin, the crickets squawking around them as if even they were happy about the rain. Did crickets squawk?

"I still don't know if I can do this..." she said into the silence.

His hip bumped her. "You're doing fine. We can take it slow."

She pinned him with a stare. "You don't seem to be."

"I've always been faster than the average bear."

"Speaking of bears, has Rhett seen any?" She pretended to scan the yard.

"No, and no moose either. Although I've become pretty fond of them."

She'd thought about giving him her motion-activated moose as a joke, but giving him a present seemed to imply something...*permanent* between them.

"Come on. Your movie awaits. Plus, I still need my popcorn."

"We need a shower."

He stopped before the French doors. Placed his hands on her shoulders. "So you're going to scrub my back?"

"If you want." Her pulse increased, imagining his muscles all wet and steamy beneath the hot water.

"I want." His hands framed her face. "You. Now."

"You changed your mind?" Her thighs clenched. "I could care less about the movie."

"We can watch it after I have you all hot and slick in the shower."

He lifted her effortlessly. The woman inside her stretched out in his arms, basking in his attention. What would it be like to wake up next to him? Have morning sex? God, she couldn't remember the last time she'd woken up that way.

"Maybe I *will* stay over next time."

His eyes smoldered. "Good."

As he carried her through the house to the shower, she waged a war with herself. She wanted him. She didn't want to want him. She could do this. There was no way she could do this.

He stripped their clothes off and nudged her into the shower.

"Stop thinking," he said.

His mouth took her nipple in the sweetest suction of her life.

Yes, make me stop, she thought, and totally surrendered to what she'd come to expect—and want—from him.

His first name fluttered out without any thought, and to her ears, it sounded perfect.

CHAPTER 27

$\mathcal{M}$ ac tapped the steering wheel in time with the rap song on the radio while Dustin fidgeted next to him. Usually their shared love of rap led to spontaneous jam sessions in the car.

"What's up?" he asked his unusually silent nephew. "You nervous about dribbling down the soccer field all of a sudden? Have you developed a phobia against giant bugs?"

Dustin kicked at the glove compartment, his shoes making a dust print. Since he didn't make a crack in return, Mac let it slide.

"What gives?"

The kid tugged on the seat belt like he was wrestling a python. "I...I have something to tell you. Just don't get mad, okay? I didn't do it."

This didn't bode well. Mac turned the music down. "We've had this conversation before, Dustin. I can't promise not to get mad, but I'll listen."

His nephew turned sideways in the car. "Seriously, this is *so* not my fault."

When was it? "Okay, let's hear it."

The kid inhaled as if he'd just emerged from deep water. "I know who made the bomb threat."

Mac's hands jerked on the wheel, and the car veered to the right. "You what?" He pulled to the shoulder and parked.

"Seriously, it's just a kid who knew I was upset about moving here. He was pissed I had to leave. I don't know why he did it. He was just...pissed."

This was...unbelievable with a capital U. Mac ejected his seat belt and turned to face his nephew. "Since I know your friends, who are we talking about here? Jeremy?"

Those familiar eyes bugged. "I don't want to give you a name. You'll kill him."

Smart. He was already ordering a gravestone. "Look, I know your friends, and I can read you like a book. Jeremy is enough of a punk to pull this shit. How did he know when the tournament finished?"

His shoulder hiked up. "I texted the play-by-play to all my friends like I always do."

A haze of red descended over him. *"Even though I'd confiscated your phone?"*

"I...kinda volunteered to hold Rhett's while he played."

Fuck. Damn. Shit. Mac's exhalation filled the car. He counted to ten. It didn't work. "Gimme a sec."

He opened his door and conducted a solo Chinese Fire Drill, circling his car, hoping it would help him rein in his desire to lose his cool with an idiot teenager. The wind slapped his face. Dustin craned his neck to follow his movements. Cars passed, probably wondering what the hell he was doing. He thought about making a sign. *Will Trade This Child.* Then Abbie came to mind. He didn't know how she was going to take this. She might laminate the sign for him. He firmed his shoulders and got back into the car.

"Please don't be mad," Dustin pleaded. 'You're right. He's an asshole, but he's my friend. He didn't mean to hurt anybody. It wasn't like there was a real bomb."

Mac's ears burned. The heat spread to his face. "*It wasn't like there was a real bomb?* And you think that makes everything okay? What universe do you live in, Dustin Maven?" His cool snapped. "I had to evacuate hundreds of people from the hotel on my opening weekend. People were terrified. Hell, even I was scared. And you think it's okay because—"

"You don't have to repeat it. I know. I'm sorry! Okay?" His T-shirt wrinkled when he yanked it. "He's my stupid friend, and he did it for me, okay? I'll make it up to you. I'm not going to be friends with him anymore, but please don't send him to jail."

Mac laid his head back against the headrest. Closed his eyes. The bomb threat had been made by some dumbass teenage friend of Dustin's. He wouldn't have put money on that one.

"Was Jeremy the one who called in the bomb threat at your old high school?"

"No, but he knew that guy. He probably got the idea there. It's not hard..."

He wisely trailed off. Mac kept his eyes clenched shut.

"How did you find out? More importantly, when?"

"A friend of ours heard about the reward. He needs money for college, so he was thinking about telling you. I begged him to let me do it instead."

His head turned, locking eyes with him. "That was brave." The menace couldn't be missed.

"No shit. You're like some black panther when you're pissed. Scares the crap out of most people. I told him you wouldn't kill me."

He made a humming noise. "Not yet."

"I've done stupid stuff before. You've forgiven me."

Oh, shit. The Forgiveness Card. Sometimes he wanted to rip it in two. "I have to. You're family. Now Jeremy..."

"He's messed up, okay? He hated me leaving, and he knew I hated it, too. He was trying to get back at you for me."

That comment was a direct hit to his heart. "You wanted to get back at me?"

Dustin ejected his seat belt and rested his elbows on his knees. "I was so pissed about coming here. Every time I get settled, we move. This time I just wanted to...stay with my friends. Finish high school with them."

Ah, fuck. Mac stayed silent for a long moment. "I know you hate it," he said after a while, "but I promised your mother that we'd always be together. Someday I hope you can understand why."

His fist punched the air. "I'm old enough now! I don't need you to pretend to be my dad anymore. I know I don't have one."

If a heart could burn, his was on fire. Mac put his hand on Dustin's arm. "Are you telling me you're totally fine with that?"

"Sure."

"Look. I had the shittiest dad around, and I'm still not fine with it."

"Maybe I'm smarter than you."

He snorted, the red-hot burn fading from acute to annoying. "Maybe you're full of shit. Dustin, I tried to give you what a normal dad might— even though I had to read about what the hell that was. It's not fun being treated like you're nothing, and I never wanted you to feel that way."

Dustin looked at his feet. "I sometimes did when we moved."

Mac pressed back against his seat. Oh, Jesus.

"I thought the hotels were more important than me."

That slap across the face made him think of the Robert Burns' quote about the best laid plans of mice and men.

"Look at me," he said. "The hotels are what I do. You and your mom are part of who I am. *Nothing* is more important than that." God, let him believe that.

Dustin's Adam's apple moved like a river changing course. "So you aren't going to squash Jeremy like a bug?"

Right. "I haven't decided what we're going to do about Jeremy yet, but the whistle blower will get his college money. Who was it? Henry?"

"Jesus, what are you, a mind reader? Yes, it was Henry."

Mac put his seat belt back on. "That kid always struck me as a rule follower."

"He wants to be a lawyer. Thinks it's his civic duty."

At least someone walked the straight and narrow. "Bully for him. You're still going to have to tell your mom. I will *not* be the messenger on this one."

"She's going to cry, isn't she?"

Buckets, kid. "She might. You'll have to hug her."

"Shit."

Exactly. Mac pulled the car away from the curb. They drove in silence for a few minutes.

"Thanks for believing me when I said I didn't have anything to do with it."

He sounded like a man who'd just been saved at a Baptist revival. Mac tried to stop thinking about all the repercussions—how he'd need to alert Aaron, figure out what to do with that punk kid, Jeremy, and tell Peg...something.

"You're welcome. Besides, you know I'm a mind reader, right? It would be stupid to try to slide something like this by me."

The kid rolled down his window. Cranked up the music. "Why didn't I get that gene?"

"Don't worry. You might grow into it." And since the lyrics provided him with the opportunity, he punched Dustin in the arm, rapping, *"And I love you like that."* That was what it came down to, after all.

Dustin bobbed his head to the music and chanted the refrain back to Mac.

He grinned at him.

His nephew might be a teenager, making mistakes, but he'd done the right thing.

Something to be grateful for.

CHAPTER 28

As predicted, Abbie cried. Dustin hugged her while Mac stood with his hands shoved into his pockets, fingering his lucky piece. He finally walked over and wrapped his arms around them both. They were a unit, a family. Dustin was right. Forgiveness was an essential ingredient.

When she pulled away, he handed her the monogrammed handkerchief he'd tucked into his pocket, knowing she preferred them in such moments. *If I'm going to cry,* she always said, *I like to have something durable to catch my tears.*

"I'm so sorry, Mom!" Dustin chanted for the tenth time. "Jeremy's a total jerk."

"So why is he your friend, then?" Mascara dripped at the corners of her eyelids. She dotted them with the handkerchief, staining the white linen black.

His foot kicked out. "I don't know. We both like soccer. Pizza. Girls."

Mac refrained from telling Abbie an eternal truth about men—they didn't over-think their friendships.

"Well, maybe you should start looking a little more closely at people."

Since Mac could feel a lecture brewing, he decided to throw Dustin a line. "Abbie, he did the right thing, coming forward. I'm sure he's learned a lot from this." Please God.

Dustin's eyes glistened suddenly. "I would never hurt the hotel, Mom! And I'll be more careful about choosing my friends. Promise."

She blew out a shaky breath. "I wonder if you would have told us if Henry hadn't called you about the reward."

"I didn't know until Henry told me, I promise." Dustin continued to pat Abbie's back. "And I'm never going to talk to Jeremy again, Mom. We're done."

Abbie sank onto the plush sofa, clutching a blue pillow. "What are you going to do, Mac?"

Dustin hunched over his knees, his eyes pleading.

"I told Dustin that Henry deserves his reward. I have some ideas about Jeremy I'd like to discuss with you."

The handkerchief formed a ball in her clenched hand. "Dustin, will you please go to your room while I discuss this with Uncle Mac?"

"Am I going to be punished?"

"Don't ask me right now. I'm too upset to see straight. We'll talk about it later."

Mac inclined his head to the stairs when Dustin opened his mouth to argue. "Okay. I'm really sorry, Mom. Uncle Mac."

Abbie didn't look in her son's direction as he pounded up the stairs.

"Let's head into the office," Mac suggested.

Her heels clicked on the hardwood as they walked down the hallway. The harsh beat of rap music interrupted the silence. Dustin was keeping the volume low at least. When she sank into the armchair by the couch, he decided to pour them a stiff drink. When he handed one to her, her mouth twitched.

"Bourbon? Yes, I suppose I need a what-a-shitty-day drink."

"Since you rarely swear, I might need to pour you a double." The couch was comfy, but he yanked aside the fluffy braided pillows she'd insisted on adding. Abbie loved having an army of pillows throughout the house. He'd bet the farm Peg didn't have any outside the bedroom.

"Oh, Mac," Abbie cried, eyes welling again. "This is a felony, isn't it?"

He sighed. "Yes, but Jeremy doesn't have a record, and he's a juvenile. This sounds like one of those shitty examples of a stupid teenager doing something stupid." He didn't care if he'd said stupid twice. The word pretty much summed it up.

"Why in the world would he do something like this? I thought he had tons of attitude, but nothing like...nothing criminal."

The bourbon swirled when he circled his hand, giving off the scent of honey, caramel, and pepper. "That's what makes me feel like shit. I guess Dustin's been venting to his friends about how pissed he is about moving. It never occurred to me that his friends would be this angry at me." Not in a million years.

"Oh, Mac. We did the right thing, moving?"

Her hand trembled when he squeezed it. "We always stick together. It doesn't mean I don't feel like shit about the whole thing." Big buckets of it.

"Me too." Her face bunched when she took a sip. "God, I don't know how you drink this."

"Wait for the warmth."

"A heating blanket might be better."

"We have one of those too. Abbie, I'm worried about how Dustin will react if we press charges against Jeremy. He's a punk, but putting him into the system with a felony is serious. If he weren't Dustin's friend, I'd throw the book at him, but I'm hoping there might be another way."

She set her drink on the rosewood coffee table. "He has to learn his lesson."

"I know. I want to talk to his parents—and him, once they give me permission. If he's remorseful, I'll suggest a legal agreement that keeps Jeremy out of trouble if he completes a whole shitload of community service at places we select. We'll set up a monitoring plan. If his attitude improves, we'll leave it at that. If not, he'll do another year of community service. He's not getting away with this scot-free, and he's not getting college credit for those hours either."

"I know his parents. His dad's a workaholic, but his mother is a nice woman. I think they'll agree. When you say a shitload, how many hours were you thinking?"

The bourbon burned his throat when he knocked it back. "Two curse words in one day. Might be a record."

"I was repeating *you*," she responded primly.

He pulled out his lucky piece and rubbed it. "Does three hundred sound about right?"

Her eyes rolled. "I was thinking a thousand."

The canary yellow chip flew into the air when he threw it. "Well, there's nearly nine-thousand hours in a year, so that's—" He caught the chip.

"Oh, stop with the math brain, please. The rest of us normal people could care less."

He smiled. "How about we start with five hundred, and if they balk, we can reduce it?"

"If they ask for less, we might as well press charges. This isn't a parking ticket."

His tie felt like a noose now, so he loosened it.

"How are you going to handle things on this end?" she asked after a moment. "Are you going to tell Peggy?"

The thought of her made his stomach burn. He was going to have to hide something from her—something directly involving her. Guilt wasn't a strong enough word. "No, I can't. She'd have to report it."

She reached for her bourbon, and studied the amber liquid a moment before draining it. "Are you in love with her?"

Ah, shit. He rubbed his lucky piece—hard. "Yes. I haven't told her yet."

Her mouth twisted, not from the bourbon this time. "Mac, I don't see how this can end up without you getting hurt. She's a porcupine."

But her needles seemed to be falling away the more time they spent together. "It's funny, but she reminds me a lot of you when it comes to men."

Her back snapped up ram-rod straight like a debutante's. "That's a horrible thing to say."

His hand covered hers. "I don't mean to hurt you, but that's how I see it. You're as much of a porcupine with Rhett as Peggy is with me."

She stood and yanked down her cream-colored jacket. "How did this become about me?"

He rose from the sofa. "Rhett loves you. He's not going away, ever. I haven't seen him this driven or focused since—"

"He beat you in the World Series of Poker ten years ago."

He inclined his head.

"Well, what he chooses to do with his life is his concern. It doesn't affect me. We're just not compatible. But what you want with this woman does. Are you planning to..."

"What?" he asked, crossing his arms.

"Marry her?"

The punch to his gut couldn't have been delivered more cleverly. He stared at her. Could he even imagine being married to Peggy? Waking up next to her, yes, but forever? Part of him said yes, but he wasn't quite there yet. Being with her was like pulling teeth—one at a time.

Abbie put her hands on her hips. Tapped her shoe on the carpet. "If you want something permanent with her, she is my concern. I've never seen you act this way over a woman. I'm not sure she's going to fit in with us. She doesn't even like Dustin."

"Dustin didn't make a good first impression. He's working on it." His temples started to pound. "Listen, she's raising a son alone, too."

"We couldn't be more different." If she yanked any harder on her jacket, she'd pop a button.

"Take a look at your own actions."

"It's Rhett who pushes my buttons. I wouldn't be this way with all men. If you and I weren't related, I'd be over the moon about you."

He snorted. "I'm more like Rhett than you'd like to admit."

"That's not true."

He took her shoulders in his hands. "When you see him again, you might want to look a little closer. He does what I'd like to do."

"And what's that?"

"Whatever he wants." The truth came out before he could stop it.

She worried her lip. "I know you've given up a lot for me and Dustin."

He held up his hand—a white flag. "Stop right there. I'm not saying I would change anything, but by God, I draw the line at you telling me what's good for me. You're my sister, not my mother. If I want Peggy in my life, you'd better find a way to accept it." Old, buried anger couldn't be squelched.

She tapped her low-heel sandal on the Persian carpet again. "You're right. I'm sorry. I don't want to see you hurt, Mac, that's all."

Neither did he. Peggy had more power over his emotions than he'd like. "And, Abbie, I know you were hurt, but that doesn't mean you should stop trying to find your own happiness. As Dustin reminded me recently, he's not going to be here much longer. He's off to college in two years. What are you going to do then?"

Her face turned chalk-white. "I...don't know. I'll have to see."

"You should start thinking about it *now.* " Like he was. "You're hurting Rhett. Doesn't that bother you even if you're fine with hurting yourself?"

She blinked back tears. He knew he'd pushed too far.

"Of course, I do. Why do you think I keep telling him to leave?"

His frustration with her and Peggy blurred as he stalked toward the door. "You don't want that. You love him. When are you finally going to admit it?"

His hand fell away from the doorknob as he realized what he was doing. He was saying to Abbie the things he wanted to say to Peggy. When he turned around, she was dabbing at the corners of her eyes. "I'm sorry, Abbie. It's not my place."

Her chin rose. Her eyes turned flinty. "You're right. It isn't."

So he just walked out.

CHAPTER 29

Abbie watched as Dustin sprayed furniture polish on the bookshelves, her current chore for him. She hadn't decided whether she thought he was a miscreant or not. He'd broken the law when they first moved to town. Now one of his friends had called in a bomb threat. She was in Mommy-Confusion Zone. Dustin whined that she was punishing him unfairly. Well too darn bad.

When someone knocked on the door, he threw his rag aside eagerly. Dust bunnies exploded into the air, catching the sunlight. He ran to the front hall like he was making a break for the goal area on the soccer field.

"It's Uncle Rhett," he yelled and promptly laughed.

What the heck did he have to laugh about? Laughing was so not on his program right now.

"Dustin. Back to dusting." Oh God, it was like the same word. Maybe that explained it. She'd named her child after dust, miniscule flecks of dirt and lint that floated until they landed indiscriminately, covering everything in their filthy wake. It had screwed him up.

"But it's Uncle Rhett!" he complained.

"He can talk to you *while* you work."

The object of her dreams and fantasies stepped into the family room, looking like a super hot normal guy in faded jeans and a white T-shirt. Was he ever going to wear animal print, snake skin, or fringe again? Did she want him to? She rather missed his cowboy hat. Correction. She missed knocking it off as she fisted her fingers in his thick, curly hair.

Her fingers rolled the fountain pen she was holding, distracting her from her sexcapade thoughts. She clutched the thank-you-for-coming-to-our-disastrous-opening cards to her stomach with her other hand. "Rhett."

His mouth turned up. "Abbie, you're looking as fresh as the lemon tart my mama likes to make."

Her yellow linen suit wasn't anything special. Why did he have to talk like that? "That's an exaggeration." One she didn't want him to counter. "What can we do for you, Rhett?"

His hand clapped Dustin on the back. "I heard the kid was having a tough spell, so I wanted to come by and see if there was anything I could do."

"You can help me dust," her son suggested. "Mom's punishing me even though I didn't do anything wrong."

"Sounds like you got off easy. Mac told me his lawyer drew up an agreement with the kid and his parents in exchange for not pressing charges."

"Yeah, Jeremy has to do a sh—butt-load of community service. And Henry gets the reward for turning him in. And me? I'm a house slave. It's so unfair."

If her kid had an off button, she would have pushed it. She hoped Rhett wouldn't mess things up by agreeing with Dustin.

Rhett squeezed his shoulder. "Well, it's a tough place for your mama and Mac. I know it seems unfair, but hell, I've gotten into my fair share of trouble for the things the people around me have done."

Abbie gave him the stink eye.

His courtly bow to her didn't soften her glare.

"Of course, my mama, like yours, is a firm believer that you are the company you keep. That's why I'm mending my ways."

Her laughter trilled out. "Oh, have you fired your poker babes, then?" She winced, realizing she had about as much control over her mouth as Dustin had over his. Asking meant she cared.

"You know they're part of my act. The fans love them. I don't know how many men have told me it's amazing what a tight sequined dress can do for a woman. You might try it sometime, Abs."

Dustin barked out a laugh and then stopped himself, realizing he was close to death by mother. He cleared his throat. "I'll go dust your bedroom, Mom."

That was probably a good choice. She wasn't sure if she could refrain from firing back at Rhett for that dress comment. As if she'd pour herself into something like that. He was just trying to get her goat since he knew she didn't approve of "his act."

"Make sure you dust under the bed," she warned as Dustin sped by.

"I'm sorry if the dress comment upset you," Rhett said. "I'd pretty much look at you wearing anything. Or nothing."

The deep timbre of his voice sent desire spiking through her, and her face flushed. Her hand accidentally knocked the cards and envelopes aside. They fluttered to the ground like paper airplanes. She stood, searching for composure. "Rhett, please stop this! You promised."

"I promised not to touch you. I haven't gone blind or lost my imagination." His large, masculine hands, the ones whose touch she craved, gathered up the stationery.

"You have pretty handwriting, Abbie. Like an elegant lady."

Mac was right. If she wasn't planning to relent, she had to make a stand. Make him listen. Her throat tightened when she imagined him leaving. "Stop it! I mean it. This isn't going to work."

He set the cards on the coffee table and rose up until he was towering over her. His musky cologne tickled her nose—calling up images of hot, steamy sex. Who wore cologne with a T-shirt and jeans anyway? Oh, right. Rhett.

"Please, I'm only hurting you, and that's the last thing I want. We had a good time together, but it's over. Please go home! Don't change your life for me. It's fine the way it is." Mac's earlier accusations made her ears burn.

His eyes regarded her steadily. "No, it's not. You're not with me, and I'll do whatever it takes to get you back. Say what you want. Do what you want. I can take it. Even if you reject me until I'm in my eighties, I'll still follow you around in my walker. Of course, I hope you'll make love with me again before I have bursitis in my hip and have to pile on the Bengay."

She shoved his chest. Thinking about them getting older made her heart race. Her already tight ribcage squeezed her breath away. "That's not funny."

"I told you, Abbie. I'm not giving up. Ever. I won't abandon you like your dad did. Or Dustin's father. Maybe someday you'll tell me what happened with him, but even if you don't, it doesn't matter. I'm here, and I love you."

He simply wouldn't listen, but she knew what would make him leave. She took a deep breath and swallowed thickly. "Dustin's father raped me on our second date. I was too stupid to know it wasn't supposed to be that way. When I got pregnant, Mac hunted him down. He told my brother I was asking for it," she whispered. "We weren't even close enough for him to technically abandon me. Now will you leave?"

His shoulders slumped. "I'm sorry, Abbie," he murmured. Then he extended his arms slowly like he intended to hold her.

She pushed them away, heels digging into the carpet as the pain rising in her chest threatened to take her down. "Don't touch me. Didn't you hear what I just said?"

His hands were gentle when he brought her to his chest. She pushed against him with her fists.

"I know I promised I wouldn't touch you, but you need to know you're loveable right now." His body cradled hers. "You need to know this doesn't change anything."

She pounded his chest. Once. Twice. "Dammit! Leave me alone."

His face pressed into her neck. "No, I love you. I'm glad you told me. It just makes me love you more. I knew someone had taken advantage of you, but I didn't know it was this bad. I want to tear him apart, limb by limb, and then leave him alive for the buzzards to finish off."

She pressed her forehead against his collarbone, silently thinking, *Please don't let me go.* "Mac already did that."

His hands caressed her spine, making the gentle up and down motions a parent used to soothe a child. "Good."

She jerked her head back, eyes frantically searching his. "You can't tell Dustin."

His face softened. "I'd never do that."

"Now can you see why this won't work?" One tear slid down, ruining her insistence.

His finger stroked her cheek. "No, I don't. You think I don't want you now that I know? That's bull. It doesn't change anything. My dad beat the crap out of me before he left. Do you think that makes me less of a man?"

Her lip trembled. "Of course not. I didn't know."

His exhalation feathered her bangs. "It's not exactly something I talk about. That's why Mac and I first became friends. We *knew* each other. Both of us got into poker to get out of a bad situation."

She sniffed, her whole chest filled with the burning need to cry—for him, for her, for them.

His shoulder lifted. "Sometimes you have to face the past. Say bullshit to the ghost."

Her mouth tried to smile. "Bullshit." And in that moment, she knew he was right. The past didn't matter. The ghost disappeared.

He pulled her against him again. "Yeah, bullshit. Christ, I love you, Abs."

The words burned on her lips. She pressed them together so she wouldn't utter them. Once she did, there would be no recanting. Was she ready for that? She needed to think things through. She'd never let herself imagine he'd do something other than walk away when he found out the full truth, saying, *see ya, you're a bit more than I bargained for.*

"Mom!" Dustin yelled.

She jumped a few inches. Eased back. Smoothed her jacket down. Took a minute before answering. "Yes, honey?"

"There's a dead roach under your bed. I am *so* not picking it up."

"Don't be a wuss. It's dead!" Rhett fired back.

Dustin emerged at the top of the stairs, a full-on grimace in place. "I said I'd dust. Not exterminate."

"I'll get it," Rhett called.

Dustin fell silent, as if sensing the mood between them. His gaze dropped to the floor. "It's okay. I'll grab a dustpan."

"That's my boy," Rhett said as naturally as he had since Dustin was little. Today, it hurt. God, how she wished it were true.

"I don't know how to tell him," she whispered, the ever-present fear clenching her diaphragm.

"You'll figure out what's best. Aside from my mama, I've never met a better mama than you, Abs."

She reached for a Kleenex. "Rhett, I don't—"

"Before you start saying something about not knowing what to say, let me stop you. I think we've had a huge breakthrough today. I'm going to head out and celebrate. Unless you want to come with me?" He held his hand out to her.

The urge to go with him made her dig her heels in place. She shook her head.

"Another time then. Thanks for finally trusting me enough to tell me." He turned and headed for the door.

"Rhett," she called, her hand caressing her dry throat.

He stopped. Spun around. "Yeah, darlin'?"

The endearment blew through her like a gentle breeze through the orange grove at their hotel in Arizona. "Thank *you*, Rhett."

His soft smile squeezed all the blood from her heart. "I'll be seeing ya, Abs."

She fell onto the couch as the front door clicked shut, raised her hands to her nose, inhaling the musky cologne that had rubbed off onto her skin.

She couldn't deny the truth.

Rhett always found a way to linger with her.

Chapter 30

Peggy was sitting at her desk when the phone rang. Her files slid like the Tower of Pisa when she picked it up.

"Deputy McBride."

"Hello, my dear," Arthur said in his gravelly voice. "I hoped I might catch you, although I thought you'd be the one to call me after our agreement."

Her brow furrowed. "Which one?"

"Remember how we agreed to tell each other if we found out anything about Mac?"

Her heart rapped against her rib. "What are you talking about?" God, he hadn't discovered they were seeing each other, had he?

"He cancelled the reward he was offering for information about the person who made the bomb threat. I thought that might mean he'd found the bastard."

She sat up in her chair. "He cancelled it?" Why hadn't he told her?

"Yes."

Surely there was a misunderstanding. "When?"

He coughed for a moment. "Jill told me this morning, so it must have happened yesterday. So, you didn't know. Hmm..."

Her gaze fell to the hotel bomb file on her desk. Even the Feds hadn't found anything. They were inclined to agree it had been a vague threat. Everyone was chasing their tale with no new news—except for Mac, apparently. And he hadn't called her. She eyed the clock. It was only ten o'clock. Maybe he was busy.

And maybe she should just call him and ask without jumping to conclusions.

"Arthur, I need to go. Thanks for calling."

"You didn't forget our deal to share anything we found, did you?"

She hadn't done a thing to dig deeper into Mac's past since she'd started sleeping with him. "No, I haven't forgotten. If I find something, I'll share."

"Let me know what you find out about the reward then."

"You've got it," she replied and said goodbye.

Hadn't Mac told her he wanted to keep their personal and professional lives separate? She dropped the file, realizing she'd called him Mac in her head. No need to freak out about that now. So she called Aaron, her *official* point of contact, to maintain protocol. Aaron didn't offer her any information. All he did was check Mac's online schedule and secure a one o'clock meeting for the three of them.

When the hour dawned, she brought a shiny new pair of handcuffs with her, hoping to bust the asshole who'd made the threat.

She saw his hotel with different eyes now that she knew him better. This was his creation. This was what he valued. She eyed it like she would a crime scene. What did she see? Elegance. Order. Decadence. And friendliness. His worker bees rushed to open doors and escort her through the halls. Hell, she'd bet they'd even hand her toilet paper if she asked.

The place between her shoulder blades itched. It had been doing that a lot lately. She'd have to buy a back scratcher or something.

Speaking of backs, she hadn't seen him since she'd washed his. Her mind immediately went into the gutter. How many times could the man make her come? They were reaching new records. The woman inside her craved more. The deputy and mother kept putting the brakes on, only responding to his text messages two or three hours after he'd sent them.

Mac and his head of security stood when she entered his office. She shook Aaron's hand, but only nodded to Mac, not wanting to utter his first name outside of the bedroom. It felt weird.

His brow winged up as if sensing her distance. "Thanks for coming, Deputy. You don't mind if I call you Peggy now, do you?"

Her mouth flattened. Well played. She paused for a moment to consider her reply. Aaron's regard made her want to fidget like a rookie. "Fine."

"Please call me Mac then." His hand gestured to a chair.

No wonder the man had won the World Series of Poker. He'd boxed her in nicely. She only nodded. Two could play that game.

After they sat, Mac picked up a crystal paper weight. "What can I do for you, Peggy?"

Hadn't Aaron told him why she was here? She crossed her arms when she couldn't figure out where to put them. "I heard you cancelled the reward. I came for an update."

He turned the paper weight like he would a baseball. "I see. Well, we all agreed that the bomb threat was vague at best, but we did our due diligence. Your folks haven't found anything. After reviewing everything on our end, we concluded there was nothing more we could do. Right, Aaron?"

Aaron's granite jaw dipped in accord.

"We've never had a threat against one of our hotels, Peggy. This has been a unique occurrence. We've decided to stop wasting my security team's time checking out bogus reward calls."

His logic made sense. He stared her straight in the eye when he said it, but she could tell something was wrong. He had his poker face up. After watching him play the game, she knew what it looked like.

"Aaron, will you give me a minute alone with your boss here?"

He stood when Mac nodded. After the door clicked shut behind him, she leaned forward, her hands on her knees. "I don't buy it. You're like a lioness with her cubs about your hotel, and you're certainly rich enough for your security team to follow up on bogus charges until the cows come home. What aren't you telling me?"

Prisms flashed on the wall as he set the paper weight aside. He looked her straight in the eye. "There's nothing here," he said. "I won't waste my time or my staff's."

She waited for him to say more. He only folded his arms.

Anger tore through her stomach in a burning sensation. She played a hunch like she would with a suspect in interrogation. "Bullshit. You know who did it."

Mac's mouth flattened. He stood. "Let's drop this, shall we? I detest beating a dead horse. No one found anything." As if to punctuate that statement, he picked up the report with her department's logo on it and waved it in the air. "Now, why don't you take a breath and have a drink with me?" he asked, laying the report down again.

"Don't try to distract me. I know you. You're lying to my face." Part of her died saying it.

"Stop this right now. You know I only have the highest respect for you."

"And yet you don't deny lying to me. You're choosing your words very carefully. And do you think I don't know most of the shades of your voice by now?"

"Under other circumstances, I'd be encouraged by that knowledge. Peg, you're reading too much into this. We all concluded it was a vague threat. I don't believe in wasting anyone's time. I want to thank you and your department for everything you did, but this is over."

Her legs shook as she rose. She wanted to lunge across the room and shake him. Instead she walked up to him until her boots touched the tips of his fancy shoes. "I want you to deny it to my face. Then I'll know what kind of man you are."

Those stoplight green eyes didn't blink. "Don't do this. Driving a wedge between us over something like this is stupid. If you're scared of how you feel about me, at least be honest about it."

"You're avoiding the real issue. Do you think this is my first rodeo? Right now you're acting like a person of interest who's hiding information that's critical to my case. Tell me again. Do you know who did it?"

He took a long moment, sweeping his gaze from her jaw to her eyes. "I stand by what I said earlier."

She almost punched him. "Then you're a goddamn liar." When he didn't respond, her hands fell to her hips. "Have it your way. We're done. *All the way.*"

And she meant it.

Her boots pounded on his shiny hardwood floor as she headed for the door.

"Peggy. Stop."

She slammed it, not caring who heard. It clicked open seconds later.

"*Peg!*"

She powered down the hallway past the dressed-up monkeys in uniforms.

Jill was waddling up the stairs as she thundered down them.

"Hey!" she called.

She passed in a blur. "Gotta get back. Talk later."

Full sentences had deserted her.

She made it to her car, her vision as red as her police siren. When she turned on the engine, Maven—never Mac again—emerged from the door to the lot. His jog caused people to stare.

She hit the gas, speeding faster than was safe in a pedestrian zone.

Her lip throbbed. She realized she'd bitten it hard enough to leave a mark. Tears filled her eyes. She wanted to blame it on the pain.

It was over.

She was stupid to have ever let it start. What had she been thinking? He had no respect for what she did, and she felt the same way about his profession. Other than sex, they had nothing in common. Another dumb infatuation for the record books. Didn't she function better alone?

She'd go to the firing range. Put fourteen rounds in a paper target. If no one was there, she'd tape a head-shot of Maven up and then fire until the paper disintegrated.

No one had *ever* made her want to cry like a girl.

The man was going to pay.

CHAPTER 31

When Mac and Dustin arrived at Peggy's house, her lawn was freshly mowed on the shortest setting. Like a buzz cut on a kid, her yard looked like shit, bald dirt patches peeking out like knobby knees. They weren't scheduled to do any yard work today, but he'd decided to come to her house nonetheless. After struggling with himself all afternoon, he'd decided he couldn't lose her. He was going to risk it all.

He hadn't been this nervous since he'd stepped into the Trump Taj Mahal in Atlantic City hoping to win enough money to cover Abbie's hospital bills.

"Jeez, what happened to her yard?" Dustin declared.

"Maybe something ate it," he supplied, wondering how much bullshit he could dole out in a day. No need to say she'd pulverized her grass wishing it were him.

"Must have been a butt-load of deer. We were here three days ago, and it looked fine then. I'll have to ask Keith."

Their little friend came through the back door when they parked and broke into a full run when he realized who his guests were. Mac scanned the house for Peggy, but didn't see her.

"Hi!" he hollered. "Mom was really mad when she got home from work, so she mowed the yard. There was dust everywhere."

Dustin gave him a fist bump. "Glad a lawn mower did this. Uncle Mac thought it might have been a flock of deer."

Keith put a hand on his little hip and shifted his weight. "They aren't flocks, silly. That's for birds. It's a *herd* of deer. I learned that in school."

"Right," Dustin replied.

Mac might have sent Keith a smile if his hands weren't so damp. His sweat glands hadn't worked like this in more than a decade. It was gross. He walked to the trunk to grab his tools. He'd brought them in case the shed was locked and decorated with a *Will Shoot Trespassers* sign. He wouldn't be half surprised if she appeared with a shotgun and ordered them off her property.

"Your bushes need a trim. Do you want to help?"

Keith lunged in the air like he was receiving a high-five. "Sure! How's soccer going, Dustin?"

"Great," his nephew answered, sounding bored. He hadn't been exactly thrilled with Mac's unscheduled yard work plan, but the kid knew he was in the crapper, so he hadn't complained—much.

"Where's your mom?" Mac finally asked.

"She's upstairs. Talking to Grandma. My Uncle David is coming for a visit."

The trimmers slid a few inches in his sweaty grip until he clenched his fist around the handle. "That's nice."

Keith shrugged. "I don't know. Mom's upset. I haven't seen him since I was a baby. I don't remember him, but Mom says he's nothing like Uncle Tanner."

Sounded like a family drama there. Great, Peggy didn't need any more personal dynamite today.

"Let's show these bushes we mean business. She'll find us when she's done talking."

"Can we make the bushes into funny shapes like on Looney Tunes?"

Dustin tapped Keith on the back in a guy pat. "That's an awesome idea! What would you—"

"No way," Mac interrupted. Peggy might have mucked up her yard, but he didn't need to add to the destruction.

"Party pooper," Dustin whined.

"We can sign you up for a landscaping class anytime, kid. Just let me know."

His nephew glared at him.

"I'd like that," Keith began and then proceeded to chatter nonstop.

He trimmed Peg's west-side bushes, keeping the back door in his line of sight. He clipped the dead, knotty twigs from their undersides. His nerves niggled at him, but he still thought this was the best approach. She couldn't avoid him forever if he was at her house. Plus, she wouldn't kill him if the kids were around. Keith was picking up twigs while Dustin sat on his knees, pulling weeds.

"Oh, that is totally gross!" Dustin whined again, flicking a translucent cut worm in Mac's direction—his new game.

Keith's squeal pierced his ears.

Mac stomped it with his work boot. *"Well now, I say, well now, you aren't afraid of a little ol' bug like that, are you? "* he asked in his best Foghorn Leghorn voice.

The kid's giggling eased the tightness in his chest a fraction. Dustin fell back on his haunches and grinned. His nephew might be sixteen, full of moving rage and hormones, but he was still a good kid.

Mac pointed his finger at Dustin. *"And if you think this ol' chicken is going to stand for any more bug throwing, you've got another thing coming. This chicken doesn't do bugs. He prefers the fancy stuff like caviar."*

His impression made Keith fall to the ground in a laughing fit. It wasn't as funny as all that, but kids had a weird sense of humor.

"Keith? What in the world are you laughing at?" Peggy called, stepping through the back door. Her mouth slammed flat at the corners.

Keith sputtered, "He's doing...the chicken voice, Mom. Your favorite."

All the moisture dried up in his mouth at the sight of her and her bad-ass body language. He almost gulped. *"Well now, I know I'm her favorite. Who doesn't like a big rooster?"* he continued, hoping like hell his act might soften her up a bit. He tucked the clippers out of view, a new patch of sweat making him wipe his hands on his cargo shorts. *"Well now, I say, well now, your mama's looking a tad under the weather."*

Fire brimmed in her eyes, hot and punishing.

Well, it was worth a shot. He walked toward her steadily. *"Maybe she swallowed one of those nasty grubs Dustin found. Perhaps that's what ya'll eat for dinner around 'ere."*

Keith clutched his stomach, guffawing. Dustin joined the fray. Peggy just crossed her arms, looking at him like he was the grub—one she'd gladly rub into the dirt.

"Why don't you come inside and see?" If words held liquid, acid would have dripped from her mouth. She jerked her chin to the house.

He followed. *"Well now, I say, that's a mighty fine offer. Dustin and Keith, you two keep on workin'. This chicken doesn't like slackers."*

When he entered the house, she clicked the door closed lickety-split. "What in the hell do you think you're doing here?"

Like a nervous teenager stuck sounding like a tenor in an all-boys' choir, he realized he couldn't stop doing the chicken's voice. *"Well, now..."*

"Answer me."

His imitation fled for cover at the ice in her voice. "Don't use that tone with me. Like I'm some suspect to you. It demeans everything between us."

Her hands gripped the back of a chair, her knuckles white. "There's *nothing* between us. In case you missed that earlier, let me be clear. We're done. Dustin's completed enough yard work around here. I don't want you to *ever* step foot on my property again."

Well, he'd nailed her dialogue. The only missing piece was a faded leather holster around her waist like a cowboy.

"I came by to explain, and after what we have shared, why don't you be adult enough to listen?" he fired right back.

She rocked on the balls of her feet, pointing at him. "I *am* an adult. You're the liar."

"Fine, then why don't you hear me out?"

"I don't want to listen to anything you have to say."

His stomach dropped like it always did when he shoved his chips forward, going all in. "You're right. I wasn't giving it to you straight earlier. I was trying to respect your duty as an officer of the law."

She shoved the chair, knocking it into the table. "You think lying to me and refusing to give me a suspect is *respecting* my career?"

His hand thrust out. "Like I told you, I despise lying. There are reasons I can't tell you what I know. You'd be obligated to report it, and I can't have that."

"This is a felony we're talking about." She rounded on him. "Someone called a bomb threat in to a major tourist venue in my town. He or she needs to be brought to justice."

At least they agreed on that, if not the terms.

"I'm taking care of it."

Her mouth parted before slamming shut. "*You're* taking care of it? Who the hell do you think you are? *I'm* the law around here."

The door popped open. Dustin poked his head in and glared at them. "Stop yelling at each other!" he hissed. "It's upsetting Keith. Why don't you lower your voices or go somewhere else and argue? He's just a kid."

Dustin's protectiveness shamed him. "Sorry. We weren't thinking." He'd lost his cool again—Peggy had a knack for making that happen. He dug into his wallet. "Why don't you walk with Keith downtown for some ice cream? I'll pick you up once we've finished."

His nephew grabbed the twenty and stuffed it into his pocket before Peggy could answer. "Whatever." The door slammed as he left.

Mac ran both hands through his hair. "Well, it seems like we've both lost the Adult gene. I'm sorry I yelled."

She didn't say anything. Her hands were still clenching and unclenching on the chair.

"Let's take a minute, okay?" he suggested. "Start again."

The fire in her eyes was now an inferno. "I *never* yell in front of my kid. Get out." Her voice could have pulverized rocks.

He covered the space between them and put his hands on her shoulders. She shoved at his chest.

"I'm not leaving. Why do you think we've both lost it?"

"I told you—"

"No! I won't leave. Listen to me. I came to the conclusion I am full-on in love with you."

She gasped like he'd just shot her.

"When you walked out on me today, it made me... Jesus." He squeezed her shoulders, trying to make her see. "I don't want to lose you over this. I'm asking you to trust me *this one time.* I have reasons I can't share."

She raised her arms, knocking his hands away. "Trust you? Who are you kidding? You're exactly who I thought you were the day you walked into town."

He nearly pulled his hair. "Bullshit! You know better. That's why you're scared. I love you, Peg. I need your trust here." And it seemed just about as far away as Timbuktu.

"Stop saying that! Tell me what you know or get out."

"Look, I took a heck of a risk telling you I knew *anything.* " His fist punched the air. "You're like a pit bull with your job. You could have me subpoenaed. I was willing to do it because I couldn't lose you without trying to work this out."

His head swooped down. His mouth crushed her lips. She elbowed him once before opening her mouth, her teeth biting at his lips, her tongue thrusting madly against his. He pushed her against the wall. Drew her hands up over her head and simply ravaged her, pouring all the love and fear and pain she'd created inside him into the kiss. She bucked wildly against him. His hips jammed hers into the wall. He wanted to take her, make her moan, make her quake. Make her love him.

He drew back from the madness and kissed her again, with tenderness and gentleness. Their foreheads pressed together. Her breath sobbed out. She tried to break free of his hold, but he wouldn't let her.

"I love you," he breathed out. "Don't send me away."

Her hands gripped his, hard enough to make his knuckles pop. "I can't be with someone who lies to me. And you don't love me. You don't even trust me to do my job."

He drew back. "I trust you too much to do your job. That's why I can't tell you."

She merely shook her head, her expression desolate.

He was losing her, and he knew it. He searched for something to make her understand. Keith's drawings on the refrigerator caught his eye. He had to tell her more, and pray the mother inside her would understand, even if the deputy didn't. They wouldn't make it with this chasm between them.

He took an agonized breath. "Okay, if that's what it's going to take, then I call your raise. Peg, the threat has something to do with Dustin. I can't follow the normal course here."

"Dustin did it? Dammit! And you sent him off with my son?"

"No, Dustin didn't do it, but it relates to him. I'm hoping the mother in you will listen to me. I struggled with this, Peg—hard—but I had to handle things behind closed doors."

She closed her eyes. "Let me go," she whispered. He heard it as a plea from the emerging woman, the one he'd hurt, the one he loved.

His heart squeezed. "No, that's the one thing I can't do. But I'll tell you everything if that's what it takes to keep you."

God, he hoped she'd understand. He knew he was putting her in a hell of a position, not to mention risking his family. But he just didn't see a choice.

Her eyelids fluttered open, and she stared at him for a long moment.

"Okay," she finally said.

"Do you promise not to slug me or run off?"

She nodded and clutched her throat when he let her go. The phone rang, but she didn't move toward it.

"Do you need to get that?"

"No, it's probably Jill."

His relief was immediate. She wasn't looking for an excuse to ignore him.

"She's been calling all afternoon. I don't know what to say."

"She was worried after the way you left the hotel." Just like he'd been.

"Peppered you with questions, did she?"

He snorted. "Jill can ask. Doesn't mean I answer."

She nodded her understanding and strode to the cupboard. "Want some water?"

"Sure."

He'd take a peace offering. God knows his mouth tasted like he'd feasted on sand. He reached for the glasses she extended and filled them with ice and water from the refrigerator, handing one to her. Then he followed her into the living room. The water cooled his raw throat.

She crossed her arms when she settled onto the sofa. He wondered if she did the same when she was interviewing a suspect. Since she didn't have a love seat, he sat next to her, turning his body toward her.

"I know I've mentioned how angry Dustin was about leaving high school and all his friends."

She didn't move a muscle.

"What I hadn't counted on was that one of Dustin's friends was mad at me for taking him away. He wanted to punish me for Dustin's sake."

"One of his friends did this?" she finally asked.

"Yes. The kid's a punk. I was furious when Dustin told me, but I thought about the most fitting punishment for a few days and asked for Abbie's input."

Her fingerprints etched the glass when she put it down on the scuffed black coffee table. She didn't say anything for a few minutes. The only sound in the room was the clinking of ice cubes as he drank.

"That was pretty brave of Dustin, telling you," she finally said.

Since she seemed to be coming down from her rocket-powered rage, he huffed out a laugh. "Well, I'm not sure he would have even found out if I hadn't offered the reward. Their other friend decided he needed the college money, so he spilled the truth to Dustin."

She picked up her glass again and rested it against her stomach. The condensation wet her simple white T-shirt. He tried not to stare.

"Prisoner's dilemma," she commented.

"Sort of. I gave the kid his reward. As for the punk, I didn't know whether turning him in was the best course, or if we should handle it between our two families. I talked to the parents and the kid himself to make sure a lesson could be driven home and his parents would hold his feet to the fire. They passed the test, so I had my lawyers draw up a legal agreement. The kid has to do five hundred hours of community service at charities selected by Abbie and me, and it can't be used on his college applications."

Her expression didn't shift, so he continued. "We have monitoring visits and check-ins set up for the next year. If I'm satisfied the kid's improved, we won't add a second year of community service, anger management therapy, or counseling. The parents and the kid know they're lucky I didn't take him to court. Everyone signed the agreement."

"Why didn't you press charges against the kid if he's a punk?"

One reason: Dustin. "I thought about it. Dammit, I wanted to hang him from the nearest flagpole for scaring the crap out of me. Do you have any idea how I felt, knowing you were inside the hotel while they searched for a bomb?"

She drank from her glass, giving it her undivided attention.

"And I had nightmares for days afterward, imagining Dustin and Abbie and all my friends and guests dying in an explosion. I can handle the money loss and the bad press, but the people... That wasn't easy to forgive."

Her eyes narrowed. "He might do it again."

He blew out a long breath slowly, like he would have with pricy Gurkha Black Dragon cigar smoke. "We all need a second chance. The kid understands this is his. Plus, this shows Dustin that there are consequences without making his friend into a martyr. I didn't want to push my nephew away. Plus, he did the right thing. He told me the truth."

Her finger circled the rim of the glass. "After the reward worked its magic."

He leaned toward her. "The reward brought the truth to light. Dustin told me as soon as he found out. He's a good kid."

"And yet, here he is doing yard work at my house for speeding and evading the law."

"Does no one get a second chance with you, Peg?"

He almost didn't want the answer.

Her lashes slid down, veiling her eyes. "No."

"Not even me?" He wanted to touch her—one simple connection to remind her of what they had—but he knew she'd push him away. "Now do you understand? Dustin might be my nephew, but I've raised him as my own. I've sat up with him when he had a fever. I've taught him multiplication tables. I've...I'd do anything for him, Peg."

She scowled and waved a hand in the air. "Fine. I get it. Okay?"

His hand covered hers. The muscles bunched before they relaxed.

"I didn't want to put you in a difficult position. Truly."

Her brow winged up. "Yet you've put me in a difficult position anyway by telling me."

His thumb stroked the back of her hand. "I couldn't lose you. I meant what I said earlier. I love you. I don't care if that makes you want to kick me in the nuts."

She stood abruptly, breaking away from him. "This isn't going to work."

"You're running because of a romantic declaration, Peg?"

Her smirk made him break out in sweat under his shirt. "Right, because I'm not an adult," she said.

He rose and grabbed her arms. "We're all insecure with someone in the beginning. I haven't handled things exactly like I wanted, but I've adjusted course. I don't want this to end, Peg, not when it's just starting. Tell me honestly. Do you?"

She stared at something over his shoulder. "Things are getting too complicated."

With a capital C. "They have been since the day we met." He tucked a strand of hair behind her ear. "Give us a chance. Haven't we been having a good time—inside the bedroom and out?"

He felt like he was arguing for a land ordinance before the town council, putting all his charm and persuasion behind his words.

"Don't *ever* pull anything like that again." Her voice was as flat as her stare.

She couldn't voice her hurt, but he could see it in the tense lines around her mouth, in her tough-as-nails gaze.

"I won't. I'm sorry I made you think I didn't respect you."

"Fine. I'm sorry too."

His arm circled her, and she didn't bolt. He curved the other one around her waist until he could lock his hands around her.

They stayed like that for a moment, and then she pulled back to look into his eyes. "What *was* that kiss earlier?"

"That was the I-don't-know-if-I'll-ever-kiss-you-again kiss."

Her liquid eyes scanned his face. "Think you could do an impression?"

So, she wasn't going to talk about him admitting he loved her. Why was he surprised? Worse, why was he hurt?

"My Foghorn Leghorn is better."

Her smile started slowly, like slight trickle from a gardening hose until it turns into a full gush. "I object to being kissed by a chicken."

His lips nuzzled her neck. "Well, then, I suppose I can practice it." The atomic clock in the family room signaled that they had more time. "I might have more than kissing in mind."

She strode across the linoleum. "Me too."

"Let me tell Dustin we'll pick them up in a while." His fingers keyed in the text. "It'll have to be quicker than I'd like." Quicker than making love to the woman he'd finally admitted to loving.

"I'm sure you'll find a way to make it memorable."

As she left the room, he stared at Dustin's face on his phone display, thought about how he'd given Peggy the means to hurt his family by doing her duty.

He'd gone with his gut by deciding to trust her.

Doing so might be the biggest gamble of his life.

CHAPTER 32

Peggy caught sight of her flushed face in the hallway mirror and pressed her hands to her cheeks. Mac's footsteps echoed behind her on the linoleum floor.

What in the world was she doing?

Another force seemed to have taken control of her body. How else could she explain letting the Big Three words make her this mushy? Her heart had expanded instantly, just like the Grinch in that Dr. Seuss cartoon Keith loved to watch.

Mac's hand covered hers when he caught up to her. He smiled, tightening his grip, as they walked up the stairs together. Her lips tingled with energy, and the tug of a smile broke free. He brought her hand to his lips and kissed it.

She picked up her pace, pulling him along to her bedroom. When she crossed the threshold, nerves popped up like gravel from a semi-truck. Her unmade bed was covered in laundry. She darted forward to gather up the clothes, her face burning now, balling up her clean, but old panties in one hand.

Mac picked up a heap of clothes. "If we had more time, I'd help you fold."

Her legs almost gave out. A man who volunteered for laundry?

"I have a better idea." He bundled the comforter and sheet into a lump resembling a bean bag, efficiently corralling the laundry. He dumped it in the corner. "There. Now we have a clear path."

Right. It's not like they'd need a comforter. She pretty much didn't care if they even used the bed.

He held out his hand to her. "Come here, Peg."

That force nudged her forward again. He framed her face with his hands, thumbs caressing her cheeks, making her feel cherished. Oh God, that's exactly why she was here. No one had *ever* done that for her before. She closed her eyes, the ground moving under her feet again, just like it had when he'd said those three damn words.

His mouth feathered her eyelids—a bit weird, but pleasant—and continued across her brow.

"I...you said we didn't have a lot of time," she said in a shaky voice, one she didn't recognize.

He made a humming sound as he caressed her face and then moved to her neck, spreading fires across her skin. "I forgot how much Dustin loves to eat and spend my money. He's going to milk this for all it's worth."

Right. His speed-happy nephew was taking care of her kid. He had a friend who called in bomb threats. And another who blew whistles. Dustin was like a black-and-white cookie. Could he be trusted?

"Maybe we should go get them now."

He pressed an open-mouthed kiss to her neck in a place that drove her wild. One knee buckled. His warm hands wrapped around her hips, and he pressed his fabulous erection into her side. "They'll be fine. Trust me."

That command again. His velvety voice vaporized her mommy-nerves and brought her further under his spell—the one he'd cast over her the first time they'd met.

"Kiss me, dammit!" she finally demanded, tired of her wandering thoughts.

He framed her face again. "Your wish is my command, love."

Not the L-word. It rattled her to the core.

His mouth sipped at hers, kissing the corners. She opened her lips and took the kiss to dark, carnal levels, rubbing her tongue against his in a silky dance, sucking on his bottom lip. She tugged on his cargo shorts, wanting to feel his hot skin against hers.

He undid her shorts and chucked them to the floor. Snagged her panties down her legs. She stepped out of them and stripped off her shirt. He did the same and came toward her—all naked, mouth-watering male. She pressed her face into his chest, nipping at the skin and following the dark trail down to his stomach.

"Oh, no you don't. I wouldn't be able to take it, and Peg, I plan to make love to you until you call out my name."

Didn't she always?

He nudged her backward until her knees hit the bed. She lowered her body, and he followed her down, guiding her legs apart. His mouth took her breast, sucking softly at first and then with increasing pressure. Her elbows gave out. She fell back onto the mattress, her heels digging into the bed. His finger dipped into her core and caressed her with unmistakable tenderness.

The emotion, the heat, and the lust brought her to a quick orgasm. She panted as his touch deepened.

"Give me more," he commanded.

Like she had a choice.

The tug from his fingers pushed her higher, the pleasure making everything inside her pulse long and hard.

A foil packet tore. She opened her eyes and watched as he slid on the condom. Rising to her elbows, she feathered his erection. He took away her hand and grabbed the other. Stretched out full length over her and pressed inside slowly, stretching her, filling her to the quick. He kissed her lips and then backed up a foot from her face.

"Don't close your eyes," he demanded silkily and began to move.

Her hips opened wider to cradle his frame, allowing him to deepen the penetration. Those stoplight green eyes held her in their thrall, making her moan with each thrust.

"Oh God. More," she called out.

His pace quickened, and she wrapped her legs around his waist, tunneling herself to him. The fire was red-hot this time, uncontainable, threatening to spill over into new territory. It was burning through any barriers she'd ever erected against him.

"Mac," she cried out.

He stopped. Her muscles quivered, waiting.

"I love you," he murmured, looking straight into her soul, the tenderness and lust merging as one in her vision.

Her heart exploded, sending a cry up her throat to her lips. "Oh, Mac." Then her body exploded too, bucking and quaking in his arms.

He thrust madly into her and took his own release, calling out her name. She curled her fingers around his and let everything become one pink mellow glow.

His rapid breathing tickled her ear, but she didn't move, didn't *want* to move. She pressed her head against his to deepen their connection. Took in the smell of sweat and cologne on his skin.

He finally drew back and rolled them to their sides. His fingers pushed back the hair flattened against her cheek and traced her mouth.

"I love you. When you start thinking about all the reasons things won't work, remember that."

Thinking. Yeah, she hated that.

His thumb traced the area around her heart. "If you let yourself, I think you'll be pretty good at loving me too."

She looked away. Talking about that after what she'd felt in his arms was too confusing.

"You can trust your heart, Peg. I do."

The organ he was talking about kicked her in the rib, almost as if it wanted more space. She brought her gaze back to his earnest one. "I don't know why."

He leaned down and kissed her lightly on the lips. "Because you're brave and strong. And when you decide to love someone, you go all in." His mouth turned up. "I respect that. I'm the same way."

His poker reference made her shoulder blades itch. She wished she could have blamed it on bed bugs.

"You're saying we aren't that different."

He slid out of her and disposed of the condom. Then he pulled her onto his chest. "Other than the obvious, no."

"You took one hell of a risk telling me about Dustin." And wasn't that why she hadn't ordered him from her house? She knew what his family meant to him, and in telling her, he had proven how much *she* meant—and how much he trusted her. God, no wonder she was a big mush ball.

His hand swept her bangs from her forehead. "If I asked you to promise never to do anything with what I told you, would you?"

Her elbows locked to her side as she thought it over. Could she really give him that promise?

What did they have after all the investigating they'd done? Nothing. It had been a vague threat. He was right about that.

And hadn't he handled the punk kid seriously? He'd used his lawyer. It was kinda like using the law, right? It wasn't like the kid was getting off scot-free, the woman inside her rationalized.

But the Feds were involved. Tons of money had been spent on the search. It was her duty to do her job, the deputy argued back

"Okay, I promise," she said, surprising herself.

When he kissed her, her darn heart glowed like Christmas lights. Even her toes curled. She wanted to lay there with him forever. He held her until their bodies cooled, kissing her long and deep, lingering over her. Finally her mommy meter pinged in. She eyed the clock and pressed her hands against his chest.

"We should get dressed. It's close to Keith's bedtime."

His finger trailed along her forearm when she sat up. "Would Keith tell Dustin that?"

The laugh she huffed out was the easiest one she'd had in his presence. Her smile wanted to expand until it was clown-size. Great, she could run off to the circus. "Probably not."

He pushed off the bed and pulled his clothes on, grinning at her. When he wadded up the big ball of bedding and laundry in his arms and dumped it on the bed, the love bubble popped. She sighed. Laundry. God, another mess to deal with after Keith went to sleep. He'd probably be so hyped up on sugar, she'd be lucky to have him settled in before ten o'clock. Summer hours sucked.

Mac tugged the comforter out and folded it neatly. Then he proceeded to snag her jeans and press the pant legs together in a perfect crease.

"What are you doing?" she demanded, her voice almost breathy with shock.

"Helping you with laundry. It won't take long. Then we can fetch Dustin and Keith."

"You can't be real," she said as she watched him sort socks, shirts, and pants with quick efficiency into two piles—hers and Keith's.

His mega-watt grin stole her breath.

"Please, who do you think does laundry at my house?"

Her shoulder lifted. "The maid?"

"We don't have one. We only have a cleaning lady who comes every two weeks. Me, Abbie, and Dustin all pitch in. We wanted Dustin to grow up doing chores, learning responsibility."

"Right," she responded, sounding like the village idiot.

"Are you planning to dress in the same clothes you had on or do you want me to fold those too?" He sounded amused. She balled up her shirt and caught him in the chest with it, and he folded it with a grin on his face. "I like seeing this side of you."

She reached for another shirt and joined him in the work. "Honestly, I like this side of *you.* " Sweat drying at his temples from their lovemaking. Folding clothes on her bed, relaxed and charming.

"I'm happy to show it to you anytime you want."

"Sometimes I think you're too good to be true," she confessed.

He stilled for a second and then resumed his folding. "And then you remember I'm a poker player. Peg, I'm going to trust you to look at the whole picture before coming to any conclusions about me."

"I'm surprised you brought that up." She'd rather be a bury-her-head-in-the-sand ostrich.

"You're going to have to come to terms with who I am and what I do."

She sank onto the bed, her knees weakening for a different reason this time—the thought of losing him. "And who are you?"

Keith's *Toy Story* shirt fell to his lap. It looked ridiculous next to his massive body, but somehow sweet.

"I'm a man who loves his family and has sacrificed for them. I had to take risks to protect Abbie and Dustin, and in the process, I discovered that I like playing the odds and making money in a structured, high-pressure game like poker. But I wanted to be more than Maven the Maverick. I majored in engineering at Princeton before I had to drop out, so it's no surprise I combined my talent for poker with my desire to build something. I found my niche in hotels, and I love it."

Her initial background check on him had given her most of that information, but hearing it from him made her darn heart power-up like Keith's old Glowworm. She rubbed her hand against her chest.

"And your flaws?"

"Well, I'm overprotective of my family." His head cocked to the side, considering. "I've been known to party hard with Rhett when I'm away from home, especially when I was younger and needed to blow off steam. I don't always think the law is the best way to handle a situation. I used to have a hell of a temper, but I've mellowed. I can be impatient when I want something, but I've worked on that, and I've gotten better at waiting for what I really want."

Folding clothes and listening to his life story. Could life turn any weirder?

"You should ask Abbie or Dustin. They'll say I have plenty of flaws."

She doubted that. The more she knew him, the more she realized that he always tried to do what he thought was right.

"What about you? What's your short suit?" he asked.

"My what?" God, she hoped this wasn't a poker thing.

He laughed. "The areas that stretch you. I like that phrase better than flaws. Flaws seem permanent."

Talk about her flaws? Jeez, was this like an interview? She gave a big sigh. "Well, as you know, I have a one-track mind sometimes."

"And when that involves sex, I wholeheartedly approve."

His easy humor loosened the knot in her chest about talking about herself. "Hah! I can lose myself in work. It's gotten better since I had Keith because I love spending time with him. He's my guy."

"You're a great mother. Tell me something about you that I don't know."

"How am I supposed to know what that is?"

His patient look made her shake out a pair of pants, folding them carefully. "Fine. I liked to play piano in the music room in high school." Part of her couldn't believe she'd just told him that. Even Tanner didn't know. She hadn't wanted her brother to take on an extra job to pay for the lessons they couldn't afford.

"So, you have an ear for music. I'd like to hear you play sometime."

She fiddled with some lint on her clothes, heat rushing up her neck. "It's been years. I probably suck."

"You might be rusty, but that's what's fun about rediscovering an old passion. It comes back to you. I have a grand piano in the hotel. You can use it anytime."

That would mean she'd have to step foot in his hotel for reasons other than sheriff business. "That's a nice offer," she said even though she knew she'd never do it.

"Well, are you ready to pick up the boys?" he asked, folding the last shirt and laying it on Keith's pile.

It wobbled and almost fell over before he righted it—rather like how she felt inside when he talked about picking up their boys like they were a family.

"Sure," she responded.

"Peg," he called quietly when she reached the door. "I meant what I said... I've learned to be patient."

As they walked out of her house, his hand bumped hers. She glanced over. There was a question in his eyes. Was she willing to hold his hand in front of her house? In public?

Her fingers flexed, but she couldn't reach for him.

His face fell before he pasted on a smile. His patience wasn't the problem. Deep down, she knew the problem was *her*. Was she capable of reconciling the man she was falling for with the poker player she feared?

She didn't know. All she could be sure of was the deep yearning she felt for the comforting warmth of his hand in hers as the sun began its dip behind the mountains.

CHAPTER 33

riends had a way of turning up like bad pennies, so Peggy wasn't surprised when Jill and Meredith appeared on her doorstep the next night. Keith whooped and hollered, basking in their kisses, hugs, and high-fives like some crazy puppy. She just crossed her arms, narrowed her eyes. They were looking for girl talk. She wasn't going to make this easy for them.

"We've brought take-out from Brian's and wine for you and Mere," Jill announced, using her pregnant frame to nudge Peggy into the house. It was a dirty, sneaky move.

"Tanner's going to take this little guy out to the ballpark," Meredith informed her, pushing on Jill's back like they were in line at a hot club, and the bouncer had just started letting people inside.

"*Et tu, Brute?*" Peggy snarled at Tanner, wondering when he'd started caving in to estrogen.

Her brother folded his arms across his chest. Stared back at her. "Like I could stop them. Plus, after hearing about your charged exit from Mac's hotel, it might be a good idea for you to talk about *it*."

Sticking to a vague reference in front of Keith was appreciated, but their unannounced visit still annoyed the crap out of her.

Keith stopped jumping up and down next to Tanner, trying to get his attention. "Why are you so mad at Mr. Maven, Mom? I really like him and Dustin."

Note to self. Vague allusions no longer worked on her kid. Darn it.

His wide-eyed gaze filled her with shame. She liked Mac. She didn't like Mac. Shit. "It's complicated."

Keith crooked his finger. Tanner knelt down until her son could put his lips to his ear. "They were yelling so loud last night Dustin took me away. He said it was for ice cream, but I know better."

His stage whisper needed some work, because she heard every word.

"You're a smart one," Tanner whispered back. "Why don't you get into the car? I'll be there in a sec."

Keith looked from one of them to the other.

She could all but hear the little gears turning in his head. "Come give me a hug."

He darted over and wrapped his arms around her waist. "I love you,

Mom. Bye."

"Love you too," she called as he sprinted off. Did everybody know she was a big ball of mess?

Tanner pointed a finger at her. "Talk to Mere and Jill, Peg. You need to get it all out. I haven't seen you this wound-up in years. I don't want you going nuclear when David arrives."

She lifted her chin, her older brother's bossiness pushing her buttons. "If I decide I need to go nuclear with David, it's my choice. I'm not as forgiving as you."

"No, you're not, but I love you anyway. If you want to talk to me about what's really bothering you—not Mac, not the hotel, not David—you know where to find me." He turned and headed off.

"And what would that be?" she demanded, feeling like a cat caught in a paper bag.

"Our jerk father, what else?" he called over his shoulder.

Something snapped inside her like a rubber band. No, that wasn't it. Her dad was dead. It was over. There was no need to dredge up all her old hurts. She was an adult, and she was over it.

And yet Mac had told her she wasn't an adult in her emotional life. Damn him.

She clenched her hands together, watching her brother and nephew drive off together. She thought about walking away from the house on foot, but while Jill wouldn't be able to catch her, Meredith would. She gave the nearby planter of red geraniums a swift kick and went inside.

The scene in her kitchen stopped her cold. They had the table decorated all Martha-Stewart- like. Jeez, why did some girls have to be so...girly?

They looked like two grown-up candy stripers—one who'd gotten into trouble (in the family way) and the other who only wanted to usher in annoying bursts of good cheer.

Jill folded a napkin into some undecipherable animal. "Come sit down. We're not leaving, so you might as well eat the spread Brian prepared for us."

She dragged her feet across the linoleum like Keith would. "You think giving me food is going to make this any less weird?"

Meredith grabbed Jill's arm when she opened her mouth—probably to spew out a Jill-ism like *weirdness is how you know you can be best friends.* "Okay, we know you don't want us here, but we're your friends. This is what friends do. They talk."

Her eye twitched when she took a seat. "*Why?*"

"Because," Jill said, shoving the platter of coq au vin at her.

"Eat!" Meredith ordered. "We're not here to debate the definition of friendship with you."

Jill scooped up some chicken. "No, we're here to help you talk your way out of your Love Confusion. This is the safe zone."

"My what?" Peggy asked. Chalk it up to another Jillism.

She took a bite of the chicken and moaned. "Mac's in love with you.

It's written all over him. He won't answer any of my questions. It's like he's gone Love Mute or something."

Peggy handed her a plate. "First, stop talking with your mouth full."

"I'm starving."

"Nothing new there," Meredith droned as she fussed over the spread of food.

"Just you wait, Mere. You're next."

Meredith made herself a plate, and then started preparing one for Peggy. "We're taking our time. Peggy, what were you saying?"

She dialed back to what she'd been saying. "Right. Second," Peggy continued, raising a finger. "Stop talking about love, okay? You might be pregnant, Jill, but I've gotta draw the line somewhere."

Jill held up a finger, chewing. They waited. "Are you saying you're this upset because Mac stopped the reward and decided to move on? When are you going to admit you have strong feelings for him? I won't use the L-word since I know you'll freak."

Peggy took the plate of food and glass of wine Meredith handed to her, determined to avoid any discussion of her feelings. "What do you know about the reward being suspended?"

"You're changing the subject. I'll let you for the moment. Mac announced to the staff that the authorities and our security team had hit a dead end. Since he's never had a threat to any of the Maven Industry properties before, and this was a vague one, we're moving on."

Peggy had been about to chow down on the chicken, but she stopped. She couldn't eat now, knowing Mac hadn't even told the truth to Jill, one of his closest friends and senior employees.

He trusted her—and only her. He hadn't exaggerated. Hadn't a part of her guessed that?

Her back started itching like she had hives. She yanked up her shirt and scraped at the spot with her nails.

"You get bit by something?" Meredith asked.

Yeah, she almost answered. *The Trust Dilemma.* She still wasn't sure how she felt about the whole thing. Was she disregarding her duty to the law by keeping his secret?

"Do you need some Benadryl?" Meredith reached for her purse.

"No, I'm fine," she replied, as if shoving your hand up your shirt to scratch your back could be considered fine.

"Mac didn't bite you again, did he?" Jill singsonged, a stupid grin on her face.

"No. Why don't you stuff some more chicken into your mouth?" she fired back.

"Thanks, I will. So, why are you all white-faced and back-scratching?"

She was white-faced? Probably the shock of realizing how deep Mac's confidence in her ran.

"Okay, I'll ask it. Have you finally realized you're in love with him?" Meredith asked, sipping her ruby-red wine.

The question made her flinch. "What? No! Ah." God, why was

everyone talking about love all of a sudden? It wasn't like she was living in the 60s in a yurt.

"*Ah...*" Jill trilled encouragingly.

Peggy gave her the stink eye. "You have even less of a filter when you're pregnant."

She gave a drumming impression on her tummy. "I know. Isn't it great? It really cuts through the bullshit. So has Mac told you he loves you yet? When a guy clams up like he has it usually means he's in The Grip."

Peggy couldn't sit still anymore. She stood and turned in a circle, yanking on her hair. "Yes! Okay, he's told me. Will that make you leave me alone?"

Meredith rose and put her hands on Peggy's shoulders, and she stopped spinning around like a top. "It's totally normal to feel like you're off your rocker when you get involved with someone new—especially when you're as busy fighting it as you are."

Jill reached for more chicken. "Exactly! Don't you remember how messed up I was when Brian and I first got together?"

"Your shrieks could have curdled milk," Peggy replied dryly.

"See! That's what we're talking about." Jill spooned some fancy herb-crusted fingerling potatoes onto her plate. "You're about ready to combust."

"Peg," Meredith said gently. "We're only trying to help."

"Look. I know you are. I don't process like this. Talking isn't my MO. I need to think about it."

"You can't think your way through a feeling," Jill commented, popping open the lid of a jar of the smallest pickles Peggy had ever seen. There was a joke there.

"Yes, I can. I'm a cop. I think my way through my feelings all the time."

"This isn't work, Peg. Won't you please sit back down?"

She threw a hand out at the table. "What? And talk about my private feelings over chicken, potatoes, and pickles? No thanks. Mac and I are doing what we need to do. That's all I'm going to say."

"You called him Mac!" Jill cried out. "That's a huge step forward." She rose, came around, and gave her a hug, bumping her with the kids. One of the twins kicked her, obviously unhappy about being squashed.

Her cheeks flamed. "Yes, I call him Mac—sometimes. Are you happy?"

"Yes, especially since you're blushing," Jill cooed.

"Jill, leave her be. You're being a pest." Meredith handed her one of the little pickles. "Suck on this."

She rolled her eyes, but did as her sister suggested.

"Tanner has told me a bit about your parents, especially your dad," Meredith continued.

"Stop right there." Her heartbeat raced like she'd done a sprint up the stairs. "Tanner can talk to you about whatever he wants, but I don't have to. That subject is off limits." Even the mention of it made acid pool in her stomach.

Meredith's face fell. Jill bit into her pickle.

"I don't want to upset you," Peggy said, her cheeks burning, "but this is not something I want to talk about. Okay?"

Jill twirled her napkin around her finger when she sat back down. Meredith joined her, so Peggy felt weird standing up. She landed hard in her chair.

"People around town are going to see you together and ask questions," Jill said "I just want you to be prepared. We're afraid you might sock someone."

Clearly she needed to dial it back a bit if they were worried she'd lose it that easily. "No one's going to talk because we aren't going to be seen like that together."

Meredith's brow knitted. "But you're sleeping together. That means you'll go out."

In Mac's world. "No. It doesn't. We don't have that kind of an arrangement."

"You're fuck buddies?" Jill's mouth formed an O.

"Jeez, well, that's blunt." She hadn't thought about that phrase. She'd had friends-with-benefits before when she was younger. This wasn't at all the same. "I wouldn't call us that." She had no idea what to call them.

"What term would you use then?"

Jill could always be counted on to push the envelope.

"I don't know. Who are you? Sherlock Holmes?"

"No, but I love the BBC version. That Benedict Cumberbun is smokin' hot."

"His name is Cumberbatch, you idiot." Peggy finally shoveled in the coq au vin. God, it was good, but the cocktail onions looked like eye balls to her. "Stop, please," she said when she finished chewing. "You're confusing me."

"So, Mac's in love with you. You're sleeping together, but you're not going out. That sounds like—"

"It's none of your beeswax," she interrupted, quoting Keith.

"Keith seems to be really crazy about Mac and Dustin... Are you sure you don't want to talk about where this is going?" Meredith asked.

"I can handle everything myself. Thanks." She piled the food in so she wouldn't have to talk. Unlike Jill, she didn't spout off with her mouth full.

"You're a tough cookie, Peg, but we love you. If you change your mind, let us know." Meredith pointed at Jill when she opened her mouth to object. "Nope. That's all she wrote, sis. Peg's made it clear she doesn't want to talk, so let's eat."

Jill made a clucking sound under her breath.

Meredith gave her a warning glare.

"Apparently she's eaten so much chicken she's starting to sound like one," Peggy commented.

"Ha ha," Jill said.

"I think it's *boc, boc, boc*," Meredith perfectly imitated.

The chicken talk reminded her of Mac doing Foghorn Leghorn—both with her and Keith and Dustin. A fuck buddy wouldn't make Looney Tunes' voices with you and your kid.

Then again she'd known that all along.

They ate the delicious food, discussing safer topics—Arthur's shenanigans at Bingo night and Jill's best story of the week from Don't Soy with Me.

Until Keith burst through the door an hour later, saying "Mom! You're never going to guess who we saw at the ice cream shop."

Tanner regarded her warily.

"Who?"

"Mr. Maven, Dustin, and Abbie. She told me I could call her that when I said it's weird calling her Ms. Maven since she and Mr. Maven aren't married. They're brother and sister and that would be *so* gross." He made a gagging sound, ever the actor. "Mr. Maven likes Cherry Garcia like I do, and Dustin let me try his peanut butter crunch. Abbie even gave me a taste of her lemon sorbet. It kinda tasted like a pie without the crust. Mr. Maven and Dustin teased her about eating girly ice cream."

"Did they now?" she asked.

"Yes, and I asked Mr. Maven and Dustin when they were coming over next time. Mr. Maven said he'd have to talk to you. I love it when they come over. Dustin's like my friend—even though he's so much older than me."

Meredith was right. Her kid was already emotionally involved.

"Keith—"

"Dustin says he'll show me how to dribble the ball and shoot it right between someone's legs. Wouldn't that be cool?"

Tanner, Jill, and Meredith all avoided her gaze.

"That's great," she managed and started packing up the food they'd brought over. It was time for them to go so she could talk to her son alone.

"I asked Mr. Maven if he'd teach me how to play poker, but he said you don't like the game. I told him you just don't like it when people play for real, and since it won't be real, he can teach me."

A potato fell off the spoon she was using and rolled across the table. Tanner caught it and handed it back, that knowing glint in his eye. She finished packing the leftovers. Leave it to her kid to come up with that logic.

"Mac's right," she responded. "It's not a game I approve of. Let's stick with soccer for now." She didn't say *until you're older*, because it wouldn't make any difference in how she felt.

"But Mom!"

"Let's say goodnight to everyone. It's getting close to the twins' bedtime." She'd have high-fived herself over that one if no one else had been around.

His eyes widened. "They have a bedtime even in *there*?"

Jill caught her pleading glance. "Yep. Me too. These two tucker me out. Come give me hugs and kisses."

Keith basked in the glow of her adoration. Peggy managed weak hugs with everyone but Tanner, who just gave her that big-brother stare, daring her to man up.

Keith continued to chatter as she shut the door behind their uninvited guests.

"Keith," she called as he pulled off his shoes and socks by the door.

"Yeah, Mom?"

"Why do you think Mr. Maven comes over with Dustin to help us around the yard?"

"I know he's making up for something he did." His grin accentuated the chocolate stain in the corner of his mouth. "But I really think it's because Mr. Maven likes you like a girl."

She gulped. "Where did you hear that?"

He ducked his head. "Don't be mad, but I heard you talking about him biting you. When you went outside, I asked him why he did it. He said he got excited like I do sometimes when I want to hug you and hurt you on accident. He said he really liked you and was sorry."

He'd talked with her son about liking her and hadn't told her? "You were eavesdropping again." God, she hoped her voice was stern.

"I said I was *sorry*. I know you didn't like him at first, but I think you like him now, right? Plus, you wouldn't let him kiss you if you didn't. Sometimes you smile after he leaves. Uncle Tanner says that's what a girl does when she likes a boy. I thought everything was okay until you two fought last night. Are you breaking up? Dustin wouldn't tell me *anything*. "

When had he become this grown up? Here he was talking to her about adult relationships. She wasn't ready for his childhood to end. She dug her fingernails into her palms.

He threw his socks aside and scurried up to her. "Mom, don't be upset. I told Mr. Maven I'd punch him if he hurt you. He might be bigger, but I'm not afraid."

The whites of his eyes made him look like a frightened horse during a storm, but the bravado and toughness couldn't be missed.

She'd seen that look in the mirror throughout her life.

"Do you need me to punch Mr. Maven?" he asked, his voice serious.

She bit the inside of her cheek. "No. He and I had a disagreement. We're back to being...friends."

The word seemed as weak as plain toast.

"You mean like boyfriend and girlfriend?"

God, who had come up with those titles? She stared into his happy face. "Adults don't use those terms, honey. Now, you should head up to take a bath." Her nose tunneled under his armpit. "You stink."

He sniffed like a little piggy. "No, you stink."

The game ensued. She repeated the phrase. He volleyed it back. And on and on it went.

When she put him to bed, she walked down the hallway to her room. Fell against the wall, exhausted from the discussion. She hadn't told Keith anything definitive because she didn't know how long she and Mac would last.

Her son was too observant by half. He'd caught her smiling at Mac? She rarely smiled, and she detested it when people sent her emails with smiley faces. Even frowned when she saw those happy faces on all the signs at Wal-Mart. Who needed smiles anyway?

Certainly not her.

CHAPTER 34

Extending a dinner invitation to your brother's... Abbie realized she didn't know what to call Peggy. Girlfriend seemed ludicrous. Love interest seemed too intimate.

She waved to a few members of the staff as she made her way to the hotel's flower cooler. If Mac wanted Peggy in his life, she was going to support him. That meant inviting Peggy and Keith over for a family dinner. And since she suspected Peggy wouldn't want to come, she was going to make it hard for her to say no. Showing up with Dustin and a bouquet of flowers to invite them in person for a casual dinner in a few hours would test the manners of even the brusquest person.

After selecting the flowers she wanted and wrapping them in white paper to match the assorted calla lilies, tying the bundle with a simple blue ribbon, she headed out to find Dustin. She had a feeling he was watching poker somewhere.

She found Aaron on the main poker floor and asked him where her son was. He told her Dustin was watching Rhett and some Silicon Valley executives in the Aspen Room. Her heart quickened. She hadn't been able to stop thinking about Rhett since their talk, and she wanted to see him again. Badly.

As soon as she walked into the room, she changed her mind. He was sitting directly across from her, wearing a partially open black leather jacket showcasing his gorgeous chest. His poker babes were leaning over his shoulders, mounds of cleavage pouring out of matching red sequin cocktail dresses.

Dear God, sequins during the day. Who did that?

Rhett, that's who.

And to top it all off, Dustin was looking at their boobs—and *not* the poker table.

The distraction she darn well knew Rhett encouraged from his "babes" clearly worked on most men, even those who weren't playing poker.

This was why they so didn't suit. She'd almost forgotten it the other day.

Rhett was so engrossed in his cards that he didn't notice as she walked along the edge of the room toward Dustin. The executives, most of them dressed in polo shirts sporting their company logos, gave her a quick glance before returning to the death-defying cleavage on display. Rhett told a dirty joke that made her blush.

Dustin was laughing right along with everyone else when she put her hand on his arm. He jumped and sent a final guilty look at the poker babes. She wanted to say, yes, I saw you ogling those women, but this wasn't the time. Who could refrain from looking when their boobs were out there like that?

"We need to go," she whispered.

"Uh...okay, let me tell Rhett goodbye."

She didn't answer, just watched as he checked his fohawk like he was Danny Zuko in *Grease*. Fantastic, she thought. Now her son was trying to impress Rhett's poker babes.

Rhett looked over as Dustin approached. And then he saw her.

She'd seen enough of his easy charm to identify when there was a crack in his composure, even if it lasted only a second. His eyelids flicked down and then he stood, causing his poker babes to quickly straighten and step back. More cleavage bounced. Abbie ground her teeth.

"Excuse me a minute, boys," he drawled out as he grabbed Dustin in a one-arm hug and came forward. "Hi, Abbie."

Rhett had been playing poker at the hotel frequently, but she hadn't really watched him since the grand opening weekend tournament. This is what Rhett was. This is what he did.

Despite all he'd said to her, nothing had truly changed. He was still the wild poker player who told dirty jokes and had poker babes named Raven and Vixen who could have doubled as porno actresses.

She still felt ashamed of this side of him and didn't want to be associated with it.

"Dustin, it was good to see you, son. Why don't you give me a minute with your mom?"

Her son must have known it was a smart move to dash off because he was out the door in three strides. Rhett grabbed her elbow and led her to the bar, motioning away the room's private bartender.

"I need to go," she told him, but he wouldn't release her arm.

"You want to run," he retorted, "and I'm not letting that happen. We got closer than I ever dreamed of the other day. You are not retreating."

She raised an eyebrow at him. "Don't tell me what to do."

"I could see you bristling from across the room. Dammit, how many times do I have to tell you that this is all an act?"

"I know it's an act, Rhett," she whispered, acutely aware of the eyes watching them. "It's just one I don't want to be associated with. My son either."

His mouth turned grim. "I would never allow Dustin to be hurt by what I do."

"And yet he was just ogling your poker babes' cleavage like every other man in the room."

"Well, *I* wasn't. The only breasts I want to see are yours, and I hate to be the one to tell you the obvious, but teenage boys—heck all men—like to look at breasts."

She set the bouquet aside so she wouldn't crush the flowers. "Which you have no qualms about encouraging in your *act*. Rhett, I have to think of Dustin here."

He growled low in his throat. "Don't use Dustin as an excuse. That kid knows this is an act, and he knows I love you."

She shook her head. "Dustin is impressionable, and recent events have proven that. I don't like him being around this kind of display."

He took off his black cowboy hat and ran a hand through his ash-colored hair. "You let him watch Mac play all the time. And me too. This is what we do, Abbie."

"I know," she said sadly, realizing any dreams she'd had about their future together were flat-out stupid. She couldn't walk into a tournament with Rhett and his poker babes. The thought was ridiculous and embarrassing.

His hand cupped her shoulder, and she felt the charge. "Don't let this stand between us. I can't stop playing poker for you. It's who I am. I love it. Just like I love you."

The entreaty in his eyes couldn't be missed, and she felt a ball of hurt lodge under her heart. "I need to go."

When she turned away to pick up the bouquet, he grabbed her arm. "I'm not giving up, you know. I'll find a way to have you and keep playing. There has to be a solution."

Raven and Vixen were entertaining the other men, weaving around the table, their husky laughter hanging in the air like smoke.

"Don't bother," she said and yanked her arm free.

Her feet ate up the floor as she walked out. Dustin was waiting for her, a penitent look on his face. She said nothing, and neither did he. Rhett was right. He was a teenager, and to ask him not to look at cleavage was silly. She'd talk to Mac about it and let him handle it. They'd agreed he would deal with that kind of stuff anyway.

As they drove to Peggy's house, she kept her eyes trained on the road, trying to keep out all emotion. She'd cried over this situation before, and she wasn't doing it again. Rhett was not going to affect her anymore.

When they pulled into Peggy's driveway and left the car, Abbie surveyed the flower arrangement in her hands before plucking out a blue daisy and shoving it on the right side to give the bouquet balance.

"Mom, relax," Dustin finally commented. "They look fine."

Fine wasn't good enough. This she had to at least get right. She rang the doorbell of Peggy's house. Tapped her foot.

The door opened. Peggy's eyes narrowed as she scanned their group, probably looking for Mac.

"Hey, Ms. McBride," Dustin said. "I'm not here to work. Not that I don't like that, but my mom wanted to give you some flowers and invite you to our house for dinner."

Her son had stolen her lines, or maybe he was trying to help her out since he knew she was upset about Rhett. Watching Peggy's jaw tense made her want to reach for her antacids.

"Here," she said, thrusting out the flowers.

Peggy eyed them like they might be infected with powdery mildew and didn't take them.

"Is Keith home?" Dustin asked.

"Yeah, he's inside, watching TV."

"Cool, I'll go hang with him if that's okay."

Dustin was probably eager to get away from her, Abbie realized.

"I told him I'd teach him how to dribble a soccer ball."

The corners of Peggy's mouth tilted up in a reluctant smile. "That's nice of you. He's really excited."

Her son kicked at the ground with his ever-growing feet. "He's a fun kid."

Peggy stepped back to let him walk by her. The flowers fell to Abbie's side, and the daisy dropped to the ground. She darted forward to pick it up and almost nailed Peggy in the head when she did the same.

"Whoa!" Peggy called, pushing out a hand to prevent the collision.

Abbie teetered on her heels before steadying herself and rising. "Dustin said you probably don't like flowers. I'm sorry. I didn't know what else to bring."

The plastic wrapping crackled when Peggy finally took the bouquet from her. "It was...nice of you."

The woman would have flunked any etiquette class with that whopper.

An awkward silence descended.

"So, you're probably wondering why I'm here." The dinner invitation needed more of an explanation.

The woman didn't say a word. Is that why Mac liked her? God knows she and Dustin always had something to say.

"Mac said he told you about the bomb threat." Her stomach churned at the very thought. "He said you'd keep it to yourself." Please God.

Peggy's mouth twisted like she'd eaten a sourball.

"I wanted to thank you. Dustin means everything to me, and this whole incident has been...crazier than I ever imagined. He did the right thing by telling us, and Mac handled the situation with Dustin's *former* friend. Trust me, Mac's a strict disciplinarian." She didn't add anything about herself. Peggy wasn't "dating" her.

Peggy's grip on the bouquet was crushing the yellow Gerbera daisies. Abbie wished she'd give them some room.

The woman still didn't speak. Well, maybe Abbie could shock her into having a conversation. "I know we don't know each other well, but my brother is in love with you."

No reaction. Great. Her poker face was as award-winning as Mac's.

"We all adore Keith," she continued. "You've done an incredible job with him, and I know how hard that is. You've been more than fair to Dustin after the car incident." She took a deep breath, pressing on her burning diaphragm. "I'd like you to come to dinner tonight at our house so I can get to know you better."

Peggy's left eye twitched. Aha. So she wasn't inhuman.

"It's only a simple dinner. Dustin would love it. Mac would too, although he wanted you to know this was my idea."

"I just got home from work," Peggy finally responded.

The refusal couldn't be plainer, but Abbie had persuasive skills of her own.

"All the more reason to be spontaneous and let someone else cook. Everything's mostly in place. Mac's going to grill steaks. Please come." She looked down at her open-toe buttercup sandals. "My brother means the world to me. He's sacrificed a lot to support us. You're the first person he's shown any serious interest in, and as his sister, I'd like to get to know you."

"Why? You don't want it to last."

Well, when the woman finally decided to talk, she could be downright bitchy.

Abbie met her hard gaze even though her heart was pounding. "As Mac pointed out, he has his own life to lead. I want him to be happy. Since you seem to make him that way, I trust his judgment. He's had more time to come to a positive conclusion about you. I'm asking you to give us both time to develop a conclusion about each other."

Peggy's death-grip on the bouquet loosened. The daisies were probably cheering over the extra space. "You didn't say positive."

Her mouth tilted up. "No, I didn't. But I'm willing to try. Are you?"

"Mom!" Keith yelled out like a banshee. His shoes pounded across the floor, and then he catapulted through the door, Dustin trailing in his wake.

"Dustin said we're invited to their house for dinner tonight. Can we please, please, *please* go? I want to see all his soccer trophies and everything."

"Gosh, a triple please," Peggy drawled. The flower wrapping crackled again as her hand clenched into a fist.

Abbie took note of her white knuckles. So, she wasn't too different from Mac and his poker players—just because she hid her emotions didn't mean she didn't have any. She thought about Rhett saying he and Mac had recognized each other. Perhaps that was how it was with Peggy and him. And then she realized she was thinking about Rhett, which so had to stop.

"Okay, we can go," Peggy finally said.

Abbie wasn't sure even Martha Stewart had any advice for hosting a reluctant guest. She'd have to check on her smart phone.

Keith lunged into the air and gave Dustin a high five. "Awesome! Can I wear this?"

"Sure, man. I'm wearing what I have on." Dustin cast a pleading glance at her. "Please tell me you aren't making this stuffy."

"Not at all. What everyone's wearing is fine." She nodded to Peggy's jean shorts and gray T-shirt. God, she hoped her face didn't show any disdain. What mother wore jean shorts?

"Great! We'll see you then," Keith popped out like a little gentleman.

Young kids always made her feel better. Abbie tapped him playfully on the nose. "I have something special for you for dessert."

"You do?" His eyes widened.

"It's only for special boys."

"Means I'm out," Dustin murmured.

Well, he knew he was on the rocks, but she still loved him.

"No, it doesn't. You just have to mind your Ps and Qs." Since he knew what she meant, she stared him down before turning back to Peggy. "How about seven?"

"Fine. Do you need us to bring anything?"

She waved a hand, back in control. "No, I've taken care of everything. Do you need directions?" she asked, her secret way of discovering if Mac had brought her to the house when they were gone.

Her gaze flicked up. "Yes. Thank you."

Yeah, Peggy had read her mind. It was good to know Mac hadn't gone that far. He'd never snuck a woman into their house before.

She wrote down the address on one of the butterfly sticky notes from her purse. Peggy gave it the stink eye like she had the flowers, but tucked it into her pocket.

"See you then."

"Mom! Can I go with Dustin now? I have lots to learn about dribbling."

Peggy gave him the Mother Warning Glare.

"Of course you can come now if it's okay with your mom," Abbie interjected. "Right, Dustin?"

"Sure, man. With those scrawny legs, it's gonna take you a while to learn." He gave his shoulder a little shove like he was a big-boy. Keith beamed.

Yeah, her son still had a ribbon of sweetness in him. Thank God.

"There's nothing wrong with your legs, Keith. Don't let Dustin tease you. He called me a lemon drop this morning," Abbie said, not wanting his feelings hurt.

Keith smiled shyly. "I like your dress. It looks pretty."

She kissed his forehead. "You're such a sweet boy."

"Can I go, mom? I'll be super good. I promise."

"Okay, you can go. But be sure to mind everyone."

He nodded and then raced over to the corner to pull on his neatly organized shoes. Her Organized Mother Gene cooed. They both liked order. Something to build on.

"We'll see you soon then."

"See ya later, Mom." Keith waved and tugged Abbie down the sidewalk.

As Abbie drove home, she couldn't stop thinking about the awkward dinner invitation. How in the world was she supposed to become friends with a woman who barely spoke? Worse, what in the world did Mac see in Peggy?

It would probably mystify people in the same way her entanglement

with Rhett would.
    Another reason why things could not go on with him.

CHAPTER 35

After a frantic call to Brian asking for a wine recommendation, Peggy darted to the liquor store on the way to Mac's house.

Mac's house.

Give her a straightjacket now, since she'd plumb lost her mind, she thought, as she walked up the path leading to the colossal mountain McMansion of stone, native wood, and rustic charm. He had to be kidding. There must be a maid lurking around here someplace.

She knocked on the door, taking in the enormous brass knocker that resembled a gigantic brass wiener. Who designed this stuff?

Mac opened the door with flourish. "Hi there," he murmured, his voice all whiskey and spice. No wonder she'd gone crazy. His voice had made her drunk.

"Your house is huge," she blurted out.

"Actually, it's about the same size as Tanner and Meredith's."

Her observational skills clearly weren't firing since it looked much bigger. "Get out."

"It's true. You can ask him."

"Tanner's been here?" she asked, hearing Keith's laughter in the background. Why was she surprised? Probably because he hadn't mentioned it—not that he would.

"Sure. He's a friend of mine. That's a nice label."

"What?" Was her tag out? She'd changed into black pants, a white shirt, and a tan jacket after seeing Abbie's yellow sundress.

His laugh huffed out. "The wine, Peg."

She held out the pricy bottle. "I asked Brian. I don't have a clue about wine. Honestly, I can take it or leave it."

"No matter. It's nice of you to go to the trouble. Besides I bought a special beer for you." A devilish gleam entered those stoplight green eyes. "You wouldn't slug me if I kissed you? All the prying eyes are in the kitchen, and I'm not sure I can make it through the evening without touching you."

Damn, that was hot.

He leaned forward, inch by slow inch. She watched him the whole way. When his lips settled on hers, her fingers tunneled through his thick hair. Who was she kidding? *She* wouldn't be able to make it through this insane evening without touching *him*.

His hand cradled her face when he pulled back. "I'm so glad you're here, Peg."

"Mom!" Keith yelled.

She jumped and stepped on Mac's foot. "Sorry. Coming, Keith."

Mac gave her another quick peck.

Her elbow connected with his rib. "Enough!"

"Don't look so guilty. Come on. Let me get you a drink so you can get settled."

Like that was going to happen. She pressed a hand to her Mexican-jumping-beans stomach.

The house's interior boggled her mind, all caramel-colored wood and sweeping arches. Like Tanner's, an enormous boulder-like fireplace punctuated the family room from floor to ceiling. The kitchen could have been on some ritzy version of *Top Chef*. The appliances sparkled, the granite gleamed.

Keith careened into her legs. "Mom. Isn't this place the coolest? Dustin showed me his trophies, and he's got like a million." He pressed a hand to his head. "Mr. Maven let me light the grill, and Abbie let me add the key ingredients to the salad, but I can't tell you what they are. It's a secret. Like the dessert, but you're gonna love it."

She scanned the others as Keith continued to summarize his exploits. Dustin was slicing red peppers on a cutting board as Abbie ground some powder in a mortar and pestle like an apothecary. Mac watched her as he uncapped a beer. When he brought it over, he made sure their fingers brushed. The label made her laugh.

"Parking Violation?"

"They don't make it anymore, but I managed to find a few bottles. I thought you'd appreciate the irony."

The sweetness of the gesture blew her away.

"I know I do," Dustin replied sarcastically.

"Be good to keep that in mind then," Abbie added, handing him a yellow pepper. "Keith, do you want to make some kebobs with me?"

"Sure thing, Abbie." He held out his arms to her.

Abbie plopped him down on the counter and showed him a skewer. "Now take a vegetable and—"

"Shove it," Dustin finished.

"*Dustin,*" Mac warned.

Keith giggled. "Mom knows how to tell people where to shove it."

Usually she prided herself on that, but...

"Keith McBride. Where in the world did you hear that?"

"Jill told me, Mom." He turned to Dustin. "You can't get into trouble when someone else says it."

The little stinker.

A pepper disappeared in Dustin's mouth. "We need that rule around here."

"Peg, why don't I show you around?" Mac said. "Keith's already had the tour."

"Yeah, Mom! It's sweet."

She squeezed the neck of her beer, feeling terribly out of place. She didn't know how to socialize like this. Heck, she didn't know how to socialize period.

The doorbell rang. Great, who else was joining this freak show?

"You didn't tell a friend to swing by without talking to me, did you, Dustin?" Abbie asked.

"Nope. I'm in enough trouble already."

"I'm happy to hear it's finally sunk in," Mac replied, amused. "I asked Rhett over. We have plenty of food, and I don't like the thought of him being stuck alone in that big old house."

Abbie's gaze could have sliced and seared the orange pepper in her hand.

"Cool!" Dustin called, racing to the door.

"I like Rhett," Keith added. "He gives me piggy-backs."

Her mouth parted in surprise. When had *that* happened?

"Who's talking about piggy-backs?" the Cowboy-on-Crack said when he sauntered into the kitchen.

"I was!" Keith jumped down and raced over. "Can I have one now?"

Peggy crossed her arms. "Mr. Blaylock just arrived. Let's not bother him."

"Well, now. If it's not our fine deputy sheriff. Ma'am."

He didn't look like a lunatic cowboy tonight. He was wearing blue jeans, a starched white dress shirt, and simple black cowboy boots. Without the hat, he looked...normal. She hadn't seen him since the poker game. What had happened? Then she caught sight of Abbie's body language. She shoved a pepper on a skewer, missed, and cried out as she stabbed her finger. Ah, so there was something there.

Rhett raced over to her side and grabbed her hand. "Did you hurt yourself?"

Her black hair swayed when she nodded. "I'm fine."

"No, let me see."

He lifted her finger. Even from across the room, Peggy could see the blood.

"Oh, that's so gross," Dustin interjected.

Rhett took a paper towel, dampened it, and gently wrapped it around her middle finger. Then he kissed it. "See. All better now."

Abbie eased her hand out of Rhett's hold, her body stiff and wary. "Thank you. I'm fine. Really."

"No, you aren't, and we both know why. This will just make it easier for me to see when you're giving me the bird when you get upset with me." He gave a naughty wink. "You know there are times when you want to, Abs. Like today."

The eye roll she gave Rhett only made him laugh.

"What happened today?" Mac asked.

"I'll tell you later," Abbie said and shot both Rhett and Dustin a look.

"We have guests."

Keith walked over and hugged Abbie. "Are you okay?"

"I'm fine," she said with a sniff, reaching for the kebobs. The paper towel unraveled from her finger.

Peggy stepped forward. The scene bordered on pathetic. "Here, let me help. Why don't you go sit down?"

"No, I invited you. The boys can do it while I supervise."

Rhett nudged her across the kitchen to the farmer's table in the corner. "I know you like hosting, but you've got a boo-boo. I brought your favorite wine to cheer you up. Let me pour you a drink. Mac, where's your corkscrew?"

"But I already have a glass," Abbie protested, which Rhett ignored.

Mac shook his head and walked over to help his friend. Peggy ran the situation over in her mind. Rhett was clearly in love with Abbie. He'd probably rented the house Peg and Mac used for their *pied-à-terre* to stay close to her. And he was no longer dressing like a crazy cowboy to make Abbie more comfortable. She sipped her beer to cover her shock.

Abbie picked at the paper covering her finger, her shoe tapping on the granite floor. Her eyes followed Rhett's movements, and then she bit her lip.

Peggy's eyes widened. Abbie was in love with Rhett—and didn't want to be.

What a kerfuffle!

Peggy was sympathetic. She sure as hell wouldn't be standing in Mac's kitchen, making small talk with his family, if she didn't feel something for him, even though she wished she could delete it like a computer virus. She fingered the beer's label, watching Dustin help Keith pile too many vegetables on the skewers as Abbie fussed over it all like she was hosting a state dinner.

Mac crossed over to her, looking mouth-watering in sand-colored cargo shorts and a black T-shirt. "Come on. I think this gang has everything under control. Let's make sure the squirrels haven't absconded with the steaks."

"You left the steaks outside? It's eighty degrees out."

He caressed her elbow as he led her out. She almost dropped her beer bottle at the pinging charge that ran down her arm.

"I'm bringing them up to room temperature."

When he closed the patio doors, the view knocked her socks off. The mountains looked purplish-green in the waning light, and the sky blasted out cobalt mixed with pink and peach. The pines cascaded down the incline like they were surfboarding.

"That's a killer view."

"I like Rhett's better."

The pitch of his voice had dropped at least two levels, full of fire and smoke. At this rate, they wouldn't need the grill. He could cook the steaks himself.

"Me too," she answered, her voice scratchy from the confession.

"I'm glad you're here, Peg."

She wanted to bury her face against his chest. Instead she crossed over to the steaks. Gave them a poke through the saran wrap.

"Me too," she repeated easily. Had he put truth serum in her beer?

She watched him grill the kebobs Keith brought out on a plate. Listened to him converse with her chattering son as he slapped the steaks on the grill. Keith's joy could have powered a light house. Part of her worried about the interaction after all his questions the other night. The other part lit up inside, enjoying the moment.

Would it be like this if they had a future together?

She drank her beer as the scenarios played through her mind. When he picked Keith up and helped him turn the steaks, her heart turned over. They looked...good together.

They ate at the picnic table Abbie had set up outside as the sun went down. Mac sprayed Peggy with bug spray when she complained the mosquitoes were biting her ankles.

He winked up at her. "Lucky devils," he whispered to her so no one could hear.

The adults didn't talk much. Keith peppered people with questions. Mac and Dustin teased each other like the guys at her office did, with Rhett joining in occasionally. Mostly, though, he just stared at Abbie, his heart on his sleeve.

"Why aren't you drinking your wine?" Rhett finally asked Abbie. "I thought it was your favorite."

Her finger tapped the stem three times before responding. "It is."

The dart was unmistakable. Rhett's shoulders slumped. Peggy almost patted his hand like she would a victim. Clearly Abbie was doing everything to convince Rhett she wasn't interested in him, but even Peggy could make out her distress in her tense shoulders and facial muscles.

"Well, if you won't drink it, I will, Mom," Dustin said, clearly missing the insult.

"As if," she primly responded, clutching the glass.

"Just kidding," he remarked, kicking back in his chair.

"You better be," Mac warned.

Keith leaned closer to Dustin. "You should listen. My mom puts people in jail who drink before they're twenty-one. Right, Mom?"

God, she loved it when her kid quoted the law. "Right."

Dustin's face fell.

After seeing him treat Keith so kindly tonight, she decided to throw him a bone. "Of course, I know Dustin wouldn't do anything like that, so you don't have to worry about him, Keith."

"Whew!" her son cried dramatically. "I don't have enough money to bail him out of jail."

Everyone laughed. Dustin's ears turned red.

Abbie served the special dessert she had mentioned—something she called a Charlotte, which made Peggy wonder why people always named recipes after girls. When they were finished eating, the men headed off to watch Dustin teach Keith more dribbling techniques. Mac sprinted across the back lawn, turning as Dustin kicked a wicked pass to him. He stopped it with his foot and dribbled it back, looking like some hot European World Cup Soccer player. The man had impressive skills.

After a moment, Abbie changed chairs and sat by her side. "They all look really good together," she commented. "Male camaraderie isn't something I understand, but I know it when I see it."

Peggy reached for her beer so she wouldn't scratch her back. Funny, it hadn't itched for a while. "Male camaraderie's about all I understand. The girl stuff—shopping and flowers—makes me as nervous as when I went through my first door."

"When you were a baby?" Abbie asked, her brow wrinkling.

"Please." Peggy smiled. "No, as a rookie."

"Oh."

Mac raised a squealing Keith to his shoulders. Her mouth dropped when Rhett did the same with Dustin.

"He's a strong one," Peggy commented, impressed.

"And stubborn as an ox." Abbie tucked her hand under her chin. "He's in love with me. He plans to stay here as long as it takes to wear me down, even though I told him it's impossible for us to be together."

Her aggrieved tone made Peggy want to laugh. "How's he doing?"

She sighed. "Before today, pretty good. Today, not so good. How's Mac doing?"

Her back caught fire. Dammit. She'd jinxed it. "He doesn't have a plan to wear me down." God, she hoped not.

"Mac isn't that devious or obvious. He's patient and consistent. He wins you over by making himself indispensible to you."

Terrific. "What's keeping you from being with Rhett? It's clear to anyone with eyes you love him."

"Pretty much the same thing as you with Mac. He's a poker player. And I have to say, even a peacock with its thousands of eyes couldn't tell how you feel about my brother."

Peggy turned her attention back toward the soccer exhibition. "Your son plays very well."

"You didn't answer my question about Mac."

Peggy stood. "You're right. When I have one, I might."

Abbie twirled her untouched wine. "Be sure. He saw what the whole thing with Dustin's father did to my trust in men. I don't know what happened with your ex, but Mac will stick by you. No one's more loyal."

"I'm going to join them. It's getting harder to see from here."

It wasn't exactly a lie. She strode across the lawn until she stood a few yards away from them. Mac waved and then dribbled in a flash around Rhett, who took him down with an outstretched foot.

"Red card!" Mac called.

Rhett launched himself at him, and they started wrestling in the grass. The boys joined in the fray, piling on. She took a step toward them before realizing the adults were orchestrating their movements to ensure no one got hurt. She stopped where she was. Watched the sun set, listening as the two voices she liked hearing most—one still high-pitched and the other low and gravely—were raised in laughter.

When Mac jogged over to her, she couldn't take it. She snuck an arm around his waist, out of Keith's line of sight. His muscles stilled, and then he settled closer.

"It's almost bedtime," he observed, all Mr. Responsible.

"Yes. We should get going."

"Can you meet me at Rhett's tomorrow? I have a powerful thirst for you."

Her mouth went dry. "When?"

He laughed. "Right now, I'd pretty much say whenever you can make it."

"Let me see if I can take off work a little early. Tanner can probably watch Keith for a few hours." Then she remembered. "Dammit. My other brother's arriving for a visit tomorrow."

"That's okay. We'll find another time."

"No. I don't know if I'm...going to see him. I'll find someone else to look after Keith."

He turned his head, his green eyes as dark as moss in the twilight. "Why wouldn't you see him?"

"Tanner's never told you about him?"

Mac shook his head.

"Well, let's just say my baby brother is an alcoholic and—"

"He reminds you of your father."

His words sucked all oxygen from her. She dropped her hand from his waist. "We need to go."

He grabbed her arm. "We need to talk about this sometime. It's the one thing standing between us."

One thing? Who was kidding who now?

She shoved at his hold. "I don't know what you're talking about."

He caressed her forearm, lowering his head until they were inches apart. She could feel his warm breath fanning her face. "You're afraid I'll turn into the man your father was because I play poker like he did."

Like a chord, his analysis pinged through her whole body. "Stop getting in my face."

He cradled it between his warm palms. "I'm hoping that if I stand this close to you, you'll be able to see I'm nothing like your father."

She stepped away. They were *not* having this conversation. "Keith! We need to go." Her voice couldn't have been shriller.

"But Mom!" he fired back, picking up the soccer ball.

"Nope. Let's go." She reigned in her anger. It wasn't his fault. "Say goodbye to everyone."

Mac gave her one last look and then walked away. "Your mom's getting tired. She didn't have a lot of downtime after work today. How about I give you a piggyback to the car?"

At other times, she would have kissed him for the tag-team, but she couldn't erase his accusation.

Her dad wasn't the problem. Mac was wrong. He had to be.

God, maybe the problem was her inability to make peace with the past. Being with Mac had ripped off all of the bandages she'd put on the old wounds. Now she couldn't seem to cover them up anymore because they wouldn't stop bleeding. Why couldn't she simply let it all go?

She said her goodbyes with a knot in her gut. The group's energy couldn't have blown out a handful of birthday candles after her abrupt departure.

Mac buckled Keith in, tickling him until he was writhing with laughter. Then he shut the door and came around to where Peggy stood. She gave an absent wave to the others by the door.

He took her hands. "Look at me. I love you. I know what I said upset you, but it was going to come out sooner or later. Since your brother's coming, I decided sooner. That way you can make your own judgments. You're a smart woman. You'll figure it out. I have faith in you."

His faith in her only made her feel ashamed. "I don't know why. I've done nothing to deserve it."

He leaned in and kissed her on the cheek before she could blink. "You only have to be yourself. I'll see you tomorrow."

"You still want to see me?" The shock in her voice couldn't have been more evident.

His finger swiped her cheekbone. "Oh, Peg, when are you going to learn that it takes a heck of a lot more than your wariness to make me walk away?" He opened her car door. "Text me when you get home."

"I'm a deputy."

He shrugged. "It's what people do when they care about each other."

She took her seat behind the wheel and buckled up, thinking over his words. As she pulled away, she thought of all the times she'd made Tanner email her after going on some dangerous mission while he was an embedded journalist in Afghanistan. He'd laughed about it, asking why she didn't just trust him to take care of himself. She'd told him it was because she cared.

She got home and texted Mac.

She knew he cared.

The big question was whether she could finally allow herself to admit the same.

CHAPTER 36

Peggy woke up the next morning grinding her teeth. She punched her pillow, her dream still sticking to her like Halloween green goo. In weird Technicolor, David had arrived at her house wearing a jacket lined with beer bottles. He'd offered her one. She'd declined. Then he'd offered one to Keith. As she was pushing him away, he turned into their father. She'd lowered her arms, a red haze closing in on her. Meanwhile, he had pulled out a deck of cards and was teaching Keith how to play poker. When she could finally lift her feet off the ground, she stalked forward to stop him. That was when his face changed again, and suddenly it was Mac who was smiling back at her.

The trembling continued throughout breakfast and her morning run-down at work. The sheriff told her she could leave a couple of hours early since she was working Labor Day. When she made it to her car, she sat in the seat with her phone in her hand. It took her five minutes before she summoned the will to text Mac to see if he could still meet her. His immediate response made her think he'd been waiting. He said he'd be there in twenty.

She headed over to Rhett's, hoping to beat Mac there, nervous at the surprise she was planning. Mac's car wasn't there when she arrived, so she unlocked her trunk and stared at the shopping bag she'd brought with her. On a shopping trip to Victoria's Secret with the Hale sisters, Meredith had bought Peggy a velvety brown nightgown, something she never would have bought for herself. The whole lingerie thing made her feel stupid, but she'd dug it out of the closet the other night.

She kinda wanted to do something nice for him, but she drew the line at modeling and saying, "Surprise." She snatched up the bag, partly hoping the doors were locked. But they weren't. Better strip before she chickened out. The nightgown shimmied over her skin in the bedroom they used. She eyed herself in the full-length mirror. The color deepened the hues of her eyes, and the nightgown clung to her curves, giving an embarrassing view of her ample cleavage. She crossed her arms over her chest and turned away, a bunch of frogs jumping in her stomach. Pacing, she waited for him.

When his car pulled up, she met him at the door. His smile widened, his gaze dipping below her face.

"Wow!" he managed before she pushed him back against the front door and devoured him.

He didn't fight her when she dragged him to the bedroom, hastily tearing off his clothes. She pushed him onto the bed and climbed onto him, needing an outlet for all her aggression and confusion.

She poured it into their lovemaking.

He gave himself to her, groaning and twisting as her hands and mouth brought him to new heights, dark plateaus.

She wasn't gentle. She wasn't tender. Moments later, she exploded. He followed her quickly over the edge.

Rising, her hands rearranged the nightgown over her aching breasts. Her skin hadn't even cooled. His gaze followed her movements as she dressed in the silence.

"I need to go," she finally said when he continued watching with that damned tender, patient look.

The urge to head to the door overtook her. He had another poker tournament this weekend, starting tomorrow. She realized she couldn't even wish him good luck. What did that make her? She couldn't offer her support to this man she cared about.

"Peg."

Her body stilled.

"I love you. If you need me, you know where to find me."

She walked out without glancing back, knuckling away the dampness from her eyes.

The drive home didn't reduce her anxiety. Usually she looked forward to holiday weekends. This time, she wanted to spend the whole weekend frozen. Someone could thaw her out after it was over like a character in a campy sci-fi movie. Tanner had invited her over for dinner tonight to see David. Meredith had told her Jill would watch Keith if she'd rather not bring him.

She had decided to go, but she was going to leave Keith at Jill's. Depending upon David's progress, perhaps she would let him see his nephew later on in the weekend.

After her day babysitter headed out, she changed out of her uniform and then followed a cheering Keith back outside the house. Conversing with him proved to be a challenge, since it was hard to concentrate. When she pulled into Jill's driveway, she told him to say hi for her. She waited until he was safely inside before pulling away. Jill waved, a frown on her face.

Right, she couldn't take whatever Jill might want to say to her about Mac or David—or anything.

The ride to her brother's place only ratcheted up her desire to flee. She bore down and pushed the accelerator, speeding slightly, reminding herself of all the dangerous moments when she'd been on the police force. She could do this.

What the hell was she so afraid of?

What Mac had said to her about her father echoed in her mind.

Tanner's dog, Hugo, careened into her when she exited the car. She reached down and scratched him behind the ears. Firmed her shoulders and headed to the porch.

Tanner opened the door and walked out, David trailing behind him like he was dragging his feet. So, she wasn't the only nervous one?

"Hey," Tanner called, kissing her on the cheek. "Glad you could come."

She turned toward David. Unlike Tanner, who favored a rougher look after years spent overseas, her younger brother had the slick style of a New York politician. He had goop in his hair and a few lines around his eyes and mouth from hard living.

"David," she managed.

"Peg," he responded.

As far as greetings went, it wouldn't make *The Hallmark Channel*.

"Let's go inside," Tanner suggested. "Meredith's got everything ready."

Her sister-in-law had to be nervous, sensing the tension between the siblings, because she'd overcompensated on the food and the presentation. First a cheese plate and hors d'oeuvres, then spinach salad, beef tenderloin, wild rice, and a mushroom medley presented with some fresh herb. Peggy thought of the meal for the Prodigal son. *Puh-lease.*

Their conversation relied heavily on pleasantries. Small talk annoyed the shit out of her—especially small talk with family.

"Feel free to have some wine or beer. It doesn't bother me," David announced as they started.

Tanner and Meredith exchanged the *married couple* look. Peggy studied her woven napkin, her gut clenching.

"Okay," Tanner finally said. "I'll have a beer. Mere, do you want some wine?"

She gave a wooden smile and nodded.

"Peg?"

"Nothing for me." She could suddenly smell her father's stale beer breath.

David had lied. It *did* bother him. His eyes flicked over to the glasses too often. She felt bad for him, but inside, an inferno raged. She was his younger sister again, listening as he came home drunk after curfew, fighting with Tanner. All she'd ever wanted was for him to stop drinking and be happy.

It hadn't worked then.

It wouldn't work now.

She was as powerless to help him as she'd been with their father.

Sweat beaded on her brow. She dabbed at it with her napkin and pushed her food around on her plate. David chattered on like the local politician he was. She'd forgotten his talent for spinning a yarn while saying absolutely nothing. Utter bullshit.

"So, I've heard there's a poker tournament at Mac Maven's new hotel starting tomorrow," he interjected as Meredith cut them pieces of the chocolate raspberry cheesecake Peggy knew she wouldn't be able to swallow.

"Maven's big time! I've watched him at WSOP on ESPN. They don't call him Maverick for nothing. Have you met him?"

Tanner's fork sliced through the cheesecake. "Yeah, we're friendly. He's a great guy."

Her brother leaned forward with a gleam in his eyes. "Do you mind if I throw my hand in at the tourney tomorrow? I can't pass up the opportunity."

"I thought AA didn't encourage addictive pursuits like gambling," Peggy said, her voice acid.

Silence descended, sharp and electric.

"I've got everything under control, Peg," David reassured her with his fake smile.

Her bullshit quotient pinged past acceptable limits. "And yet, you keep staring at the alcohol like it's your be-all-end-all."

"*Peg—*" Tanner warned.

She ignored him. "David, do you think I don't know the signs? I'm a cop. If you can't drink alcohol, you fulfill the urge with something else. Gambling is a popular vice. Just like it always was with dear ol' Dad."

Tanner's hand crashed onto the table. "Peg, that's enough."

She stood, her napkin falling to the floor. Fire engulfed her. "No! It has to be said. Playing in a poker tournament is a stupid idea, David. If you won't resist temptation for yourself, do it for your family."

Why couldn't he see how much he was hurting them?

David's eyes narrowed. "I'm an adult. I make my own choices."

Her fist punched the air. "Not on this. You come here to...what? I still don't know why. Make-up with Tanner after your last indiscretion? I show up here to give you another shot, and the first thing you say is that you want to join a poker tournament. How can you forget alcohol and gambling addictions run in the family?"

"I know that better than you, Peg," he muttered, lowering his gaze.

"I doubt that. All three of us lived in the same slice of hell. But that doesn't mean I'm going to let you make another stupid mistake while you're in my town."

Tanner jerked his head in warning. She ignored him.

"Your town? You're my *sister*. Stop acting like the Deputy Sheriff." David stood. "I can take care of myself."

Her hands clenched on the chair. "How many times have we heard that? Your wife has stuck by you, just like Mom did with Dad until he finally left her. What about your kids? What about *them*? "

She thought of Keith and thanked God she hadn't brought him. She couldn't be more grateful that he didn't have to deal with a father like this. Like her own.

Tanner walked over until he was in her face. "That's enough," he growled, deep grooves around his mouth. "You're only making it worse."

Meredith cast her a pleading look, but what the hell did she understand? Her father was a sweet man who gushed over his two girls. He'd never put booze and cards before them.

"He's just like Dad," she whispered, the hurt of it breaking her heart wide open again. "Can't you see?"

Tanner put his hands on her shoulders and rubbed. "Why don't you head home? You're not thinking straight."

She clenched her hands at her sides, wanting to make him see. "You're the one burying your head in the sand. He hasn't changed. When are you going to stop enabling him?"

David shoved his chair aside, the violence causing Meredith to jump. "Stop talking about me like I'm not here. I'll play poker if I damn well feel like it."

She thought of his two young daughters. They deserved a better father. "Not if I have anything to say about it."

Her arms pumped as she slammed out of the house. She couldn't stop her father, but she could stop her brother. Save his kids from growing up the way she had.

And she knew just who she could go to for help.

CHAPTER 37

The intoxicating smell of popcorn permeated the house. Mac microwaved the butter, trying not to worry about Peggy and their earlier interaction.

Rhett had come over under the pretense of watching a movie with Dustin and him, but it was obvious he was trying to regain the ground he'd lost the other day in the Aspen Room. When Abbie had talked to Mac about Dustin and the poker babes' cleavage, he'd raised his hands and said he was staying out of it. She hadn't been too happy about that.

Dustin hadn't let his mother's determined attitude about Rhett affect him. He'd turned into a teenage Cupid, and it was pretty amusing to watch.

The timer went off, and Mac dumped the melted butter all over the popcorn.

Abbie cringed. "*Mac.* Some of us don't have a crazy metabolism like the rest of you."

"Please," Rhett drawled, rubbing his thumb over her hand before she could yank it away. "You're beautiful. Sleek as a sea lion."

"Don't those things have whiskers?" she tartly replied.

"Rhett, man, you need major help," Dustin interjected. "Animal references so don't work with chicks."

Abbie's gaze flew to Dustin. "And you'd know that—"

"Beats poetry. *You're as beautiful as a rose,* " Mac interrupted his sister in a British accent to save his nephew. "Seriously. Now, who's up for the movie?"

Dustin jumped off the bar stool. "Since I picked it, I'm in. Mom, why don't you and Rhett stay in here and talk?"

Her hand flew to her neck. "Dustin! Enough."

"I'm game if you are, sugar," Rhett murmured, waggling his eyebrows. "I told you I'm not giving up."

She narrowed her eyes. "Since it's another blow-everything-up movie with aliens, I'll pass."

"Me too, then," Rhett said. "I'll keep your mom company."

"But I thought you came over to watch a movie."

He shrugged. "It was only a ruse to be close to you."

"Nice one, Rhett!" Dustin snagged the bowl of popcorn. "I'm going to have a field day with you two. Right, Uncle Mac?"

He wiped the butter off his hands with a towel. "Leave me out of it. Dustin, we'd better make a break for it before your mother decides to hit us," he said, his face breaking into a wider grin.

"I'm too much of a lady for that," Abbie replied, fingering her butterfly lapel pin.

"Amen," Rhett agreed.

"But I'm not above dying your white soccer socks pink." Her finger pointed at her son for emphasis.

Mac chuckled. "Now, you're in trouble."

His phone buzzed as he slung an arm around Dustin's shoulders. "I guess it's just you and me, kid." He glanced at his phone. Peggy. His stomach plummeted. Somehow, Peg calling him—something she never did—rung the alarm bells in his system.

"Hello," he answered.

"I'm outside your house. Can we talk?"

He cupped the phone and slapped Dustin on the back. "Peggy's here. Why don't you go play a game for a minute? I need to see what she wants."

Dustin studied him. "She still pissed with you after last night?"

"Probably."

"Don't call her a sea lion."

"Smart ass. I'll find you in a bit."

"Do you need me to help you two get together like I'm doing with mom and Rhett?"

"You haven't done it yet." Mac headed to the door.

After a fortifying breath, he turned the knob. His muscles clenched at the blast of fury emanating from her. Any attempt at a poker face had melted away. Then he saw the wetness around her eyes. The thought of her crying made his insides clench.

"David?" he asked in a gentle voice.

"I need to talk to you. In private."

Her posture was so rigid he was afraid she'd crack if he touched her.

He dismissed his office as too formal. "Let's head up to my room. Abbie and Rhett are in the kitchen. Dustin's in the family room playing video games."

"Fine."

Yeah, she wasn't interested in saying hello. He schooled his features as they ascended the stairs. He'd need to tread lightly tonight. Disaster hovered all around her. She preceded him into his room and froze beside him.

"*This* is where you sleep?" It was almost an accusation.

Having seen her undecorated white walls and utilitarian navy bedspread, he knew his bedroom had to look like a sultan's palace to her. The plush burgundy curtains and bedspread made a dramatic impact against the gold walls. His king-size sleigh bed and hotel linens looked plush.

"I read in here too," he replied, his belly a maze of swirling nerves. "But I don't watch TV. I don't believe in having one in the bedroom."

Her eyes widened at that, but she didn't say anything. It was weird—and oddly nice—to see her standing in his room. He'd hoped to show it to her.

This wasn't how he'd imagined it.

He fought the urge to take her in his arms. "What happened?"

Her posture snapped into military precision. "My brother wants to play in your tournament tomorrow. I want you to deny him entry."

She might as well have slit his guts open. He studied her. There was a frantic gleam in her eyes that he'd never seen before.

"Tell me what happened at dinner tonight."

She flew into action, pacing on his Turkish rug. "David tried to make light of it, but he still wants a drink—bad. I could smell it on him."

He clenched his hands to stop from reaching for her. "Keep talking."

"He said he knew about you and your hotel. Wanted to play. Hell, he even asked if we'd run across you." Her laugh was dry and shrill. "Isn't that funny?"

He'd lost his funny bone. "And what did you say?" he asked, even though he knew the answer.

"Nothing. That's not the point. The point is he's in AA for the second time, and gambling is *so* not on the program."

Mac crossed his arms, striving for calm. "Perhaps that's for him to decide. I learned a long time ago you can't stop anyone from doing what they want."

She thrust her chin out, her eyes filled with fire. "Bullshit! I can too. *You* can deny him entry."

His head buzzed as if all the oxygen had been sucked out of the room. He knew what his answer had to be, and he knew what that would do to them. He could already hear the death knell.

"I can't do that, Peg," he said as gently as he could. "Everyone can enter so long as they're eighteen and can pay the fee."

Tell me what's really bothering you here, he wanted to say, but he knew she wasn't ready.

She strode forward until she was inches away. "He could fall off the wagon if he does this. Gambling is another addition, and he's an addict."

Her fear ate at him.

"Do you have any idea how many addicts come through my hotels per year?"

She looked at him blankly. "No."

"Neither do I. Because it's personal, Peg. I'm not a morality checker. People need to make their own way."

Sometimes the God's honest truth hurt like hell.

"He's my brother, Mac." Old hurt coated her voice, making it crack.

He stilled. It was the first time she'd used his first name outside the bedroom. He knew it. She knew it.

"I know he is, but you can't save David, Peg." He put his hands on her shoulders and massaged the rigid muscles, unable to fight the urge to touch, to comfort. "Anymore than I could have saved my old man or you yours."

She broke his hold. "That's not what this is about!"

He leaned down until he was close enough to see the frantic pulse in her neck. "Yes, it is. No one likes to feel helpless, but this isn't something you can fix. Even if I stopped him tomorrow, he'd find another way to play if that's what he wants to do."

"Not while he's in my town."

Oh, she was so damn tough. It broke his heart.

"You can't legislate this away, Peg."

She clutched at her shirt. "If your damn hotel wasn't here, he wouldn't even be thinking of it!"

The vicious cut made him lock his knees to stand upright. "If not my place, then another."

"That's what your kind always says."

The venom couldn't be missed. He supposed it had always been there. He'd heard those words before. He'd fought against other people's judgment his whole life. He'd built things. He'd given money to charities. He'd helped his sister raise her son. But it was never enough to convince narrow-minded people Mac Maven was anything but a *kind*.

Apparently Peggy was no different—despite all they'd shared.

Inside, he started building a wall to keep the hurt out, laying brick after brick to buffer himself from her words. He executed extreme control of his facial muscles, not revealing anything. "I'm sorry you think that way, but if you and Tanner can't talk him out of it, there's nothing I can do."

"Then you really don't love me."

His wall rose as high as the Empire State Building. All around him, the world went numb. "Loving someone isn't always about doing what that person wants."

Her finger thrust into his chest. "No, it's about supporting them. And you won't support me in this."

Why couldn't she understand? If he did what she wanted, he'd be throwing away everything he'd tried to become. "No, I won't. It's not your life, Peg. It's his."

Her face fell. "He's my baby brother! He has a wife and two kids. They don't deserve this."

Ah, here was the crux. "Neither did you. Neither did I."

She stalked away. "Stop talking about me! Think about how you'd feel if this were Dustin."

Her attempt to manipulate him packed a punch. He girded his walls with steel. "I can't deny anyone from my tourney on these grounds, Peg. David hasn't done anything to be disqualified. Please understand. My reputation is at stake here."

She fell back a few steps, like she'd lost her balance. "Then I don't mean any more to you than your businesses. I guess that's why they call luck a *lady*. I can't compete against her."

Inside he was filling with iron, becoming an automaton—completely unfeeling. "I'm not asking you to compete against her, but this business means as much to me as being a deputy means to you. Would you refrain from arresting someone if I asked?"

Her brown eyes blinked. "There's no comparison." Then they narrowed. "We're done here."

Her tone's finality blasted a hole through his walls, piercing his heart. He put a hand on her arm. "Don't leave like this. I *do* love you, Peg. Even though it pretty much hurts like hell right now."

She shrugged him off. "Not enough."

Why wouldn't she listen? He wanted to shake her. His rage sealed the hole like a blow torch, making him impenetrable again. "Well, then we're even because that's how you feel about me. You've never said you love me. Not once. You've never even called me Mac one *goddamn* time outside the bedroom until now. What does that say about you?"

Rage overtook heartbreak.

He strode forward, armor in place, realizing he needed to get her the hell away from here. All his patience was gone. "I've *never* been good enough as I am! And I'm fucking tired of it. *I'm* nothing to be ashamed of." His fist punched his chest. "I'm someone, dammit! You just refuse to see it. It's easier to brand me as a poker player and a maverick than it is to get over your preconceived notions. Fuck that. I'm more than that."

Her jaw clenched. She waved a hand dismissively. "Fine! Be yourself. I don't want you anymore. But you *will* do what I want."

The death knell sounded a second time, harsher and more damaging.

"No, I won't." If she wanted to lock horns, he wouldn't back down. He couldn't on something this important.

Her mouth twisted. "If you don't stop my brother from entering your tournament tomorrow, I'm going to call the Feds to tell them I have new information on the bomb threat."

He sucked in a breath. The foundation of his tower of steel cracked inside him. The walls he'd built to protect himself fell in resounding destruction. His heart pulsed, naked and vulnerable in the aftermath.

"You promised me," he ground out.

She threw both arms into the air. "Which was stupid of me. I'm a deputy, first and foremost."

He stalked over to her. "No, you're a scared, frightened woman who's now resorted to blackmail. What in the hell did I ever see in you?"

"I don't care what you think of me as long as you do what I say."

How could he have forgotten the depths to which she'd stoop to get what she wanted? Hadn't she attacked him and his family at the town meeting to stop his hotel?

His rubbery legs obeyed him as he walked across the room. He reached for his land line phone, his ears buzzing. "If I gave into blackmail, I'd become every horrible thing you ever accused me of being. I won't do that. You want to take it to the Feds, go ahead. I'll tell my legal representative in Colorado, Bill Perkins, to expect a call." He picked up the receiver.

She gasped. "You think I'm bluffing? What about Dustin?"

"I know you're not bluffing." His stomach churned at the thought. "I'll talk to my family and my lawyer. As for Dustin's friend, he'll have to stand on his own. You want to go after him, that's your prerogative. I'll protect my family and my interests. I won't be blackmailed, Peg—not by what I told you in confidence or how I *felt* about you."

His deliberate use of the past tense made her eyes narrow. "Oh, *goodie*, you've finally realized you don't love me. I knew it all along."

Her cruelty knew no bounds. It was time to put a stop to this. "You can believe whatever the fuck you want. Get out of my house."

"I hate you!" She stalked to the door and turned, a sneer on her face. "I only wanted you for the sex anyway."

She couldn't have fired a more killing shot to his defenseless heart. His pulse slowed as all possibility of reconciliation vanished. "Then I hope you got your fill. I don't do repeats, and I always learn from my mistakes."

Her chin lifted. "Then we agree on something."

The beating of his heart stopped. Emptiness spread throughout his body.

She left in a blur of motion.

His body fell back onto the bed, and he stared up at the blank ceiling.

It was over.

It never should have begun.

After all the lucky breaks he'd gotten in life, how could he have fallen in love with someone who despised everything he was? And then tried to blackmail him using what he felt for her?

He pushed himself into a sitting position. He couldn't stay in Dare anymore. Not with her here. The town was too small, and he couldn't bear to act distant when he ran into Keith. The boy wouldn't understand.

He'd leave Cince here for the year to train Jill and handle the hotel when she went on maternity leave.

They could all move back to Arizona. Dustin would be thrilled, and Rhett had made it clear that he'd follow Abbie to the moon and back. Mac could work from there until it was time to create a new hotel. Perhaps in Jackson Hole this time.

He reached for the phone, but exhaustion overtook him. The call to his lawyer could wait a few minutes. Since Bill's office was in Denver, he could drive up in the morning to be present when the Feds descended. He would call in his corporate legal team if it came to it.

God, the Feds.

He closed his eyes to stop the images of them swarming his hotel, Peggy accompanying them in her uniform, a sneer on her face.

The numbness he strove for wouldn't come in all the way. Goddamn her.

His ears picked up the sonic boom coming from *World of Warcraft*. He'd forgotten all about Dustin.

He firmed his shoulder and headed downstairs.

Peggy might have killed his heart, but he still had a family, people who needed him.

233

He'd never neglect that—despite what she thought of him.

CHAPTER 38

Peggy was having trouble reading the Saturday edition of *The Western Independent* when something smacked her front door. She cocked her ear. It didn't sound like a hand, but she went to investigate. Keith continued to watch cartoons in his animation-induced trance. She opened the door and realized what had made the sound—Arthur's cane.

He rubbed his grizzled beard. "Hope you don't mind me coming over unannounced."

Did anyone ever say *yes* when asked that question? She felt like a drug dealer had tortured her all night after learning she was undercover. She probably didn't look too hot either.

"No, of course not," she lied. "Keith will be delighted. He'll probably make you play checkers until your eyes roll back in your head."

He huffed. "I hope not. When you're my age, that usually means you've had a stroke or died."

The urge to tug at her clothes was strong. She'd slept for maybe an hour before throwing on her police academy shorts and a T-shirt dotted with holes. Arthur looked pressed and polished in navy slacks and a white button-down shirt. Her clothes were a reminder of comfortable days, days when she hadn't questioned who she was. After last night, she wasn't sure she knew anymore. Regret had descended on her like a shroud as soon as she'd left Mac's house and cooled down. Her attempt to blackmail him had been a new low. And it wasn't something she could take back.

She was fighting a battle with herself over whether or not she wanted to know if David was playing in Mac's tournament. She couldn't pick up the phone and ask Tanner, though—not after last night.

Arthur tapped his cane, bringing her back to the present. "I'm here to see you actually. Can we talk somewhere?"

The ongoing electricity in her back surged. "Is anything wrong?"

His hand fell to her shoulder. "No one has died, but Jill's holding something of a wake. I just came from the coffee shop. Let's take this inside. My hip's starting to bother me. Bursitis."

Her muscles tensed. She let him pass while questions swirled in her mind. What had happened? Hadn't enough shit gone down in her world in the last twenty-four hours?

"Mom! Who is it?"

"It's Mr. Hale, but he needs to talk to Mommy. You keep watching your show. We'll be in my office."

Her gaze counted the stairs and then fell to his cane. "Ah, maybe we shouldn't use my office."

He growled. "Don't insult me. I can handle a few stairs."

Keith's feet pounded across the floor as he came running. "Hey, Mr. Hale." He gave him a careful hug, just like she'd taught him.

Arthur patted the boy's head and then reached into his pocket for one of his ever-present red hots. "Here you go. Better get the checkers out. I'm going to beat you when I finish talking with your mom."

Keith didn't rip the candy from its wrapper as quickly as he usually did. He studied Arthur. "What's the matter?"

Arthur winked. "Newspaper stuff. Your mom's gonna be my source."

His mouth popped open. "Cool. Is her name going to be in the paper?"

The look the veteran journalist gave her made her think of her first police captain. Something was *so* not right.

"She might be a confidential source—the best kind. Now, off with you. You might want to go practice for our game. It's the only way you're going to win."

Keith rolled his eyes. "I've beaten you *plenty* of times."

"Don't remind me. Now, off with you. We'll find you in a bit."

Keith trudged off. Arthur's cane tapped each stair as he slowly climbed to the second floor. Peggy held her hands out as she followed behind him, ready to swoop in if he stumbled.

He took a moment at the top of the steps. "I'd like to shoot whoever invented stairs."

She was too nervous to reply, so she just showed him into her office. The board she'd taken out of the closet last night sat in the corner now. Her gut clenched. She darted over to cover it.

Arthur's chuckle stopped her.

"Do you think I don't know a police board when I see one? Mac's a pretty photogenic fellow."

Her hands clenched when he appeared beside her. The whole board had her back itching again. Looking at her collection now, all she could see was her shame. She'd treated Mac like a criminal—and he'd done nothing to deserve it. She was a horrible human being and a total failure as an officer. She'd tried to blackmail him with personal information to do something she wanted for her personal life. She'd broken every oath she'd ever made.

Even though her stomach burned, she firmed her shoulders. "What did you want to discuss?" She couldn't bring herself to utter Jill's name. Her friend would hate her if she found out what she'd threatened to do. Hell, everyone would.

"We made a deal a while back," Arthur reminded her. "You said you'd give me the scoop if you found out anything about Mac."

Her mouth dropped open. "What? I mean…I thought this had to do with Jill." God, had Mac already told Jill what she'd threatened?

He gestured to her office chair. "Can I?"

"Please sit down." The urge to pace made her root her feet in the carpet.

"Jill's holding a wake at the coffee shop because Mac told her this morning that he and his family are moving back to Arizona this week, leaving Cince in charge with Jill as his deputy. Jill's in a tizzy—she thinks you must have broken his heart."

Her own heart broke from the truth. How could she have broken his trust so horribly after all he'd done for her?

Arthur fingered his cane. "Mac assured her everything will be all right, but he wouldn't tell her why he's leaving. I figure it's gotta be more than a broken heart. Mac wouldn't make an about-face over something like that. He's too much of a man. I figure you found out something to make him leave. I came over to follow through on our deal and find out what it is. I want to run it in tomorrow's paper if I can confirm everything today."

Shock rolled over her like fire through tumbleweed. "He's leaving?" she said out loud. She couldn't imagine not seeing him again.

Arthur's bushy eyebrow winged up. "You didn't know? Well, now, that makes this reporter mighty curious about what you did to drive him out."

His frankness knocked her back a step. *Drive. Him. Out.* Then she looked at the board. She'd fallen under his spell as she'd looked for ways to destroy him. There weren't enough bad words in the dictionary for her.

She pressed her hands to her face and spun around. "Arthur, I can't talk...right now. Please. Go play...with Keith."

Something clawed up her throat. Her nails dug into her palms.

The hand on her shoulder made her jump. Her eyes popped open to the sight of Arthur's furrowed brow.

"Here now. I've comforted many women over the years. I know a distressed woman when I see one. Talk to an old man."

Her lip started to tremble, years of reserve cracking. "No. I...can't. Arthur, you've gotta leave me alone."

He shook his head and reached to embrace her. She was too afraid of injuring him to push him away. His bony arms circled her. The pain, the shock, and the hurt all broke through the ice. She fell apart, a big ball of ugly cry.

His murmurs and pats were distant in her mind as her emotions swept through her, leaving her light-headed, stuffy, and sick to her stomach. When she couldn't breathe through her congested nose, she pulled back. Arthur pressed a cloth handkerchief in her hand.

"Let it all out. You'll feel better."

She thought about Keith and prayed he couldn't hear her over the TV. She didn't want to scare him. He'd never ever seen her cry before—because she never did, not even after Frank had left.

Now she couldn't stop.

When her forehead fell onto Arthur's shoulder, he shifted his weight. Was she hurting his hip? She stepped away and wiped her nose.

"I'm mortified, Arthur. I *never* do this."

His mouth twitched. "I know. You can always tell who the tough ones are. When they finally cry, they pretty much howl like the coyotes in the canyon. I've seen a lot of people cry. I can take it."

"Please sit down," she managed over the buzzing in her ears.

He did. Her body sank to the floor since she couldn't stand upright anymore.

His elbows rested on his knees. "Why don't you start from the beginning?"

Her hands pulled at her T-shirt, indecision overwhelming her. "I can't tell you. You'll have to report it."

He pushed his glasses up his nose. "Why would you care if I report it?"

Her throat closed. "Because I don't want to go through with it."

Mac had kept his integrity all along. She'd thrown hers away last night.

"How about this?" Arthur continued. "I'm not a journalist right now. I'll just be your grandpa for the day. You're the same age as Jill and Mere. Talk to an old man. You'll feel better."

She sat Indian style and stared at her feet. Then the words tumbled out. Her throat hurt. Her voice was scratchy, but she kept talking. He nodded as she spoke, his somber blue eyes never leaving her face. He rolled forward until he could put his hand on her shoulder. She knuckled a shitload of tears away from her eyes. She was like a geyser in desperate need of a shut-off valve.

When she finally finished, she gripped her thighs and waited for condemnation.

Arthur patted her gently. "Families have a way of making all logic and common sense head for the hills. Some of my greatest misjudgments have come in my relationships. My wife would tell you stories if she were still here with us. I punched one of my best friends in the face when we were first married because he looked at my wife for a little too long in her new white dress and stockings. He'd always had a thing for her. It ruined our friendship."

He sighed, long and deep. "There's a lot of shit to wade through when you're involved with someone, and as I told Brian when he was having trouble with Jill, when there's shit in the way, you simply have to shovel harder and more often. The main question is the only one that *ever* matters. Do you love Mac?"

Her chest split apart as the woman inside broke free, holding her heart. The answer came through with more tears. "God. Yes. I just don't know..." Her hand turned in an impatient gesture. "How."

Arthur's laugh huffed out. "No one really knows *how*. There's a bunch of manuals out there, but there aren't any secret, foolproof instructions for how to love the people in our lives. My wife didn't like presents like the other women I knew. She also hated my long hours at the newspaper. She knew I had to make it a success, though, so she made a habit of packing up a picnic every day and bringing it to my office. We'd eat around five o'clock. Then I'd work for a few more hours. We found a rhythm. Loving is about listening, being together. You do that with Keith without even thinking about it."

"It feels...weird with someone else," she confessed.

His knobby fingers scratched his face. "Yes, that's to be expected. Loving someone is an ongoing process since we all change. The weirdness you describe is only showing you that you're growing in your mastery of it. When you get it right, nothing is more perfect."

She thought of the moments with Mac when things had seemed perfect between them—easy. Suddenly, she knew exactly when she had fallen in love with him. It was that moment he had held the apple out and told her to shoot it. Racing across the yard into his arms had been the most perfect feeling in the world. She never would have gone to bed with him otherwise.

The enormity of what she'd done fell into her lap like punishing hail. "Mac hates me now. He'll never forgive me."

"You were trying to protect your brother and save him like you couldn't save your father. You just took it further than most." He set his cane on the floor and scooted closer. "Seems like a forgivable offense to me, particularly if he loves you. And he does. You can't turn it off in a few hours."

Hadn't he decided to leave? He might still have feelings for her, but he was doing everything he could to break free of her. "I don't know about that."

His soft smile brought tears to her eyes. "Well then, now's the perfect time to find out. I can't tell you how many times I said 'I'm sorry' to my wife or her to me. You're a brave woman, or you wouldn't have chosen law enforcement. If you can put your life on the line, you can probably handle an apology."

"But he's leaving! How do I stop that?"

Arthur patted her on the shoulder and then stood. "You stop him anyway you can." His cane tapped the floor as he headed for the door. Then he looked over his shoulder. "I'll give you a hint about men. When a woman tells a man she loves him for the first time, he'll pretty much do anything for her if he loves her back. Mac loves you. Be honest with him. I think he'll surprise you."

"Yeah, he'll surprise me by throwing me out of his hotel," she muttered, fear strangling her throat.

Even his chuckle couldn't make her smile. "I've always enjoyed covering the stories of people who handcuff themselves to a building for a sit-in, refusing to leave. There are all sorts of options, my dear, and you strike me as a resourceful woman. I'd be happy to spend the day with Keith if you'd like to execute your plan immediately. The sooner the better, I think."

The door closed behind him.

The board of Mac mocked her, so she closed her eyes. She'd been making the wrong moves with Mac from the beginning. How could she fix that? Telling him she loved him didn't seem enough. He'd told her he didn't do repeats. Maybe Arthur was wrong. Telling him she loved him now might only make her look more stupid.

She felt like raising her hand as she had when she was in kindergarten, so she could ask her teacher what to do. She was in Love Kindergarten with no teacher in sight.

God, she felt so sick and bruised. She studied the board again, looking for an answer in the patterns like she would with a crime.

Something shifted inside her. She began to see a new line of information—one she'd missed or hadn't wanted to see. The stories and pictures she'd cut out had little to do with him playing poker. In one, he was cutting the red ribbon to a new hotel with the mayor and a sea of people behind him. He wanted to be a part of the community. In another, he was giving away his prize money from a poker tournament to a women's shelter. Yes, it had come from poker, but he'd used the money to help others and build things.

Mac was right. He was nothing like her father, she finally realized. Nothing like David.

He'd supported Abbie and Dustin, adjusting his own life and pursuits to be there for them no matter what. He trained people like Jill so they could become more successful. He made himself a part of the communities where he lived, learning people's names and life stories. Hadn't she seen how much he enjoyed talking to people in Dare, even after they'd approved his business plan? It hadn't been an act. He genuinely cared about people.

He'd loved her and treated her so patiently, even when she'd done so little for him in return.

How could she convince him she loved him? What did he want more than anything from her?

It came to her like a flash.

She knew what she needed to do.

CHAPTER 39

Mac's poker vision was laser-sharp as he won another hand. The other players at the table had grown silent, sensing his mood. He was a shark, eager to rip apart anyone in his way. He played without mercy, deliberately trying to reduce the amount of time he had to sit at the table.

He had things to do, orders to finalize for the move to Arizona.

He didn't have time for this.

Raking in the chips as he won yet another hand didn't bring its usual spark of joy. Peggy had taken everything from him, and he'd be damned if he'd let her. She might be winning now, but he was a street fighter. He wouldn't go down like this.

After he left Dare, he would shuttle back and forth to ensure everything ran smoothly at the hotel. Play in a few tournaments here a year. And hope he never ran into Peggy again. It would be pretty easy if he never went into town.

If he could will himself to win—and he did—he could will himself to erase Peggy from his mind.

Mac looked at the next two cards the dealer handed him. They weren't the best cards, but he'd play. He could probably bluff his way through every hand now. No one at the table had the balls to challenge him. Two had cut out early. He hadn't so much as looked at them.

Every now and then he scanned the room, keeping an eye on Peggy's brother, who was playing three tables away. David McBride wouldn't last long. He was too vain and compulsive to handle the pressure. Most addicts cracked. He wouldn't be any different. Still it gave him a jolt to see the man's determined chin and brown eyes, so like Peggy's.

He steeled himself against feeling any sympathy for the McBrides today. Tanner wasn't playing and had only nodded at him. He was standing against the wall, his jaw clenched, his face revealing nothing as he watched his brother lose his chips in record time.

The Feds hadn't arrived yet, but he didn't doubt they would. He'd told Abbie to prepare herself, assuring her that their lawyer would take care of the problem. She'd cried and then become enraged, calling Peggy all the names he wouldn't. When she calmed down, they had agreed to tell Dustin about moving home after today's event.

Abbie had agreed to tell Rhett with him, saying he needed to know she'd be leaving so he could make other plans. Rhett had said he'd follow them, and then he'd pulled Abbie in for a long hug. She'd leaned on him, which Mac thought was a good sign. Then Mac had found Cince and told him too.

They were a family, after all.

Jill was another matter. He'd outlined his plans for her, but he hadn't shared the reasons for them. She was too close to Peggy, and even without the full story, she'd gotten emotional on him. Still, he'd held firm against the barrage of questions about him and Peggy.

He wasn't discussing that with anyone.

Aaron wove toward him through the sea of tables. His presence indicated that the Feds had arrived. Mac had told him to find him immediately. His gut burned with rage. So, she had really done it. A last piece of him died. He'd never trust another woman again.

He signaled to the dealer, who nodded and stood, smoothing his jacket. Time to play a different game with higher stakes. They could charge him with obstruction of justice and a whole slew of other things. They'd probably revel in it. The law hated his kind. If Peggy thought he was just going to confess everything for a plea bargain or hand Dustin's friend over with open arms, she had another thing coming. He wasn't a snitch, and he wouldn't give her the satisfaction. He and his lawyer could stonewall with the best of them. There was no hard evidence.

Mac met Aaron in the corner.

"Deputy McBride is here. She tried to enter the hotel, but the guards stopped her per your orders. She's demanding entrance. When I told her she'd been banned, she asked if we had a judge's order."

"Are the Feds with her?"

"No."

Mac's jaw clenched. So she wasn't going to handle this above-board. The Feds hadn't gotten here quickly enough to stop her brother from playing, so she'd decided to kick things off herself. What was she planning to do? Arrest him? He ground his teeth to keep the pain in his heart from spreading.

"Clear the front entrance of all guests. I only want your guards out there. Re-route any traffic to the garage. I'll deal with her, but I'm not going to give her the scene she craves. Tell Bill to meet me downstairs."

Jesus! A part of him couldn't believe this was happening.

He headed downstairs with Aaron, taking the steps two at a time. "Clear the lobby too. Offer everyone a free drink in the bar. I don't want anyone to overhear us."

"Yes, sir." Aaron started moving toward the guests, smiling easily, gesturing toward the bar.

Mac headed to the entryway. His doorman hurried to open the door, and Mac stepped into the harsh noonday sun, wishing he had sunglasses. He scanned the drive. Two of his beefiest security men towered over Peggy, hands on their hips. Her finger was thrust in the direction of the hotel, and she was arguing with them.

Taking a moment to compose himself was essential. She wasn't in uniform, which didn't make sense. Wasn't she here as an officer of the law? Instead she was wearing that damn yellow dress with the red dragons from Jill's closet and low-heel black sandals. The sun picked up the red highlights in her dark hair. Sunglasses rested on her nose.

He strode forward, muscles locked, pushing all emotion away. If she thought seeing her in that dress would make him weak, she was delusional.

She stopped arguing with the guards when she spotted him.

He came forward, his hands on his waist. "Give us a little space," he said to his guys.

They fell back to the entryway, but knew better than to go inside. Aaron had told them he wanted witnesses to whatever she had planned.

"You need to leave my property right now," he informed her. "I told you I wouldn't stop your brother if he showed up, and I haven't. Tanner's inside watching him play, but I'm afraid that's all the McBrides my hotel's willing to host today—or ever."

She removed her sunglasses and made a healthy dent in his armor. He had never seen her wear makeup before. But then he noticed her bloodshot, puffy eyes. He swallowed thickly, realizing how much she was hurting. It shouldn't sway him, but it did.

"If it's any consolation, your brother won't last long. He sucks at poker."

Her mouth lifted, a ghost of a smile. "So did my father. That's why we never had any money. I don't know why, but that strikes me as rather funny right now." Her laughter barked out, slightly hysterical.

His alarm grew. "Are *you* drunk?"

Her laughter died. "No. I thought about downing something before coming up here, but that would make *me* like my father. Besides, I'm not here about David."

Right. Nice cover. He steeled himself. No, she'd say she was here about the bomb threat.

"My lawyer, Bill Perkins, is standing inside those doors." He pointed to the front of the building. "He's listening to everything we say."

She looked up at the cameras positioned discreetly across the entrance. "I see."

"I know you're going to do what you have to do, but I won't have you make a scene at my hotel. You can leave now, or we can see how far you want to escalate things. We can start by making a harassment complaint to the sheriff. If that won't deter you, I'm prepared to move for a restraining order. It's your call."

The pulse in her neck beat like the wings of a hummingbird, fast and strong. She opened her purse and dug out her handcuffs. "You can try and make me leave, but I can tell you, I'm just as determined to stay and make you listen."

He folded his arms across his chest. "So you're planning to arrest me for obstruction of justice before the Feds get here? What, were they playing golf today?"

Bill came through the doors. Mac held up his finger to stop him from coming forward, wanting to hear her answer. If she actually tried to arrest him, she'd be dead to him.

"Aren't you playing poker today?" she asked, her voice cracking.

He narrowed his eyes, not understanding what game she was playing.

"I was until you showed up. I left the table and invoked a penalty."

Her breath shuttered out. "Well, then, you'd better go back. I was planning on standing by your table, watching you play."

He couldn't fight it anymore. He met her gaze. Her brown eyes didn't look...normal. The wariness and mistrust had vanished. The gold ring around her iris radiated...warmth.

"I don't understand. Why would you watch me play?" He slapped a hand to his forehead. "Oh, I see. You want to make me lose again. Well, Deputy, I think I've given you enough of my time. Are you going to arrest me? If not, I'm going back inside."

He didn't wait for an answer. Couldn't bear to hear what it was. He turned and walked away, sweat beading his brow. Bill walked toward him and then gasped. There was a distinctly metallic clink. Mac's body spun around.

Peggy had handcuffed herself to the brass guard rail by the parking station.

He ran back to her. *"What are you doing?"*

"I'm following a friend's advice. I'm staging a sit-in until you listen to me."

Flabbergasted didn't begin to describe what he was feeling. "Stop this!" The hurt started to spread as his walls crumbled again. "Peg, please. You're only making this worse for yourself. You're leaving me with very few options. There's no need for us to go to war against each other."

The very idea made his gut tremble.

Suddenly Abbie rushed out of the building. Bill grabbed her arm and held her back.

"Please don't do this, Peggy!" his sister cried out.

Her distress rooted Mac to the spot. "Abbie, go inside! I'm handling it. Bill, take her to Rhett." His sister fought to release herself from his grip, ripping Mac to shreds.

Peggy waved her free hand. "Abbie, I'm not here about that. I'm just here to talk to Mac. Calm down!"

Mac gave her a sneer. "We're done. I don't talk to people who set out to destroy my family." He turned and started to walk away again.

She lunged for him and caught his jacket with her free arm, jerking her other in the cuffs. Her pained cry halted him in his tracks.

"God! Please stop this, Peg. Can't you see what you're doing?"

A tear slid down her face. "Will you please listen to me now, Mac?"

Her tears—and the sound of his name whispered from her lips—rusted his armor. He could feel himself falling even as he tried to shore up his reserves. "What?" he finally demanded. "What is it you want to tell me?" he asked even though he wasn't sure he could take it.

Her whole face changed, the muscles tensing and narrowing like she was trying to figure out what to say. "I'm sorry! For what I did and for what I said..."

"Jesus!" he replied, her hoarse words cutting his belly wide open. An apology from her had never entered his mind.

"I don't know if you can ever forgive me." She exhaled sharply, but kept her gaze pinned on him. "Oh, God, this is harder than I...Mac, I..." The handcuffs clanked against metal as her arms wrenched by her sides. *"I love you. "*

Her gut-retching confession silenced him, the pain from his heart obliterating any cogent response.

"I'm sorry!" She pressed her free hand to her face, hiding it from him. "I did everything wrong, and last night I became the worst person on the face of the planet."

He studied her bent head and agonized body language. Let her tone and words filter in all the way. Something had changed. He could feel it. His armor dropped to the ground as his control crumbled. If she was here to make amends, he couldn't deny her.

"Maybe not the *worst* person."

She lowered her hand. Her tear-dampened eyes made his legs tremble. He'd never imagined her crying, and the sight of it almost brought him to his knees.

"Well, I'm the worst person I've ever known, and I hate myself for it. I'm sorry. I don't know what else to say."

Neither did he. Mac realized the silence was so great he could have heard a pin drop. And everyone was listening to their conversation since he'd added mikes in strategic areas of the hotel in preparation for the Feds' arrival. Suddenly, he felt exposed.

"Aaron, cut the goddamn security feed!" he barked. "Everybody, get inside."

Abbie's fevered gaze held his for a long moment, and then she nodded, signaling her trust in him. Her faith had always helped him move mountains.

He turned to the other woman who held his heart. "Let's start over. Why don't we remove these handcuffs?" he suggested, reaching for her wrist, wanting to caress away the red marks where the metal had dug into her skin.

"You aren't going to throw me off your property?" she whispered, fumbling inside her purse.

He ran his hands through his hair and went with his gut. "You said a few things earlier that need more explanation. Like when you said you love me."

She dropped the key to the cuffs. Her hand was shaking so hard he decided to help her. He fought against the need to hold her when he freed her. He pocketed the handcuffs in his jacket and studied her again. Her lips were trembling.

He reassessed the situation.

She'd worn the dress and makeup not to weaken him, but to impress him. And since it was so out of character, his heart came back to life and began to beat again.

"You were saying..." he suggested.

She wiped her runny nose. "Right. I'm a fool and a failure—all around. I'm a horrible—"

"You've covered that. I'm more interested in *why* you came here to watch me play poker." They'd start there. He folded his arms to keep from reaching for her.

Her shoulder lifted. "I wanted you to know I accept you for who you are and am willing to let everyone know it."

The harsh wave of past rejection rolled through him, and her acceptance washed him up on a new shore.

"You *are* a good man," she whispered. "I'm sorry I didn't tell you that before."

"Shit. When you go all in..." He unbuttoned his jacket, awash in emotion.

"You said you want me to accept you for who you are." She opened her hands palm-up. "I'm here to show you I can."

He couldn't take it anymore. He yanked her to him, burying his face in her neck. "Jesus, you kill me," he muttered before crushing his mouth to hers.

She responded with a desperate yearning he could taste. He fed on her, letting all the pain go. When he felt her tears wet his face, he pulled back and brushed them away.

"Tell me again," he demanded.

"I was wrong. I'm sorry. And I love you." She said it like she was reading a telegram.

He framed her face. "You might have been wrong," he agreed, "and you might have been slow to catch up." His smile couldn't be contained. "But you did. You always come through in the end."

She shook her head. "But what I said last night. I don't know how we can ever forget that. It's always going to be between us. Your sister probably hates me. I wouldn't blame her. I'd feel that way if someone threatened Keith."

His finger pressed her lips, silencing her. "Stop. Yes, we have some things to sort out, but it's going to be okay."

"I didn't want David to turn into my father, but I finally realized I can't do anything about that."

His hand cupped her cheek. "Not an easy revelation. I'm proud of you."

A tortured laugh bubbled out. "The whole thing made me go crazy, but when it came down to it, I realized I wasn't willing to lose you over it. You make me...happy. I don't..."

"You don't what?" he encouraged, amazed at how much she was opening herself up.

"I don't want you to leave Dare, even though I don't have the right to tell you not to go."

"I was only leaving to get away from you." He finally grabbed her reddened wrist and caressed the mark. "Didn't you know that?"

She shook her head, another tear slipping out. "I hoped so."

"Last night..." He had to take a deep breath. "It was a bad night."

"Can you...forgive me?"

He stroked her hot brow, kissed her cheek. "Yes. You'll have to apologize to Abbie, though, and explain things to her. It might be hard, but I think she'll understand. We share a similar upbringing."

Her hand covered his, warming his heart.

"What about Dustin?"

"We haven't told him yet."

"Good!" She laughed nervously. "I didn't have much hope of being forgiven by a teenager."

He pulled her close, cradling her body against his. "Maybe if you let him drive your car. So this means you're willing to be seen in public with me?"

She rubbed her forehead against his chest. "Nothing would make me prouder."

Music to his ears. "What about your reputation and people's opinions?" he made himself ask, running his hands over the yellow material outlining her curves.

She pushed back. "I'll say I was wrong. It'll be awkward...and it'll probably make me grouchy, but it's the way it has to be."

"Last night I thought everything I'd ever seen in you was a lie." He cupped the back of her neck. "Then you showed up today and proved that deep down I know what makes people tick."

Her mouth tipped up. "Well, it *is* an invaluable asset in your professions." She put her hand on his heart. "You're a poker player and a business man."

His lips feathered her brow. "I'm glad you can finally see that."

"I'm just a little slow."

"But you're gaining speed," he encouraged, done with the self-deprecating talk. "I'd say you caught up to me today."

"I'd like to tell Keith about us, if that's okay." She looked away, her vulnerability stark in her eyes.

Keith. How lucky could a man get to have a beautiful woman and sweet kid in his life? "I'm glad. Maybe you can come over to the house for dinner with Keith tonight."

"I'd like that."

He gave her a long and lingering kiss. "Of course, I'm giving you fair warning that once we settle things between us and our families—and you and Tanner and David, by the way—I'm going to start suggesting that *we* get married. What do you think of that?"

Her shudder rocked her against him. "Since I swore I'd never get married again, it might take me a little while to come around, but I promise I'll try to speed things up."

His hand gestured to the dragon on her dress. "Breathe fire on the past, Peg. We'll make it work, I promise."

Her mouth parted. "My back isn't itching anymore. Huh."

He had no idea what she was talking about. "I'm glad. I guess..."

"I'll explain later." Another fire sparked in her eyes, not the kind to burn away the past, but one to build a future on.

He extended his hand. "Are you ready to head inside?"

She nodded and took a deep breath. "I'm ready."

He remembered that her brother was still playing inside. "You don't have to do it here, you know. We can go out somewhere else."

Her chin lifted. "No, it's okay. I have to make my peace with the past—and the present. Tanner's probably upset with me, but we'll work through that. I don't know if I'll ever be okay with David, but I'm done comparing him to my father."

"That sounds wise. And Peg, Tanner will get over it. Those of us who love you always find a way."

She took his extended hand, and they walked through the door together.

And made his tournament the most talked about event in town for reasons that had nothing to do with poker.

ℰPILOGUE

A few months later...

$\mathcal{M}$ac and Dustin hauled the trough of beers onto the deck to keep them chilled. With the temperatures dipping into the teens and snow swirling across the valley, Peggy wondered why anyone would want to drink anything cold. Personally, she only wanted to keep sipping her warm, alcohol-laced drink.

"What's this called again?" she asked when they returned.

Mac crossed the room and put his hands on her shoulders. Gave her a gentle squeeze. "A hot toddy."

"It's like the Ole Miss cheer," Dustin informed her. "Be sure to have Rhett sing it to you when he arrives. He's already sung it for Keith. Everyone in the family *has* to know it."

It made her smile when he included them in his definition of family. She seemed to be smiling all the time now. The weirdness was wearing off.

"I forgot how it goes!" Keith said, jumping off the bar stool where he'd been sitting, a pickle in his hand. "Teach it to me again, Dustin. Pleeeeease."

Mac winced. "I'm not sure Peggy's gonna like it."

Dustin rolled his eyes. "Mom didn't either, but that didn't stop Rhett. I'm glad he's decided to stay until Mom agrees to marry him. Party all the time."

"Party all the time," Keith parroted, pretty much like he always did. Dustin was his hero.

"Who's going to party all the time?" Abbie asked, emerging from what she called the powder room.

Even though they'd made their peace with each other after Peggy had profusely apologized, they still didn't always know what to say to each other. Peggy had wisely refrained from asking Abbie what the heck "powder" had to do with the john when she'd excused herself.

The doorbell rang. Keith raced for the door. "They're here!"

Abbie tugged her apron off and smoothed her navy wool dress.

Peggy looked over at Mac. "Remind me why we agreed to host Thanksgiving." And darn if she wasn't proud of herself for calling them a "we."

His finger caressed the necklace he'd given her the previous week.

ـnere was an engagement ring on it. It was his way of letting her decide when she'd wear it and tell everyone she'd *finally* agreed to marry him.

"Because it's what families do."

Right. And hers was ever expanding, delighting her more than freaking her out.

Jill and Brian hustled inside—each holding a baby carrier—with Tanner and Meredith behind them, carrying the casserole dishes. Abbie efficiently took care of everything. She truly was in her element as hostess. Made it easier for Peggy, who had no desire to be Martha Stewart.

Keith leaned down and stared at Violet and Mia, decked out in hot pink matching onesies. "They're still pretty small."

Jill hugged him to her side. "They're not as big as you yet, but they've each gained eight ounces."

"That's not much," he responded, making everyone laugh.

Meredith and Tanner pulled Keith in for hugs after Jill had finished tickling him. Then both of them embraced Peggy warmly. Jill's bear hug lifted her two inches off the ground.

"Whoa" she cried.

"Oh, don't be a wimp. I'm a mother now. Super human strength."

"I could use some super human sleep," Brian said, elbowing Jill aside to give Peggy a gentle hug. "These girls don't like to sleep, just like someone else I know."

"What can I say?" Jill responded. "I've always been a night owl. That's why you need to hire another chef, babe. So you'll have more time."

"I'm getting there, hon," Brian responded, walking over to greet their hostess. "I'll likely pull in someone I went to school with if they're ready to move to Dare. Hey, Abbie, thanks for doing all the heavy lifting on the cooking."

"My pleasure," she responded.

Abbie was still getting used to everyone, but she gave them all hugs. Tanner shook hands with Mac and then wrapped his arm around her. "Hey, sis. This must be a record. Two Thanksgivings together in a row."

They'd found their balance again after David left. Tanner had admitted that their brother hadn't changed much, but he was happy he'd made the effort. Peggy knew she hadn't, but she'd made her peace with that. They didn't have anything in common except the past, and she didn't want to live there anymore. Neither of them had talked to David since his visit. They only knew about his life from their mother, who still blindly refused to see him for what he was, rather like how she'd been with their father.

Arthur came in behind Linda and Alan Hale in the next batch of company. "Colder than a witch's..."

He stopped before saying, "tit," but his eyes gleamed with humor. He made the rounds, saving her for last. Since her total meltdown in front of him and his wise counsel, she'd taken to thinking of him as her grandpa. She hadn't told anyone except Mac, who'd kissed her and said it was sweet.

"How's my favorite deputy?" Arthur asked, handing her a red hot.

She crunched on it, the cinnamon flavor exploding in her mouth. "Pretty good. How's my favorite journalist?"

"Hey," a chorus of reporters protested from all around them.

"*I'm* your brother. I thought *I* was your favorite." Tanner gave Keith a wink before plucking him up on his shoulders.

"I can't help it," Peggy found herself answering. "I have a thing for older men."

Joking had become easier with practice. With Dustin and Mac around, it was either joke or drown. Thankfully, Abbie took her side once in a while.

Mac's eyebrow winged up. "Good thing for me then."

She didn't stop to consider whether she should grin or not, the smile practically flew across her face. "Yes, you're practically ancient. It's no wonder I like you best of all."

The kitchen exploded with activity around the twins, who were fast asleep in their carriers. Keith kept peeking inside, asking when the girls would be ready to play.

The men grabbed the beer. The women opened the wine. Jill frowned as she drank her soda, complaining about breastfeeding.

Dustin pulled Mac aside. "Please make her stop."

Peggy almost laughed. Jill didn't have a filter about anything, which was part of her charm.

Mac snorted. "Good luck with that."

Tanner punched the teen lightly in the arm. "Man up, kid. You're going to hear plenty of that kind of stuff with this crowd. How's school, by the way?"

His tennis shoes kicked the bar stool. "It's okay. My soccer team is way cool."

"And he's not doing so badly in school," Mac murmured. "Not that that's important or anything."

"Right," Abbie commented. "Not important at all."

But even Peggy knew she was thrilled at how well Dustin was settling into Dare after the initial rough patches.

Dustin's hip bumped his uncle's as he tried to throw him off balance— their usual game. "Mom's happy because she likes my friends here better. But I think that's just because she's so crazy in love with Rhett."

"Dustin!" Abbie gasped, even though everyone knew she was still fighting hard against her feelings for Rhett. "You need to zip it up, or you won't get any pie."

"Yeah, mind your manners, kid." Mac lifted his drink to Peggy in a salute.

She gave him a wink, rather hoping no one noticed. Smiling was one thing. Winking was another.

Mac stared straight at Peggy. She could read his mind from a mile away. He wanted her, and he'd probably talk her into allowing another sleepover for Keith and Dustin tonight. Which meant she was spending tonight in his bed. The woman inside wanted to cheer.

Ava Miles

"Stop it, you two. You're making me gag," Dustin pleaded.

The kid seemed to have an inner radar about their interest in each other. She looked away from Mac, somewhat embarrassed at being called out by a teenager for, well, acting like a teenager.

"Yeah, gag," Keith repeated.

Jill came up behind her and tickled her neck, making her jump in her chair. "Is this new?" she asked, tugging on her necklace.

Peggy's hand grabbed the chain to keep it under her shirt. "Cut that out."

"You *never* wear jewelry," Jill said with a suspicious glint in her eyes. "Is that a present from Mac? Show, show."

Peggy nudged her with her foot. "Hey, isn't that Violet?"

"Nice try, but I have Violet and Mia's cries down pat. Mommy radar. Plus, you can't sidetrack me."

"Brian!" Peggy called, hoping for backup.

Jill's hubby only held up his hands. "Sorry, can't help ya. She's feeding my kids."

Peggy gave him the evil eye. "Jill, let go. I don't want you to break it."

Meredith came over. "I think the lady doth protest too much. What do you think, Jill?"

"I think we need to get to the bottom of this. Grab her, Mere."

"Abbie, help!" she cried.

"Sorry, you're on your own. Those two mean business."

Meredith tickled her ribs, and dammit if she didn't hiss out a giggle and jerk in her chair.

"You're ticklish!" Jill cried out.

"Yep," Mac and Keith responded at the same time.

"Help me, Keith," she called, trying to fight them off and protect the necklace.

Her son didn't budge—he was sticking with the men, the little traitor. She was going to have to work on that.

Meredith and Jill finally plucked the chain out from under her shirt. She froze in her chair, her eyes seeking Mac's. Those stoplight green eyes glowed with that incredible patience.

"Oh my God!" Jill cried. "Is that an engagement ring?"

Meredith's mouth dropped open. "Oh, Peggy, I'm so happy for you."

Tanner ambled forward and put a restraining arm around both women. "I'd check yourselves a minute before jumping to conclusions, ladies. An engagement ring goes on a finger. This ring is simply on a necklace. Pipe down."

She could always count on her big brother. "Thank you."

A quick glance at Abbie told her she wasn't surprised by this. Well, Mac had made no secret of his intentions.

"I thought all rings went on your finger," Keith mused, coming to her side.

No one laughed. Everyone in the kitchen was staring at her.

Peggy stood, her legs trembling a little. Her back gave an itch like it wanted to flare up after these many months. In that moment, she knew what she needed to do.

"Keith, let's go into Mac's study for a minute." She needed to tell him before everyone else.

Her son put his hands on his hips. "Mom, I know Mac wants to marry you. He asked me a long time ago if it was okay. I told him, *of course.*"

The adults laughed.

Her gaze flew from her son to Mac. "You asked him?" she croaked, the sweetness of the gesture swirling through her like the chocolate ribbons in Brian's pain au chocolat.

"He asked me too, Peg," Tanner informed her, coming closer. "I wasn't a pushover like Keith here." Her brother tossed Keith in the air.

"What's a pushover?" her son asked.

Tanner chuckled. "Someone who falls down easily."

"I stand up all the time," Keith informed him.

"Sure you do."

"And he told us, too," Abbie said, putting her arm around Dustin. "We couldn't be happier."

Everyone fell silent. Peggy raised her hand and held it out to Mac. His smile started out slow and then spread across his face.

"I guess we're engaged then," she declared, her stomach doing Olympic backflips.

His hand squeezed hers. She gripped it and then was yanked into a new round of hugs.

Someone pounded on the door, and then a cold blast blew through the house.

"Is dinner ready yet?" Rhett called, carrying a massive bouquet of those red Amaryllis flowers Abbie loved so much.

Everyone called out a greeting right away, except for Mac's sister, who clutched a blue hand towel.

"Happy Thanksgiving, Rhett," Abbie finally said as he strode toward her.

"Thanks, Abbie. It's nice to be here." He handed her the flowers and darted forward to kiss her cheek, causing her to blush.

Watching them, Peggy had no doubt Rhett was going to keep after Abbie until she caved. It was going to be fun seeing what Rhett came up with. And what he was going to do about the poker babes. Peggy agreed with Abbie. They were embarrassing.

When Rhett turned around, he clutched his chest suddenly like he was having a heart attack. "Oh my God! Mac Maverick Maven, do my eyes deceive me or did you finally hit the jack pot?"

Peggy didn't know what he was talking about until she realized Rhett was pointing at her.

"We're engaged," she confirmed, holding out the ring, awkwardness making her duck her head.

Rhett shot across the room and man-hugged Mac off the ground. "You old coon dog. Good for you!"

Mac slapped him on the back. "You call me a coon dog again, and I'll start in with the Liberace remarks."

He staggered back, clutching his chest. "Not the Liberace remarks," he cried, making everyone chuckle.

Peggy played with the ring in her hand. Mac had known she wouldn't go for big and bold. The simple diamond in its elegant setting worked for her. She expected the diamond was flawless because it radiated enough rainbows to keep a leprechaun happy.

"Did everybody know but me?" she finally asked.

"I didn't," Jill and Brian answered in unison.

"Probably because you wouldn't keep your mouth shut," Meredith interjected.

"This old man had his suspicions," Arthur interjected. "Congratulations, my dear."

"Perhaps it's time to put it on your finger now, Mom," Keith said. "It's kinda dumb wearing a ring on a necklace."

Her laugh sputtered out. "Yes, it kinda is."

Mac squeezed Keith's shoulder before reaching for the ring. He slid it on her finger and then rubbed it with his thumb. His head dipped to kiss her, but instead, he leaned into her ear.

"It's official."

She kissed his cheek. "Yeah. Who's lucky now?"

Rhett barreled in, arms flying. "Wait! I *have* to tell this story. When I first met this lady, she had on a sexy sheriff's outfit—oops, I'm going to have to clean that up, aren't I?" He threw an absent kiss to Abbie. "Okay, let me start over. I met Peggy at her *very* professional office, and she told me she didn't believe in luck."

Dustin sucked in his breath. "No way! You don't believe in luck?" The kid made it sound like not believing in Santa Claus.

"I didn't." Peggy turned her hand to make her ring flash. "But I do now."

Her fiancé tugged her to his side. *Fiancé.* Man, that word would take some getting used to.

"Like I said, you might start off slow, but you always catch up."

She leaned her head against his side, surveying the group. With her extended family all around her, she realized she was the luckiest girl in the world.

Dear Reader,

I have to admit that it was really hard to see Peggy and Mac's story end. They became my best friends, and I might have fallen a little in love with Mac—although I'm a bit afraid of what Peg might do to me if she finds out.

Your opinion really matters to me, so I would love for you to post a review and let me know what you think of THE GRAND OPENING. Additionally, your review helps other readers find my books.

In other awesome news, I have been designing my own Dare Valley swag. If you sign up for my newsletter at www.avamiles.com and connect with me on Facebook at www.facebook.com/authoravamiles, you'll know when we're having a contest so you can enter to win our fun prizes. Jill has lots of ideas, trust me.

Okay, now onto the big question: do Abbie and Rhett ever get together? I totally fell in love with Rhett and really sympathized with Abbie's struggles, so they had to have their own story. It's called THE HOLIDAY SERENADE.

I also have had so many people tell me how much they love Grandpa Hale that he's going to have his own novel called THE TOWN SQUARE. Who was the woman who stole this journalist's heart? I like to call their story "Mad Men" in a small town with a happy ending. Both of these books are e-only, but I want my print-only readers to be happy so you can buy both books in my print anthology called DARING DECLARATIONS.

With so much incredible feedback about the characters of Dare Valley, I have a lot more planned and look forward to sharing their love stories and amusing antics. Thanks again for reading!

Lots of light,

Ava

The Dare Valley Series continues...
Book 4: THE HOLIDAY SERENADE
Rhett and Abbie's story

Professional gambler Rhett Butler Blaylock is everything Abbie Maven doesn't want in a man—flamboyant, flashy, and unreserved. After a horrible experience in her youth, she has spent her life trying to make all the right choices, pouring her energy into being the best possible single mother to her son. But though Rhett doesn't seem to be husband and stepfather material, he awakens emotions in her that are as frightening as they are powerful. They had a fling she's never forgotten, and now he has followed her to Dare Valley, Colorado with the intention of winning back her heart...this time, forever.

Rhett's determined to show Abbie he can be the man of her dreams. He'll do whatever it takes for the woman he loves, including giving up his flamboyant lifestyle and bad-boy image. As Christmas approaches, he prepares a special surprise for her, hoping the holiday will work its magic and grant him a miracle. Will his holiday serenade heal Abbie's heart and convince her to give love a second chance?

Book 5: THE TOWN SQUARE
Harriet & Arthur's story

1960 is ushering in a new decade of change, and journalist Arthur Hale is determined to be on the forefront of it. A successful New York City journalist, he returns to his hometown of Dare Valley, Colorado to start a new newspaper that will channel the voice of the West, joining the ranks of prestigious papers like The New York Times and The Chicago Tribune.

But the bigger the dream, the higher the price. Arthur's ambition and drive isolate him, and the only person who can break through his self-imposed solitude is Harriet Jenkins, his talented and mysterious secretary. Though Arthur's sixth sense as a journalist tells him the beautiful and complicated redhead is hiding something, he can't stay away.

What he doesn't know is that Harriet Jenkins is actually Harriet Wentworth. A newspaper article ruined her father and sullied her family name, and now she's out for revenge on the journalist who wrote it: Arthur Hale. As she gets to know Arthur, Harriet discovers he's not the monster she thought he was. He's a man of integrity, committed to uncovering the truth at all costs. Soon the impossible happens, and she finds herself falling for the man she set out to destroy, but can the two build a future on a foundation of lies and ugly truths?

ABOUT THE AUTHOR

USA Today Bestselling Author Ava Miles burst onto the contemporary romance scene after receiving Nora Roberts' blessing for her use of Ms. Roberts' name in her debut novel, the #1 National Bestseller NORA ROBERTS LAND, which kicked off her small town series, Dare Valley, and brought praise from reviewers and readers alike. Ava has also released a connected series called Dare River, set outside the country music capital of Nashville.  Far from the first in her family to embrace writing, Ava comes from a long line of journalists. Ever since her great-great-grandfather won ownership of a newspaper in a poker game in 1892, her family has had something to do with telling stories, whether to share news or, in her case, fiction. Her clan is still reporting on local events more than one hundred years later at their family newspaper, much like the Hale family in her Dare Valley series.

Ava is fast becoming a favorite author in light contemporary romance (Tome Tender) and is known for funny, emotional stories about family and empowerment. Ava's background is as diverse as her characters. She's a former chef, worked as a long-time conflict expert rebuilding warzones, and now writes full-time from her own small-town community.

If you'd like more information about Ava and her upcoming books, visit http://www.avamiles.com and connect with her on Facebook, Twitter, and Pinterest.

If you enjoyed reading this book, please share that with your friends and others by posting a review. Thank you!

Made in the USA
Middletown, DE
27 May 2020